santiago garcía · david rubín

BEOWULF

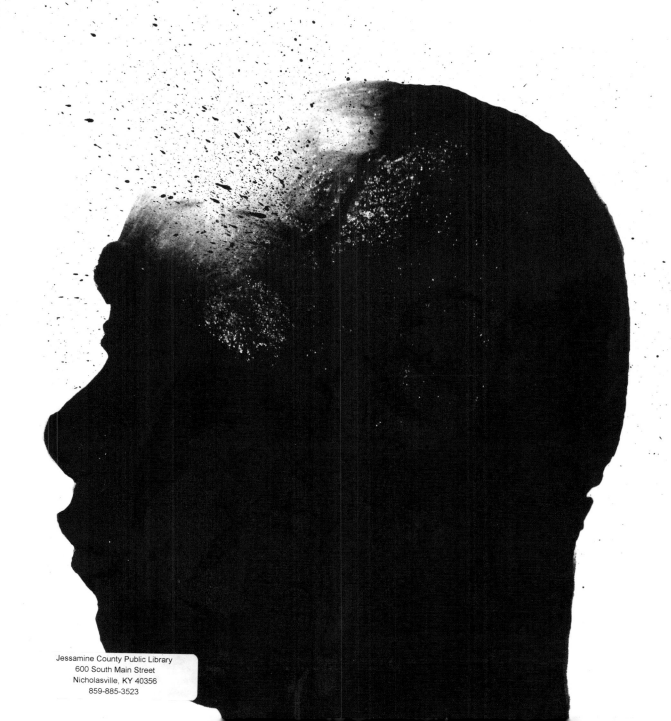

BEOWULF

A graphic novel by Santiago García and David Rubín
Edited by Image Comics

Scans:
José Domingo and Sara Solano

Design: David Rubín
Layouts: Manuel Bartual
Translation: Sam Stone and Joe Keatinge
Lettering: Jared Fletcher

David Rubín
daredeivid@gmail.com
www.detripas.blogspot.com
@davidrubin

Santiago García
mandorlablog@icloud.com
www.santiagogarciablog.blogspot.com
@mandorlablog

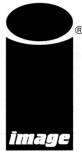

IMAGE COMICS, INC.
Robert Kirkman – Chief Operating Officer
Erik Larsen – Chief Financial Officer
Todd McFarlane – President
Marc Silvestri – Chief Executive Officer
Jim Valentino – Vice-President
Eric Stephenson – Publisher
Corey Murphy – Director of Sales
Jeff Boison – Director of Publishing Planning & Book Trade Sales
Jeremy Sullivan – Director of Digital Sales
Kat Salazar – Director of PR & Marketing
Branwyn Bigglestone – Controller
Drew Gill – Art Director
Jonathan Chan – Production Manager
Meredith Wallace – Print Manager
Briah Skelly – Publicist
Sasha Head – Sales & Marketing Production Designer
Randy Okamura – Digital Production Designer
David Brothers – Branding Manager
Olivia Ngai – Content Manager
Addison Duke – Production Artist
Vincent Kukua – Production Artist
Tricia Ramos – Production Artist
Jeff Stang – Direct Market Sales Representative
Emilio Bautista – Digital Sales Associate
Leanna Caunter – Accounting Assistant
Chloe Ramos-Peterson – Library Market Sales Representative
IMAGECOMICS.COM

BEOWULF
First printing
December 2016
ISBN: 978-1-5343-0120-7

Published by Image Comics, Inc.
Office of publication: 2001 Center Street,
Sixth Floor, Berkeley, CA 94704

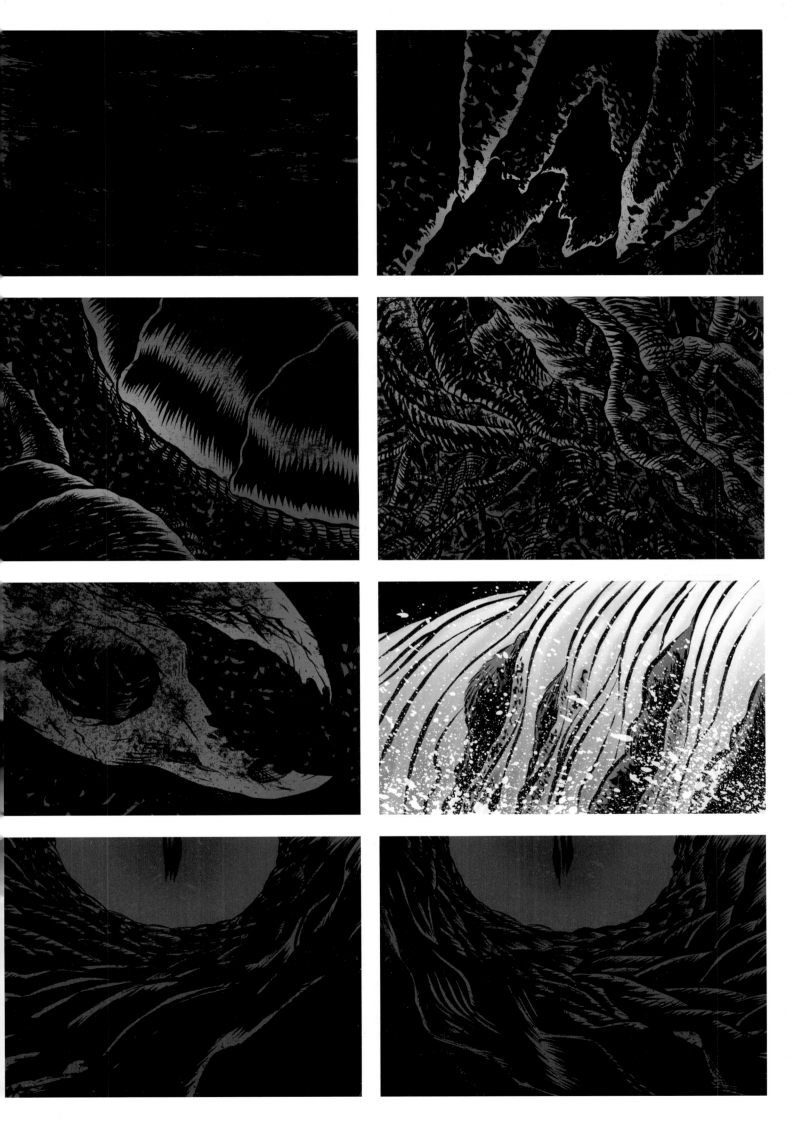

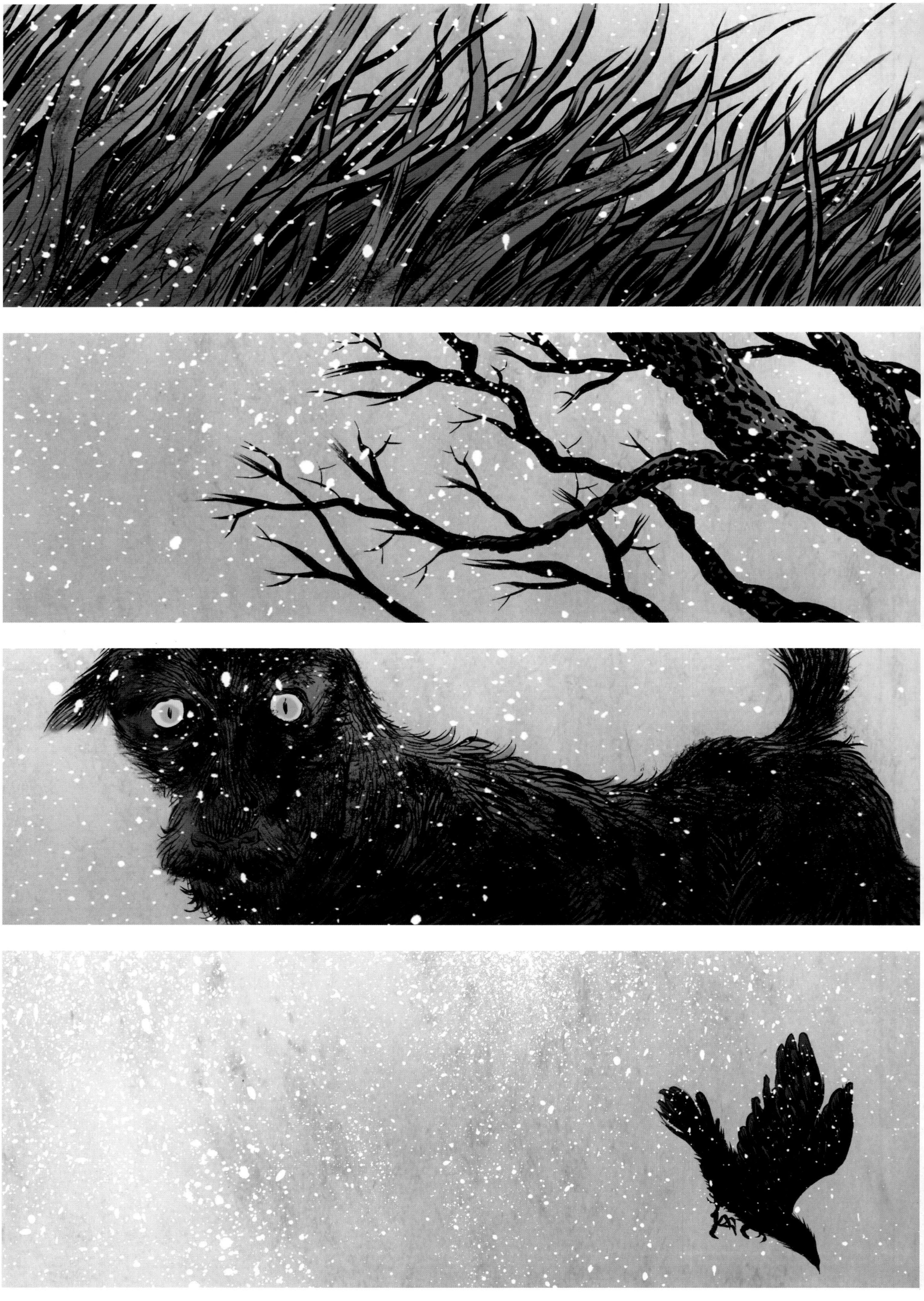

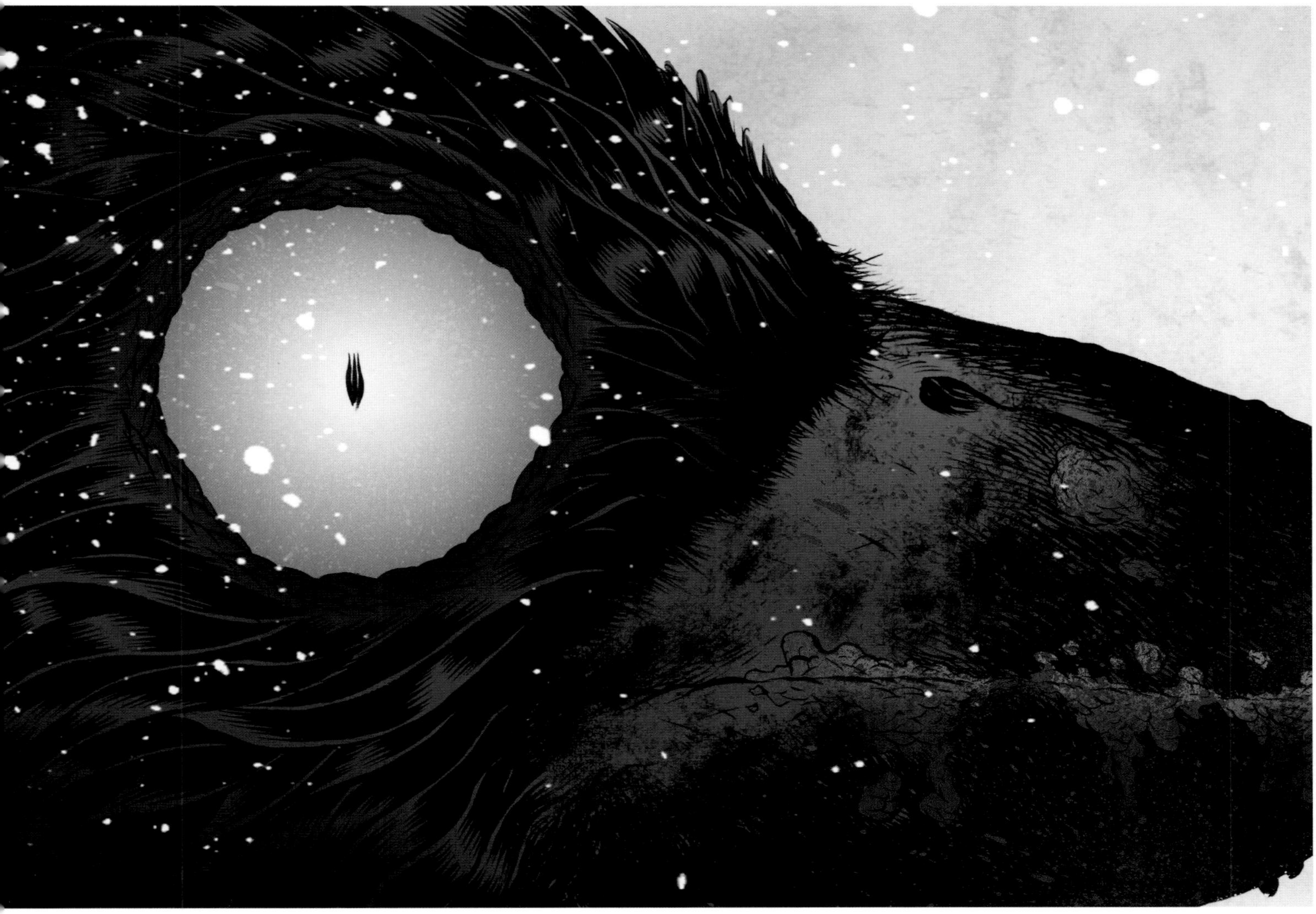

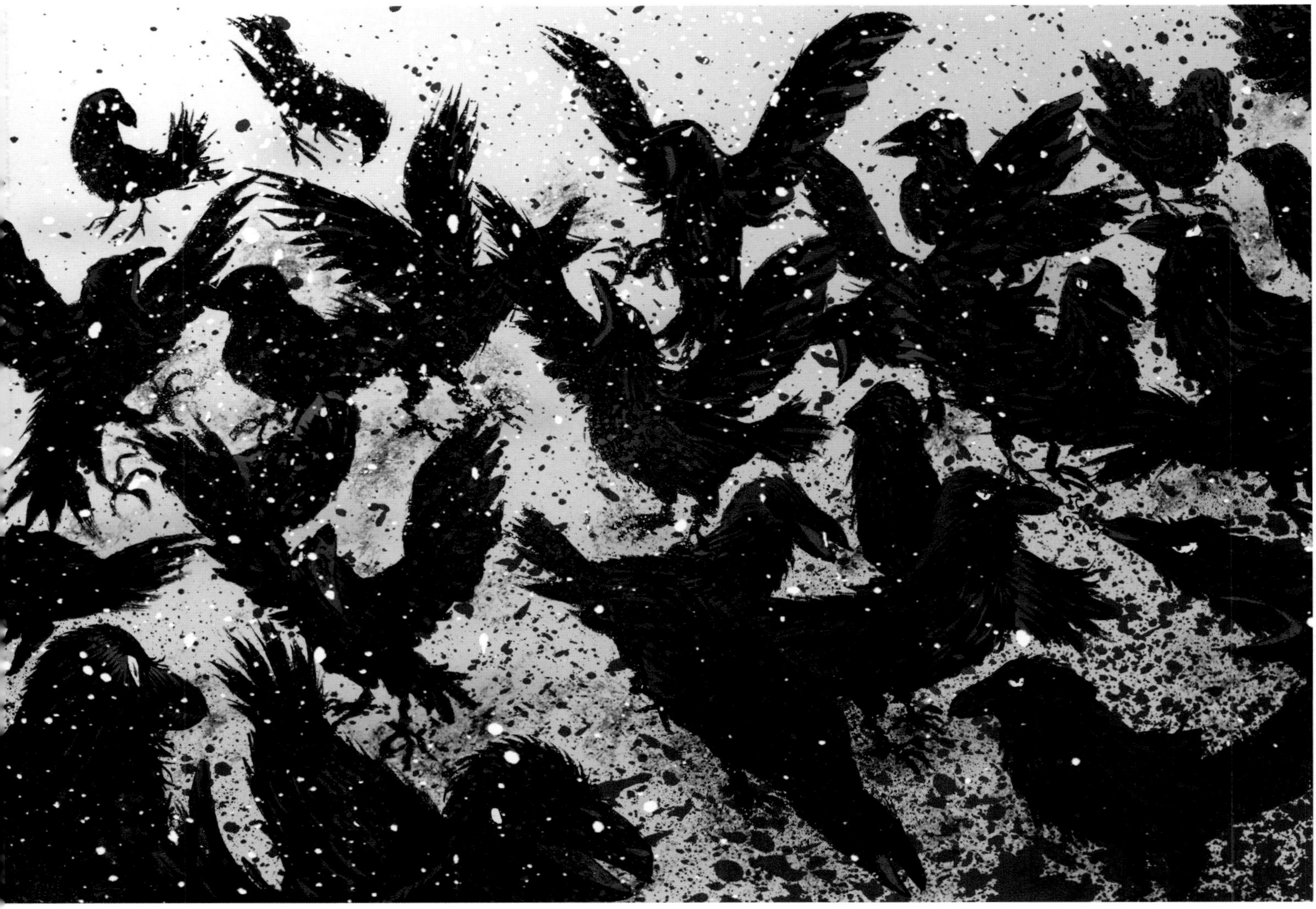

1. A MONSTER

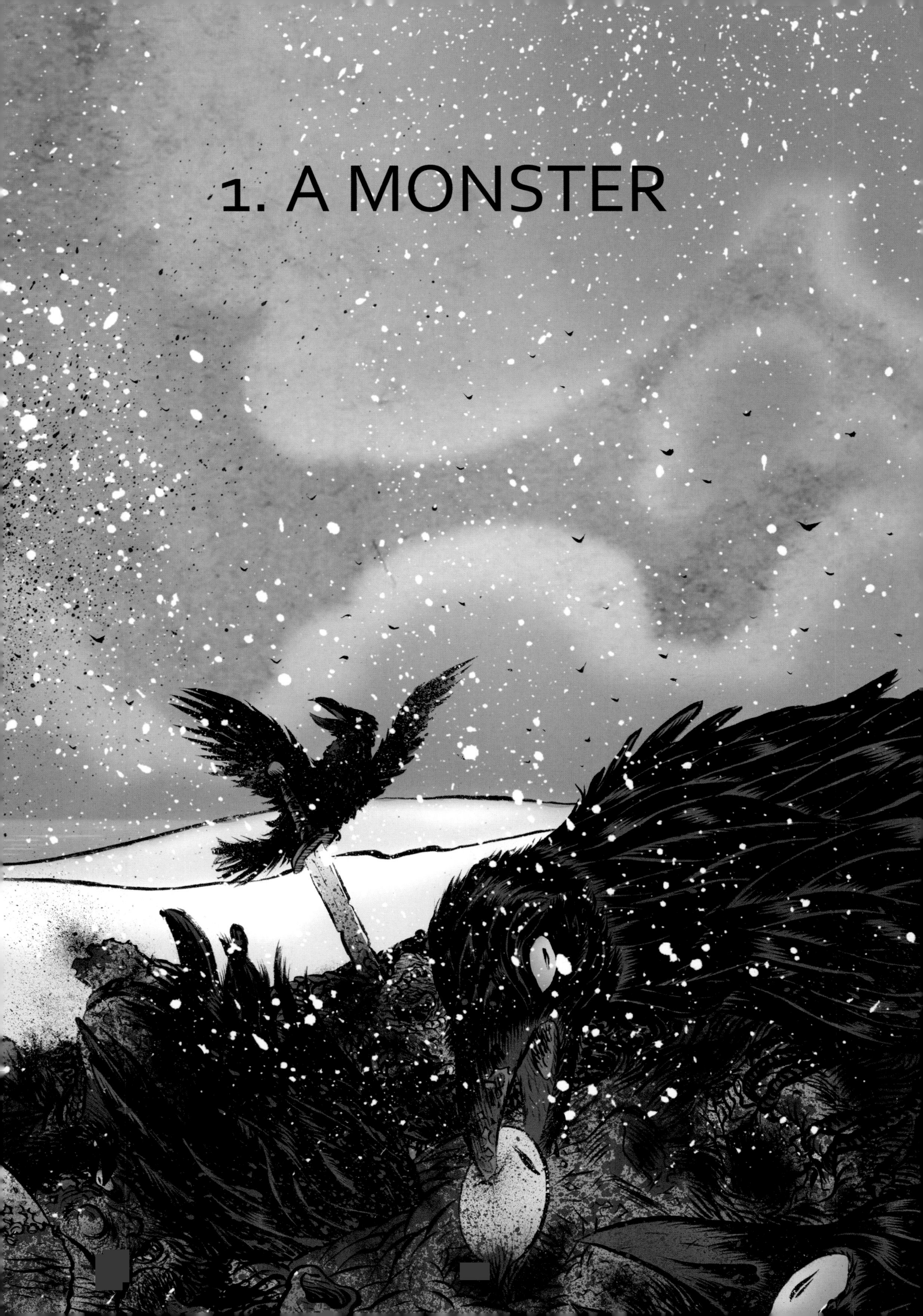

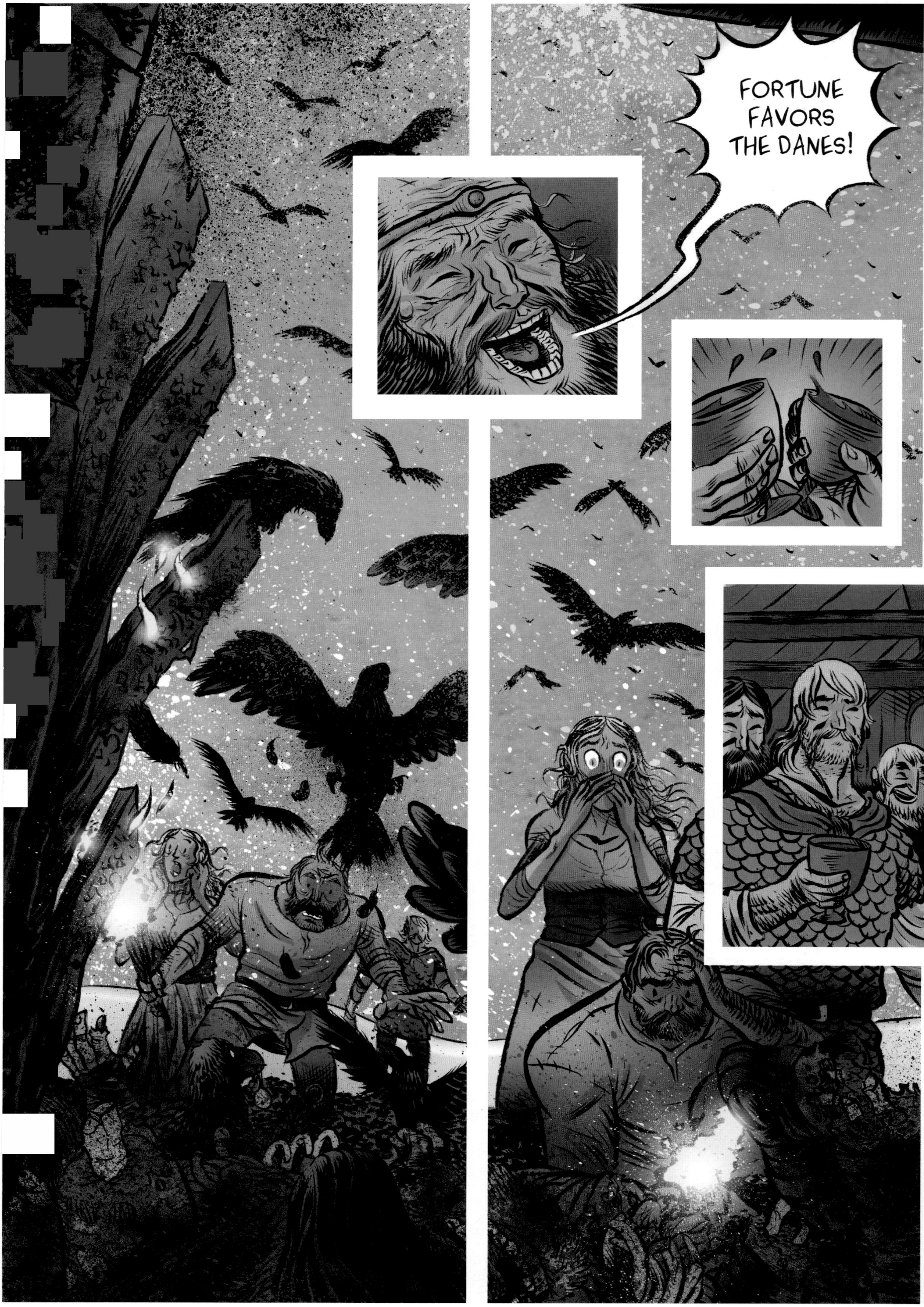
FORTUNE FAVORS THE DANES!

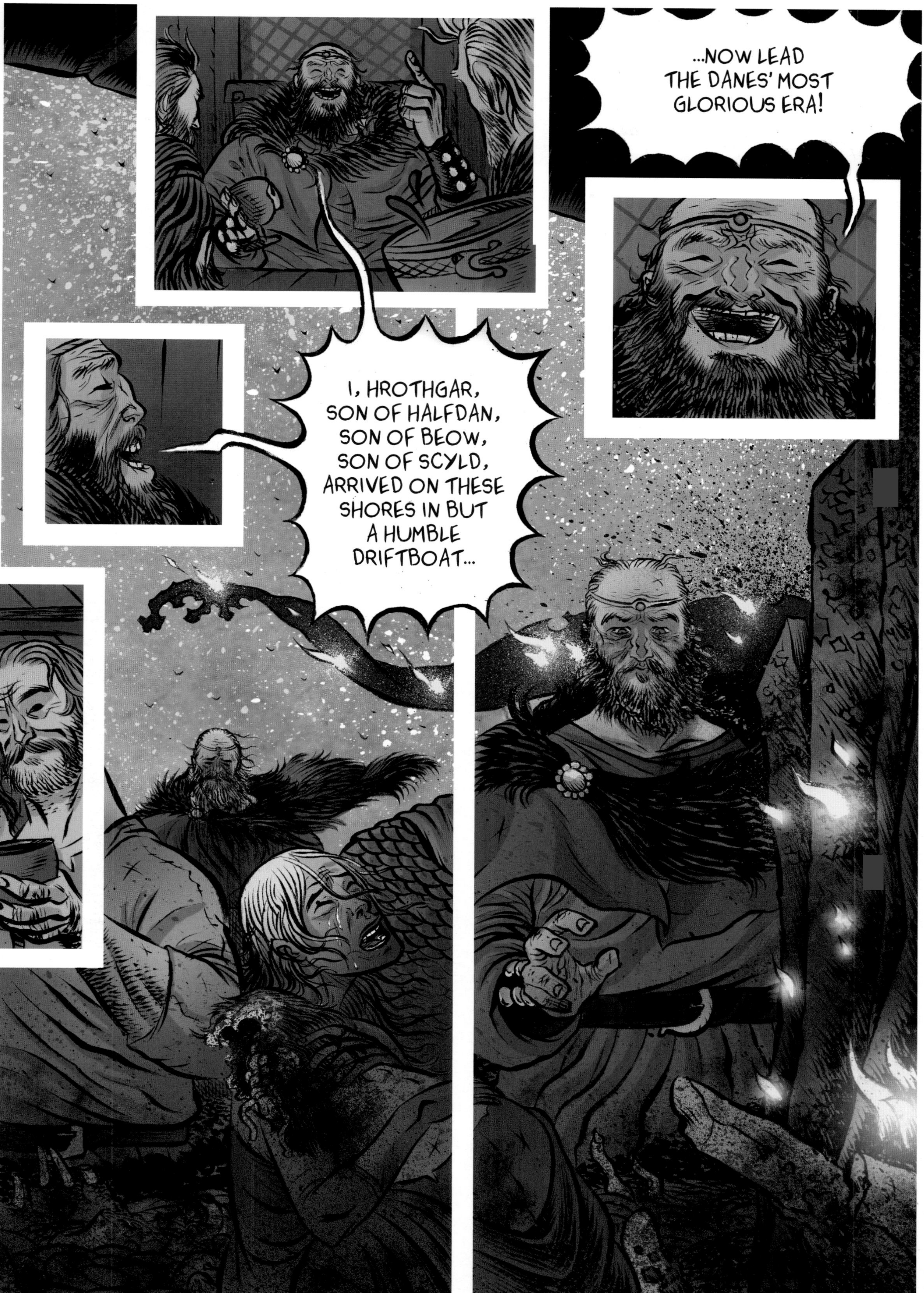
I, HROTHGAR, SON OF HALFDAN, SON OF BEOW, SON OF SCYLD, ARRIVED ON THESE SHORES IN BUT A HUMBLE DRIFTBOAT...
...NOW LEAD THE DANES' MOST GLORIOUS ERA!

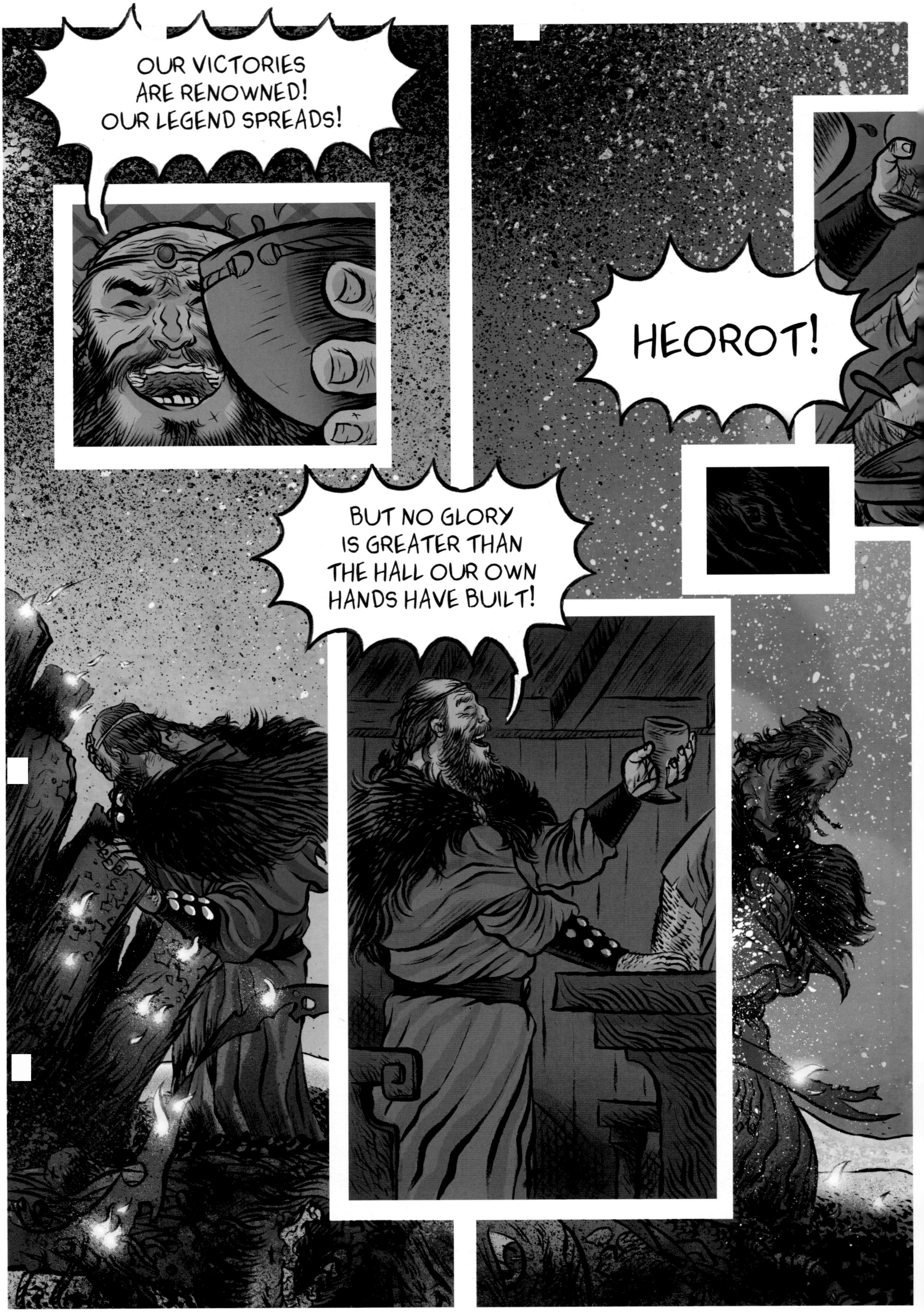
OUR VICTORIES ARE RENOWNED! OUR LEGEND SPREADS!
HEOROT!
BUT NO GLORY IS GREATER THAN THE HALL OUR OWN HANDS HAVE BUILT!

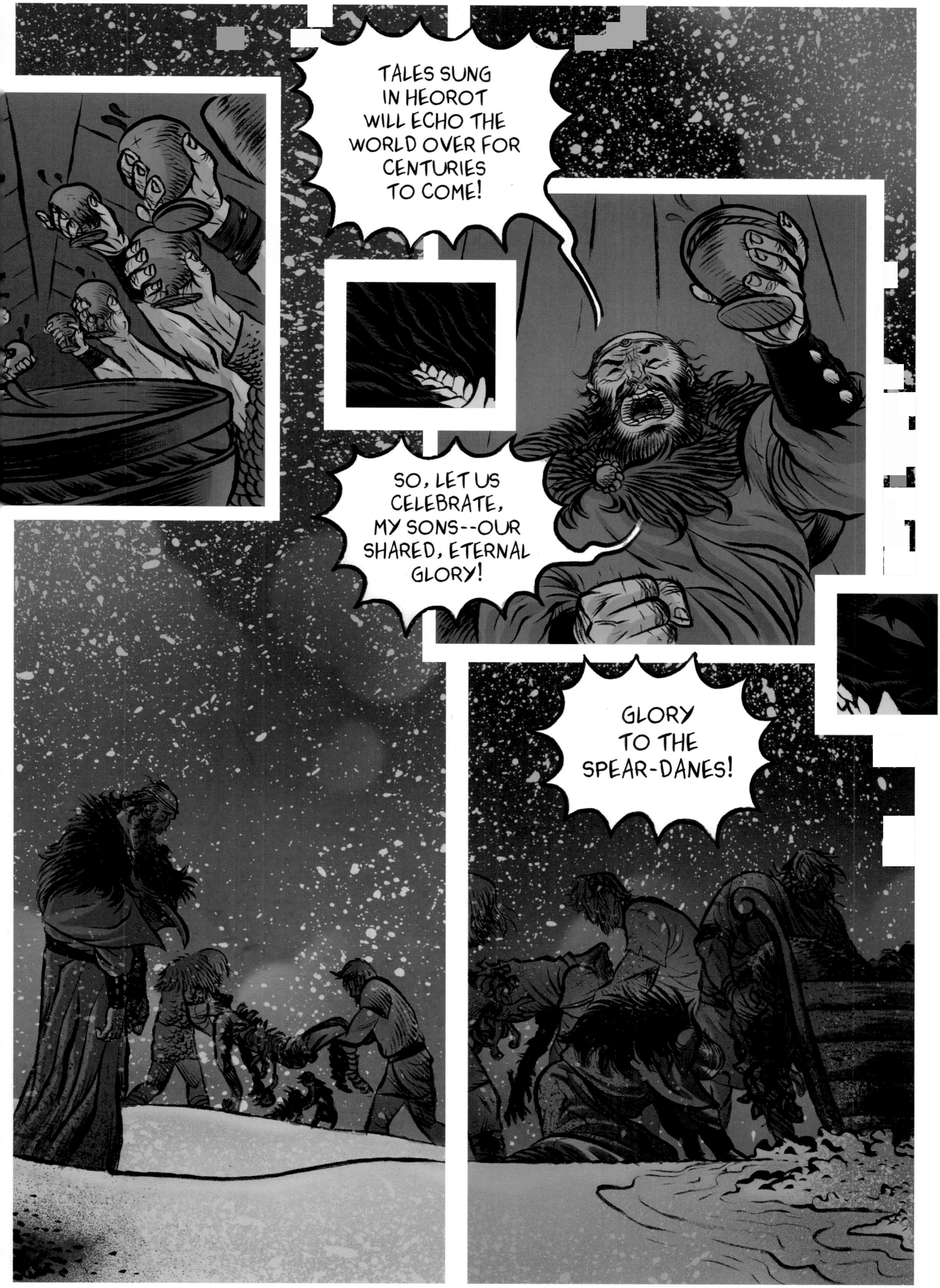
TALES SUNG IN HEOROT WILL ECHO THE WORLD OVER FOR CENTURIES TO COME!
SO, LET US CELEBRATE, MY SONS--OUR SHARED, ETERNAL GLORY!
GLORY TO THE SPEAR-DANES!

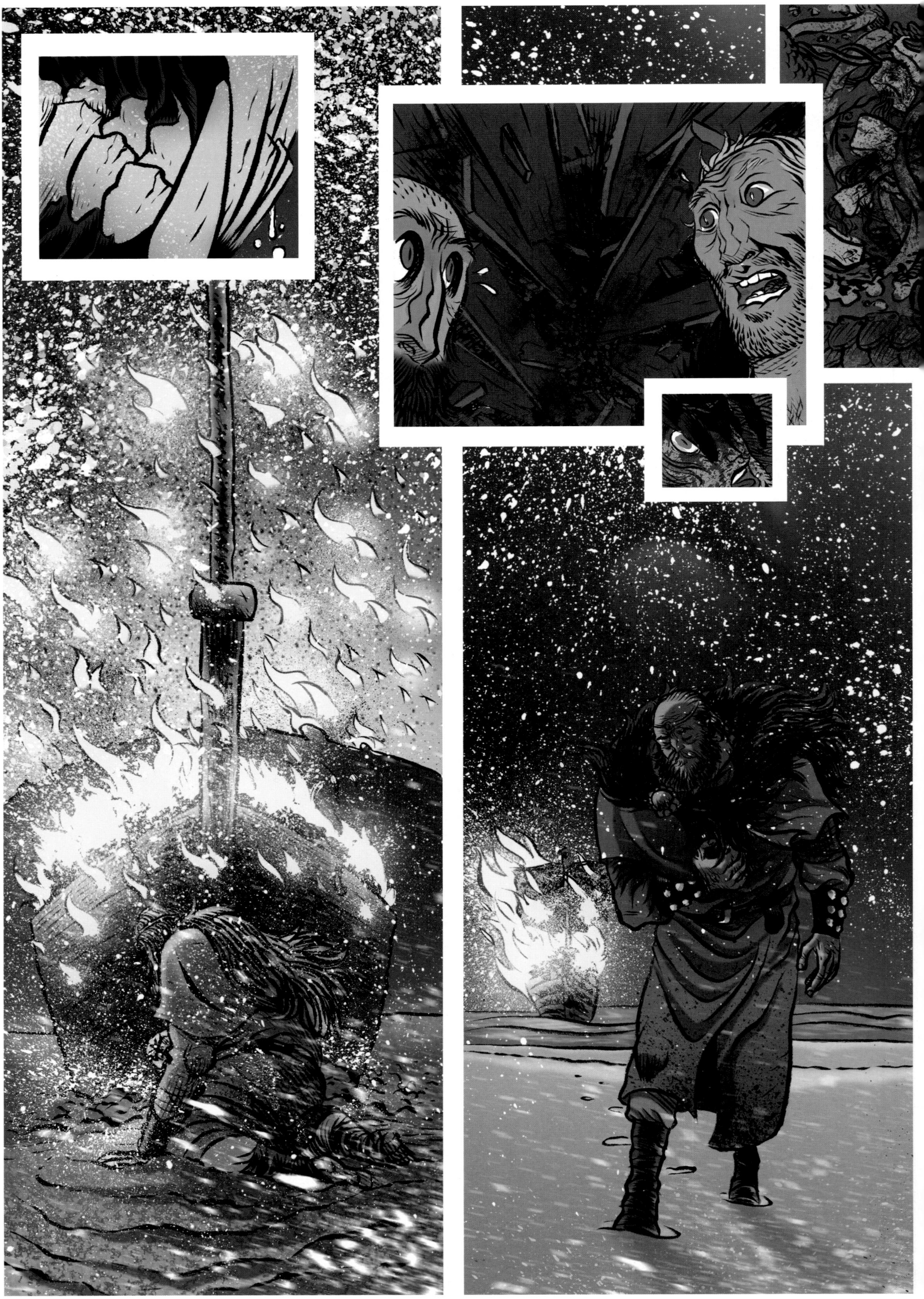

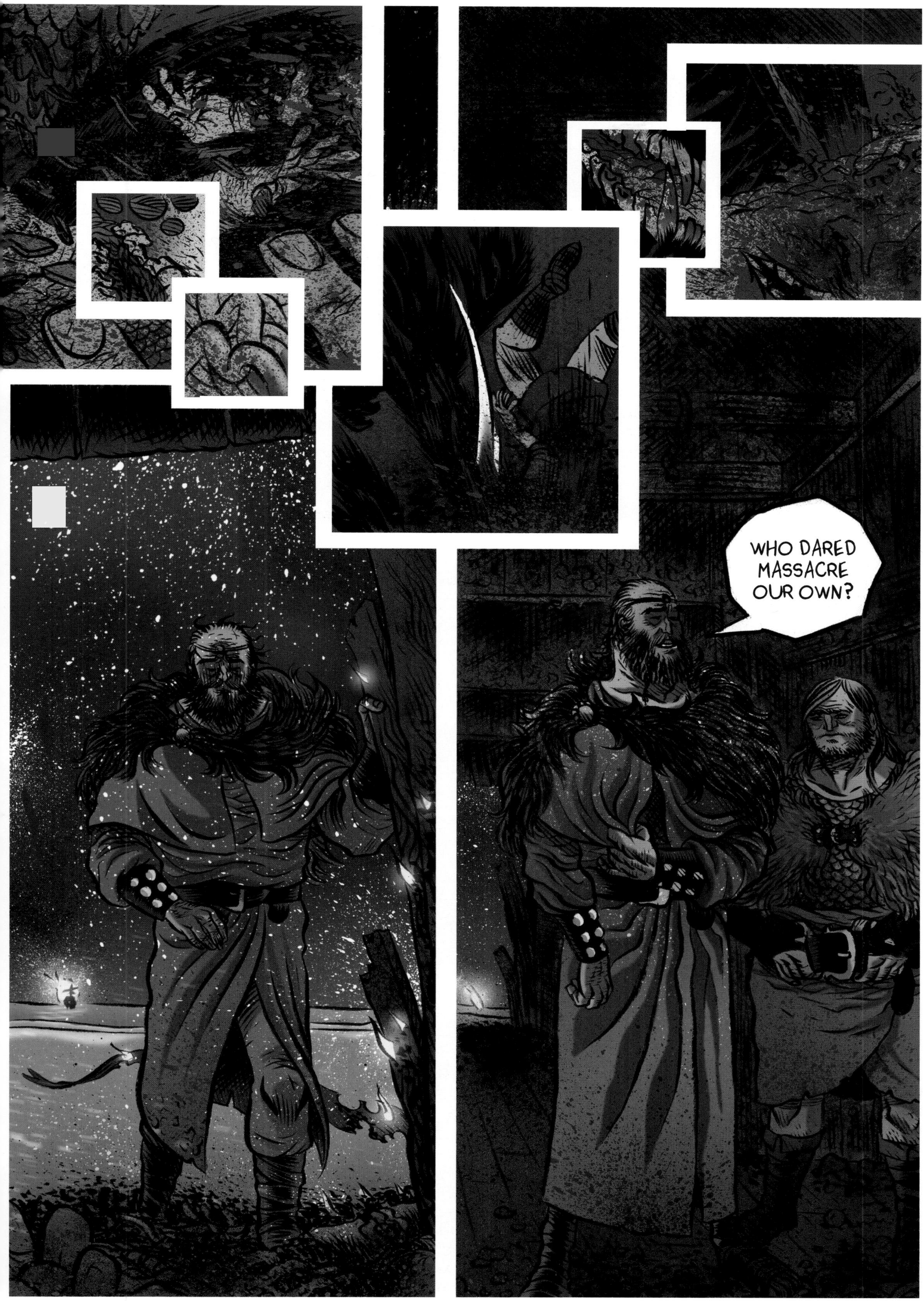
WHO DARED MASSACRE OUR OWN?

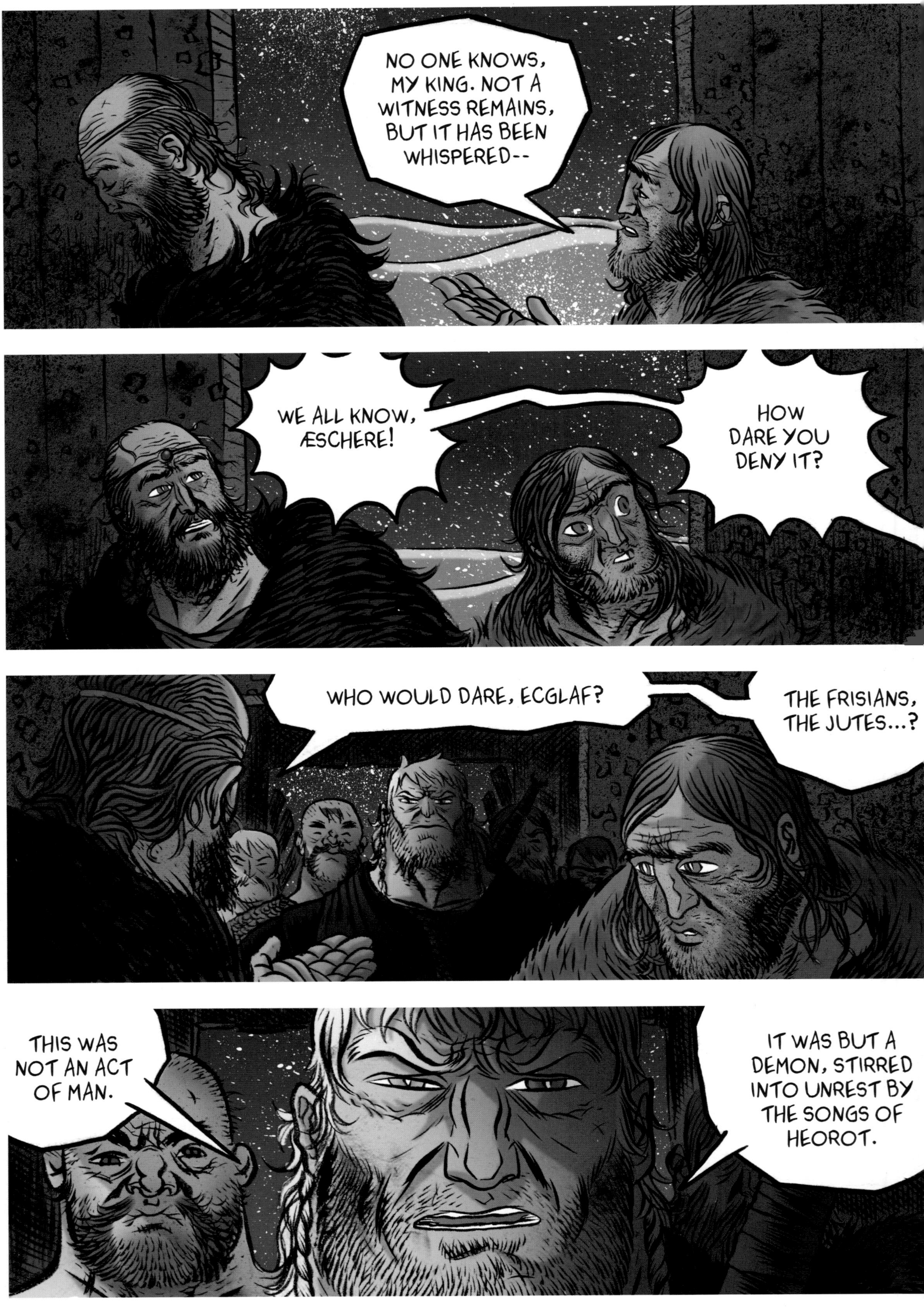
NO ONE KNOWS, MY KING. NOT A WITNESS REMAINS, BUT IT HAS BEEN WHISPERED--
WE ALL KNOW, ÆSCHERE!
HOW DARE YOU DENY IT?
WHO WOULD DARE, ECGLAF?
THE FRISIANS, THE JUTES...?
THIS WAS NOT AN ACT OF MAN.
IT WAS BUT A DEMON, STIRRED INTO UNREST BY THE SONGS OF HEOROT.

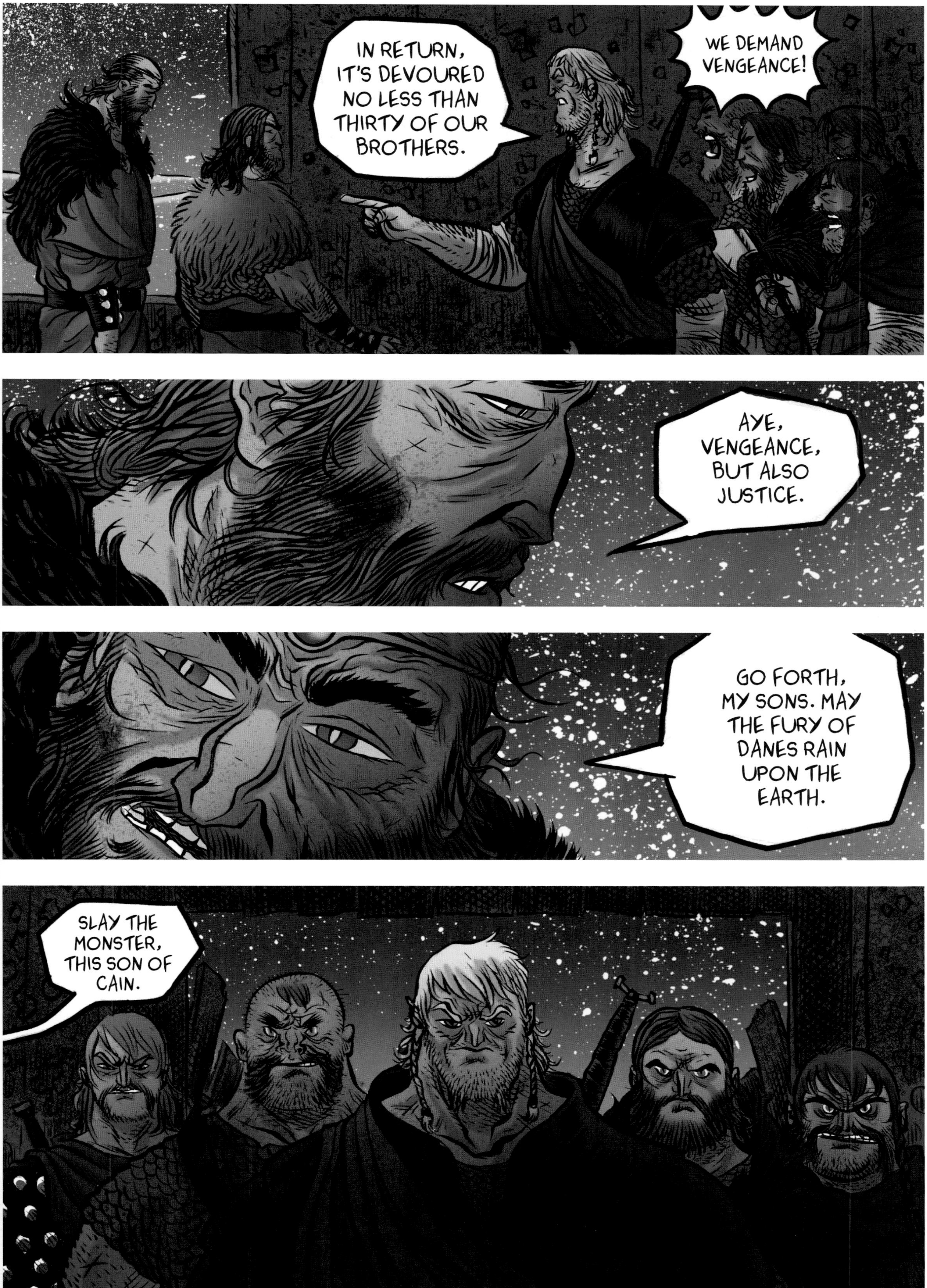
IN RETURN, IT'S DEVOURED NO LESS THAN THIRTY OF OUR BROTHERS.
WE DEMAND VENGEANCE!
AYE, VENGEANCE, BUT ALSO JUSTICE.
GO FORTH, MY SONS. MAY THE FURY OF DANES RAIN UPON THE EARTH.
SLAY THE MONSTER, THIS SON OF CAIN.

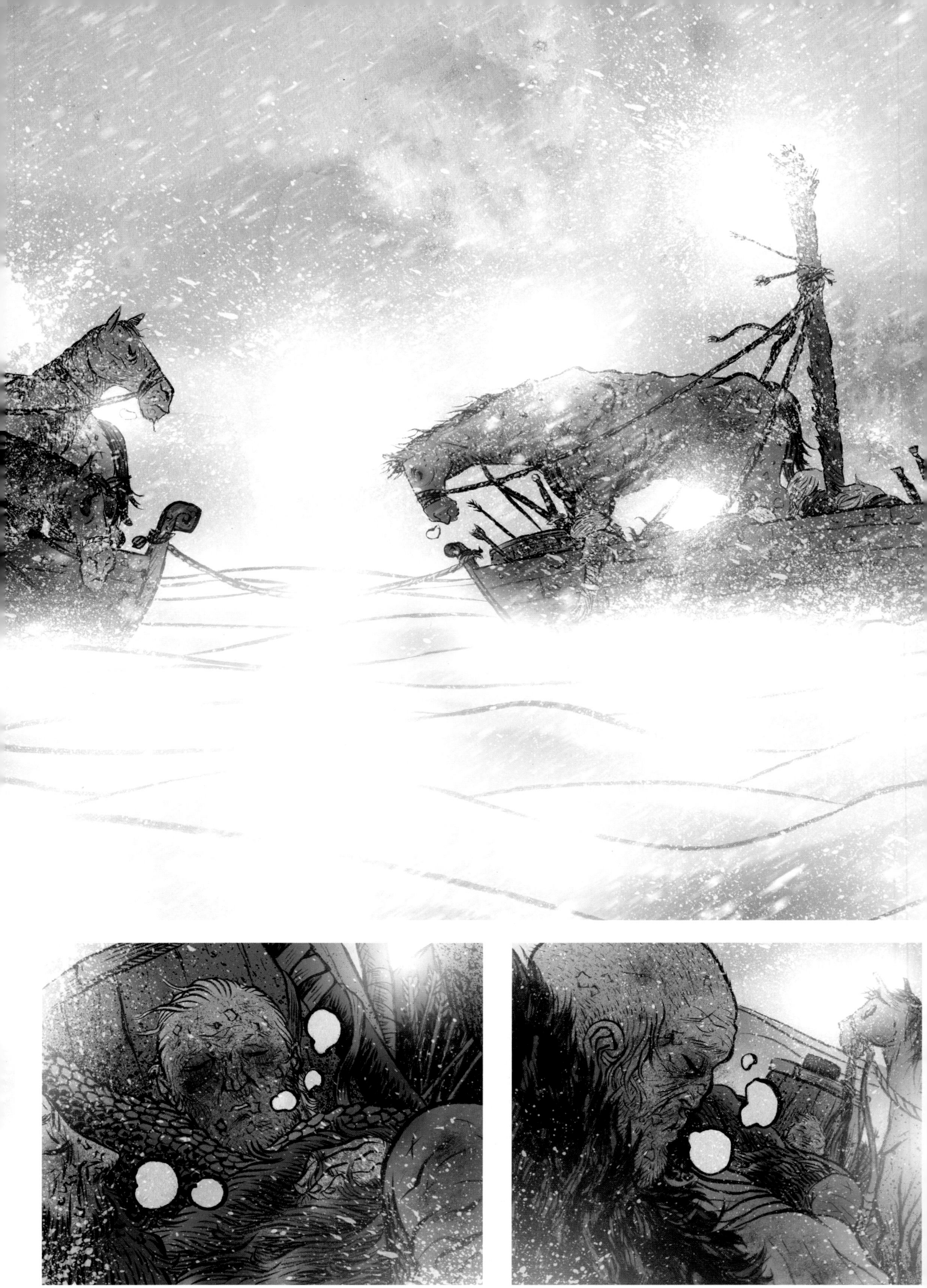

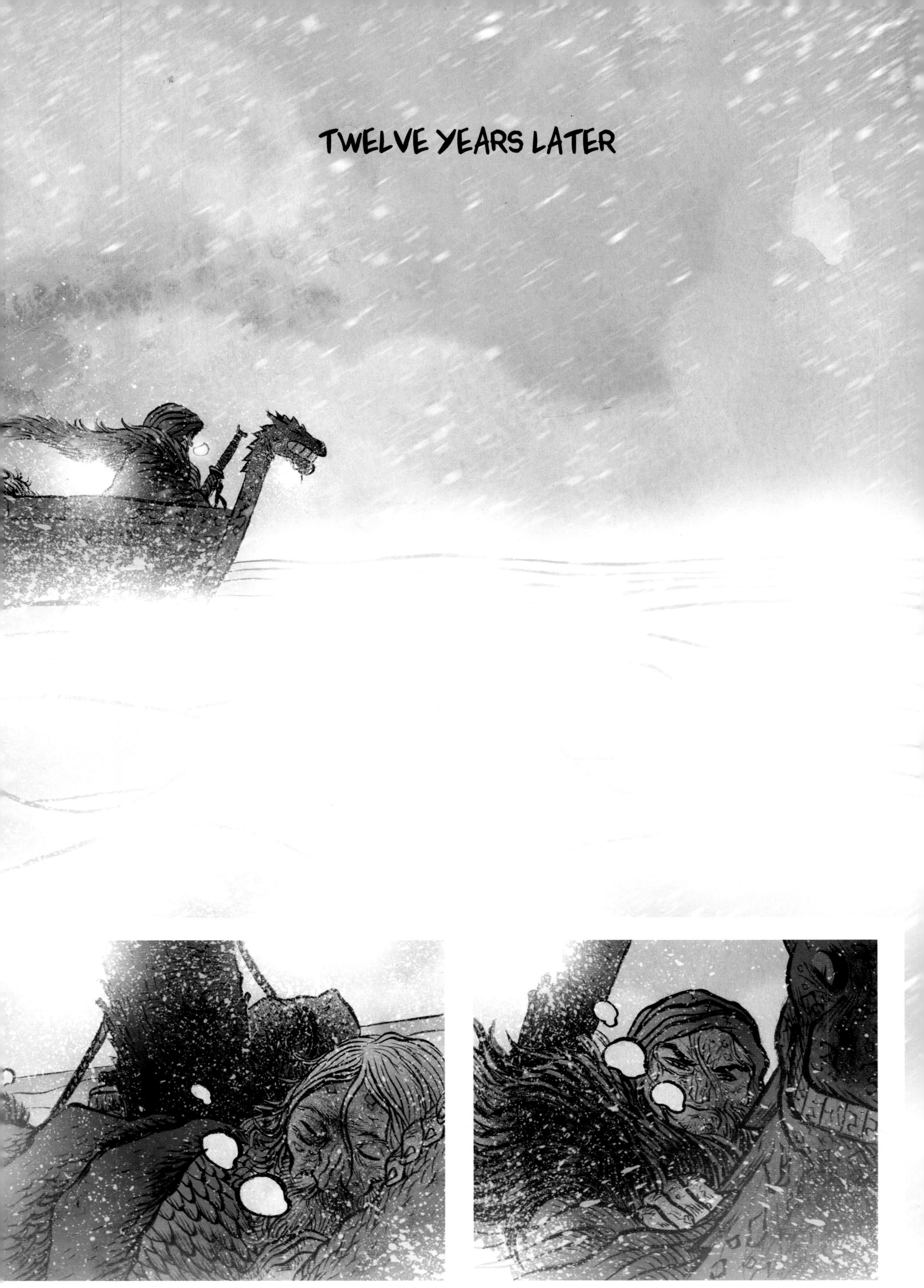
TWELVE YEARS LATER

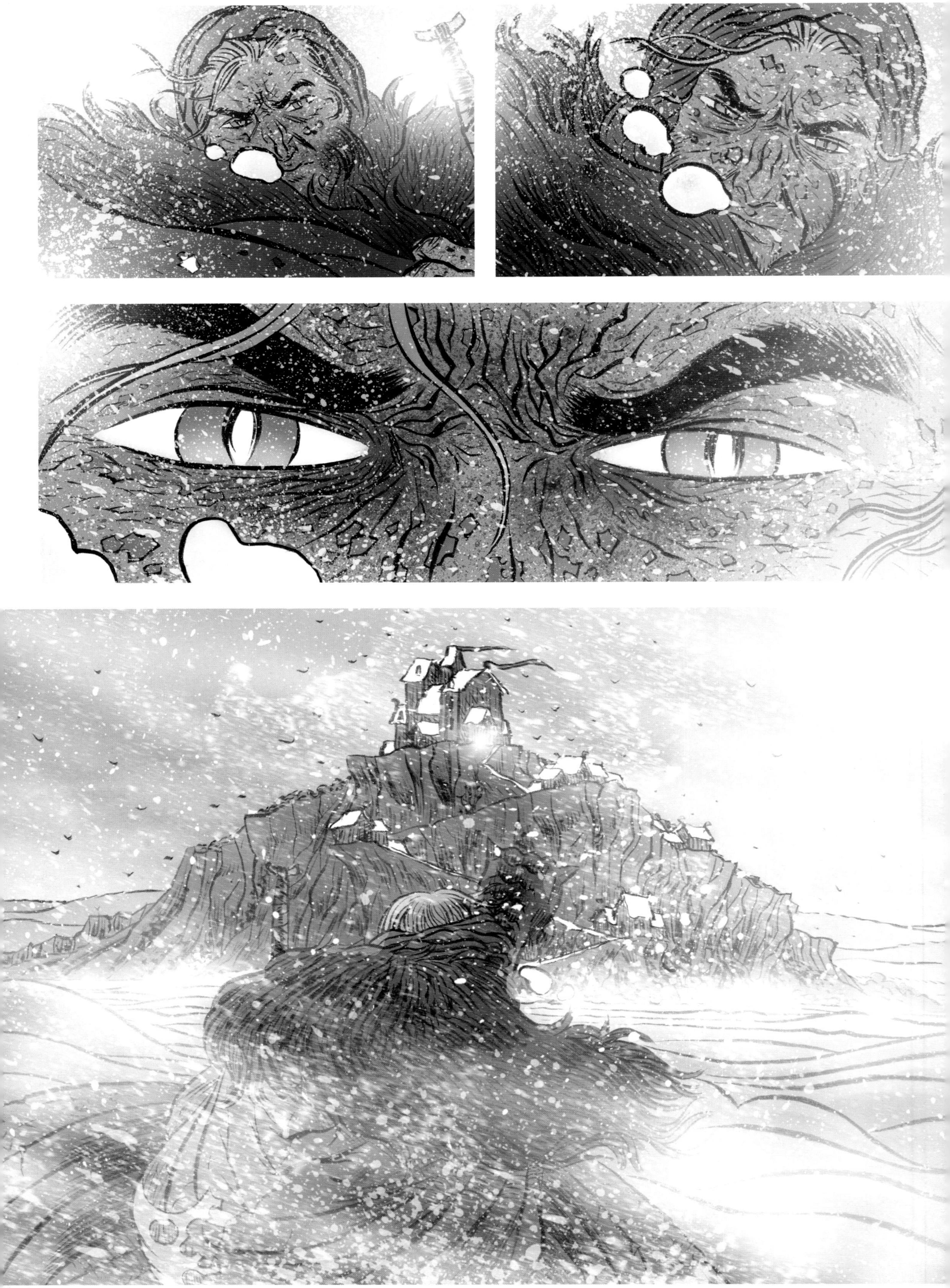

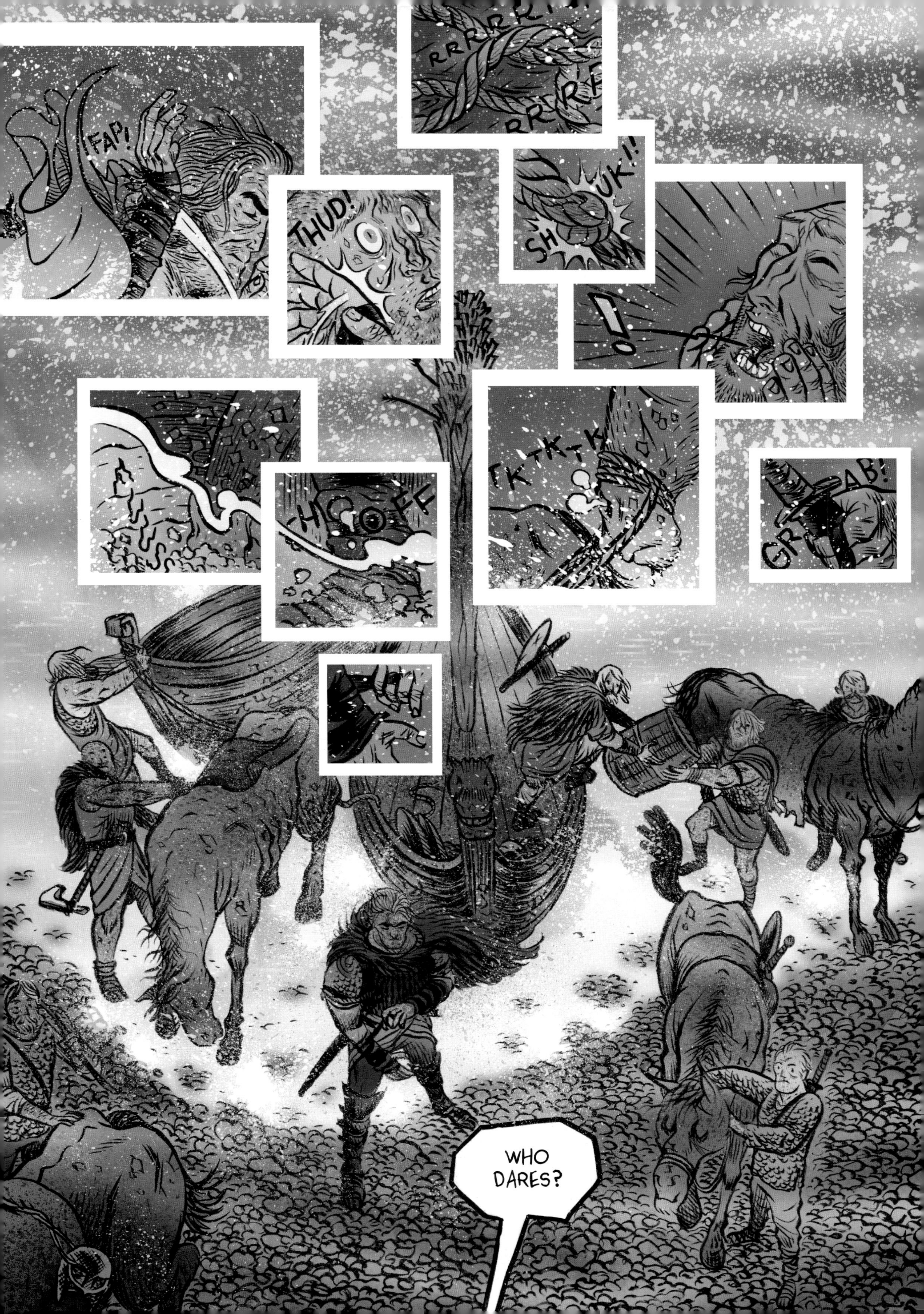
FAP!
RRRRRK!
RRRRR
THUD!
SHUK!!
!
HOOFF
TK-TK-TK
GRAB!
WHO DARES?

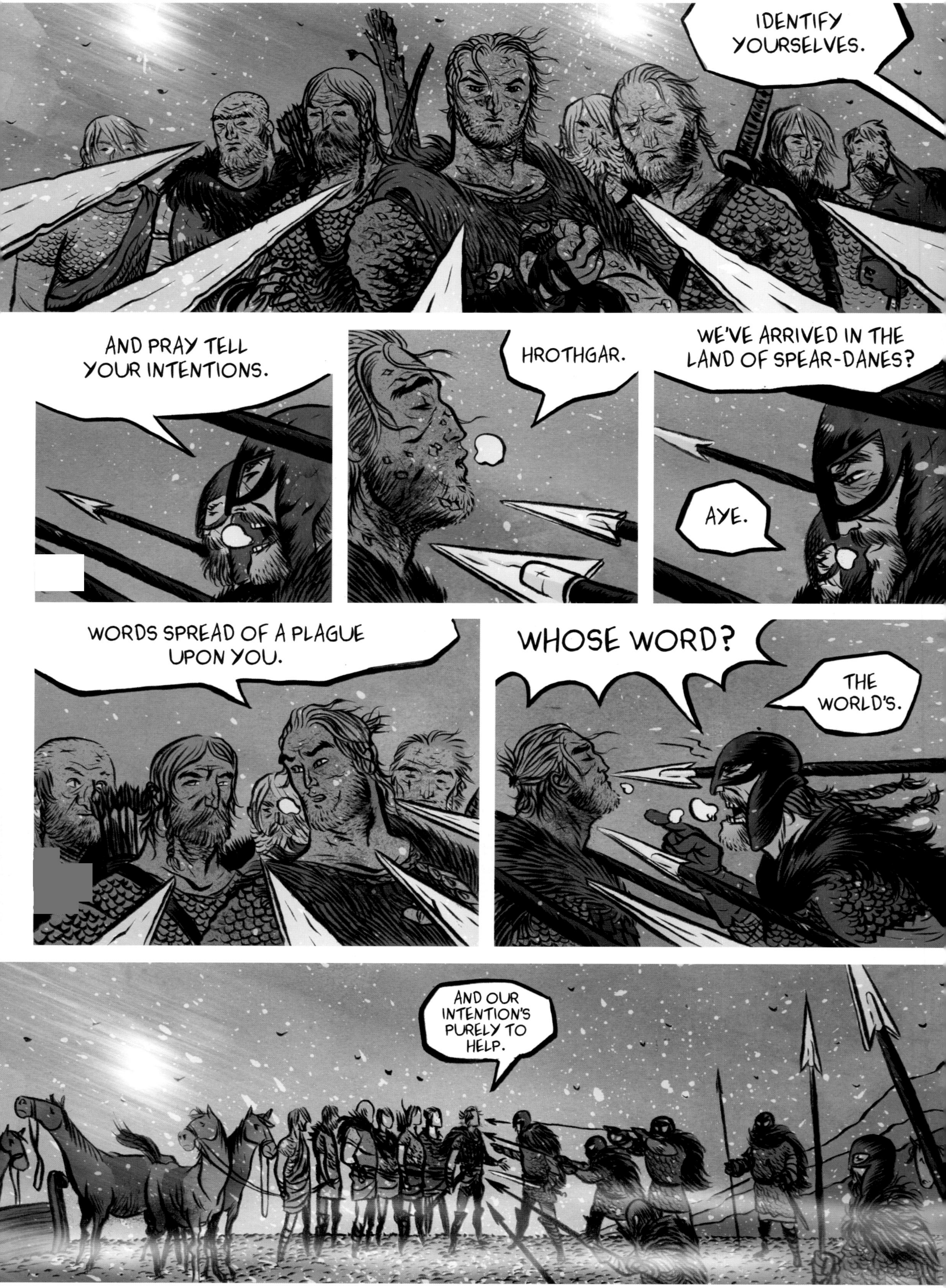
IDENTIFY YOURSELVES.
AND PRAY TELL YOUR INTENTIONS.
HROTHGAR.
WE'VE ARRIVED IN THE LAND OF SPEAR-DANES?
AYE.
WORDS SPREAD OF A PLAGUE UPON YOU.
WHOSE WORD?
THE WORLD'S.
AND OUR INTENTION'S PURELY TO HELP.

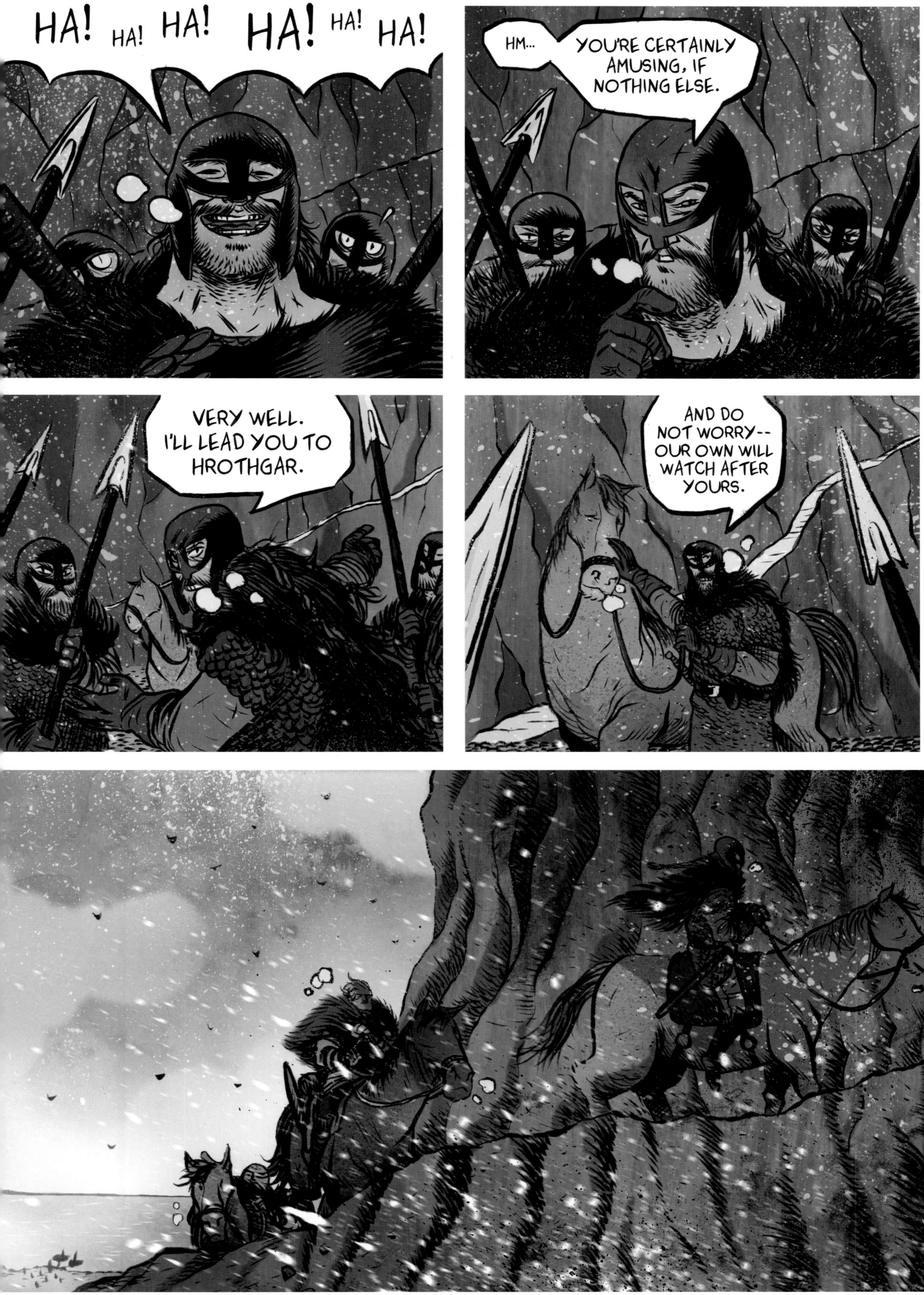
HA! HA! HA! HA! HA! HA!
HM...
YOU'RE CERTAINLY AMUSING, IF NOTHING ELSE.
VERY WELL. I'LL LEAD YOU TO HROTHGAR.
AND DO NOT WORRY-- OUR OWN WILL WATCH AFTER YOURS.

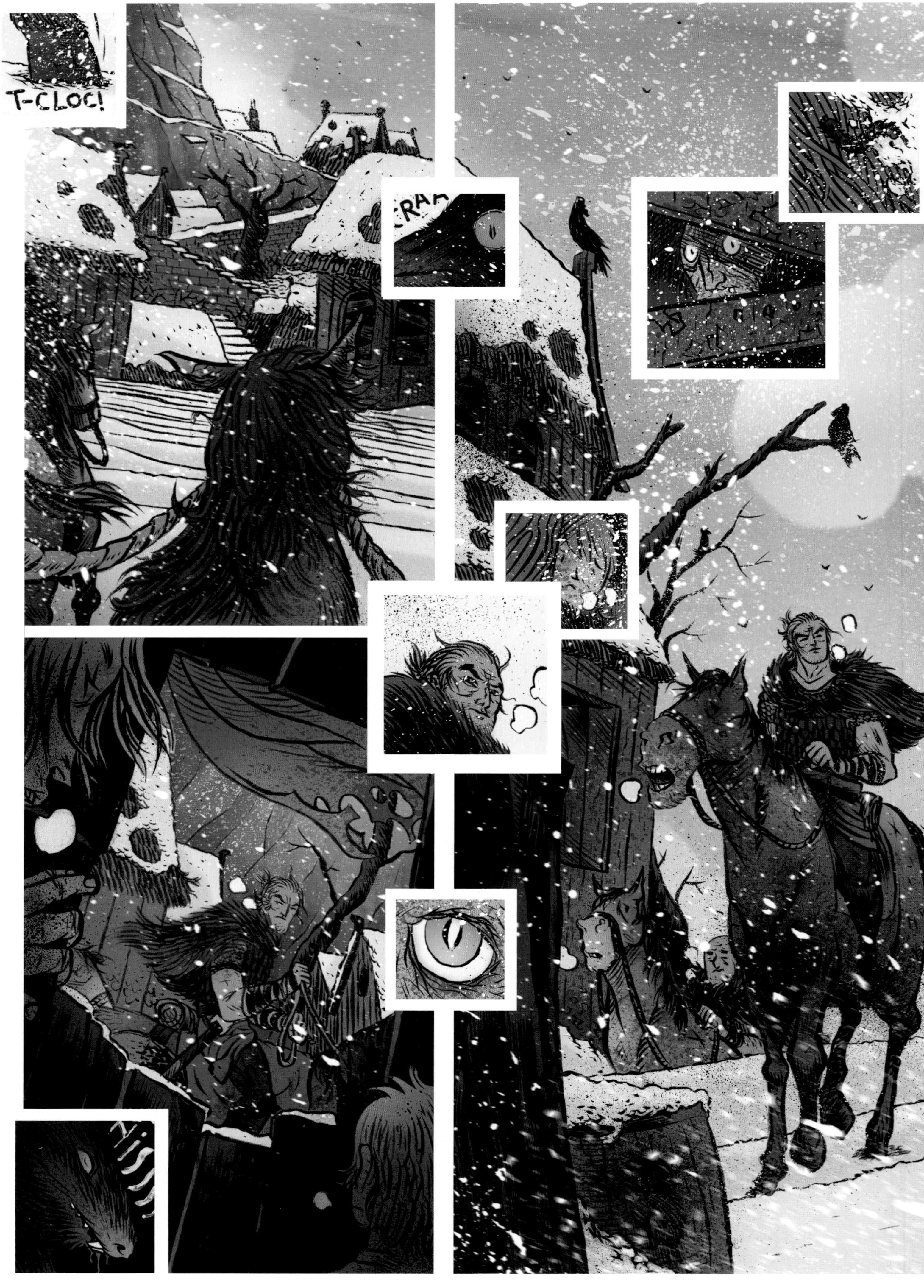
T-CLOC!
CRAA
HISS

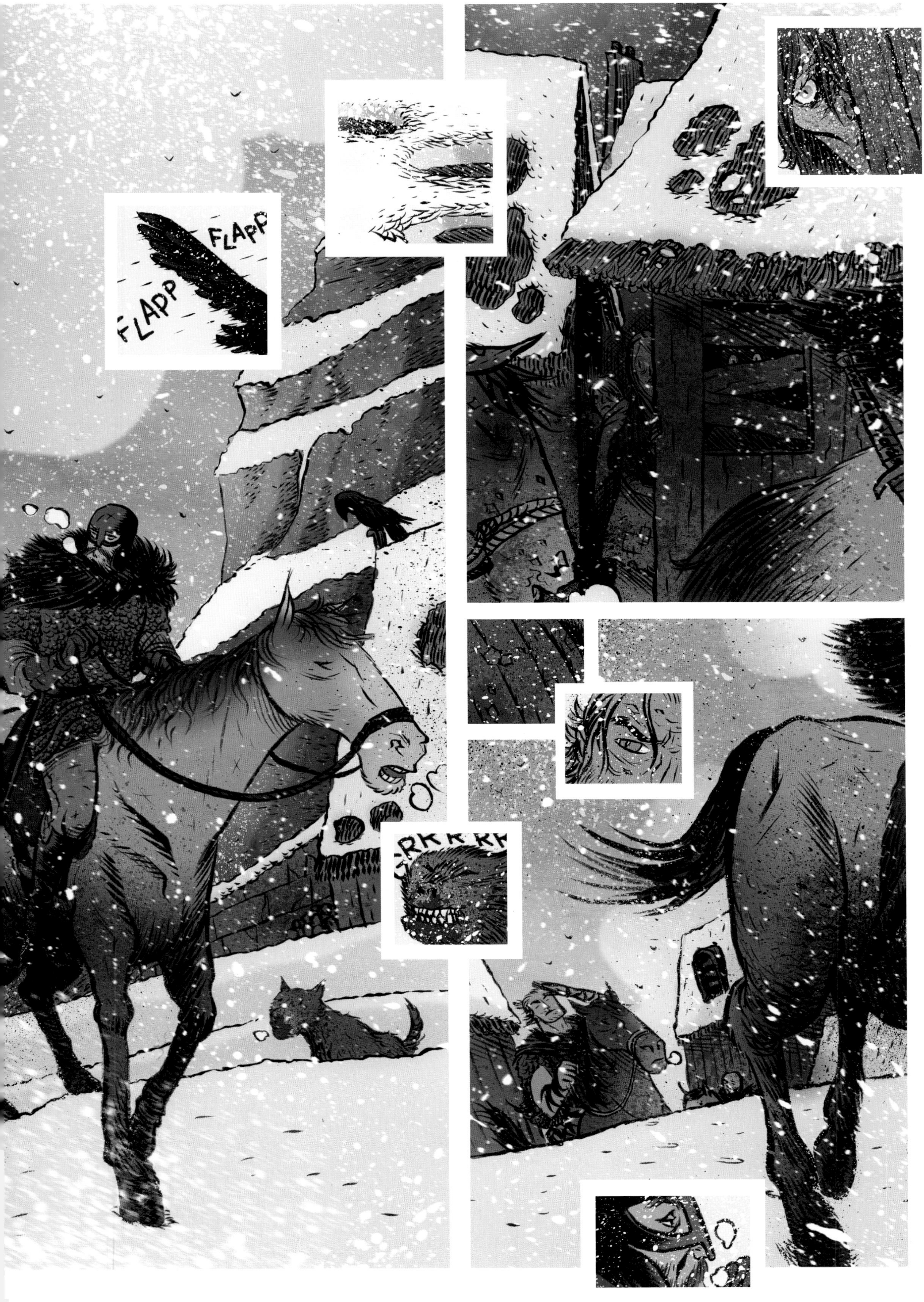
FLAPP
FLAPP

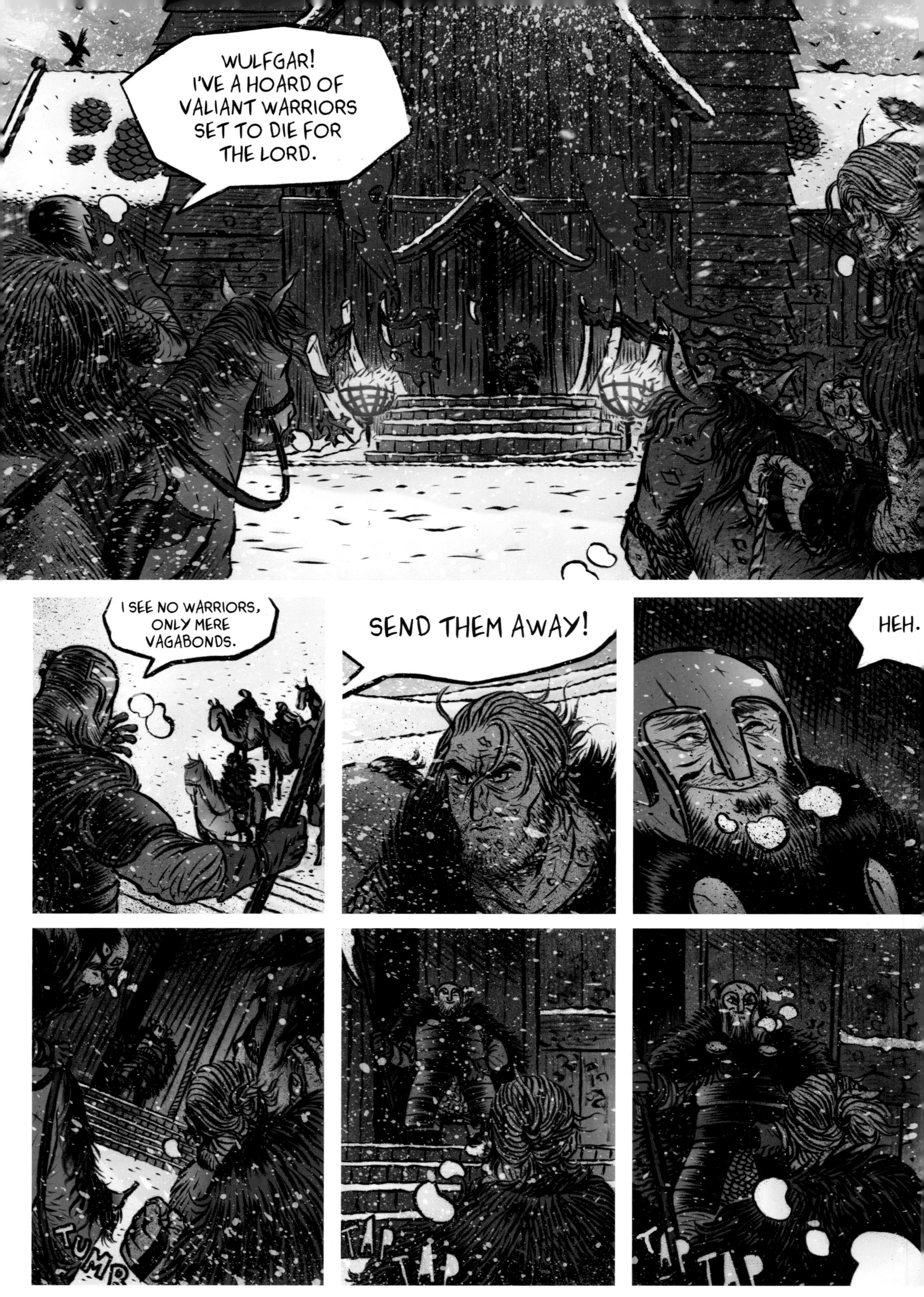
WULFGAR! I'VE A HOARD OF VALIANT WARRIORS SET TO DIE FOR THE LORD.
I SEE NO WARRIORS, ONLY MERE VAGABONDS.
SEND THEM AWAY!
HEH.
TUMB
TAP TAP
TAP TAP

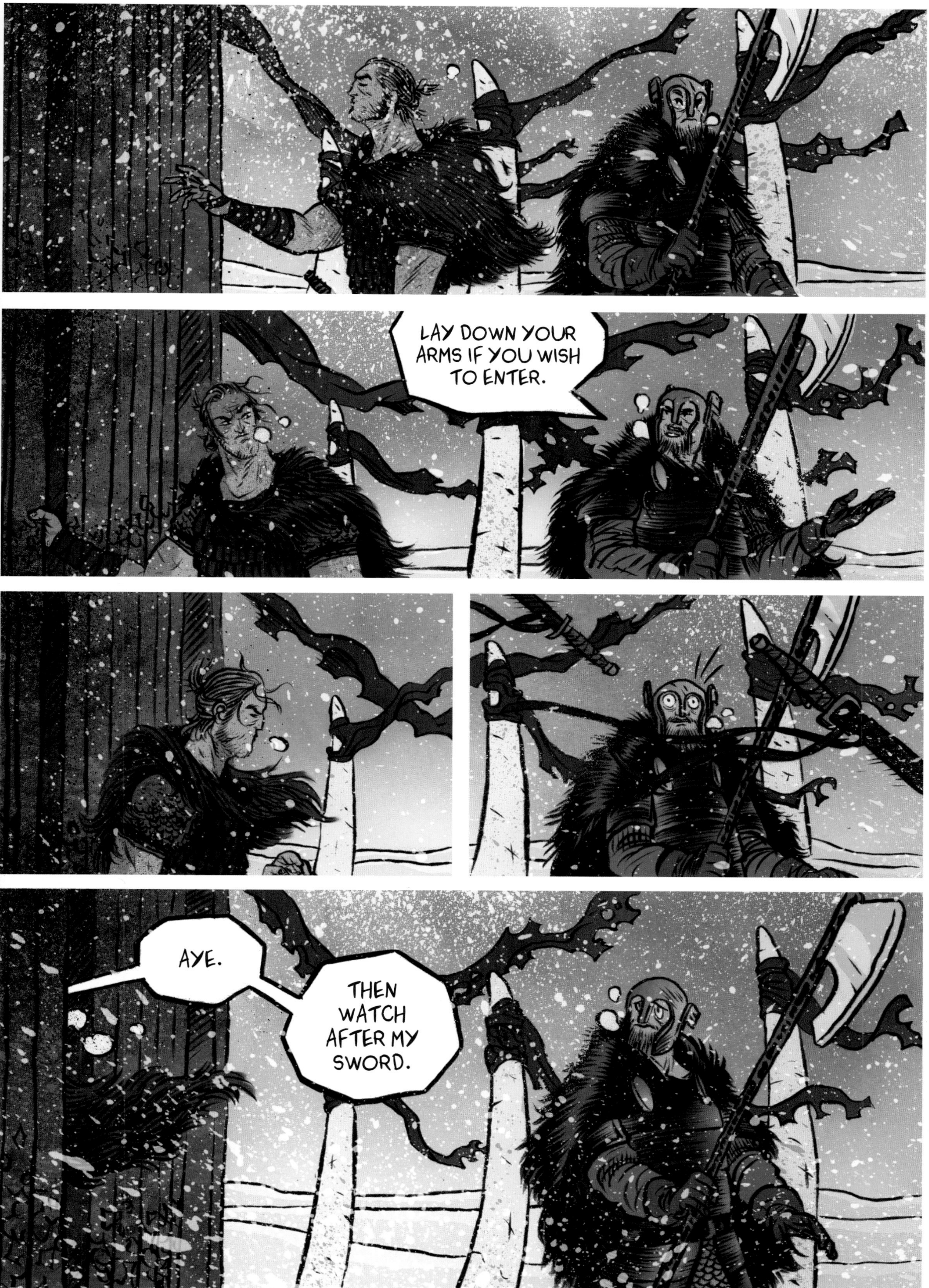
LAY DOWN YOUR ARMS IF YOU WISH TO ENTER.
AYE.
THEN WATCH AFTER MY SWORD.

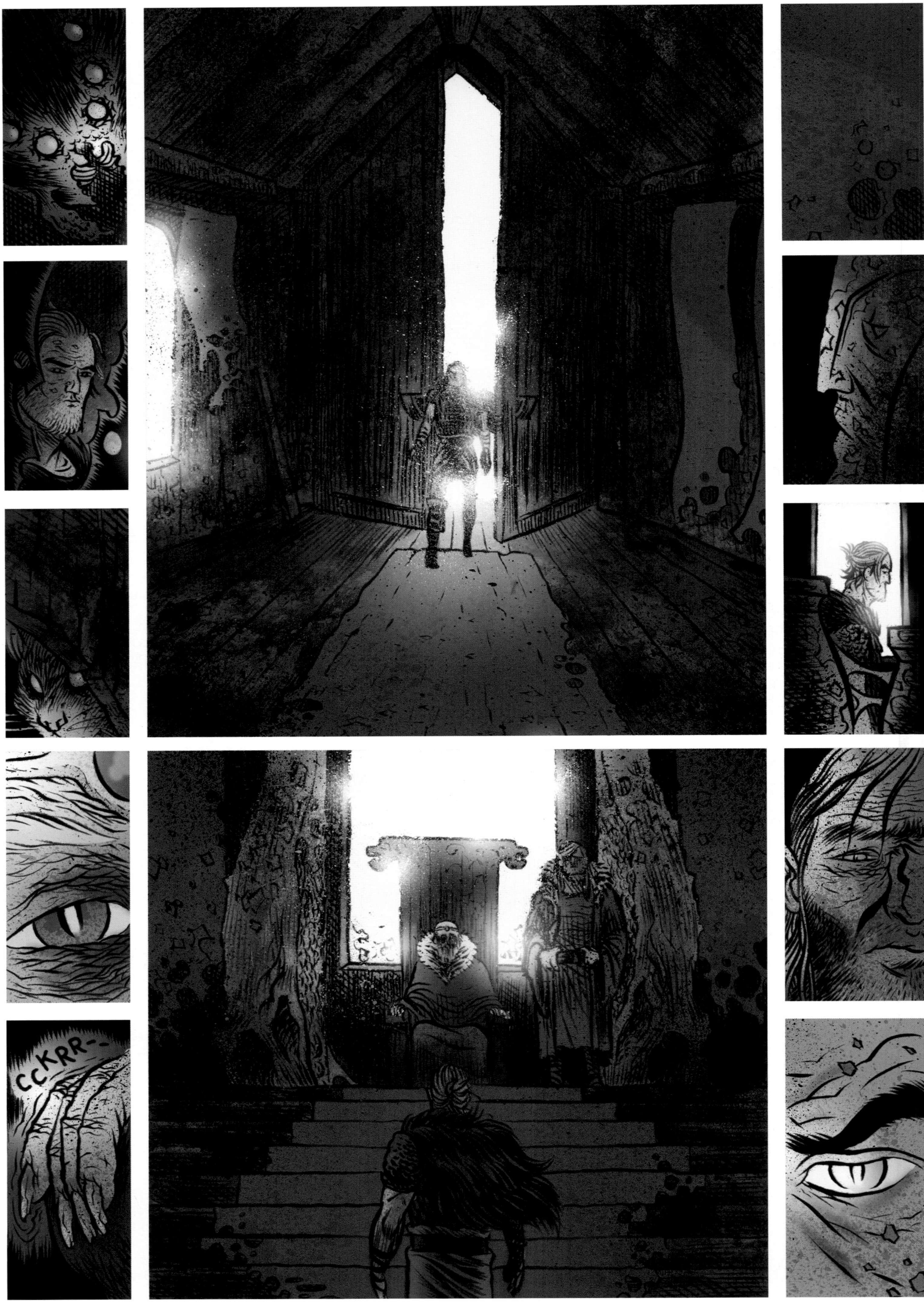
CCKRR--

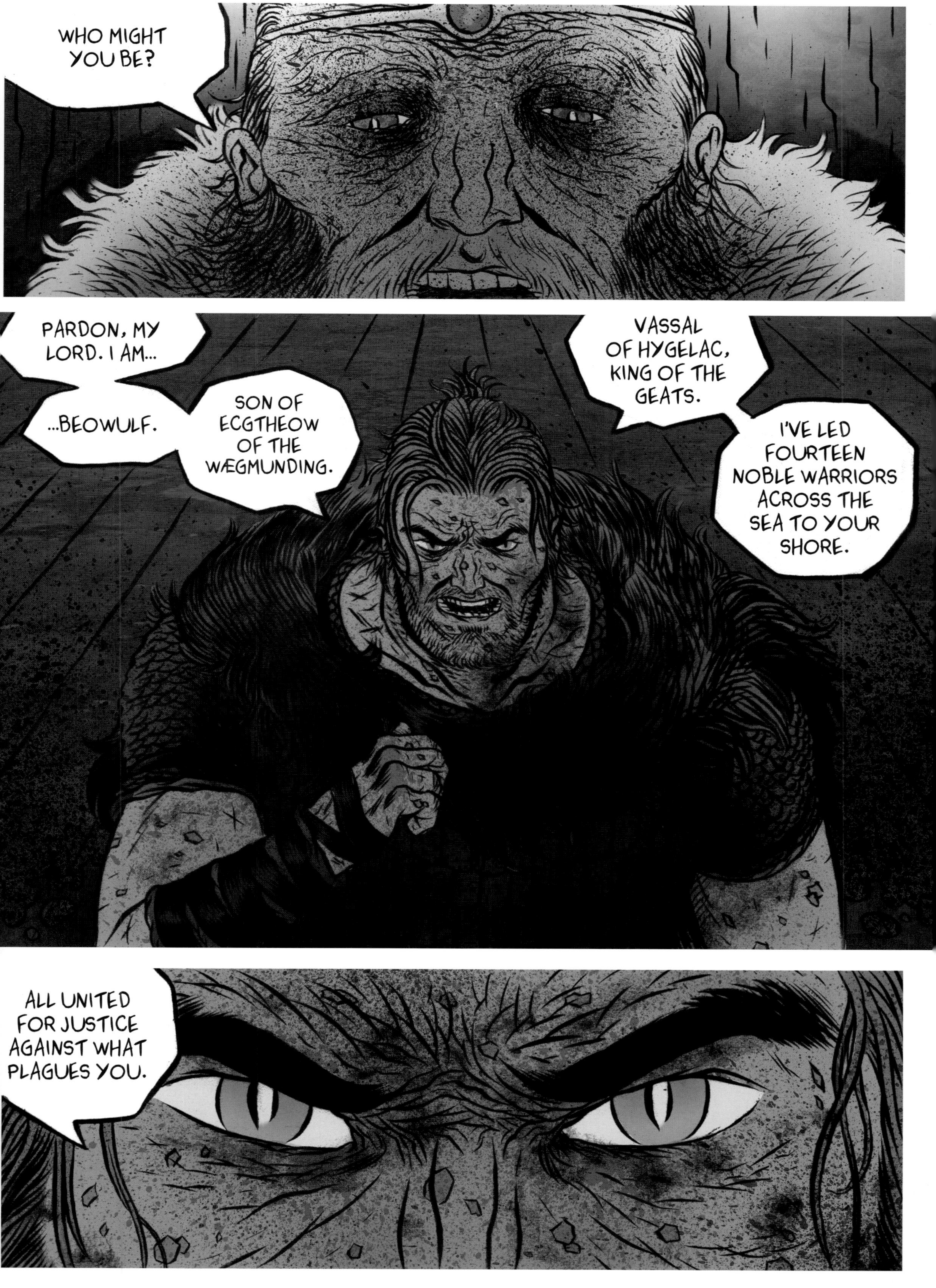
WHO MIGHT YOU BE?
PARDON, MY LORD. I AM...
...BEOWULF.
SON OF ECGTHEOW OF THE WÆGMUNDING.
VASSAL OF HYGELAC, KING OF THE GEATS.
I'VE LED FOURTEEN NOBLE WARRIORS ACROSS THE SEA TO YOUR SHORE.
ALL UNITED FOR JUSTICE AGAINST WHAT PLAGUES YOU.

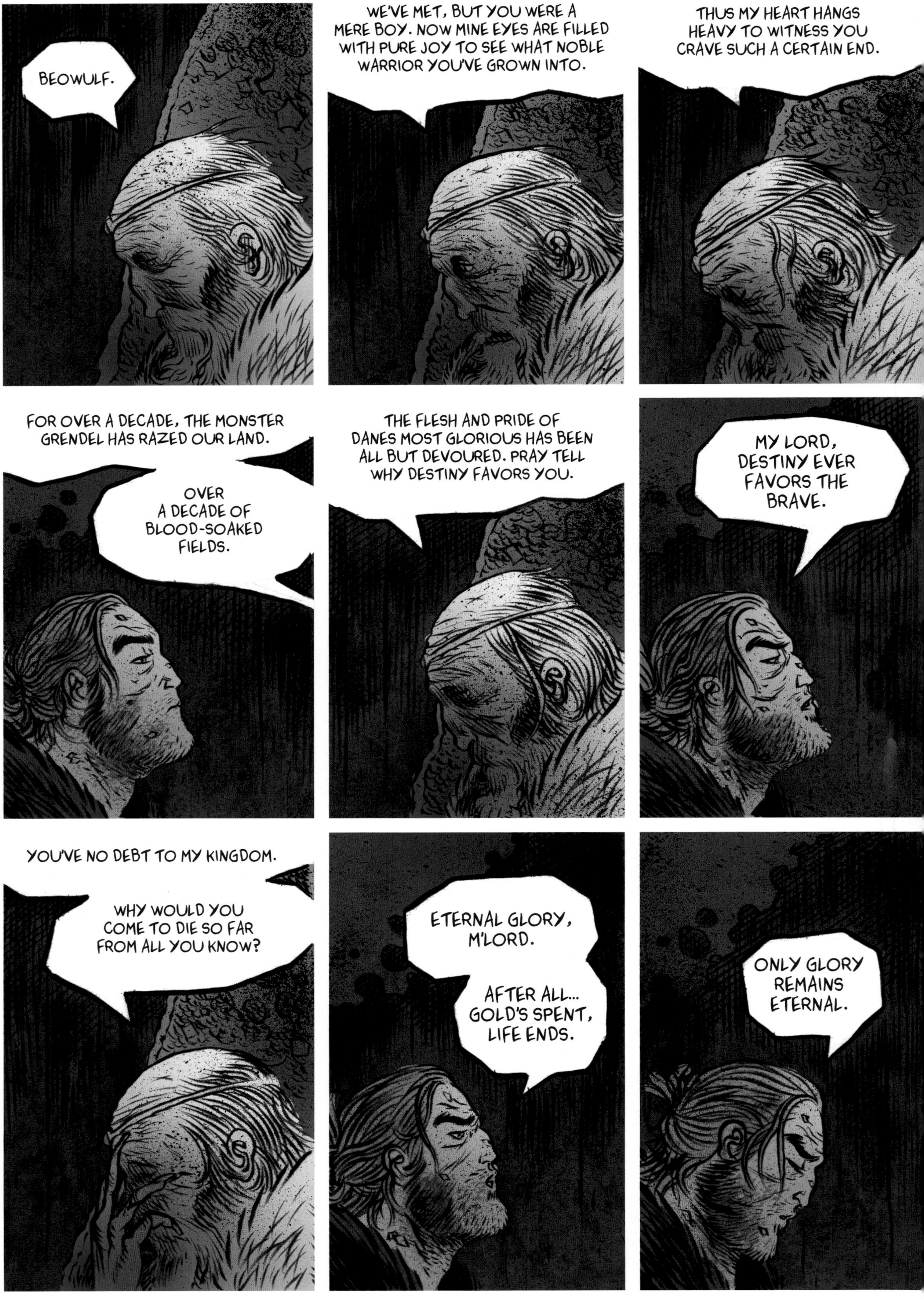

BEOWULF.
WE'VE MET, BUT YOU WERE A MERE BOY. NOW MINE EYES ARE FILLED WITH PURE JOY TO SEE WHAT NOBLE WARRIOR YOU'VE GROWN INTO.
THUS MY HEART HANGS HEAVY TO WITNESS YOU CRAVE SUCH A CERTAIN END.
FOR OVER A DECADE, THE MONSTER GRENDEL HAS RAZED OUR LAND.
OVER A DECADE OF BLOOD-SOAKED FIELDS.
THE FLESH AND PRIDE OF DANES MOST GLORIOUS HAS BEEN ALL BUT DEVOURED. PRAY TELL WHY DESTINY FAVORS YOU.
MY LORD, DESTINY EVER FAVORS THE BRAVE.
YOU'VE NO DEBT TO MY KINGDOM.
WHY WOULD YOU COME TO DIE SO FAR FROM ALL YOU KNOW?
ETERNAL GLORY, M'LORD.
AFTER ALL... GOLD'S SPENT, LIFE ENDS.
ONLY GLORY REMAINS ETERNAL.

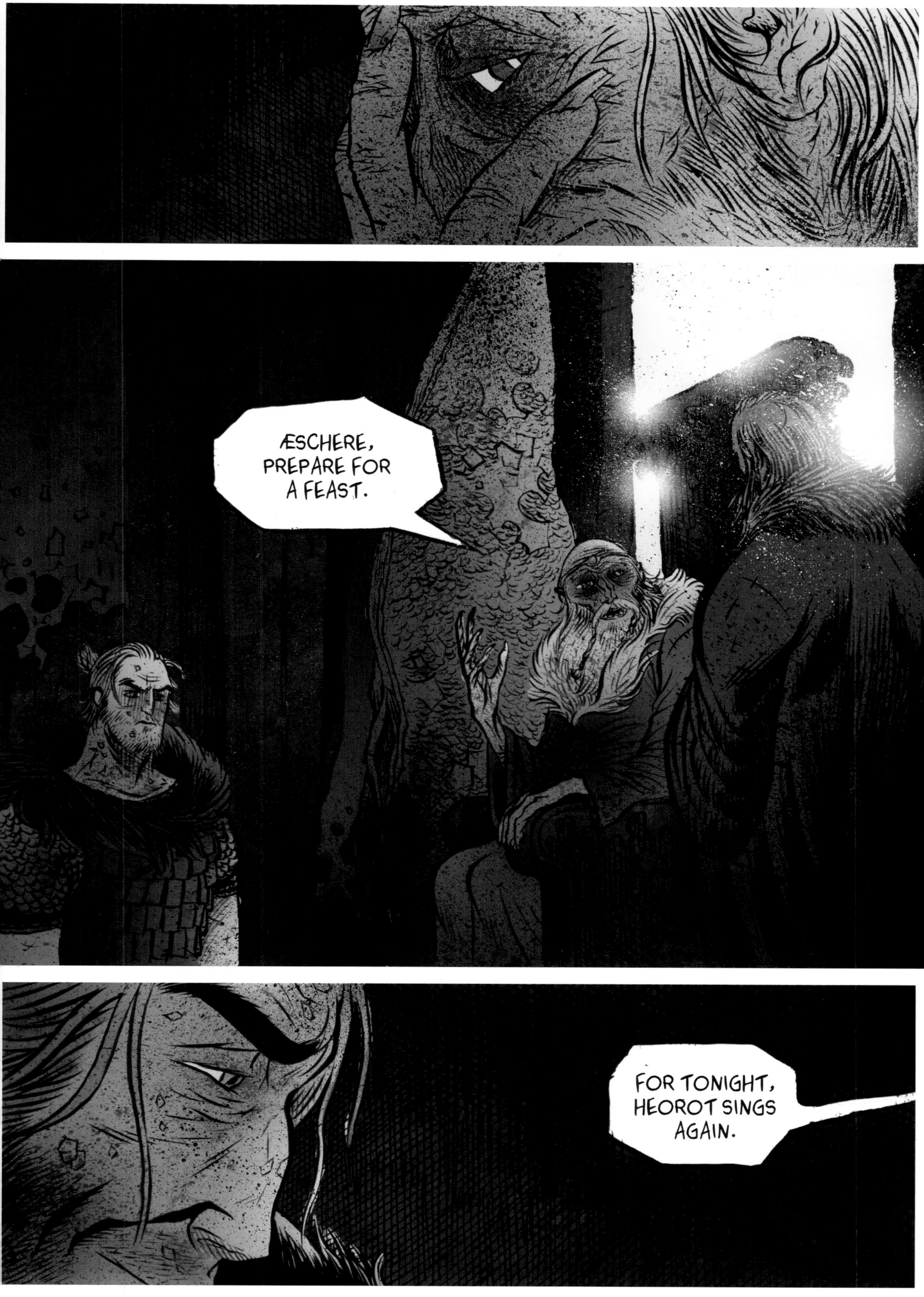
ÆSCHERE, PREPARE FOR A FEAST.
FOR TONIGHT, HEOROT SINGS AGAIN.

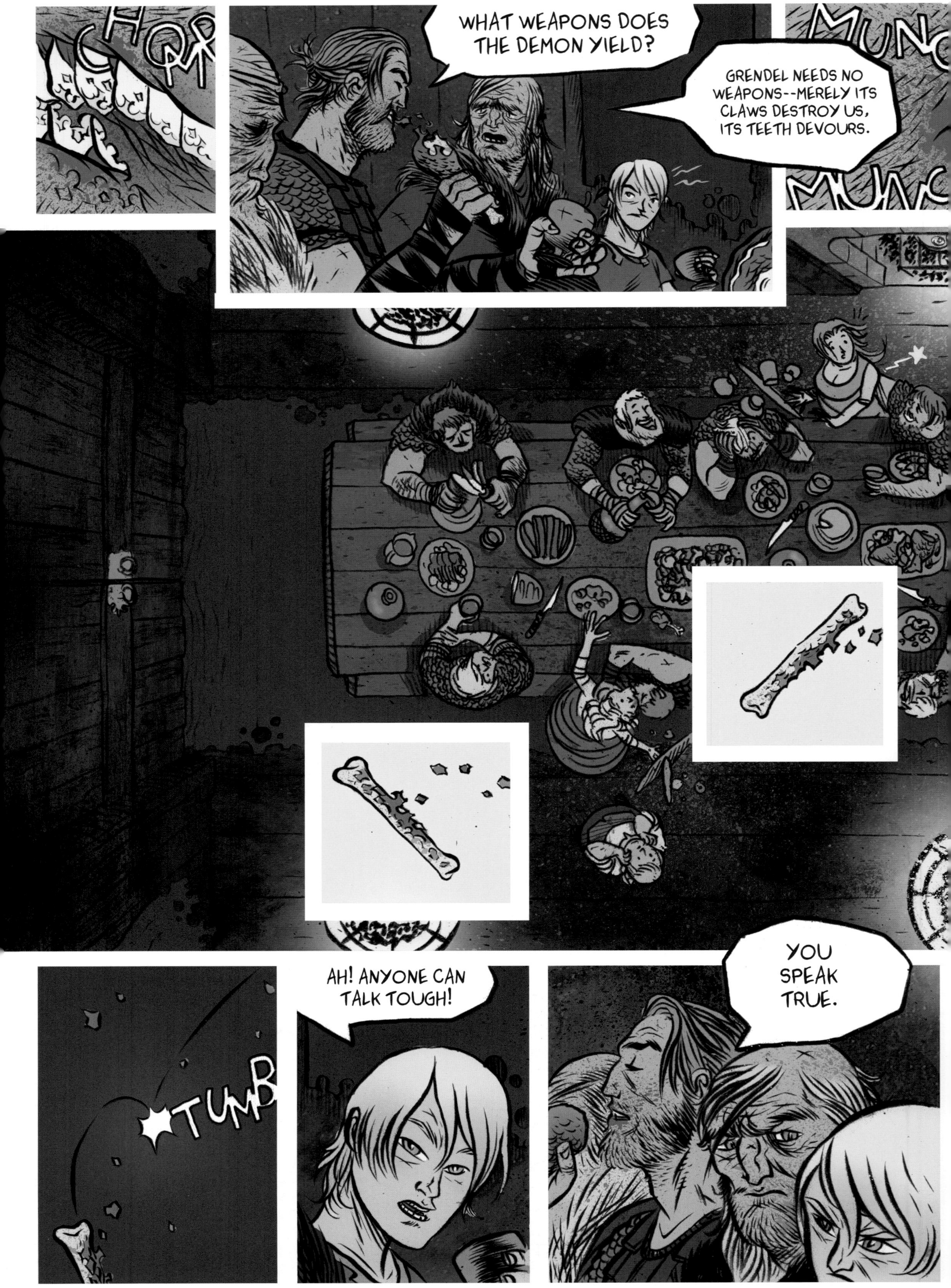
CHOM
WHAT WEAPONS DOES THE DEMON YIELD?
GRENDEL NEEDS NO WEAPONS--MERELY ITS CLAWS DESTROY US, ITS TEETH DEVOURS.
MUNC
MUNC
TUMB
AH! ANYONE CAN TALK TOUGH!
YOU SPEAK TRUE.

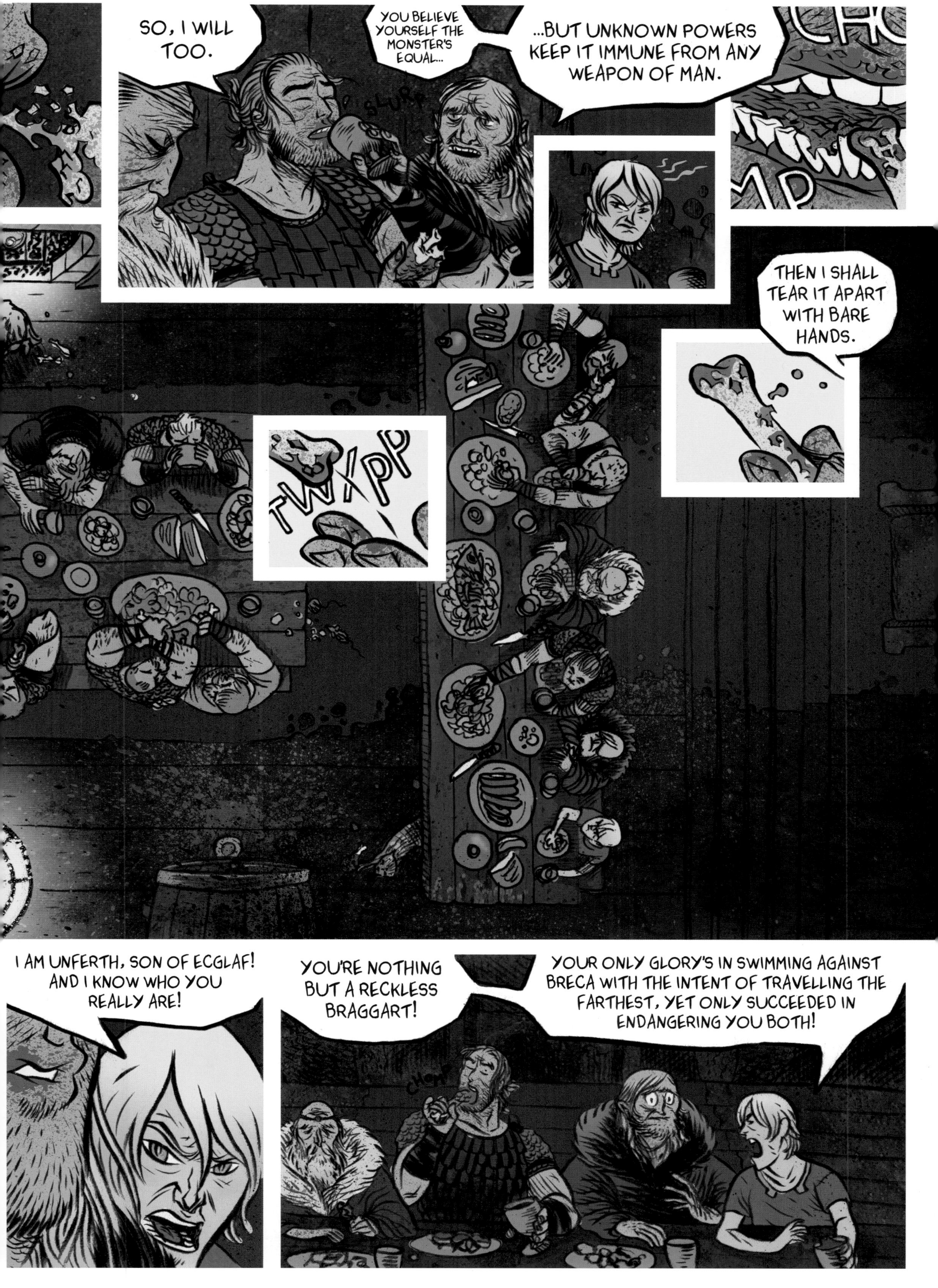
SO, I WILL TOO.
SLURP
YOU BELIEVE YOURSELF THE MONSTER'S EQUAL...
...BUT UNKNOWN POWERS KEEP IT IMMUNE FROM ANY WEAPON OF MAN.
THEN I SHALL TEAR IT APART WITH BARE HANDS.
TWXPP
I AM UNFERTH, SON OF ECGLAF! AND I KNOW WHO YOU REALLY ARE!
YOU'RE NOTHING BUT A RECKLESS BRAGGART!
YOUR ONLY GLORY'S IN SWIMMING AGAINST BRECA WITH THE INTENT OF TRAVELLING THE FARTHEST, YET ONLY SUCCEEDED IN ENDANGERING YOU BOTH!

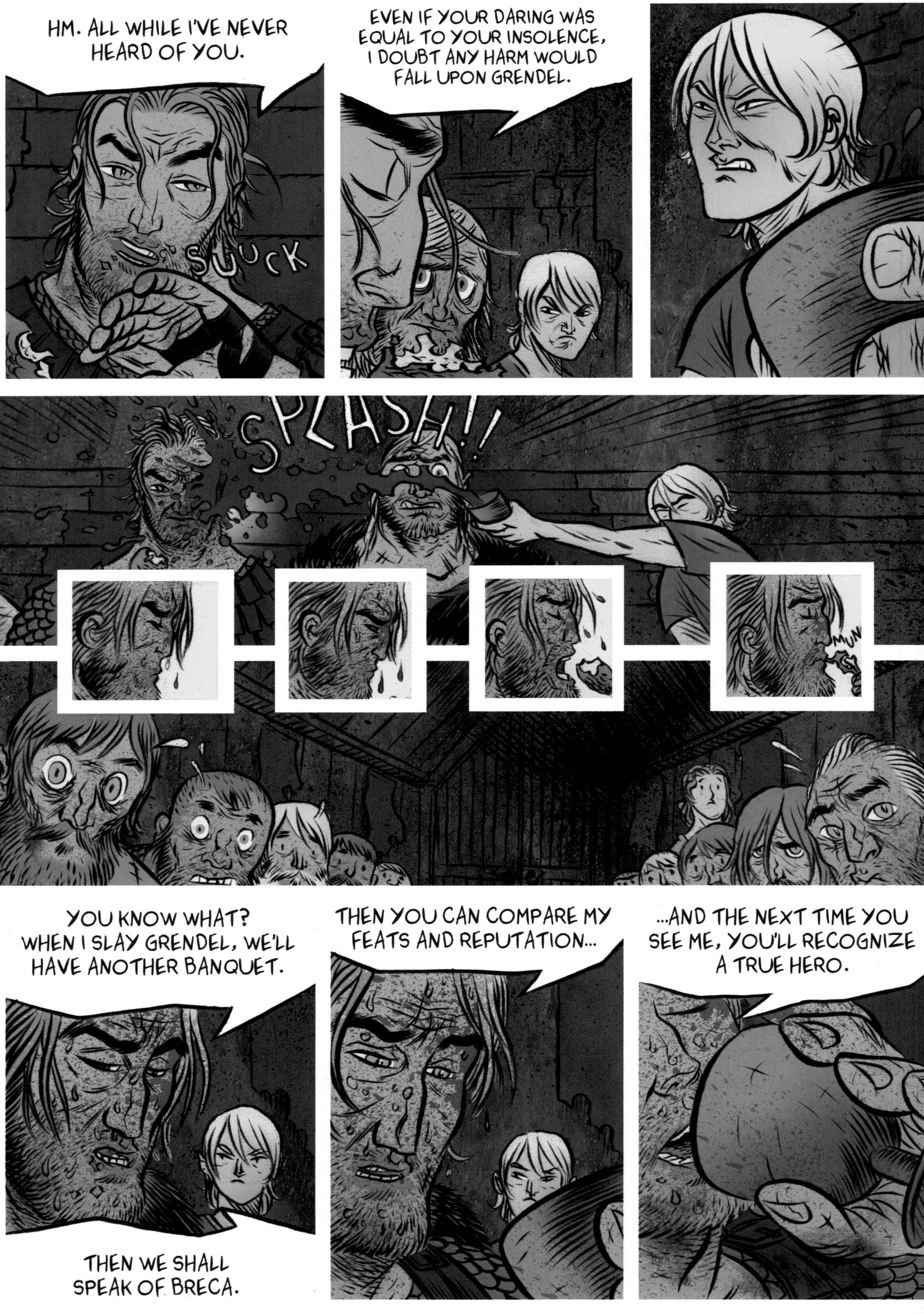
HM. ALL WHILE I'VE NEVER HEARD OF YOU.
SUUCK
EVEN IF YOUR DARING WAS EQUAL TO YOUR INSOLENCE, I DOUBT ANY HARM WOULD FALL UPON GRENDEL.
SPLASH!!
MUN
YOU KNOW WHAT? WHEN I SLAY GRENDEL, WE'LL HAVE ANOTHER BANQUET.
THEN WE SHALL SPEAK OF BRECA.
THEN YOU CAN COMPARE MY FEATS AND REPUTATION...
...AND THE NEXT TIME YOU SEE ME, YOU'LL RECOGNIZE A TRUE HERO.

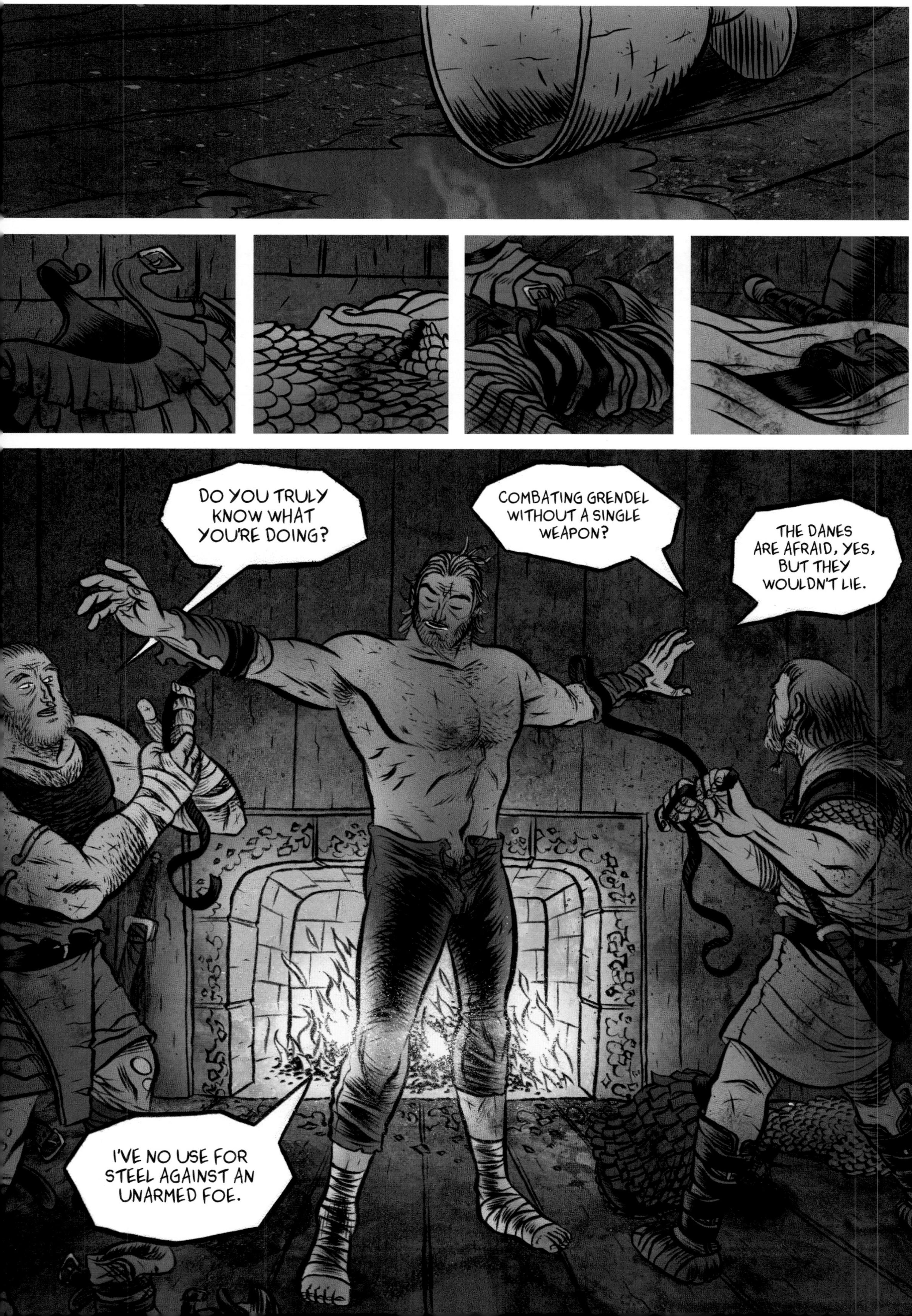
DO YOU TRULY KNOW WHAT YOU'RE DOING?
COMBATING GRENDEL WITHOUT A SINGLE WEAPON?
THE DANES ARE AFRAID, YES, BUT THEY WOULDN'T LIE.
I'VE NO USE FOR STEEL AGAINST AN UNARMED FOE.

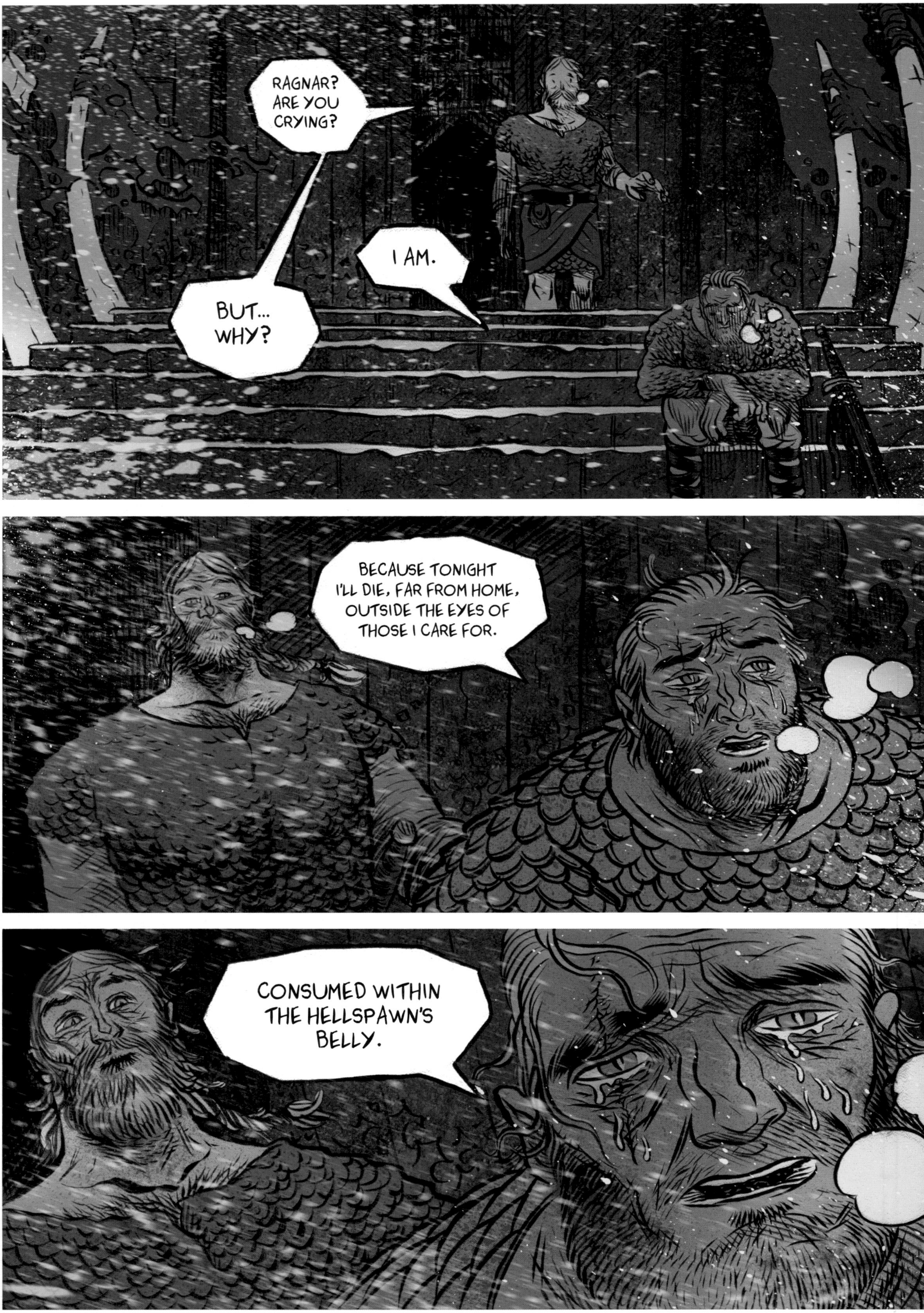
RAGNAR? ARE YOU CRYING?
I AM.
BUT... WHY?
BECAUSE TONIGHT I'LL DIE, FAR FROM HOME, OUTSIDE THE EYES OF THOSE I CARE FOR.
CONSUMED WITHIN THE HELLSPAWN'S BELLY.

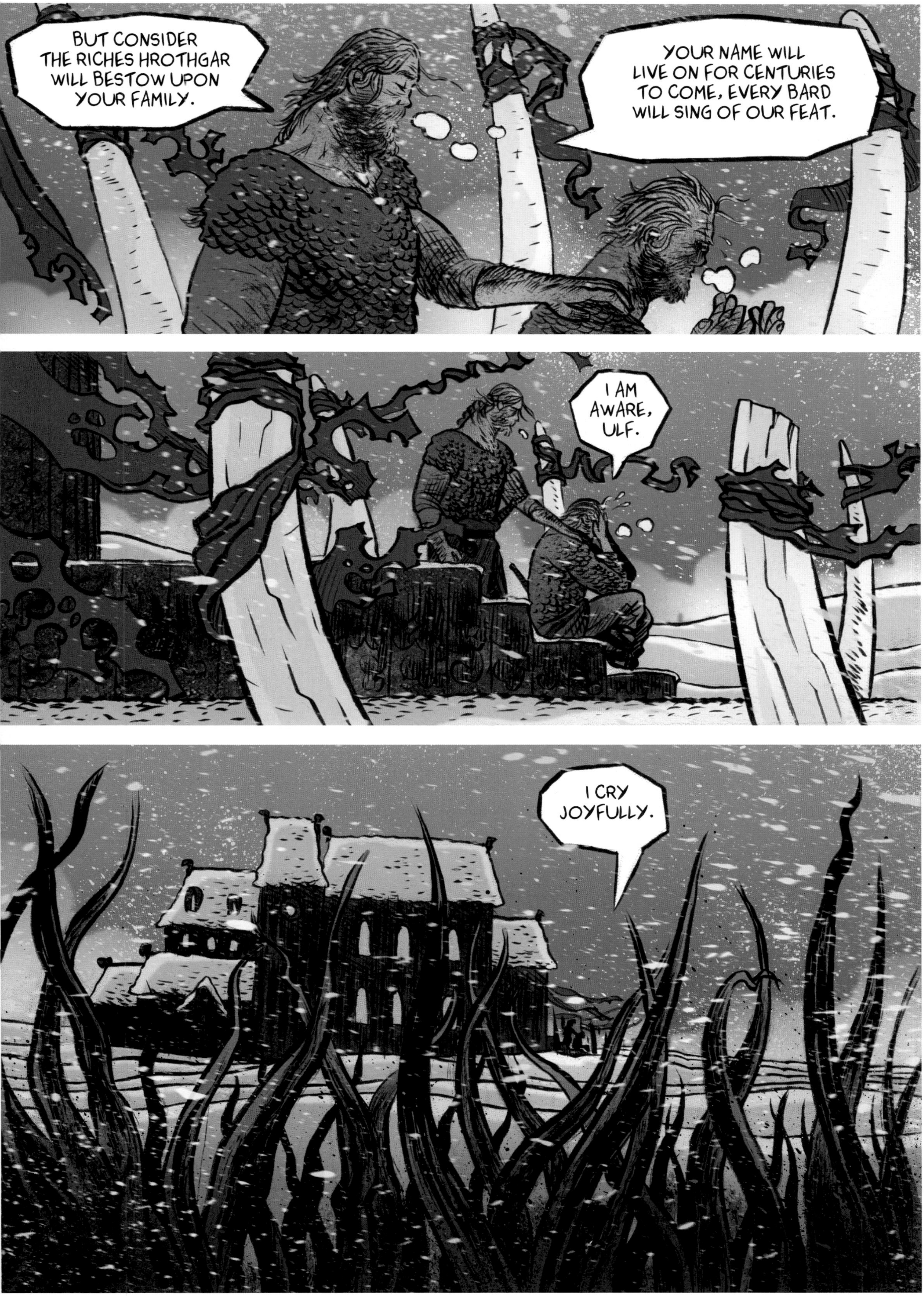
BUT CONSIDER THE RICHES HROTHGAR WILL BESTOW UPON YOUR FAMILY.
YOUR NAME WILL LIVE ON FOR CENTURIES TO COME, EVERY BARD WILL SING OF OUR FEAT.
I AM AWARE, ULF.
I CRY JOYFULLY.

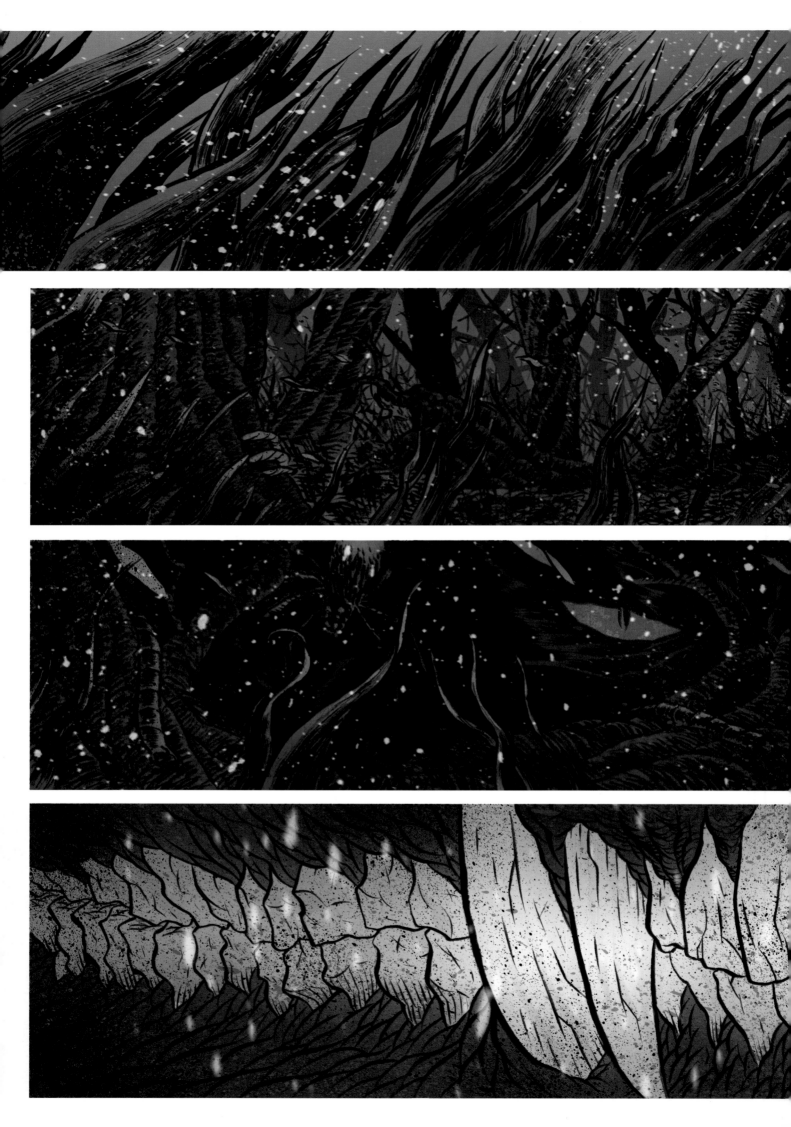

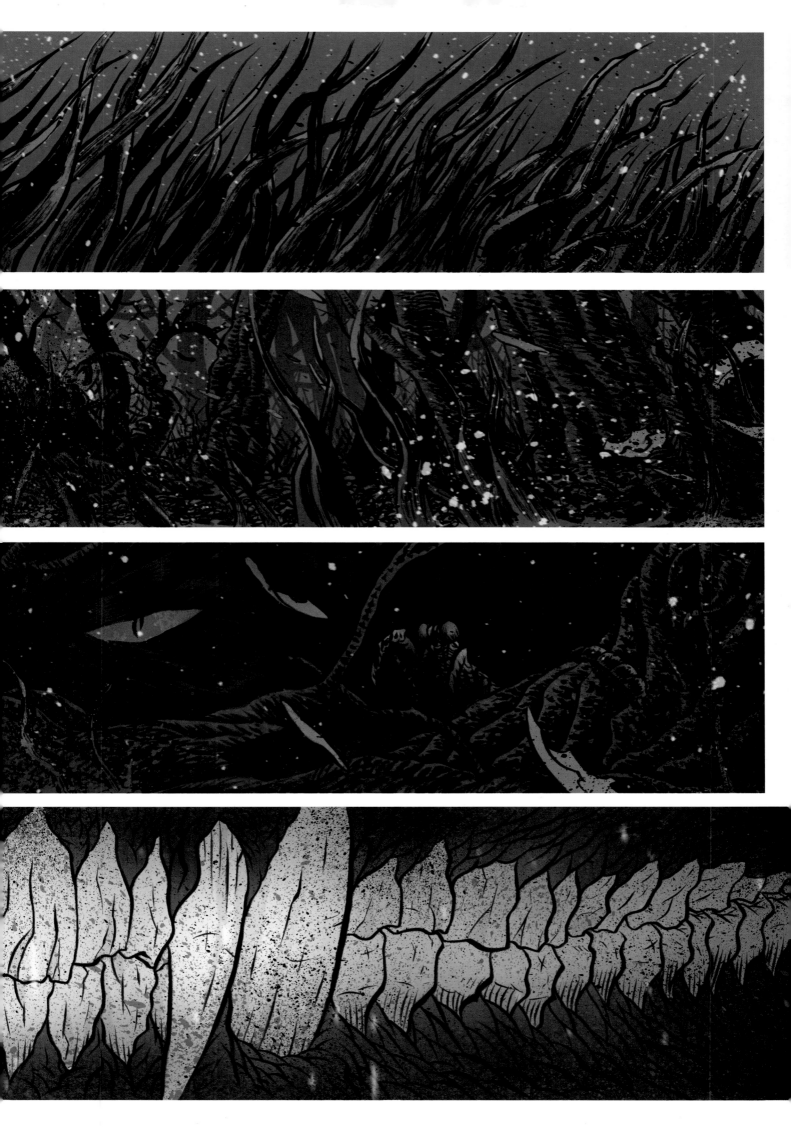

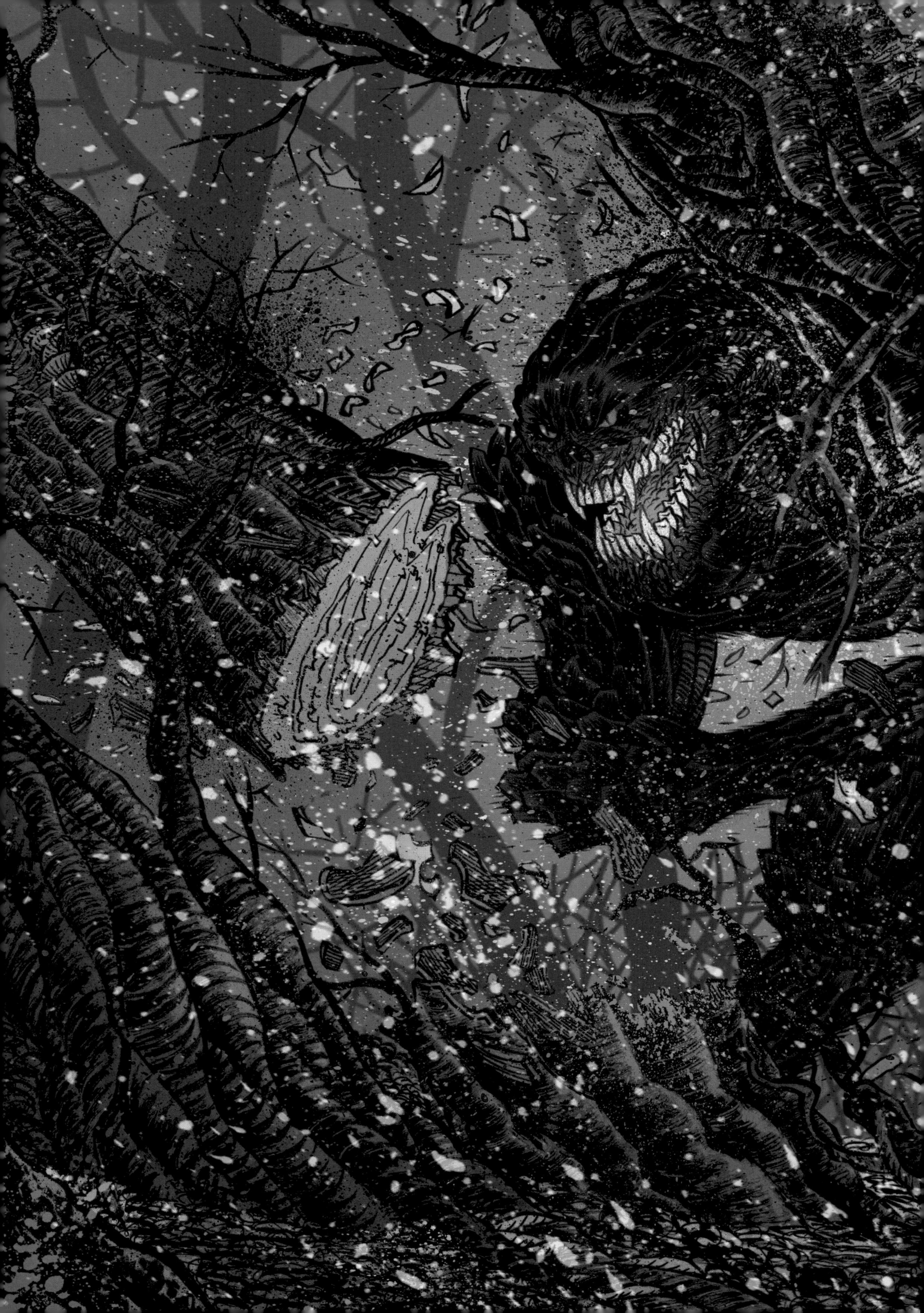

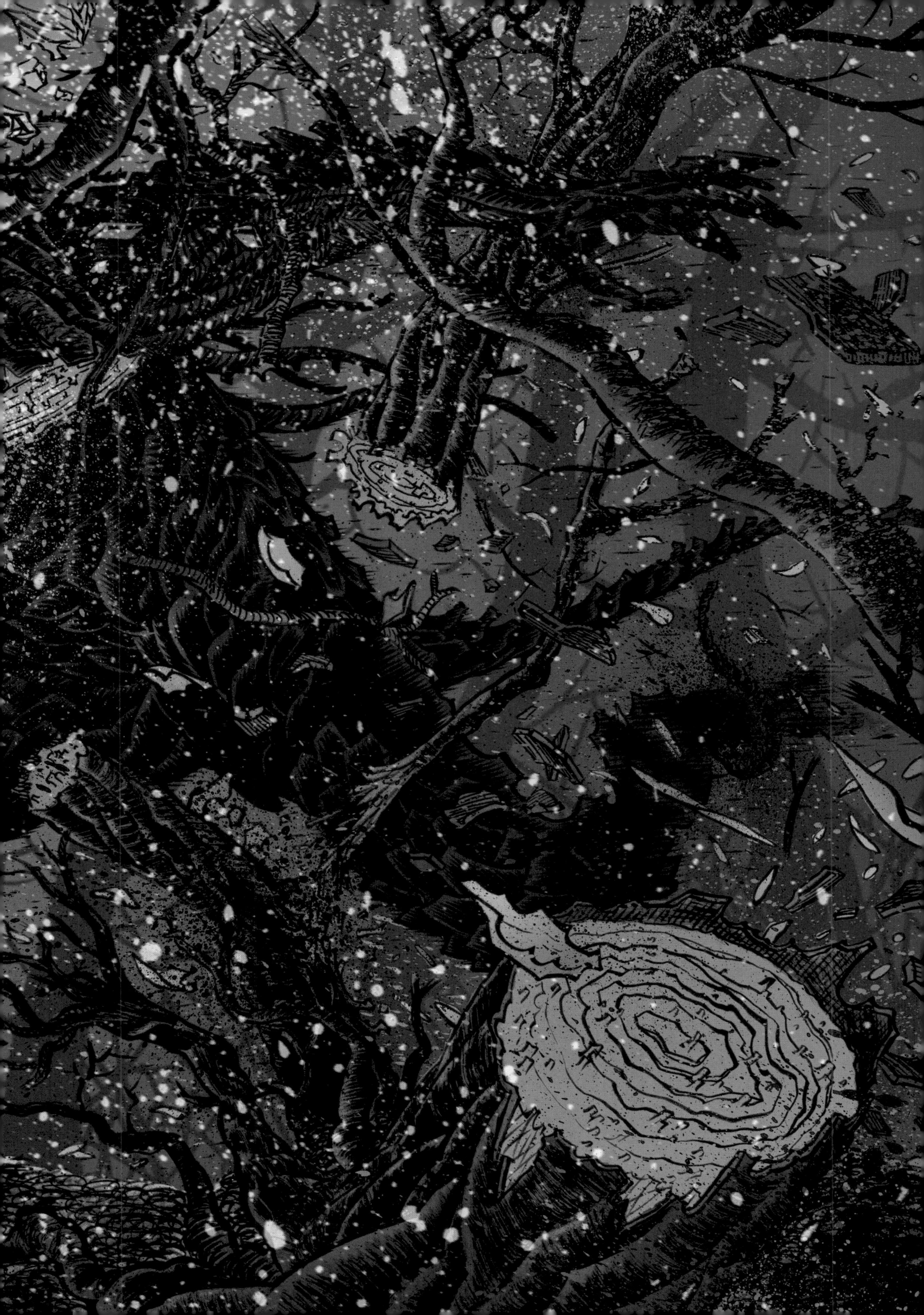

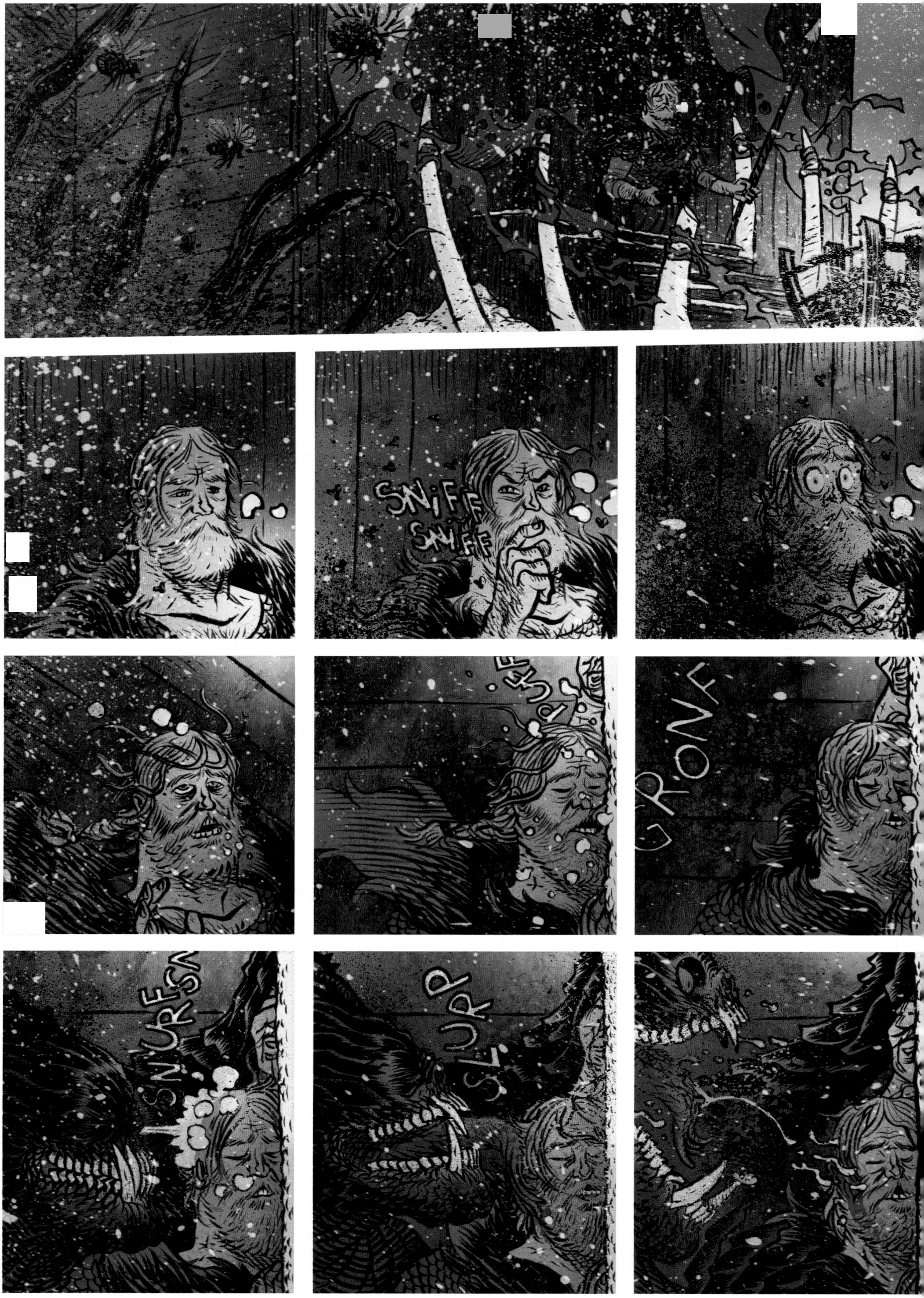
SNIFF
SNIFF
GRONF
SLURP

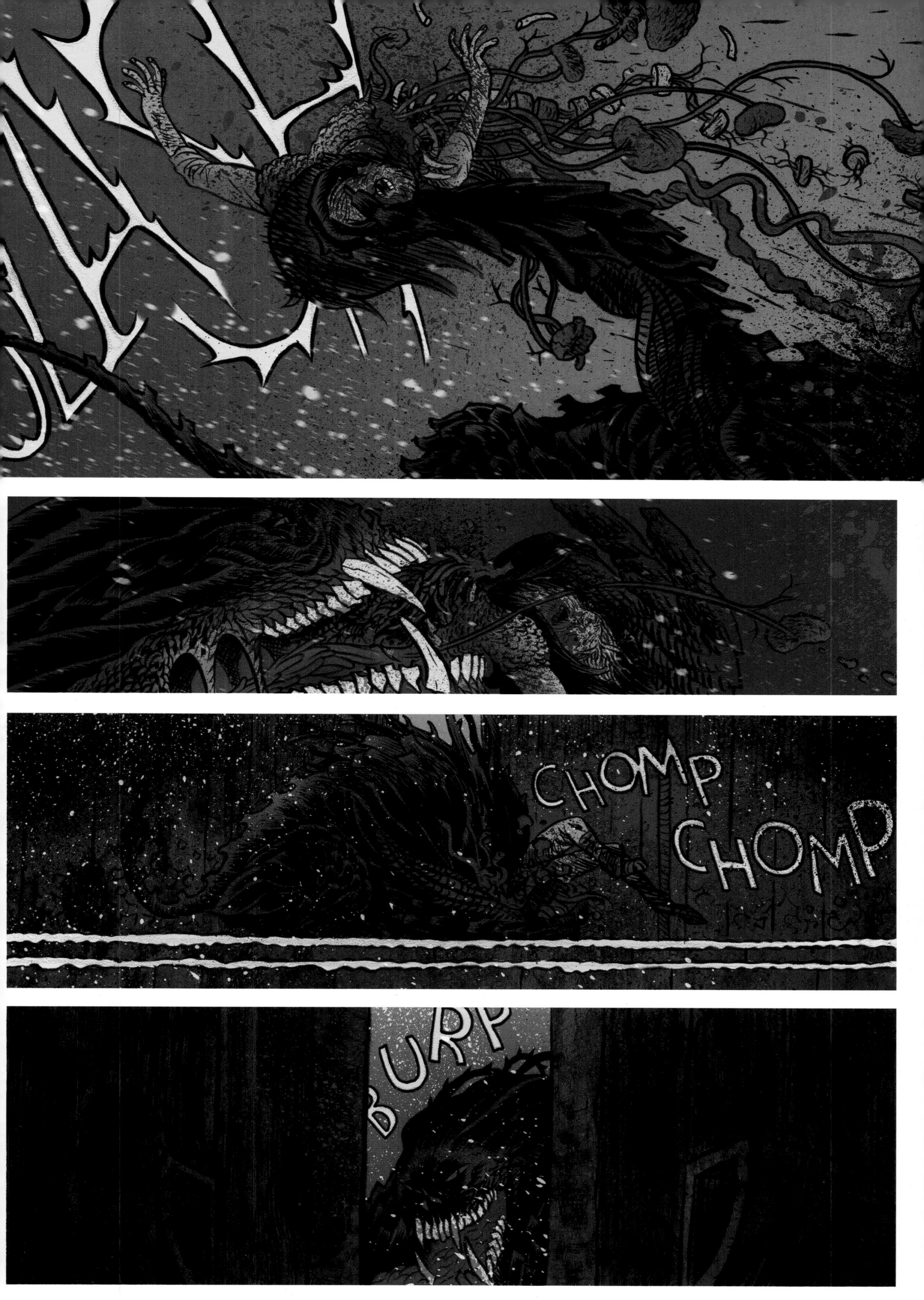
CHOMP
CHOMP
BURP

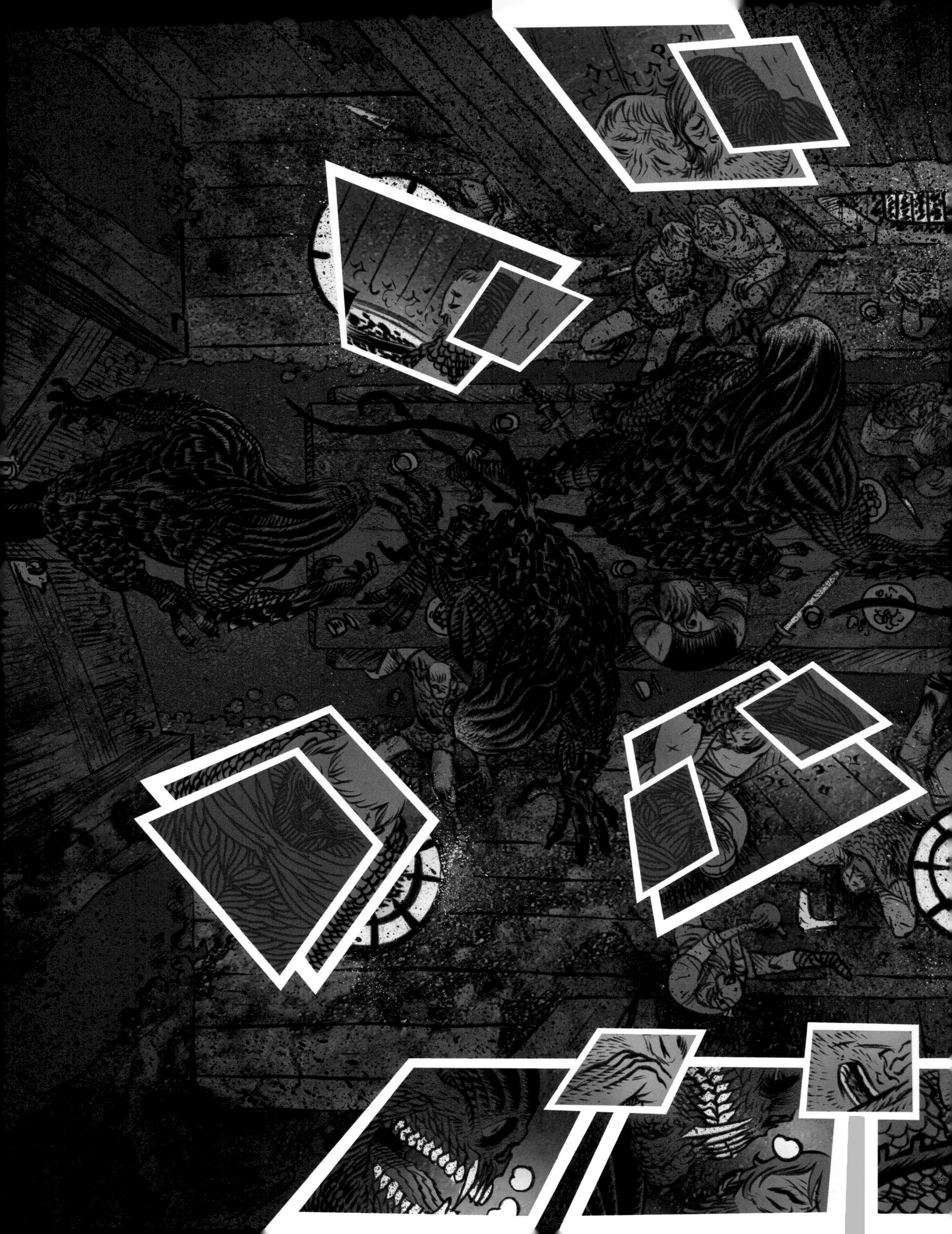

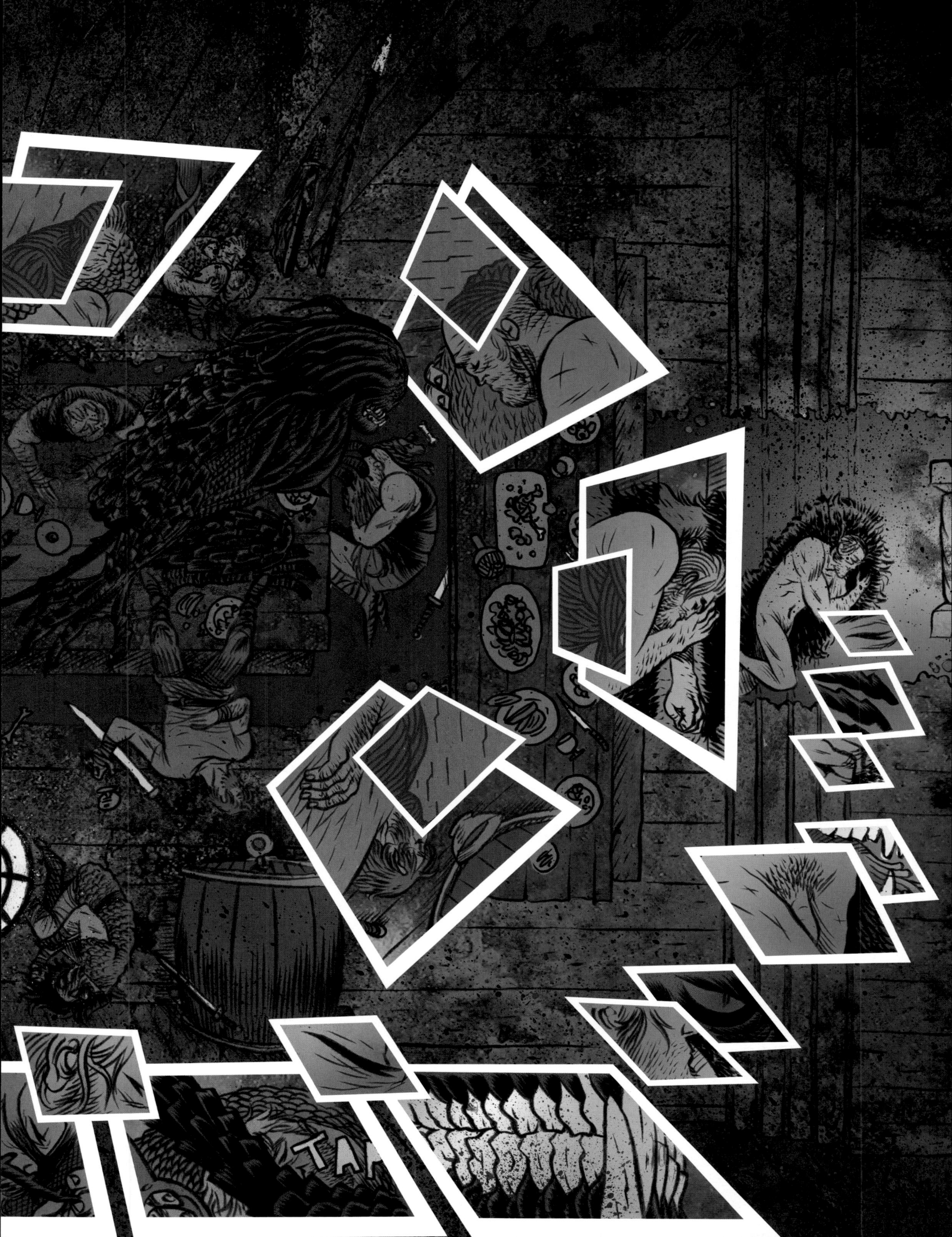
TA

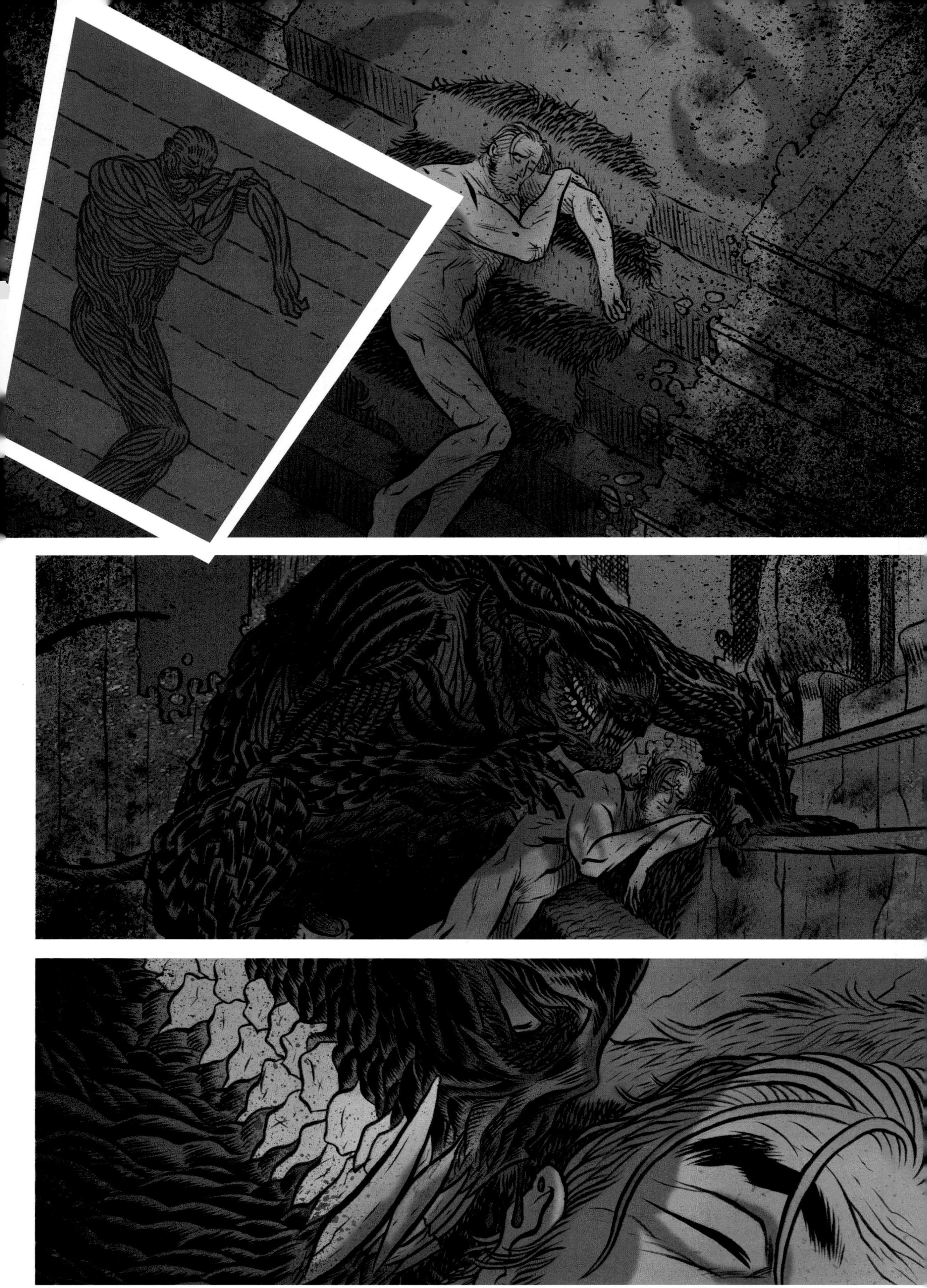

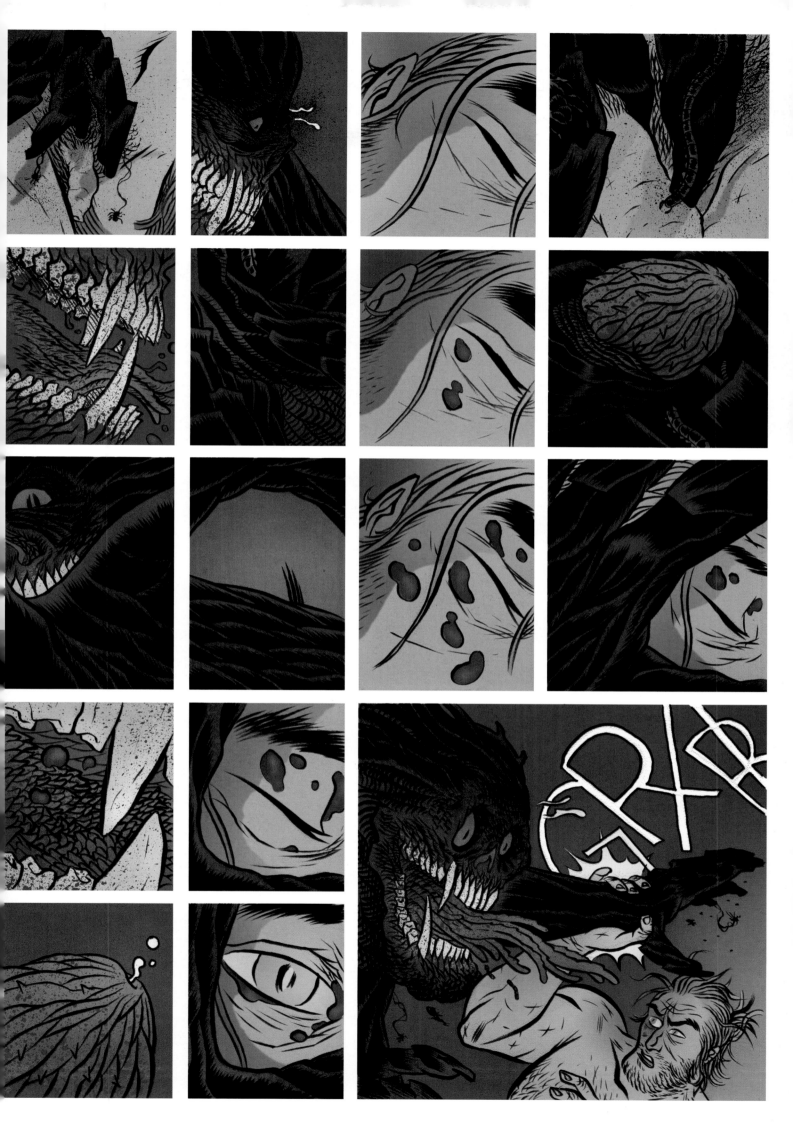

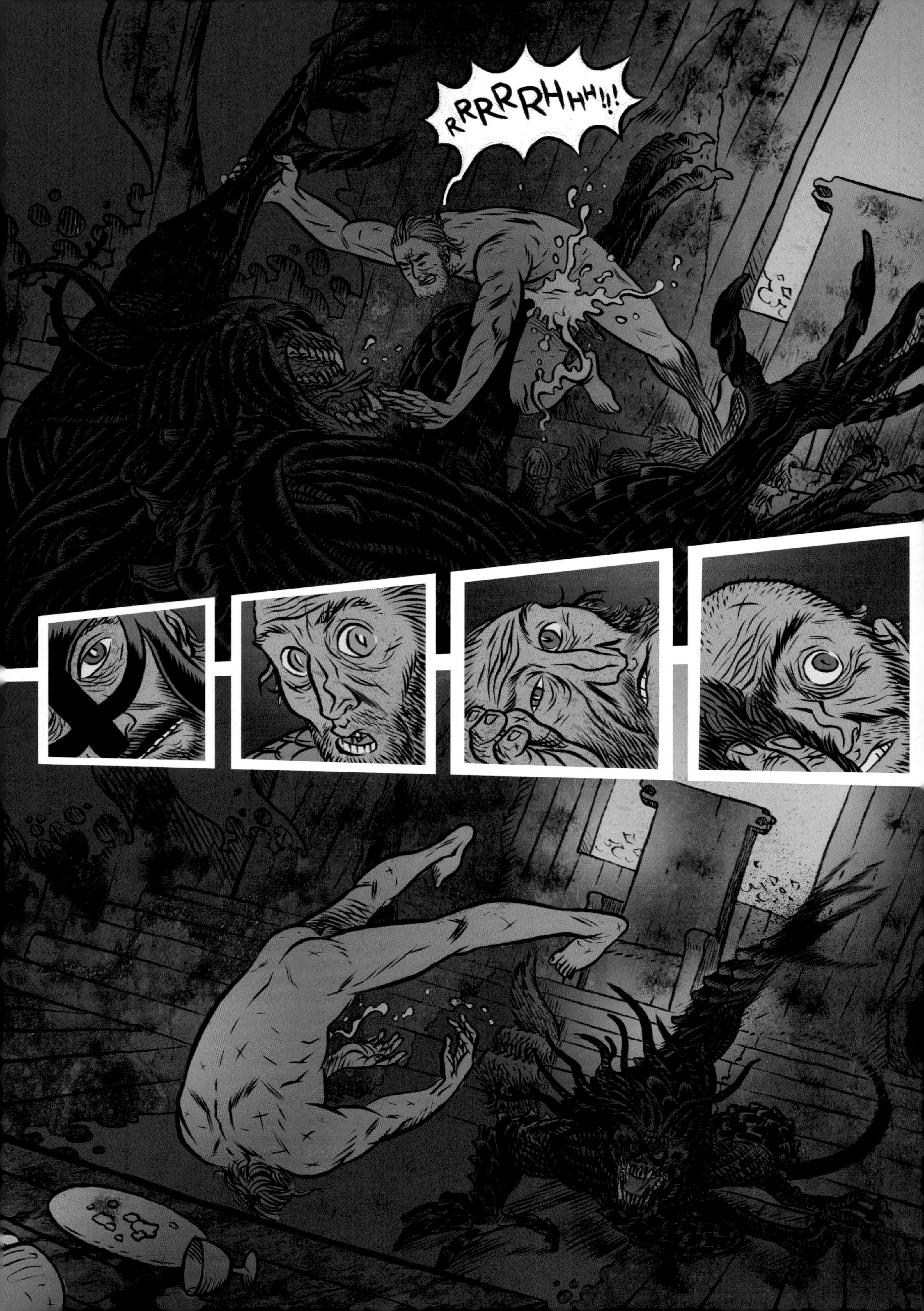
RRRRRHHH!!!

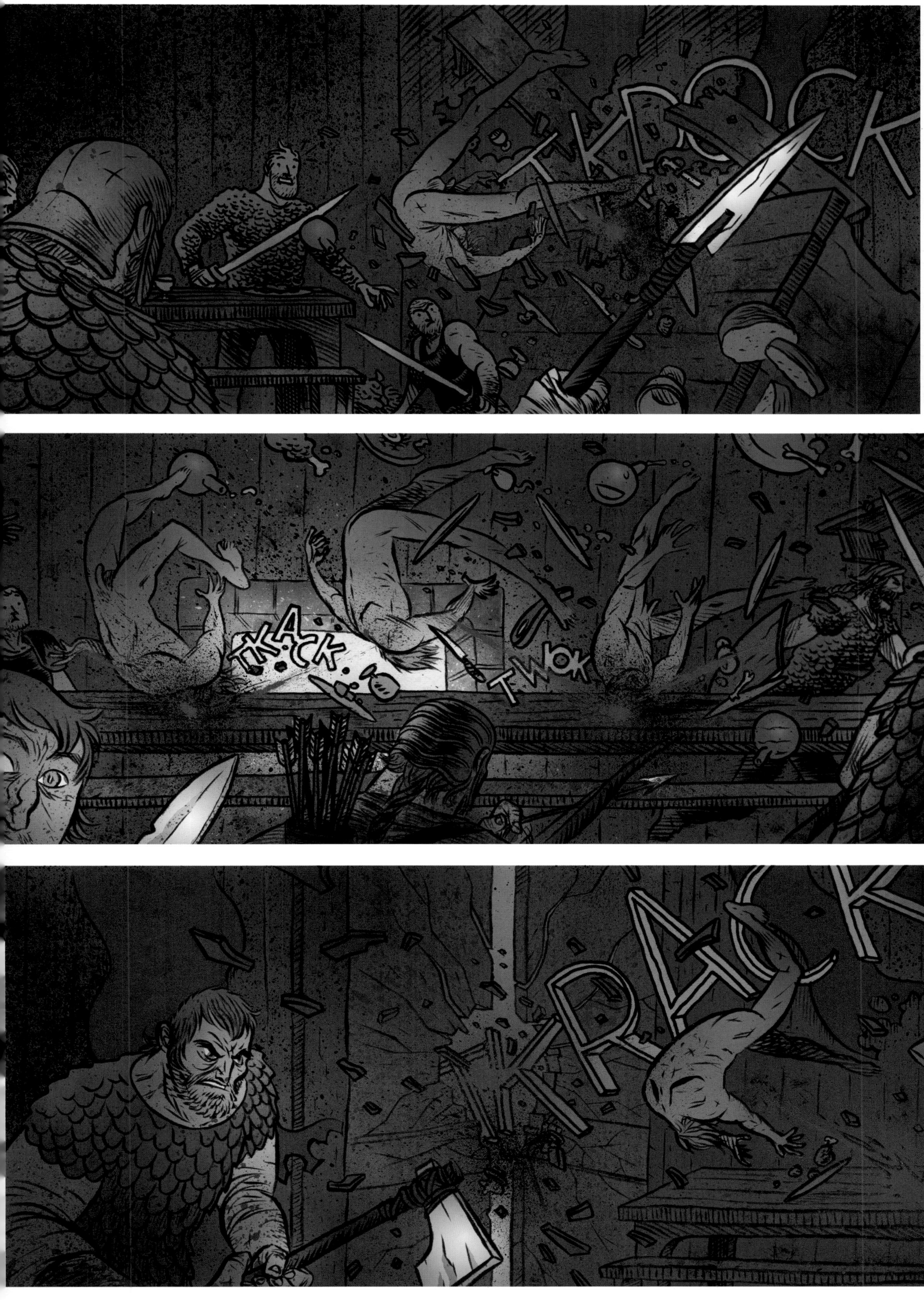
TKDOCK
TKACK
TWOK
KRACK

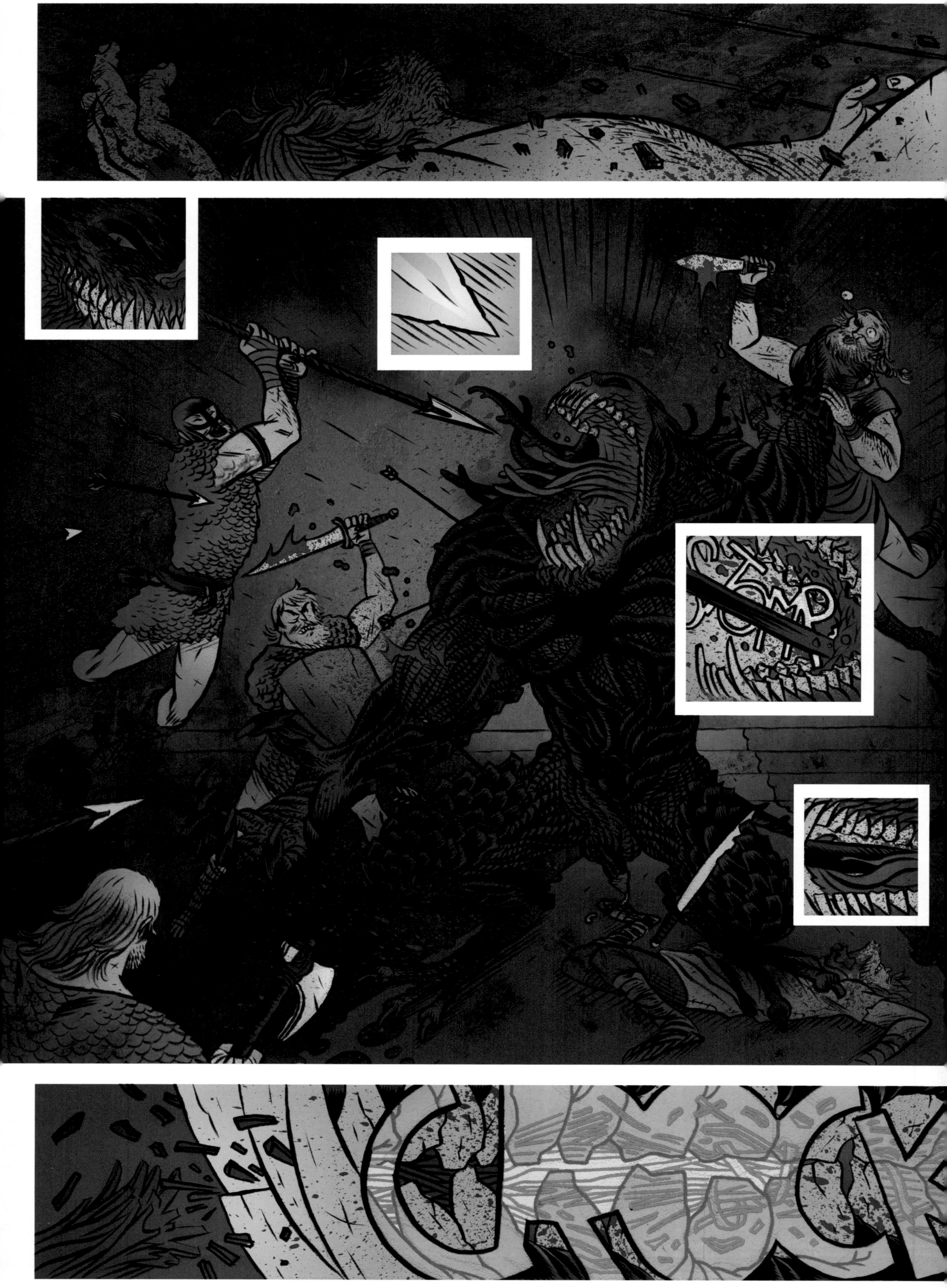

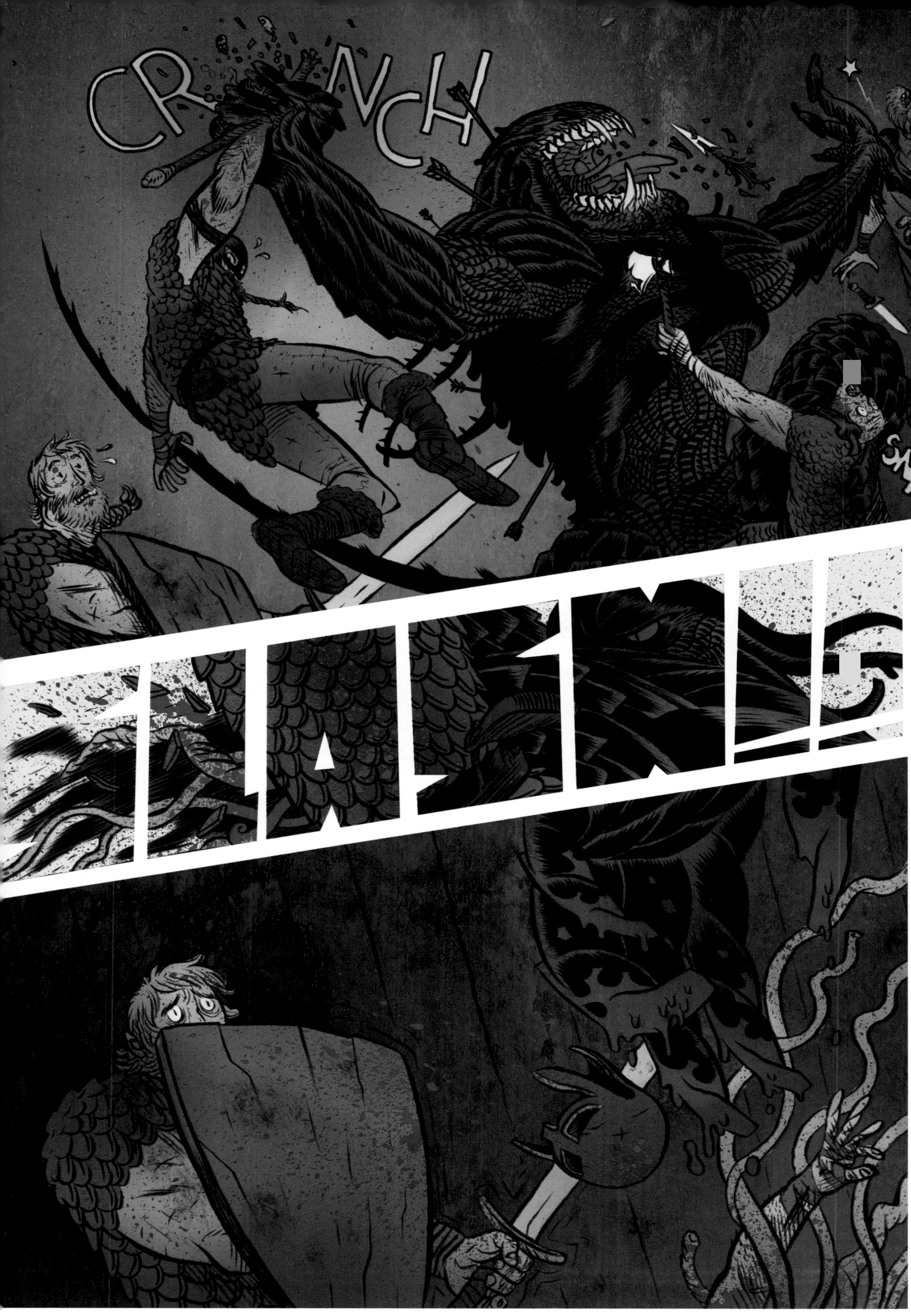
CR NCH
SNAP

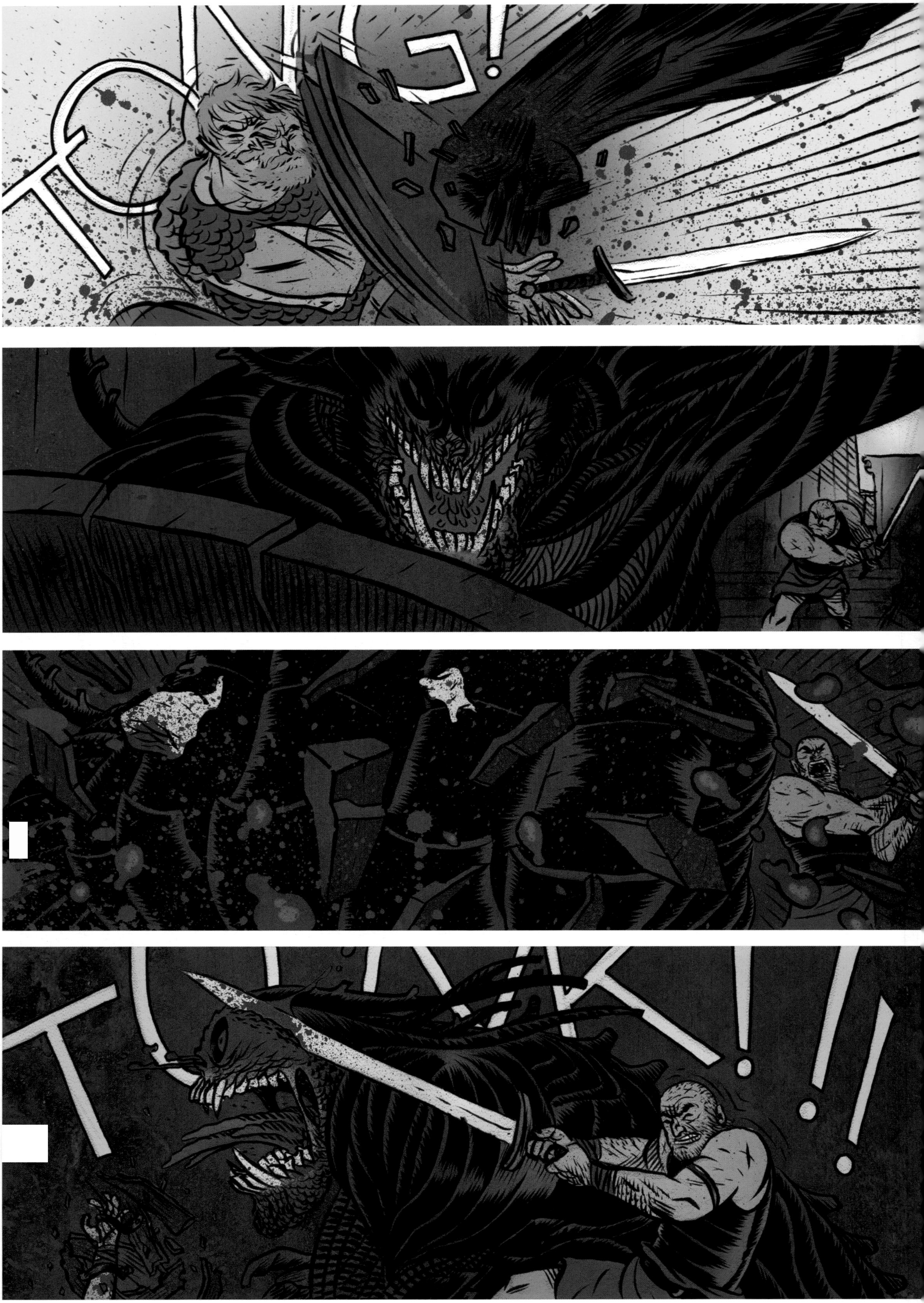
TONG!

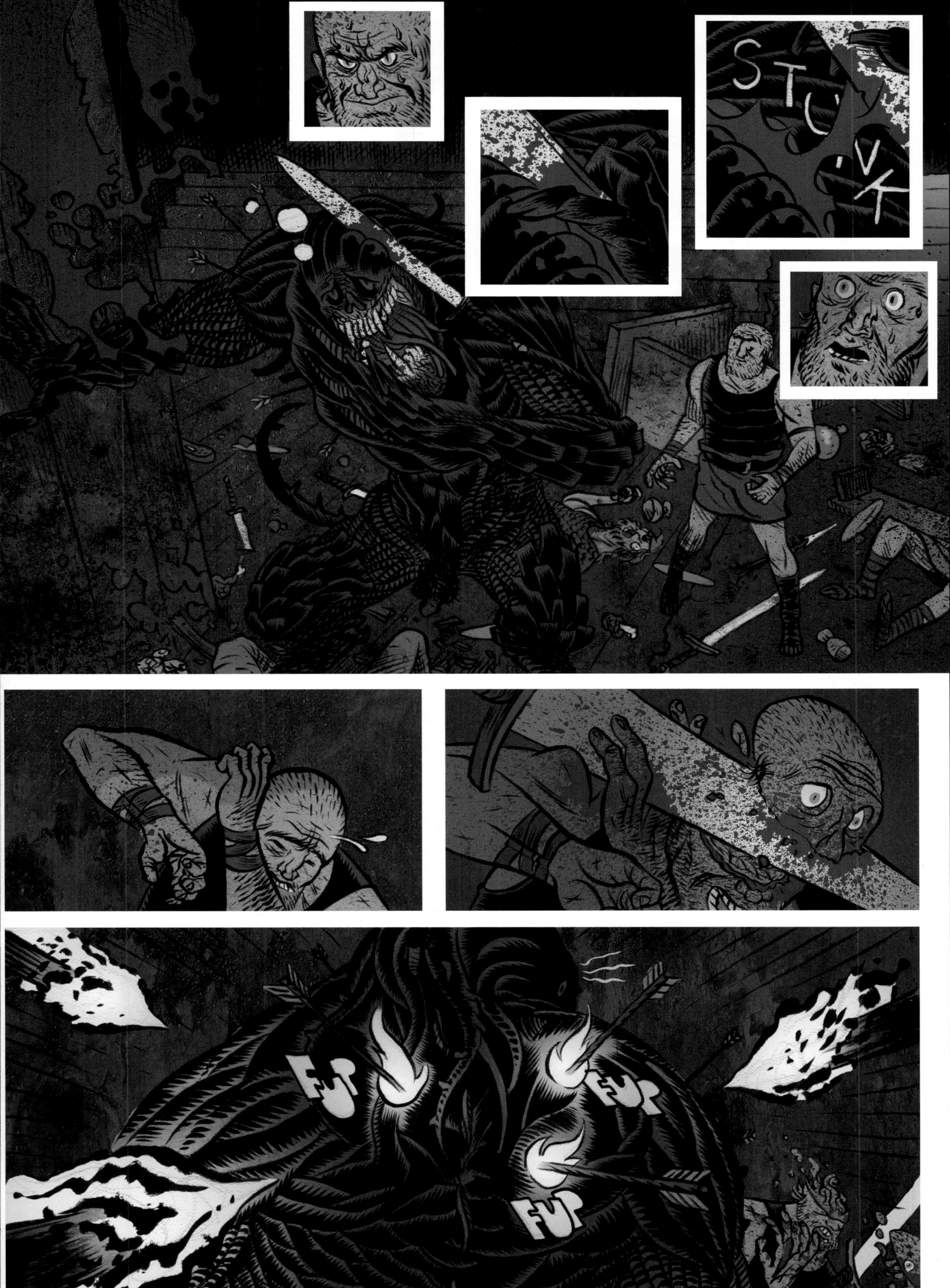
STUVK
FUP
FUP
FUP

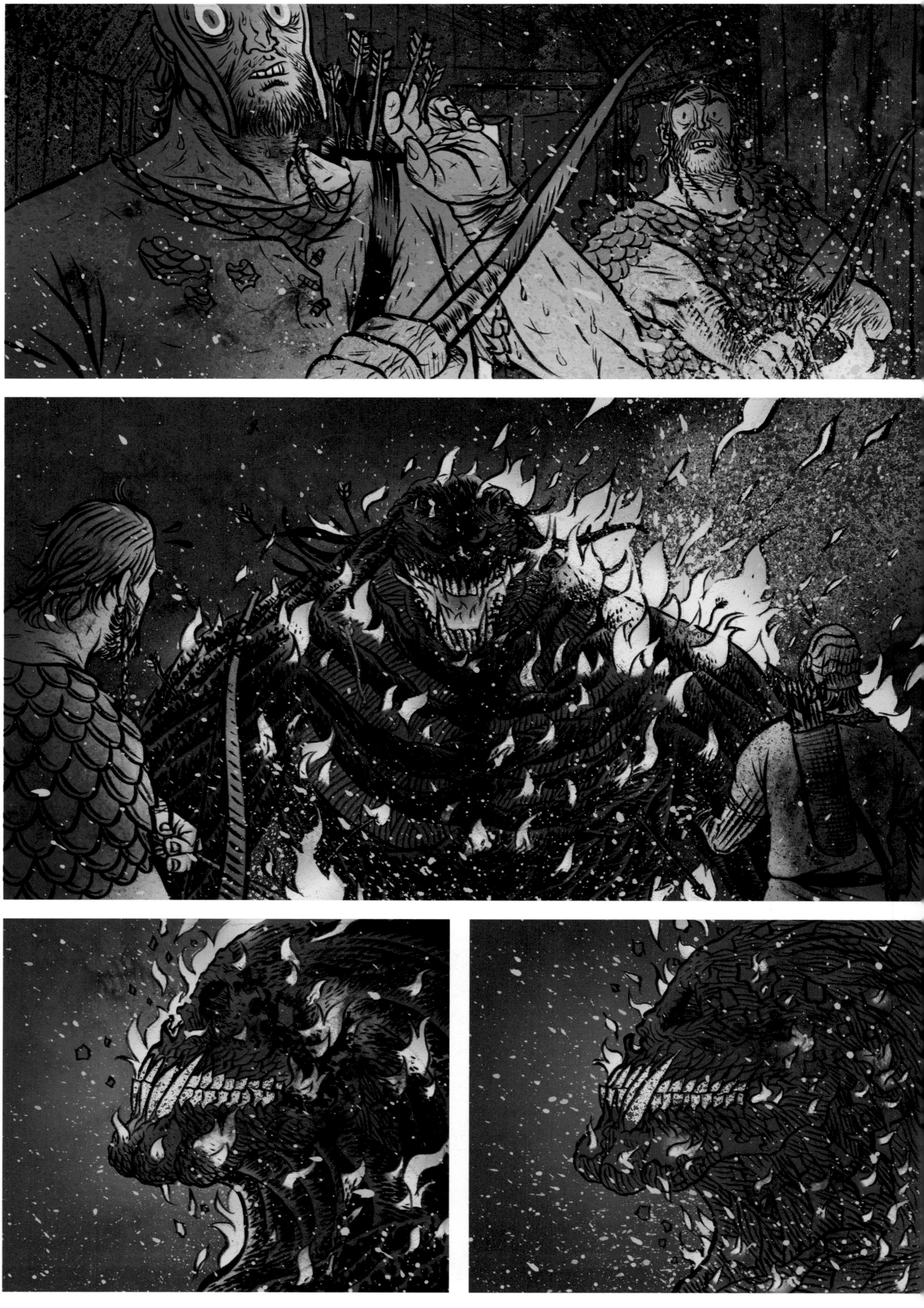

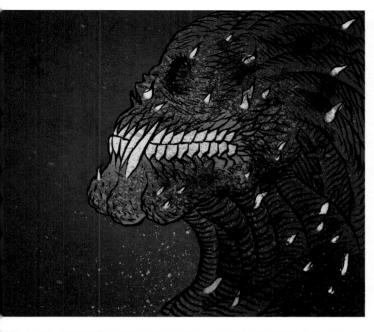

RRRAAAARRRGGHH!

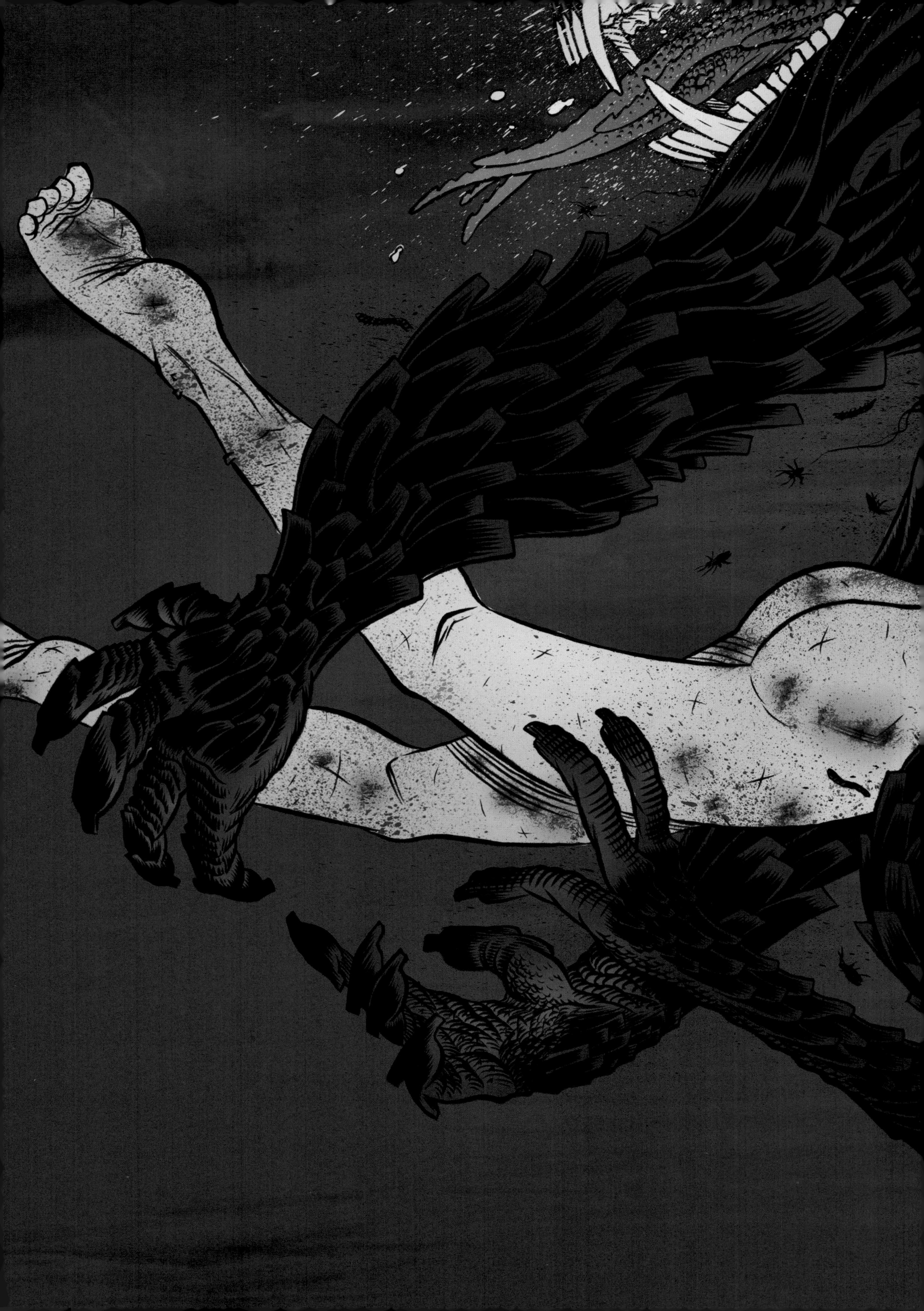

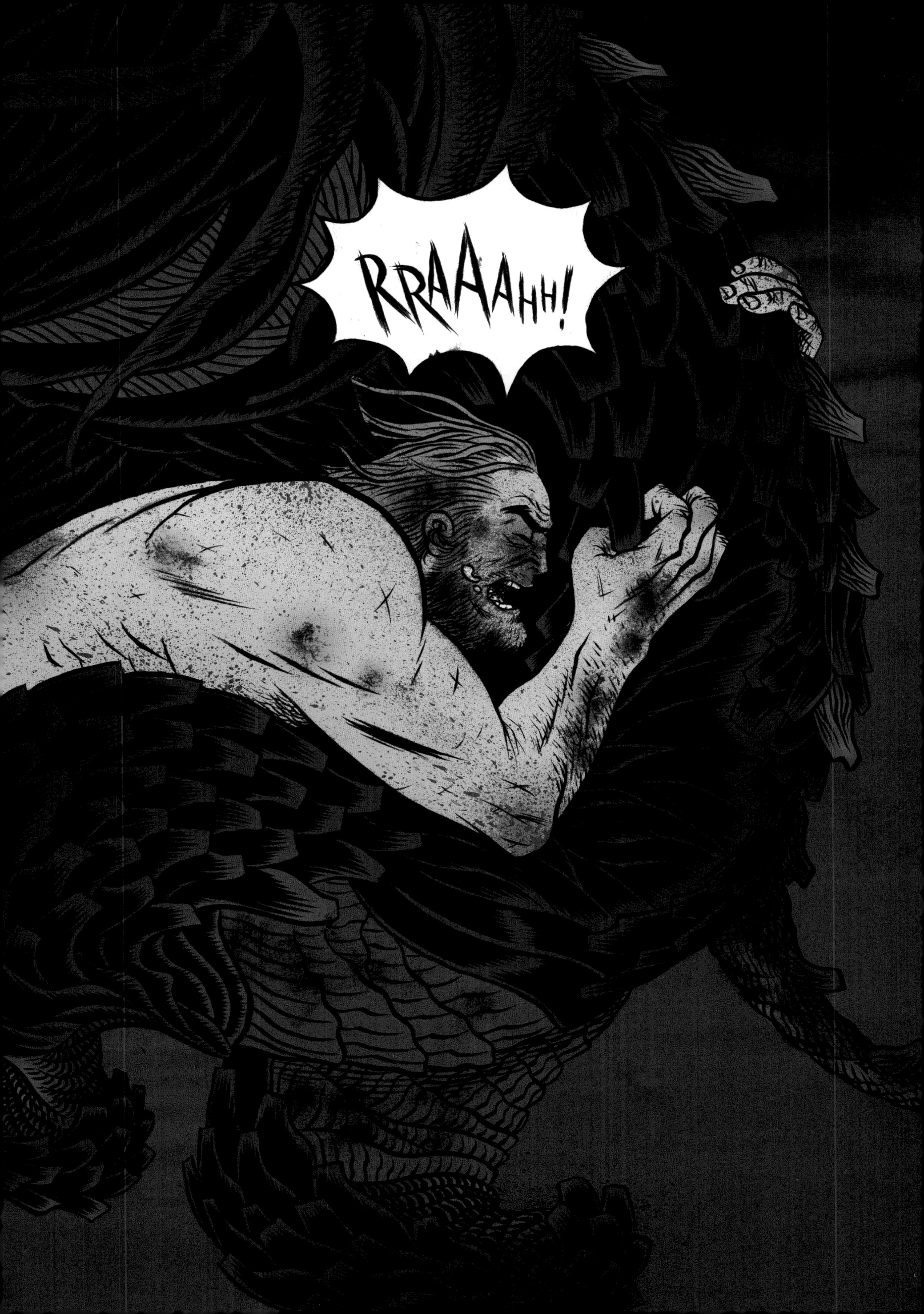
RRAAAHH!

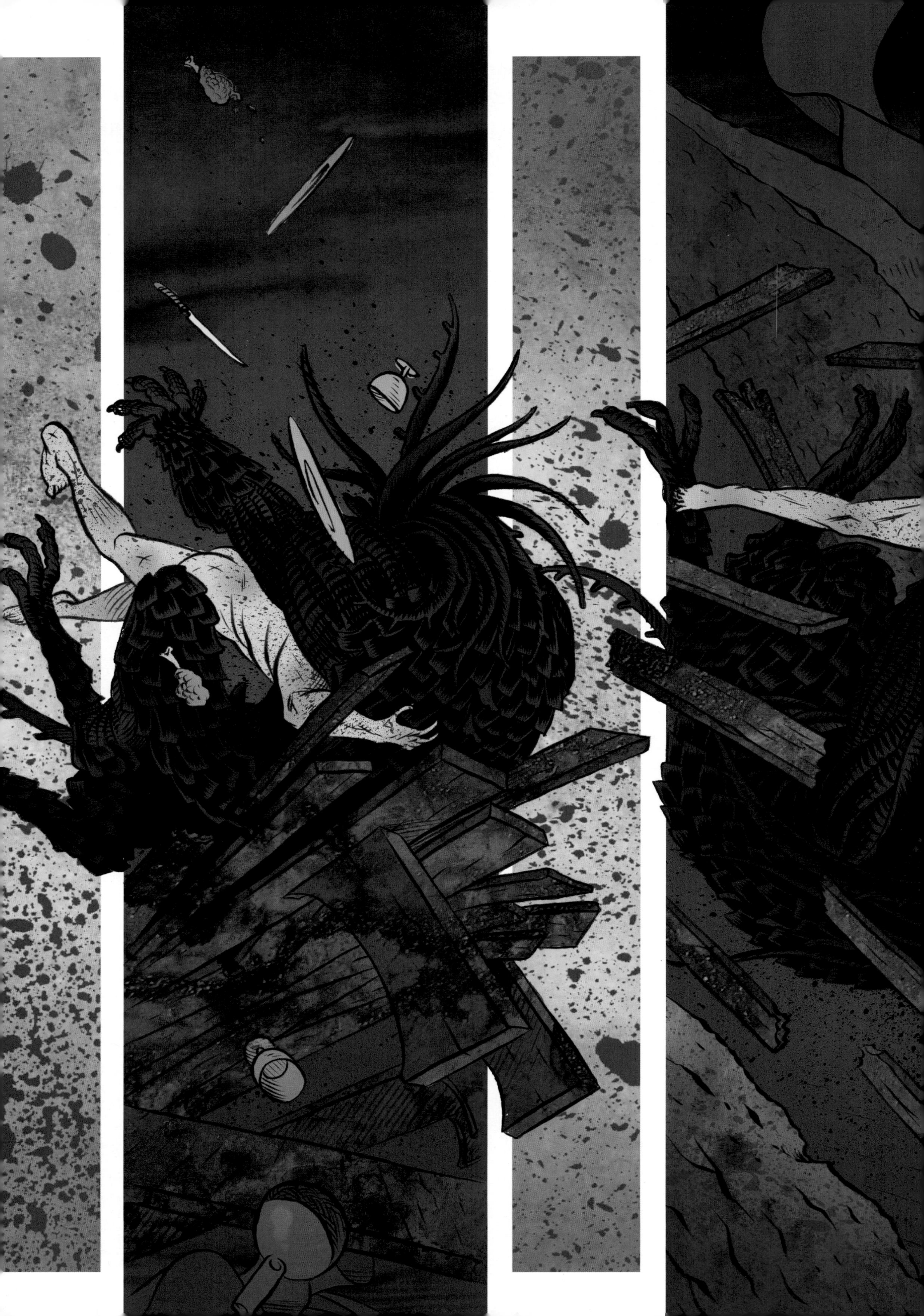

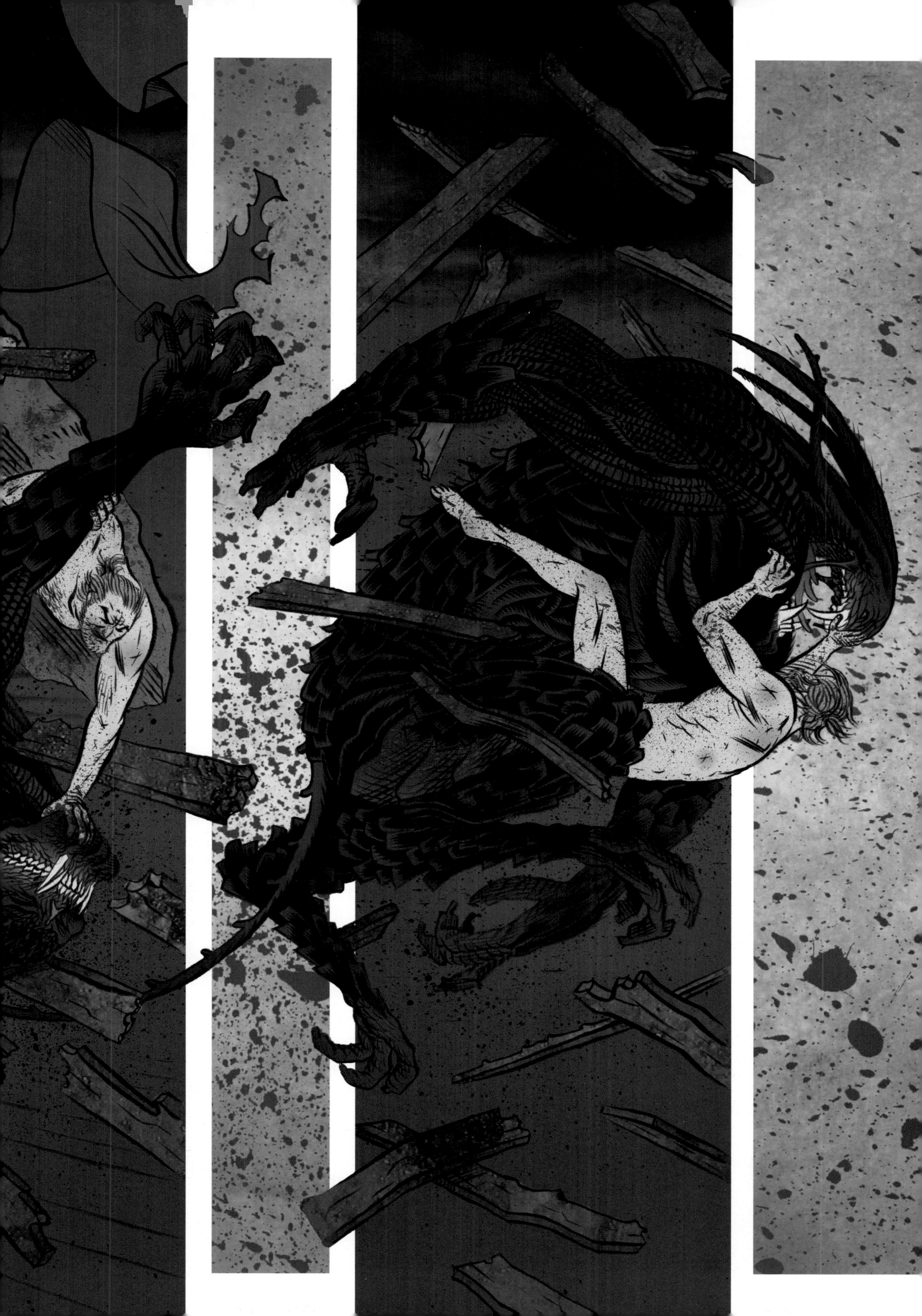

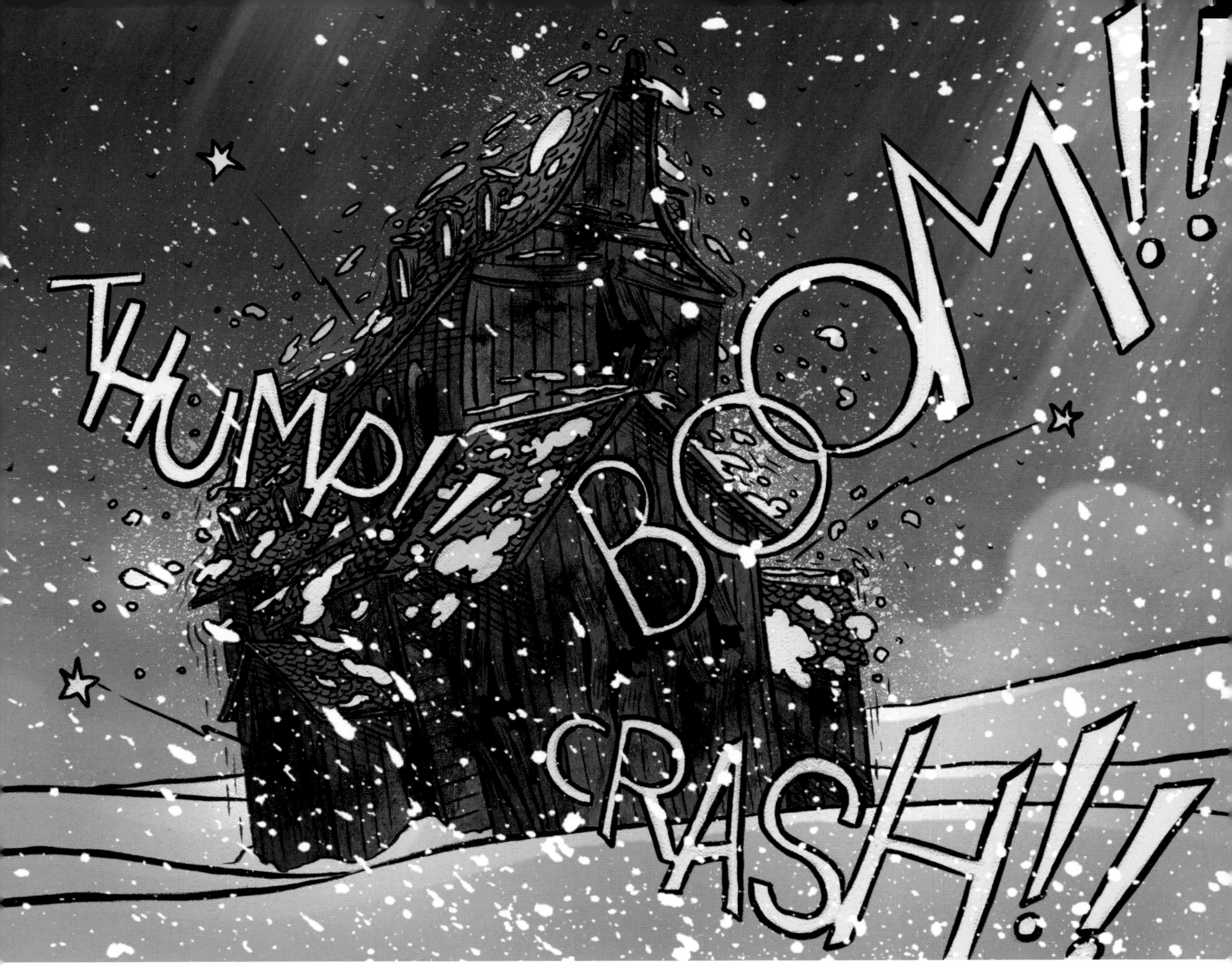
THUMP!!
BOOM!!
CRASH!!!

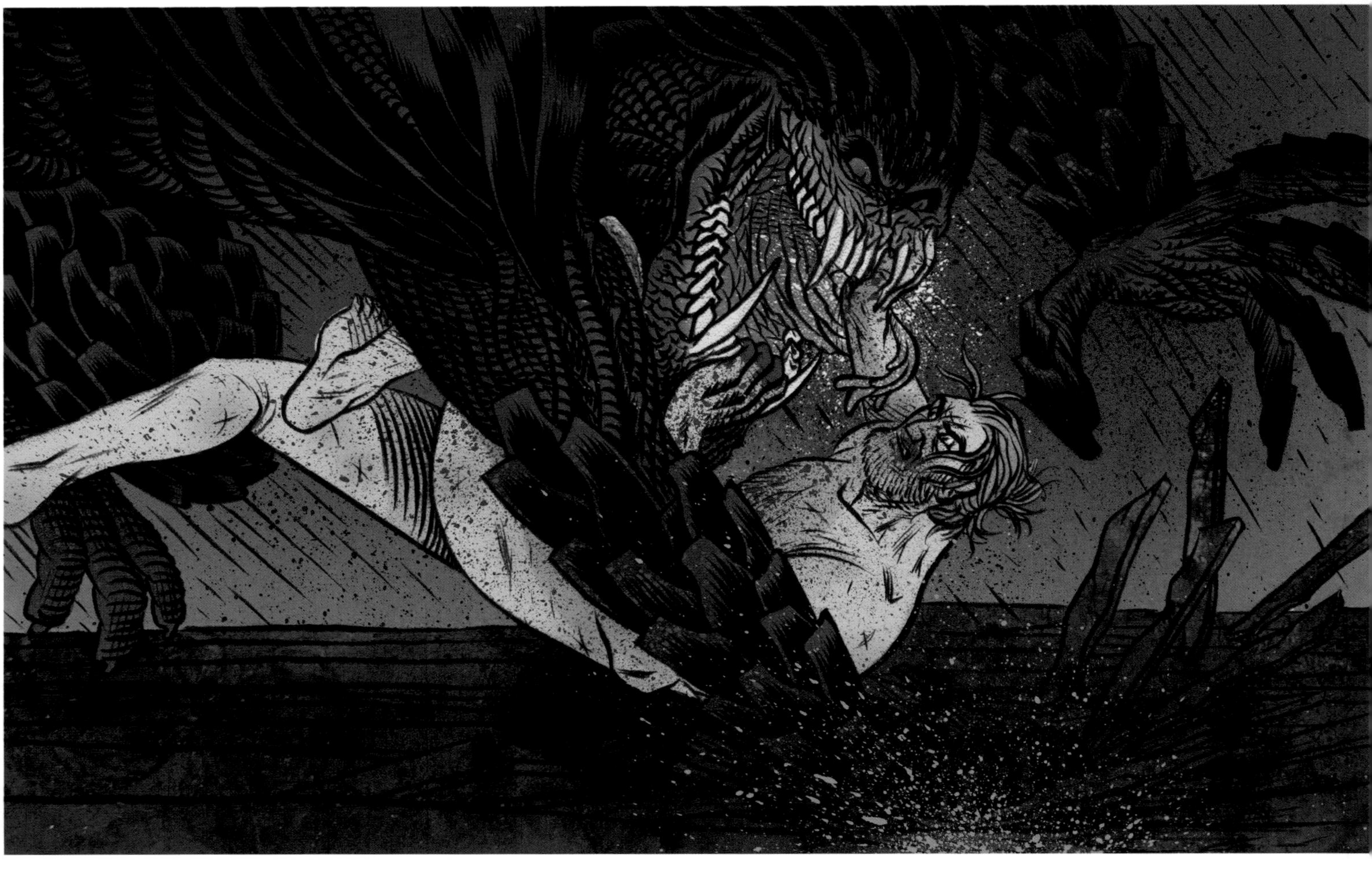

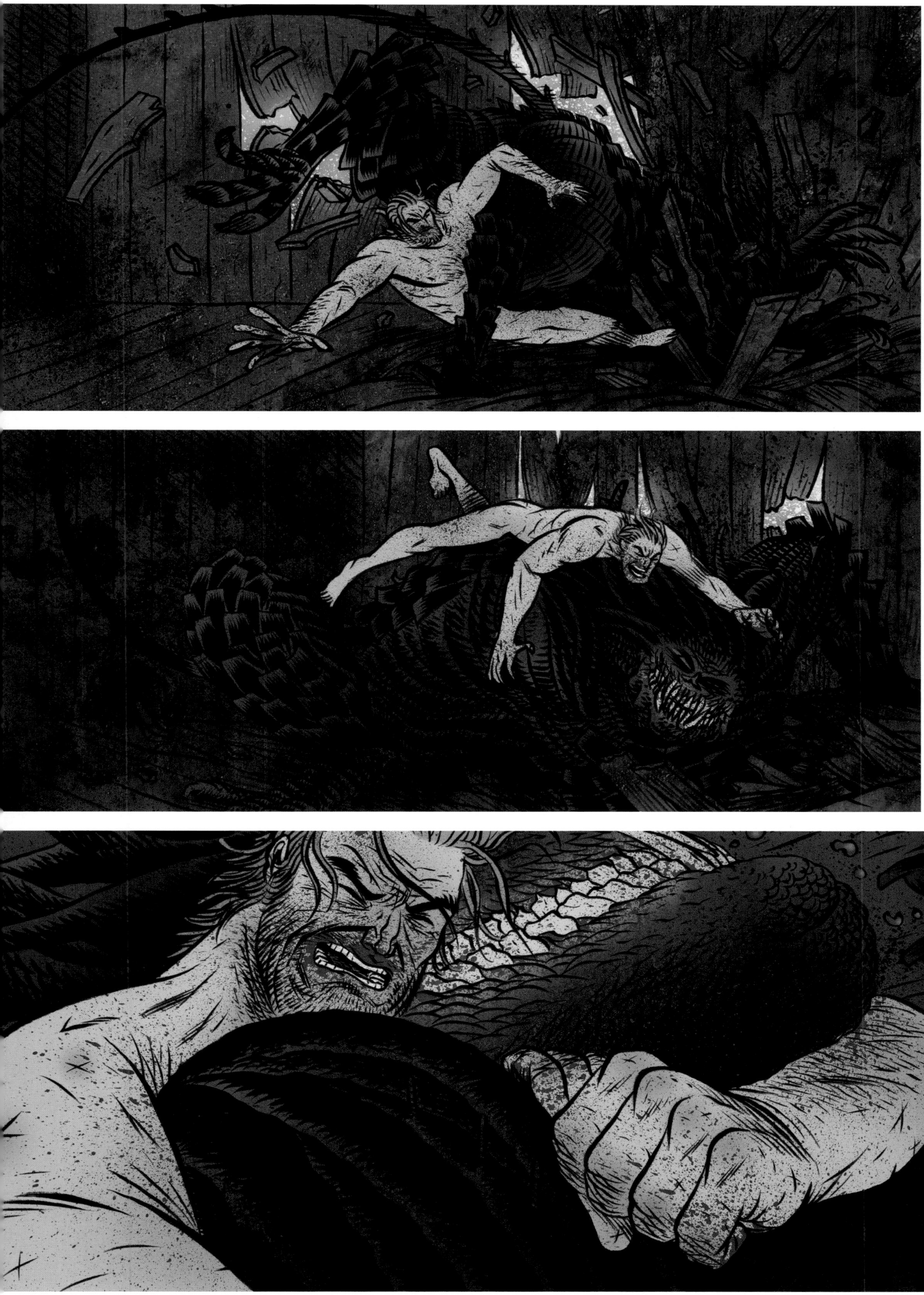

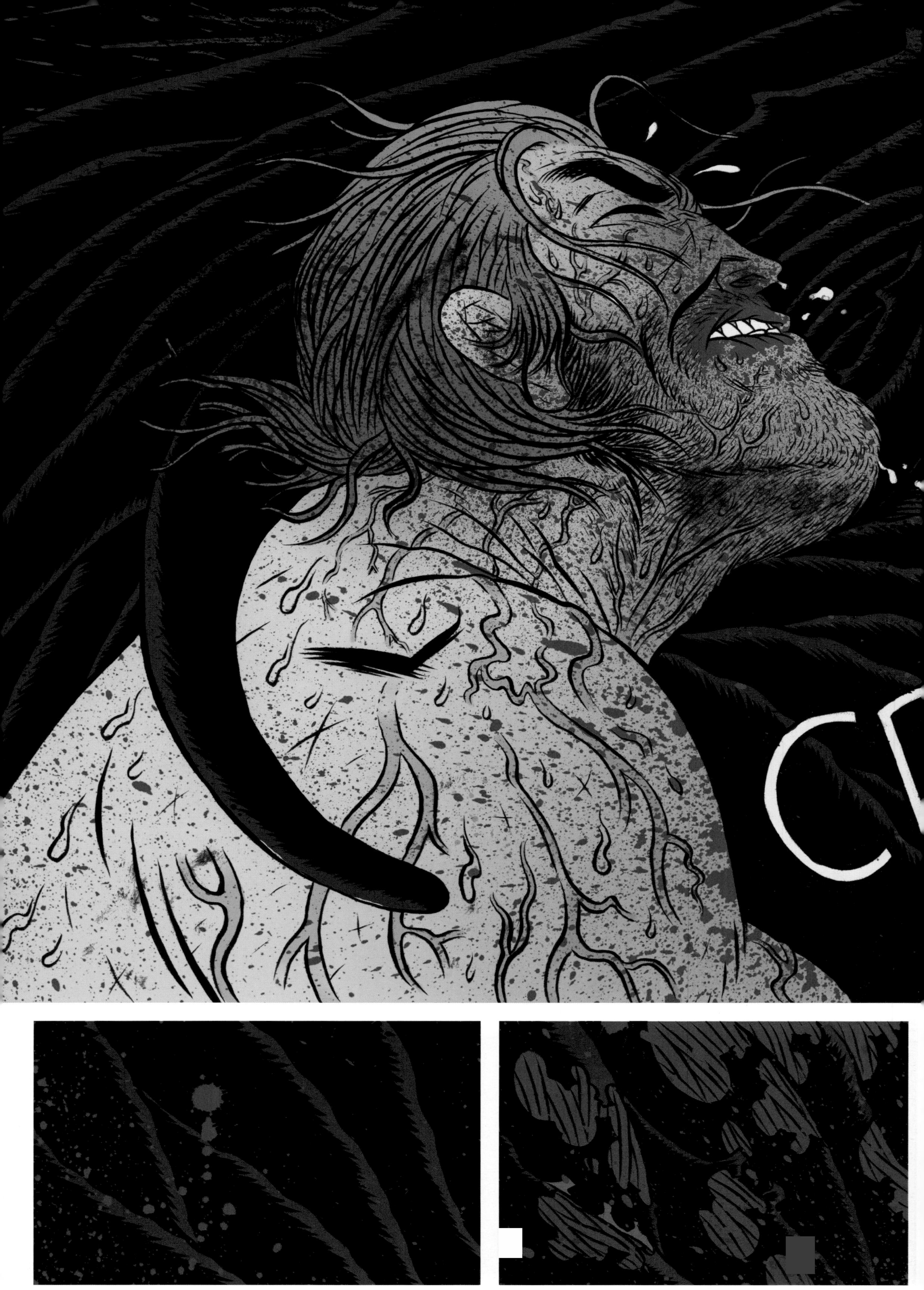

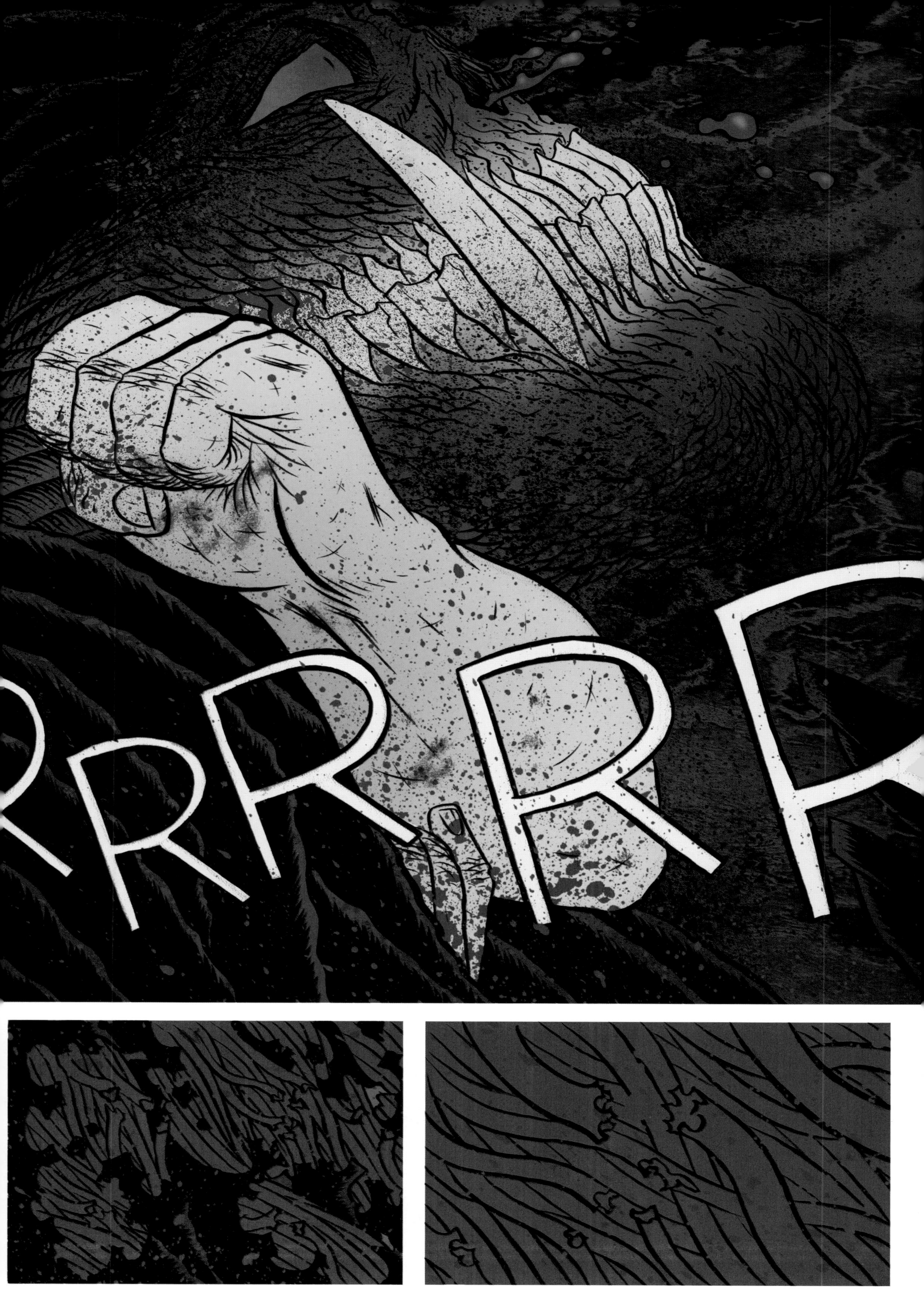
RRRRR

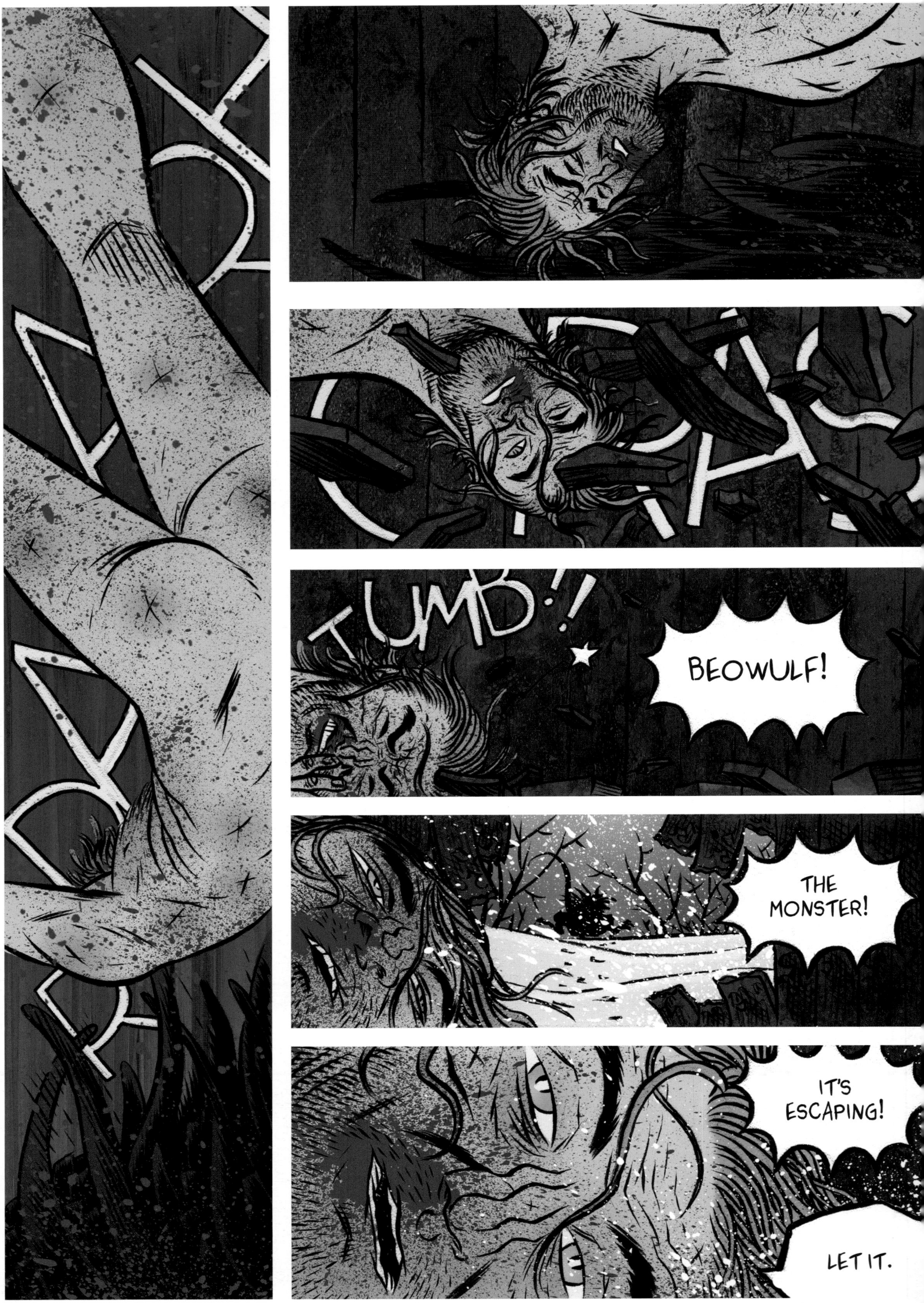
TUMB!!
BEOWULF!
THE MONSTER!
IT'S ESCAPING!
LET IT.

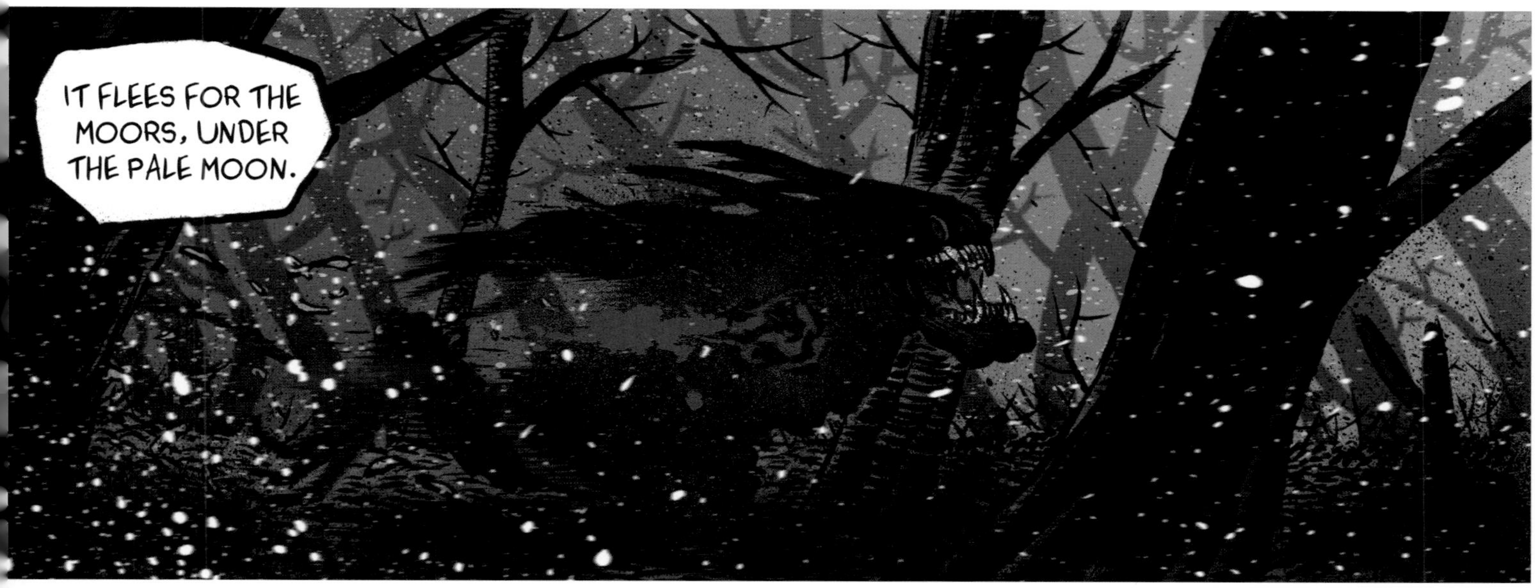
IT FLEES FOR THE MOORS, UNDER THE PALE MOON.

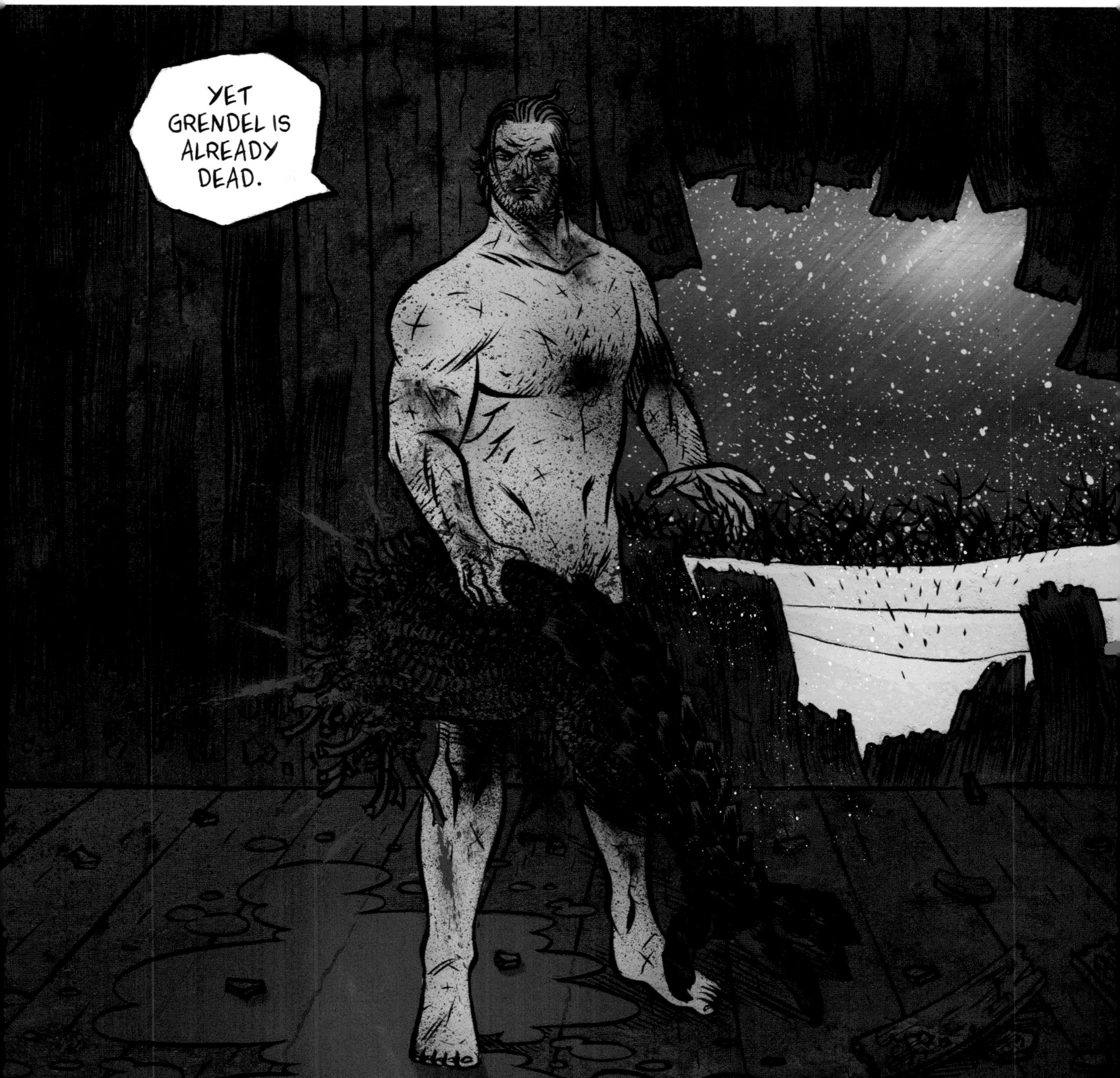
YET GRENDEL IS ALREADY DEAD.

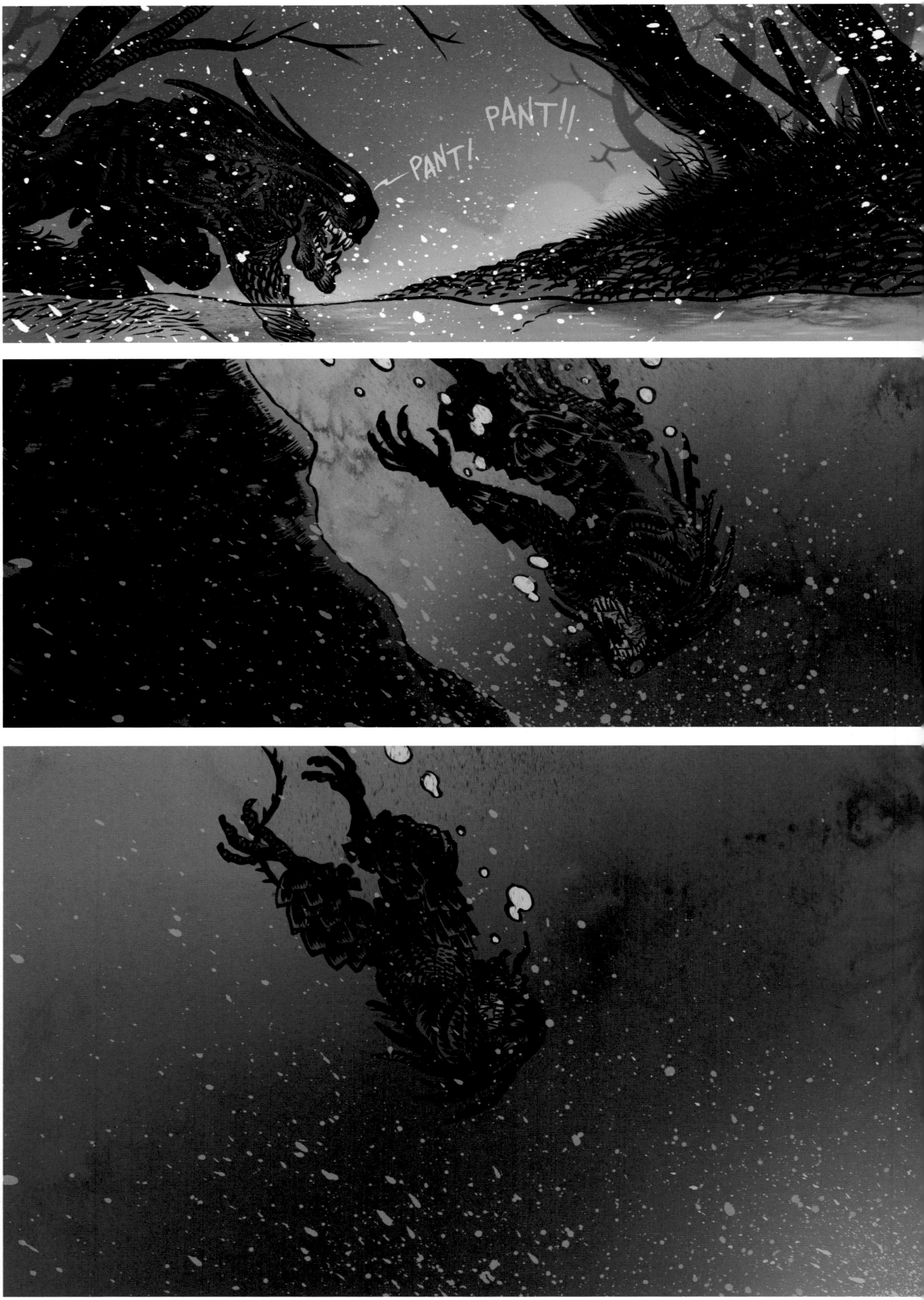
PANT!
PANT!!

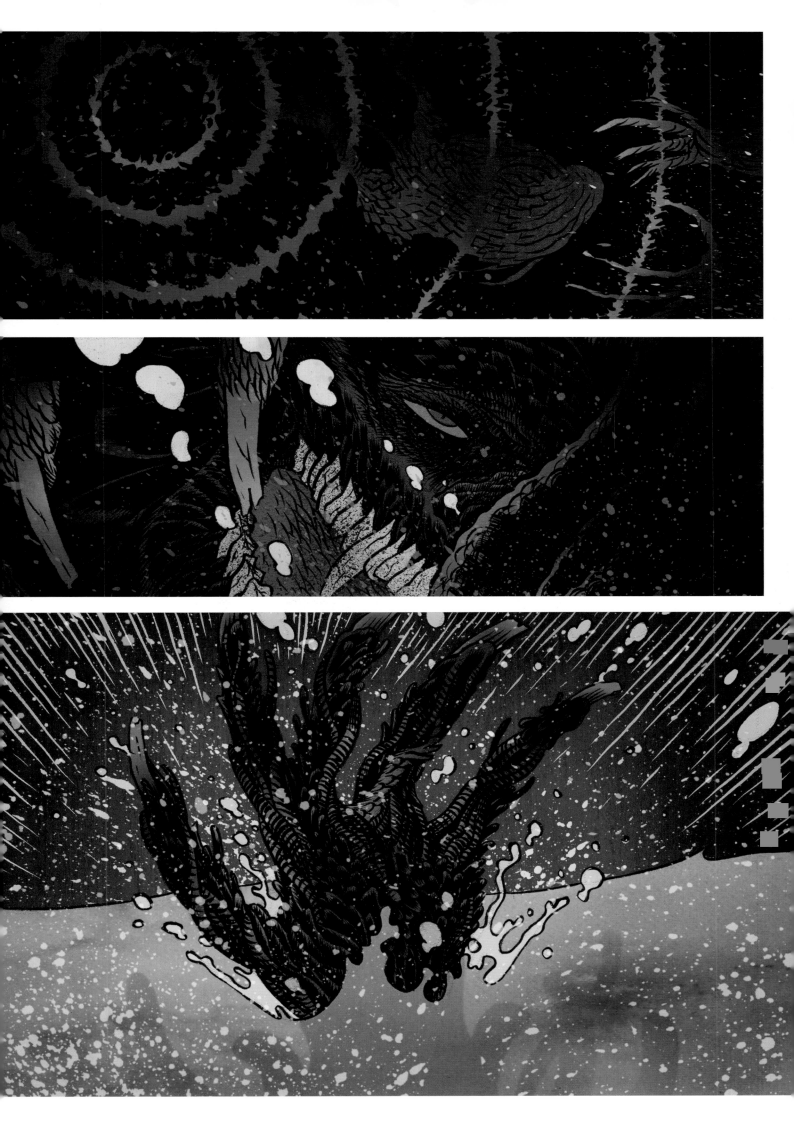

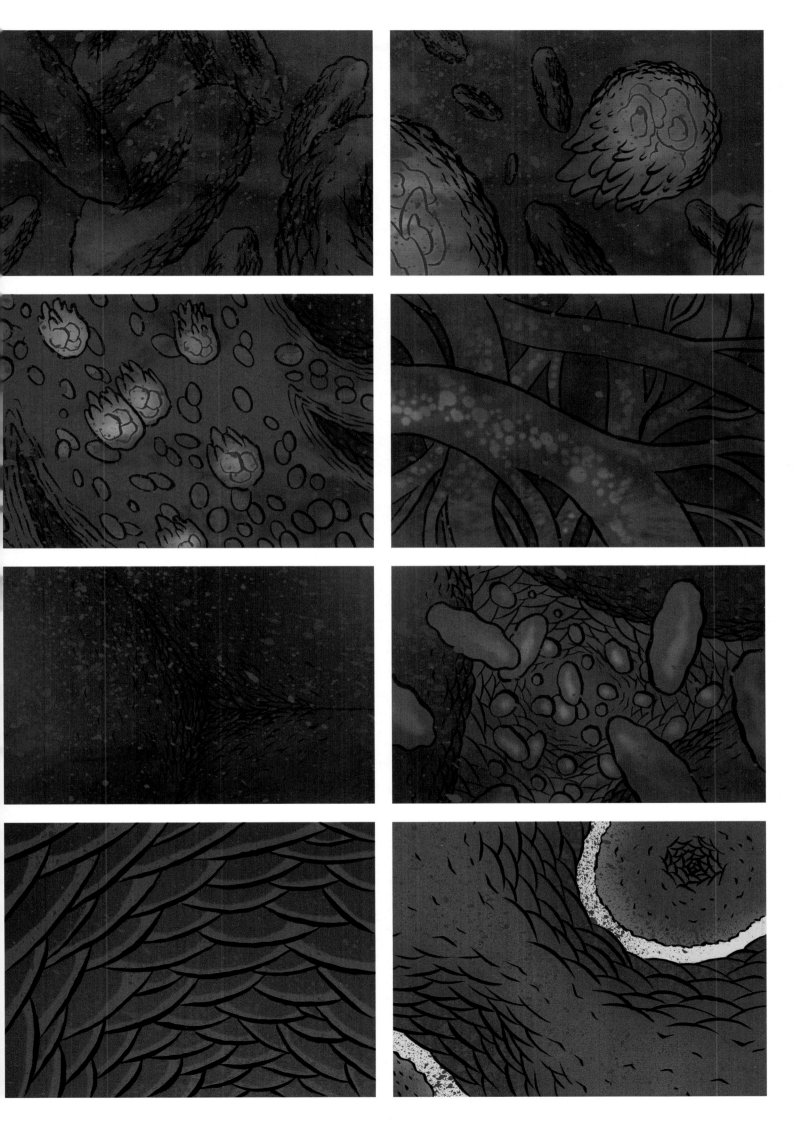

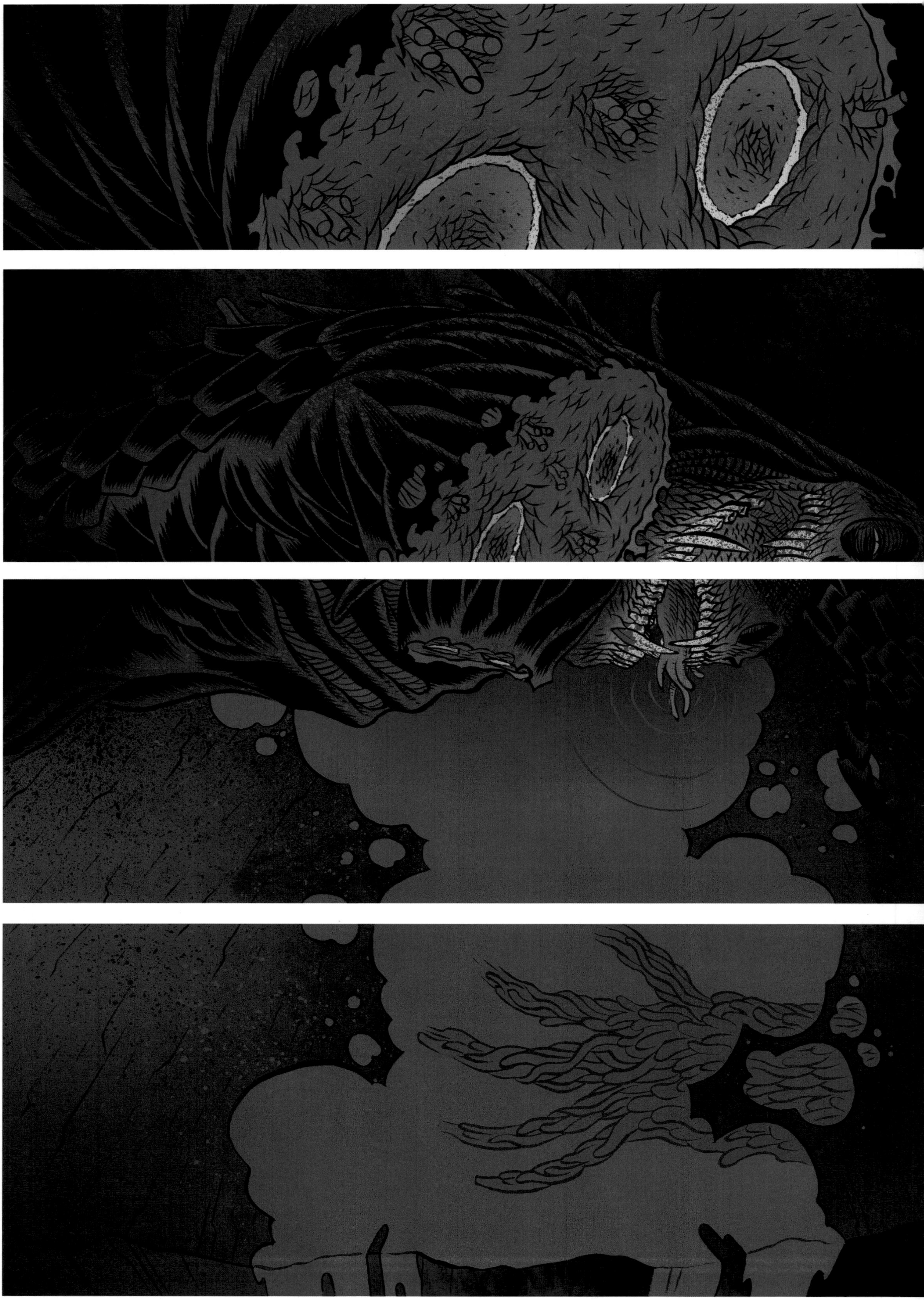

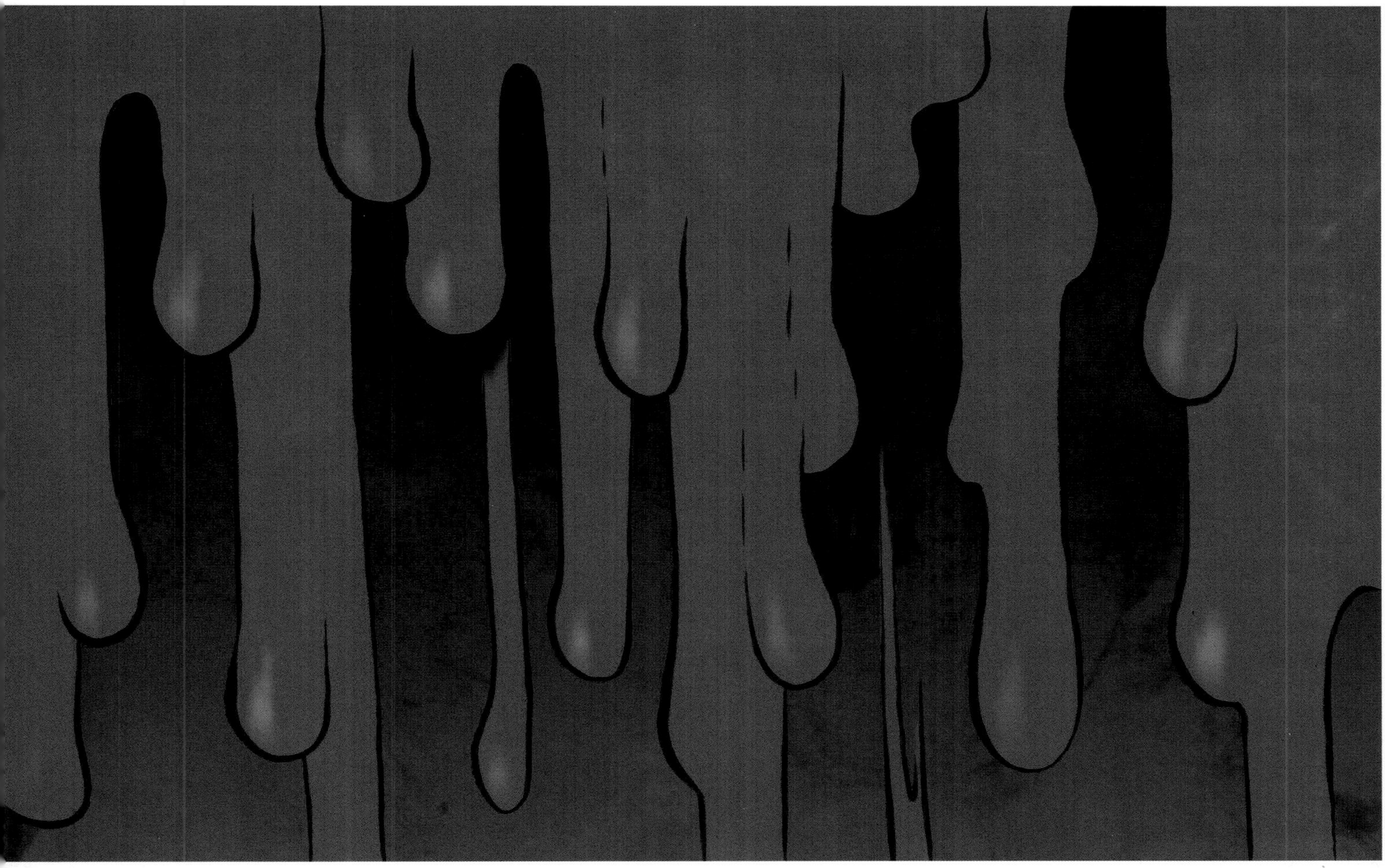

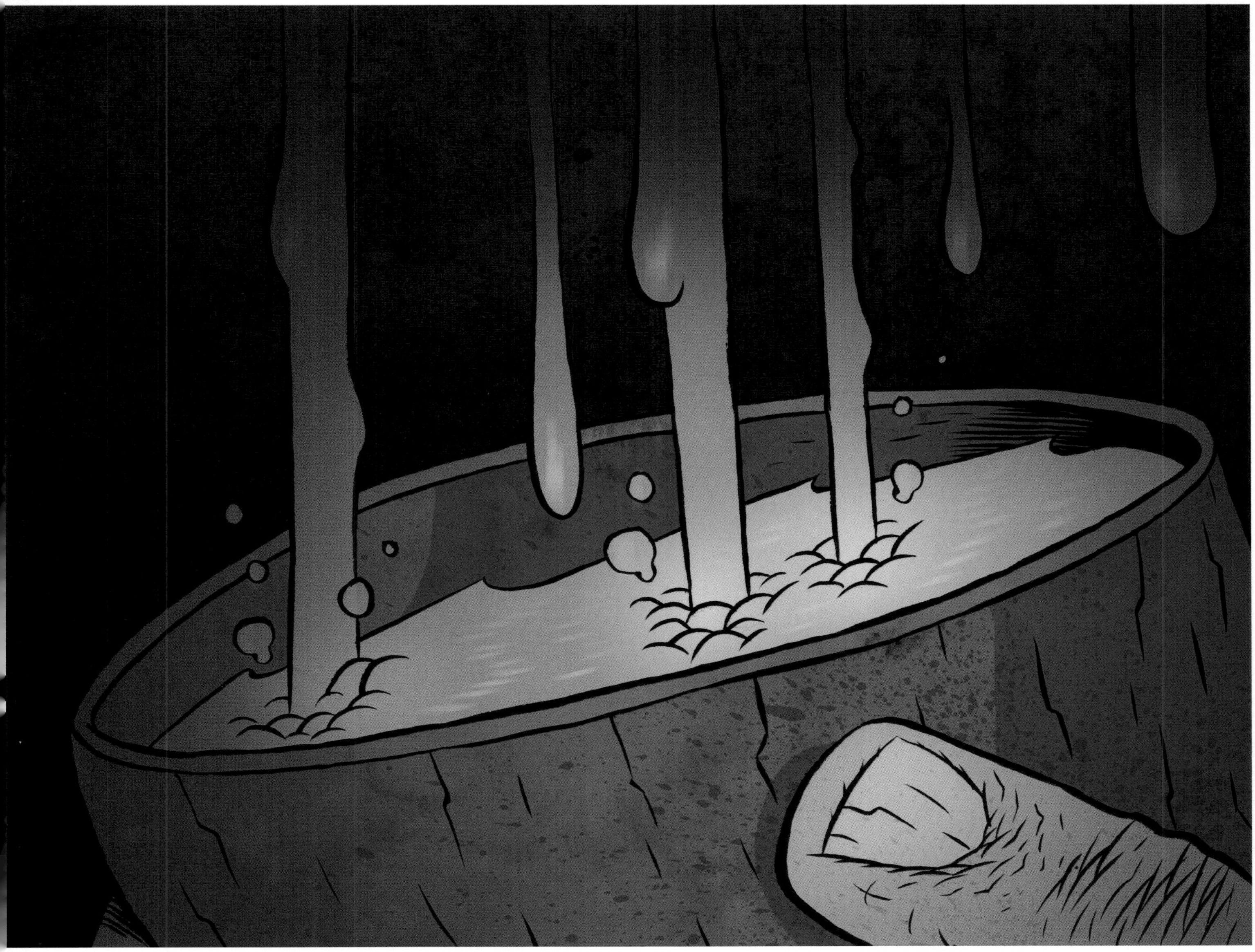

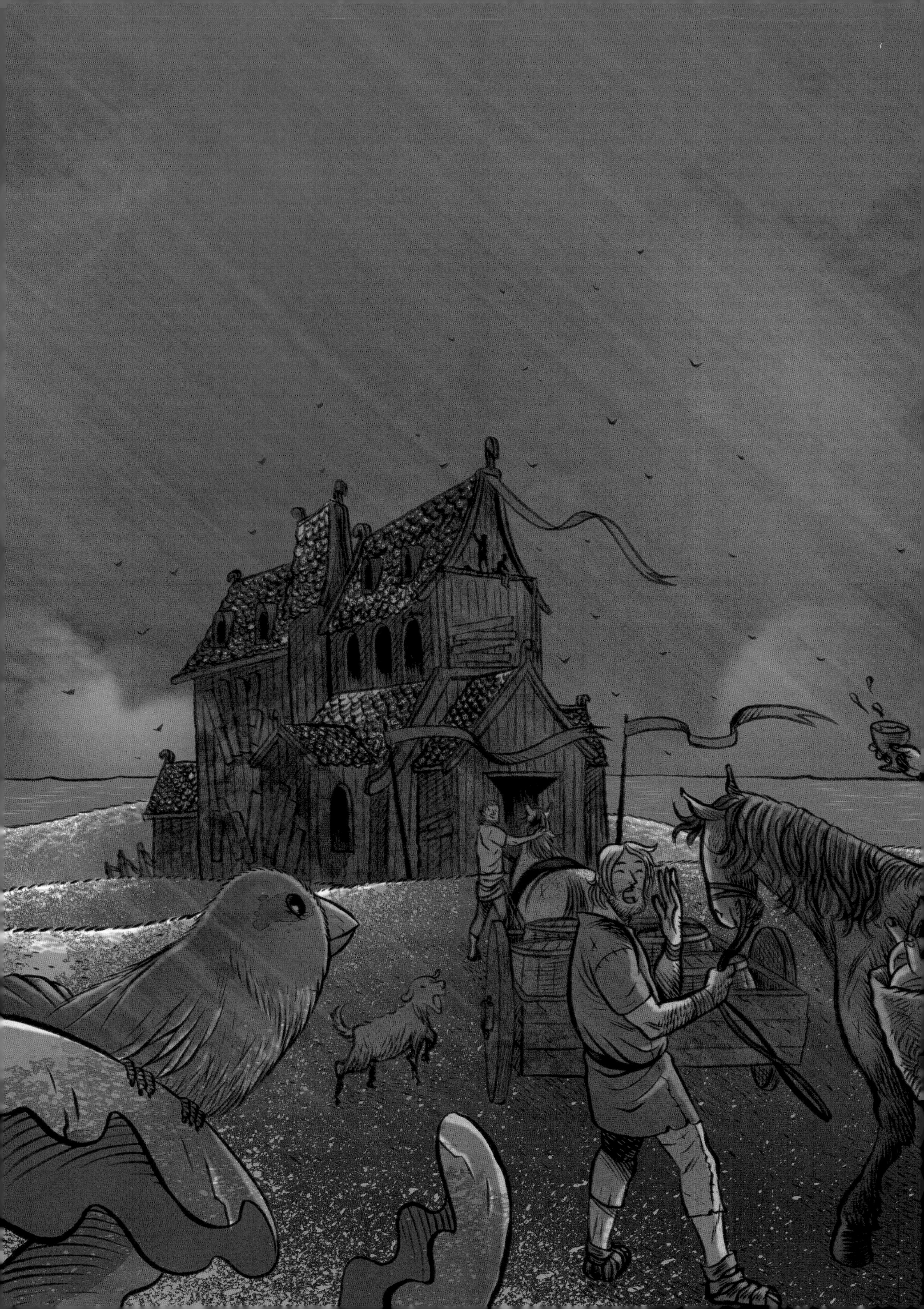

2. MOTHER

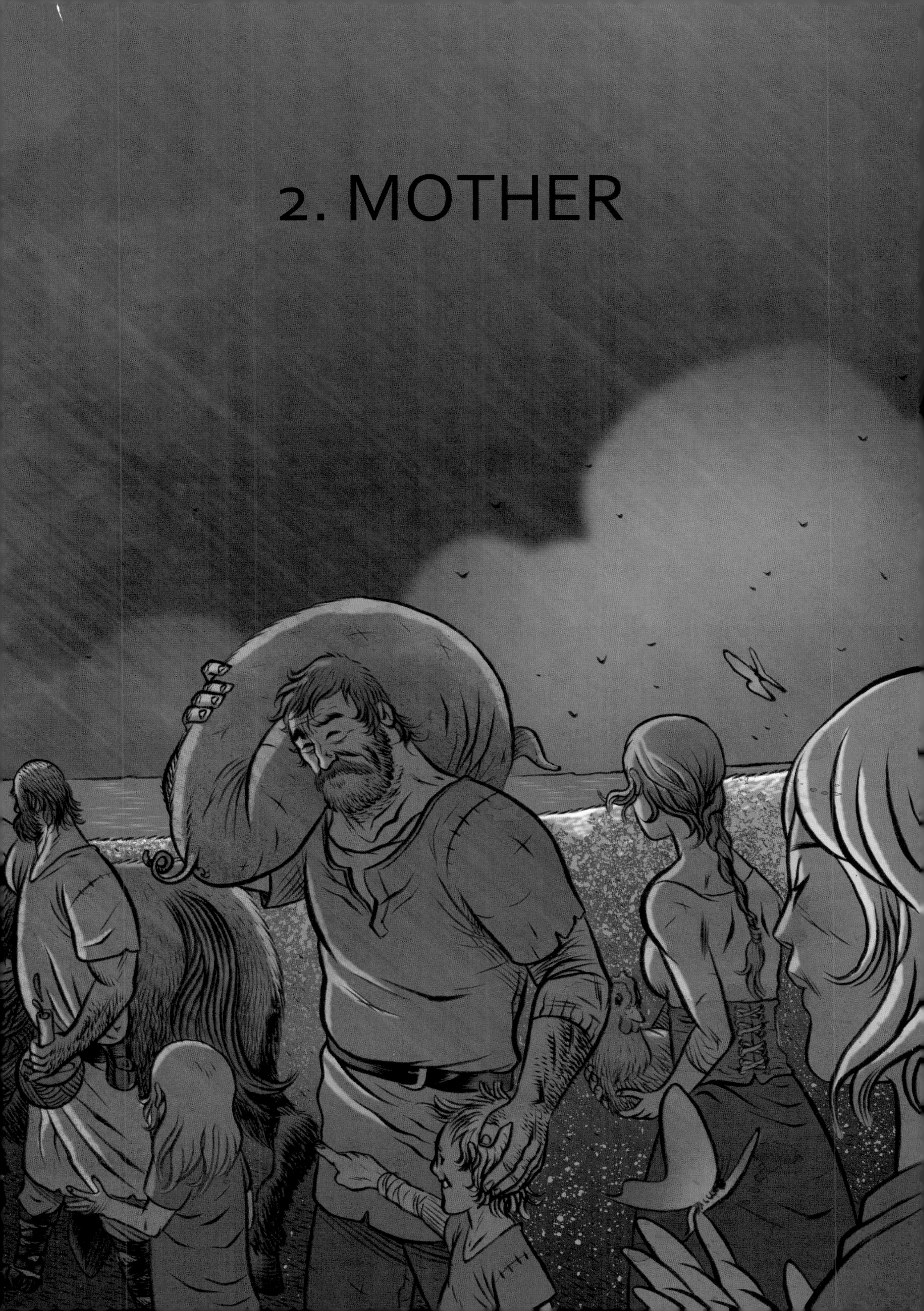

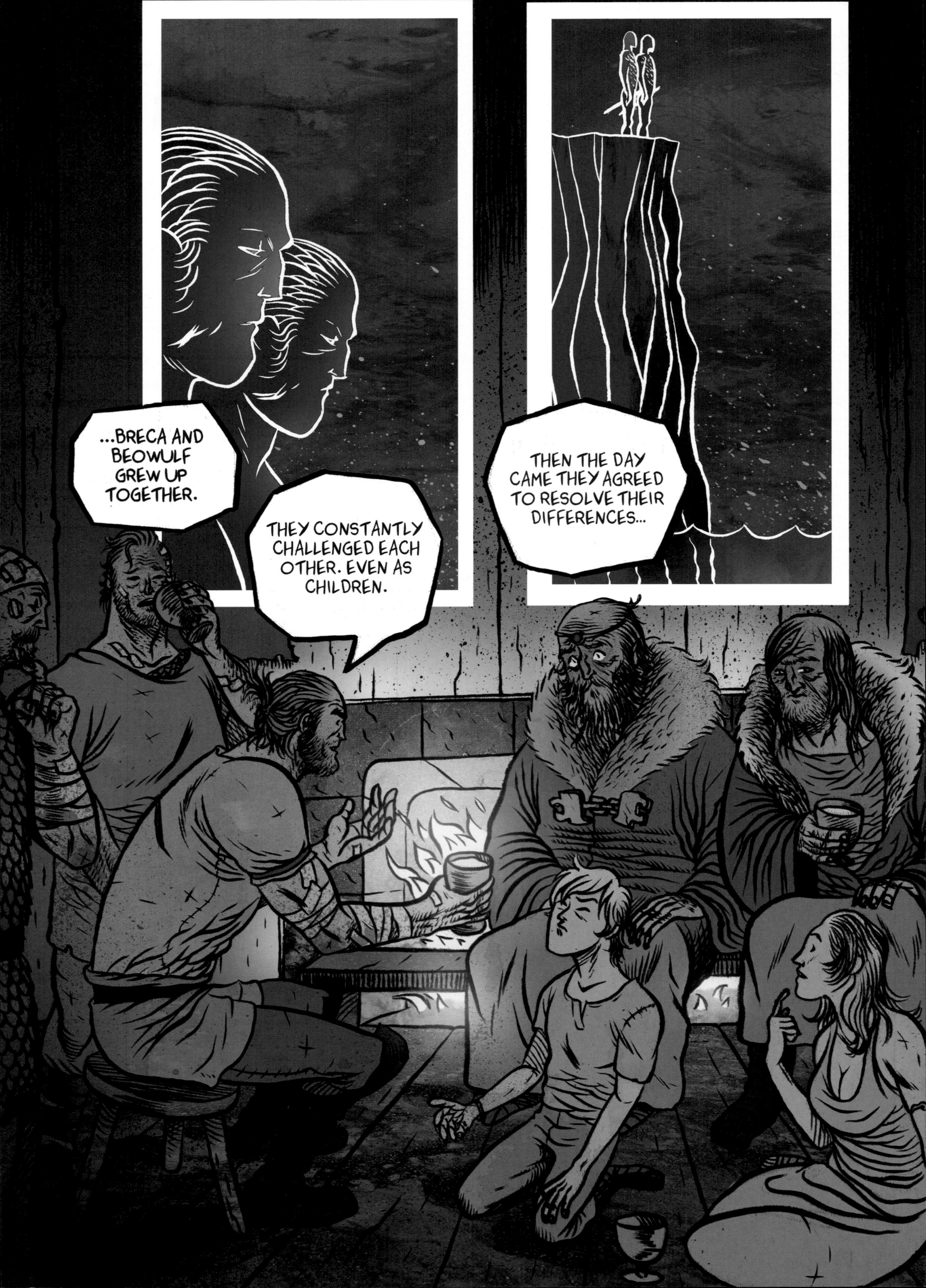
...BRECA AND BEOWULF GREW UP TOGETHER.
THEY CONSTANTLY CHALLENGED EACH OTHER. EVEN AS CHILDREN.
THEN THE DAY CAME THEY AGREED TO RESOLVE THEIR DIFFERENCES...

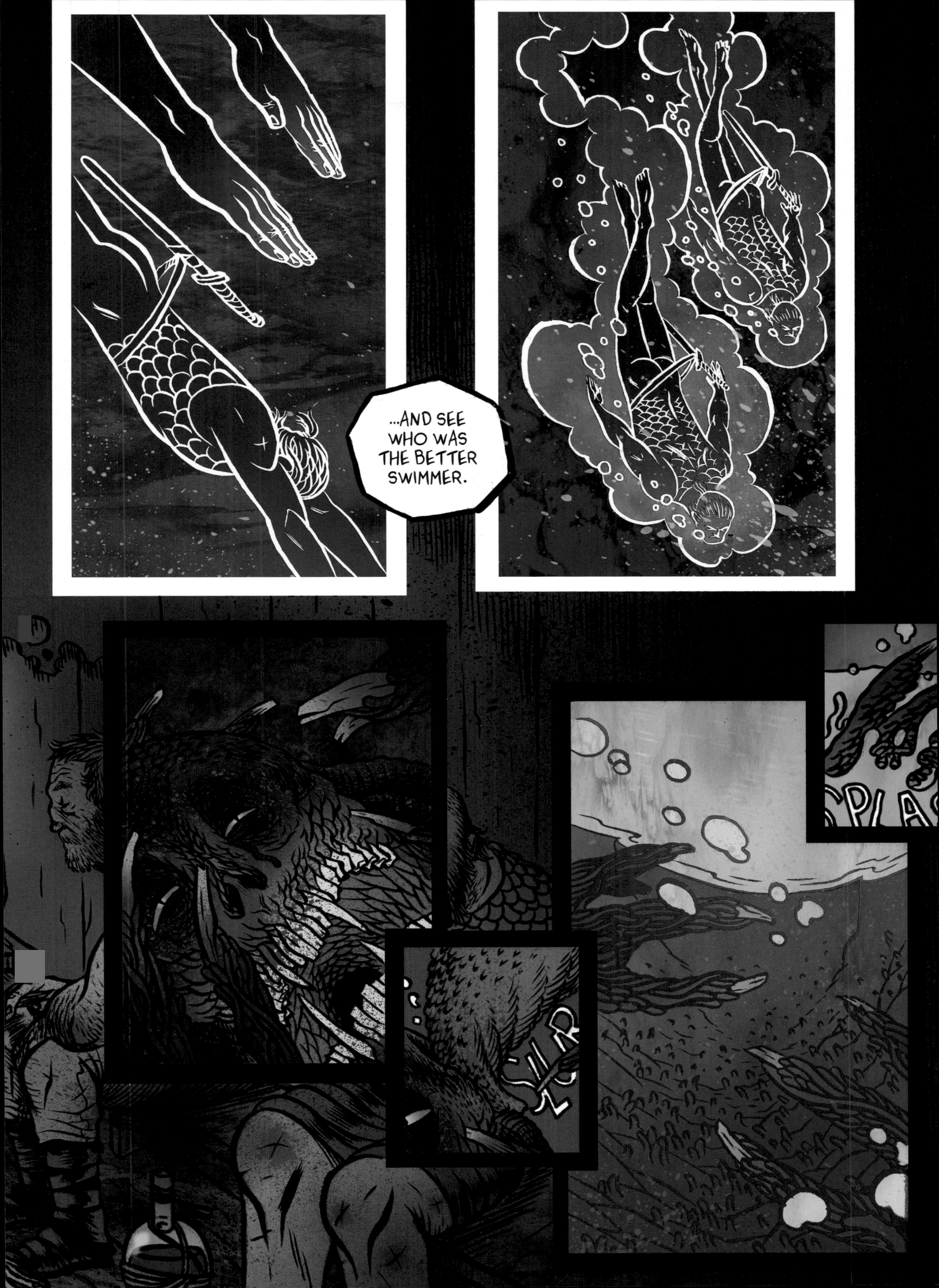
...AND SEE WHO WAS THE BETTER SWIMMER.
SPLAS

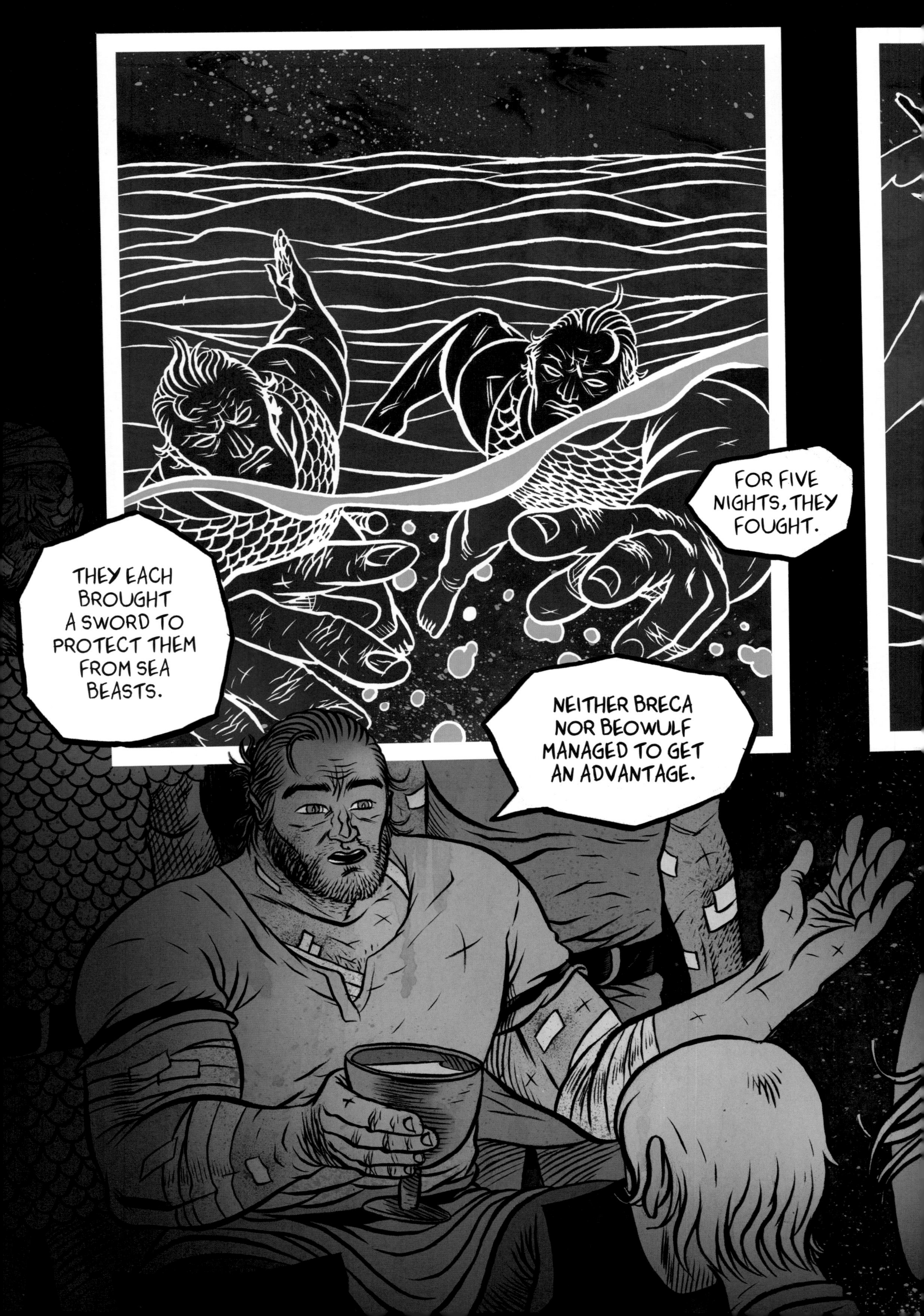

FOR FIVE NIGHTS, THEY FOUGHT.
THEY EACH BROUGHT A SWORD TO PROTECT THEM FROM SEA BEASTS.
NEITHER BRECA NOR BEOWULF MANAGED TO GET AN ADVANTAGE.

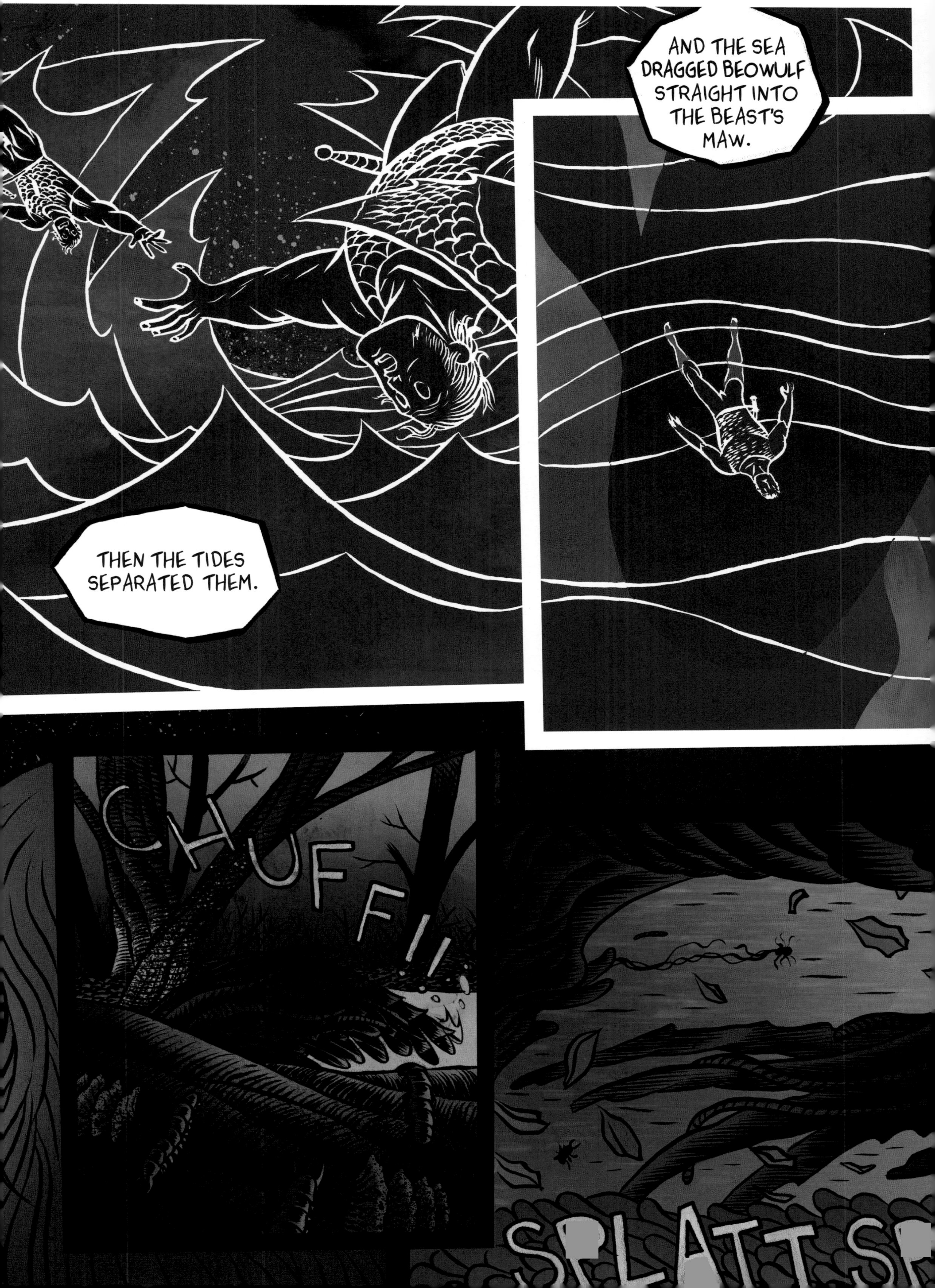
THEN THE TIDES SEPARATED THEM.
AND THE SEA DRAGGED BEOWULF STRAIGHT INTO THE BEAST'S MAW.
CHUFF!!
SPLATT

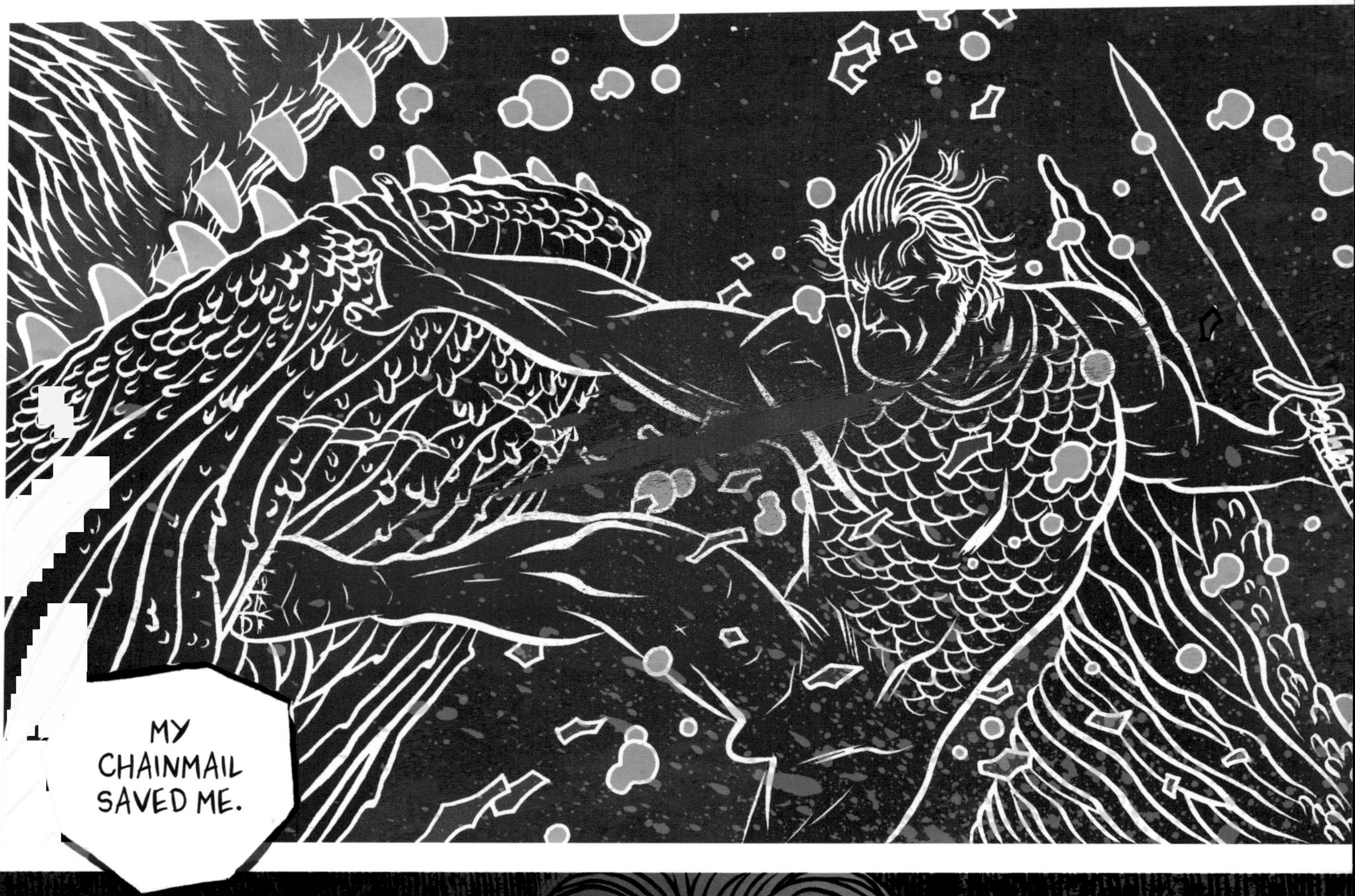
MY CHAINMAIL SAVED ME.

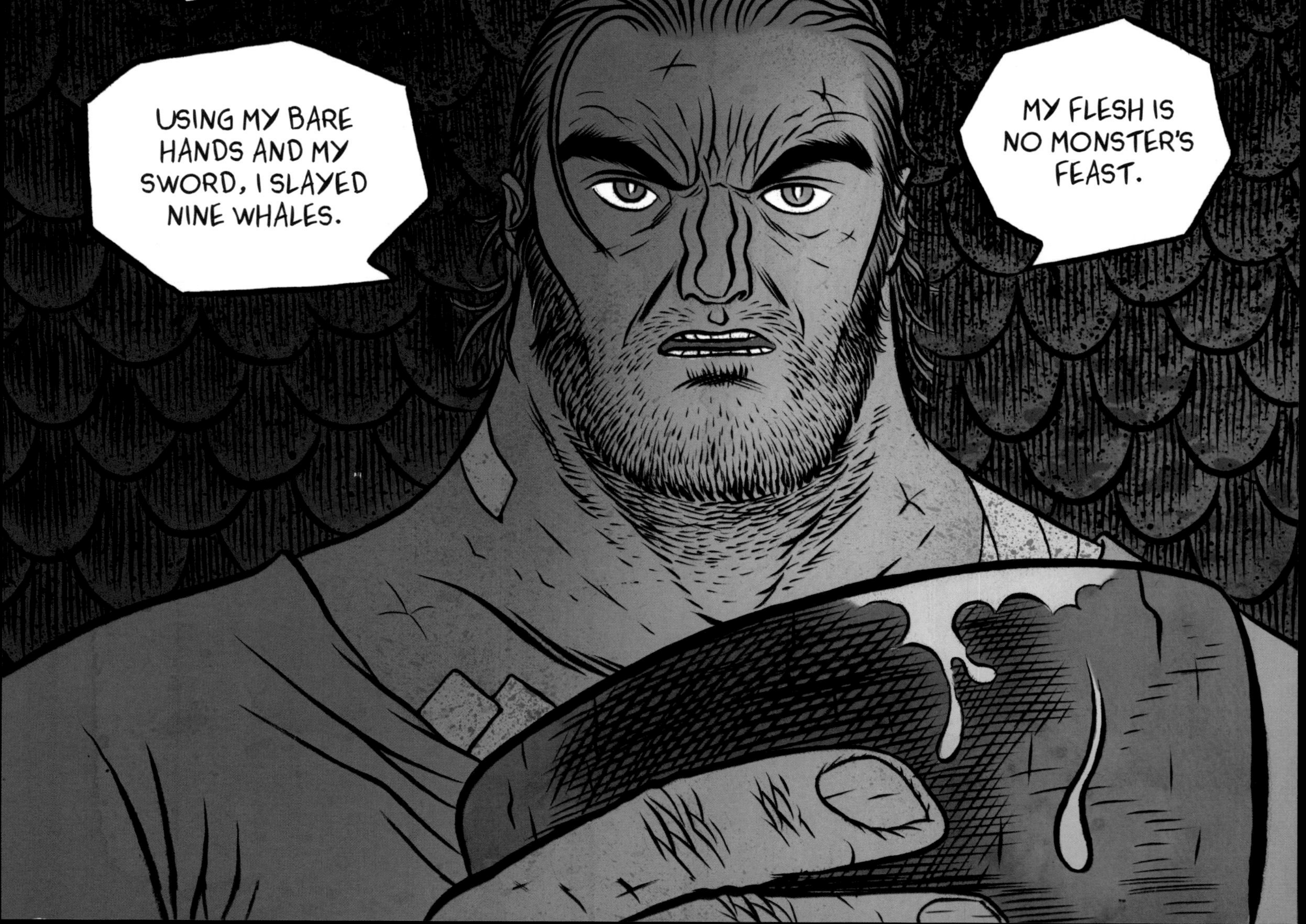
USING MY BARE HANDS AND MY SWORD, I SLAYED NINE WHALES.
MY FLESH IS NO MONSTER'S FEAST.

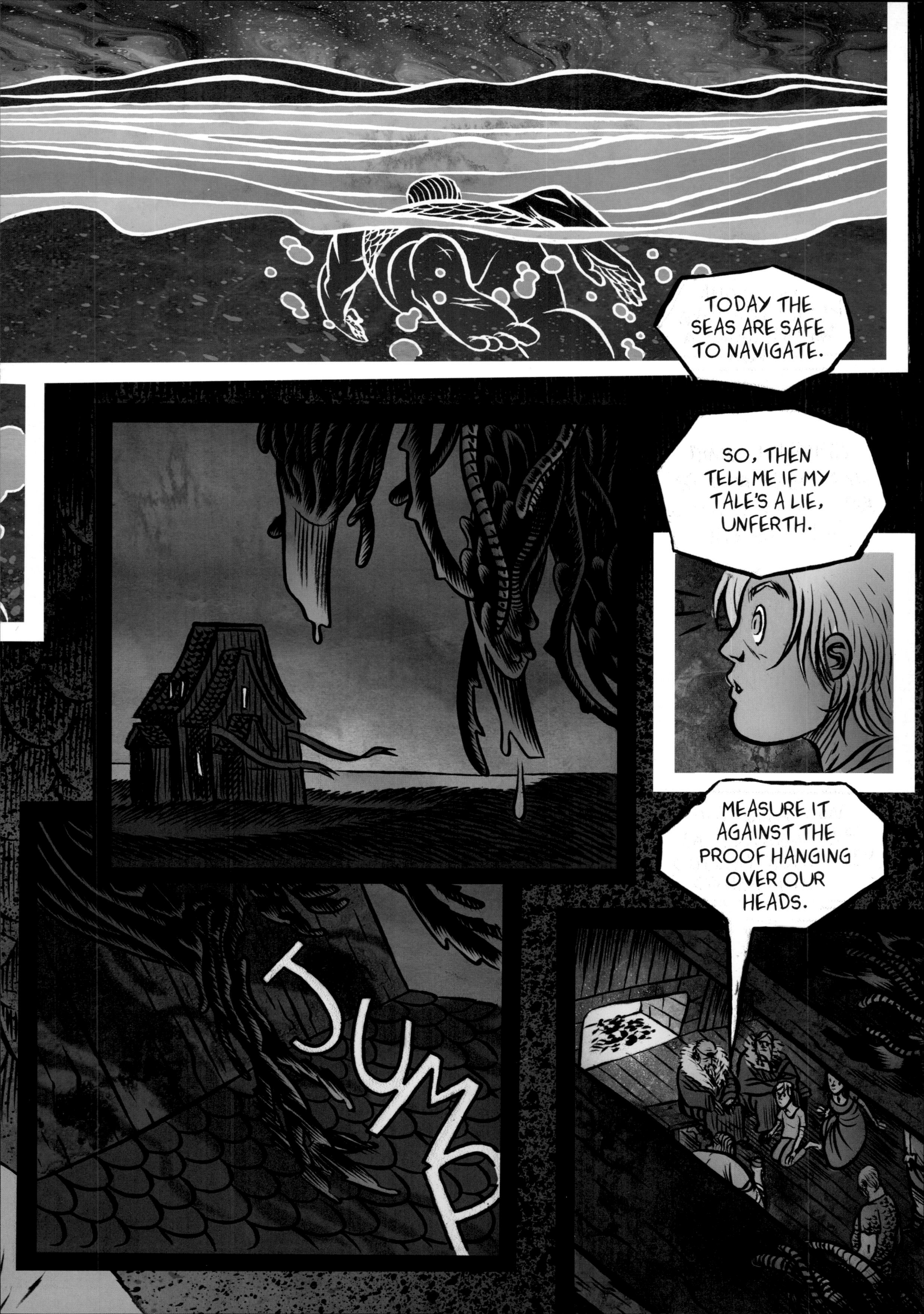
TODAY THE SEAS ARE SAFE TO NAVIGATE.
SO, THEN TELL ME IF MY TALE'S A LIE, UNFERTH.
MEASURE IT AGAINST THE PROOF HANGING OVER OUR HEADS.
JUMP

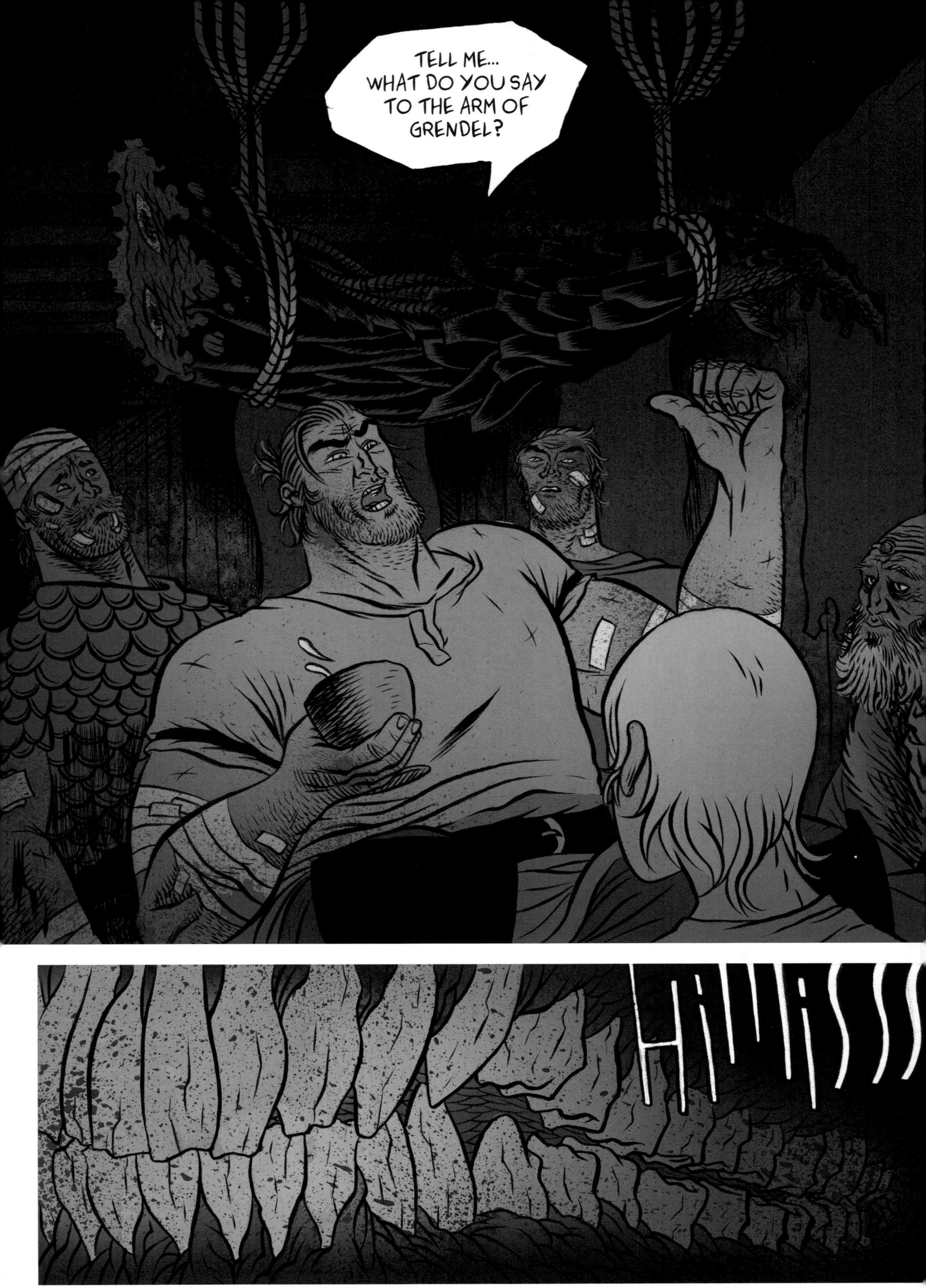
TELL ME... WHAT DO YOU SAY TO THE ARM OF GRENDEL?

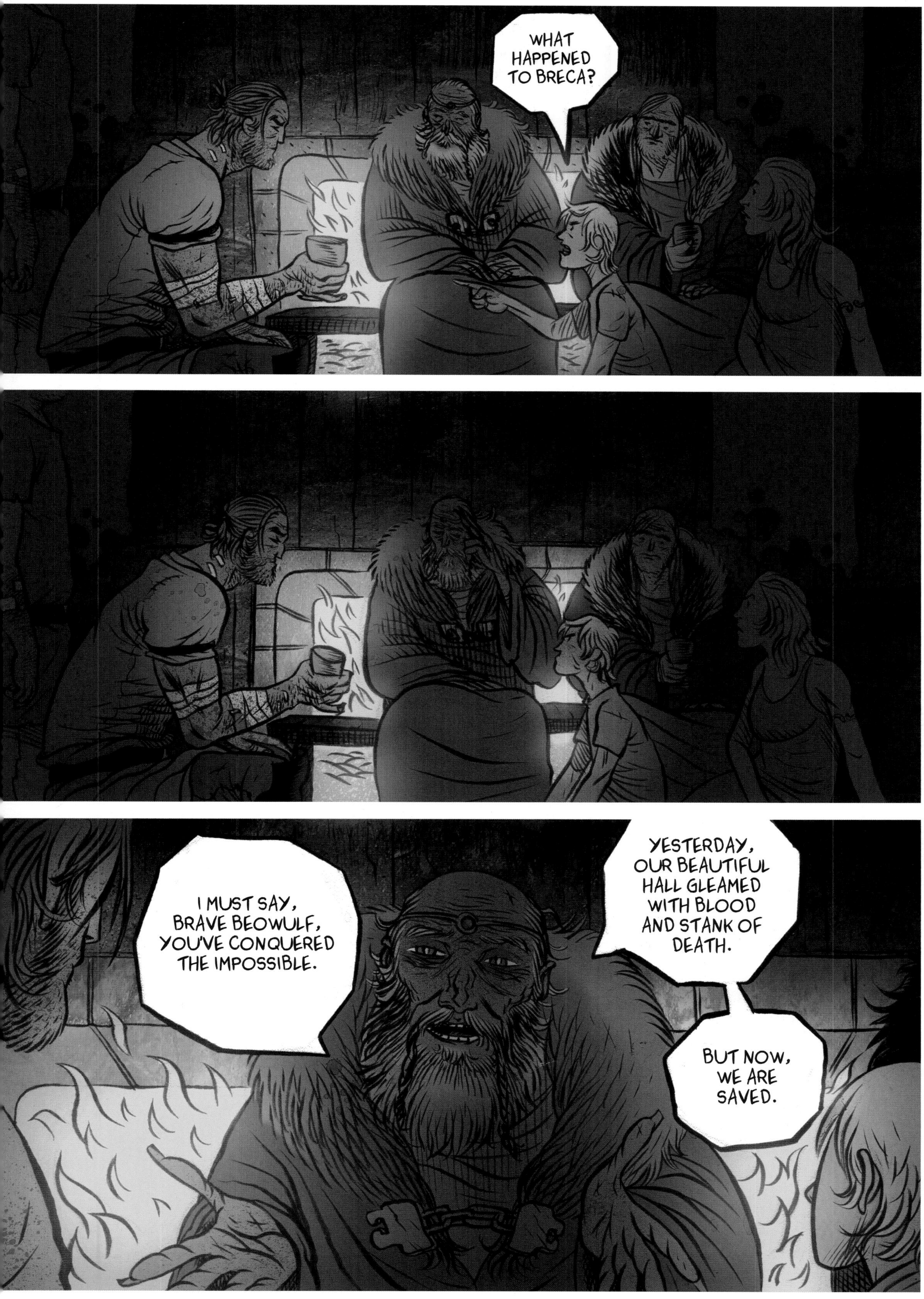
WHAT HAPPENED TO BRECA?
I MUST SAY, BRAVE BEOWULF, YOU'VE CONQUERED THE IMPOSSIBLE.
YESTERDAY, OUR BEAUTIFUL HALL GLEAMED WITH BLOOD AND STANK OF DEATH.
BUT NOW, WE ARE SAVED.

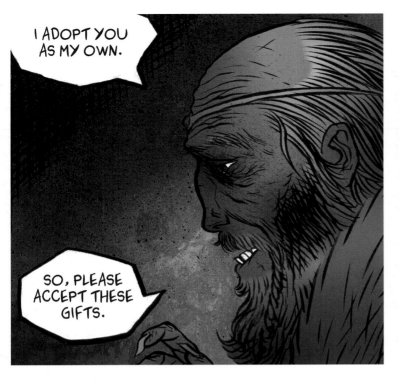

I ADOPT YOU AS MY OWN.
SO, PLEASE ACCEPT THESE GIFTS.
A BANNER OF GOLD WITH AN EMBROIDERED PENNANT.
CHAINMAIL AND A HELMET.
A SWORD.
EIGHT HORSES WITH FINE SADDLES.
AND TREASURE FOR EACH OF YOUR MEN.

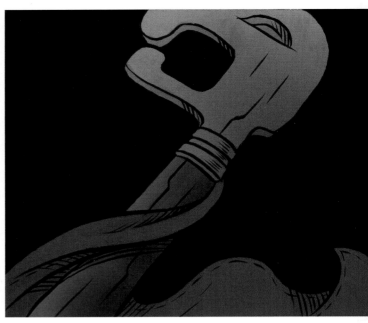

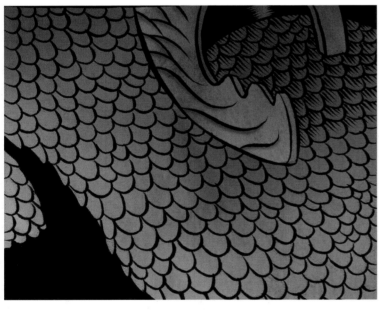

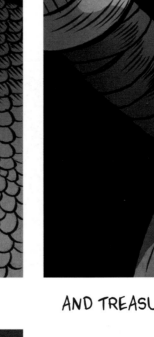

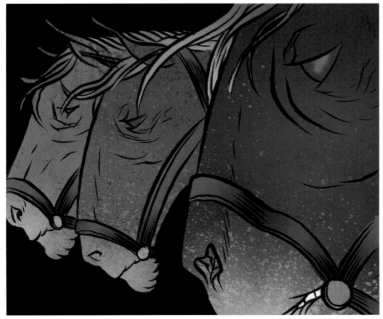

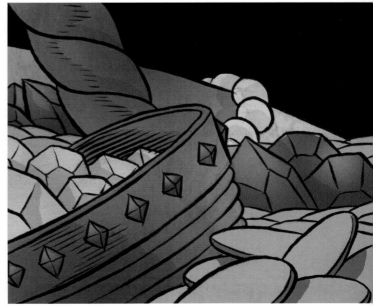

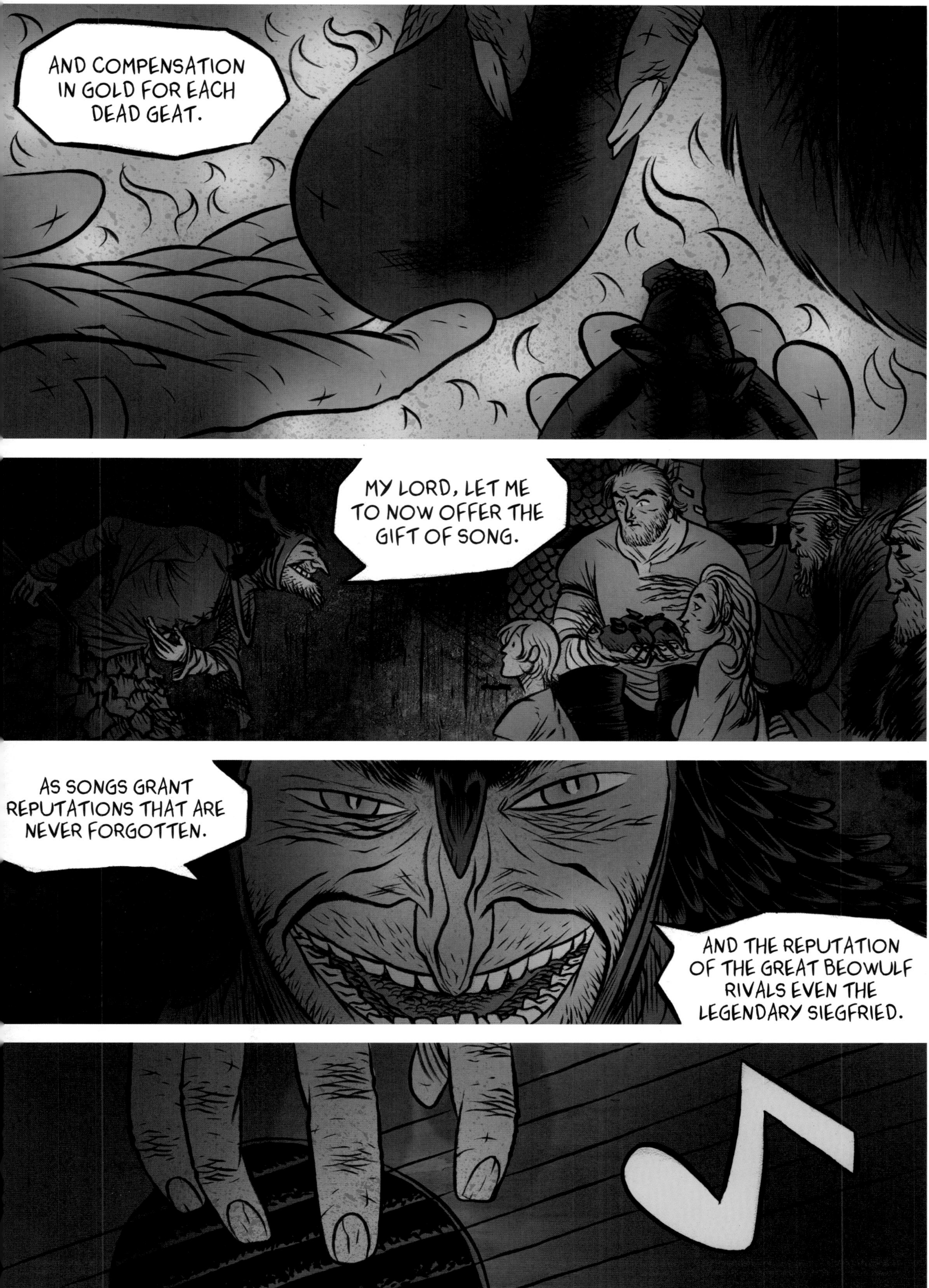
AND COMPENSATION IN GOLD FOR EACH DEAD GEAT.
MY LORD, LET ME TO NOW OFFER THE GIFT OF SONG.
AS SONGS GRANT REPUTATIONS THAT ARE NEVER FORGOTTEN.
AND THE REPUTATION OF THE GREAT BEOWULF RIVALS EVEN THE LEGENDARY SIEGFRIED.

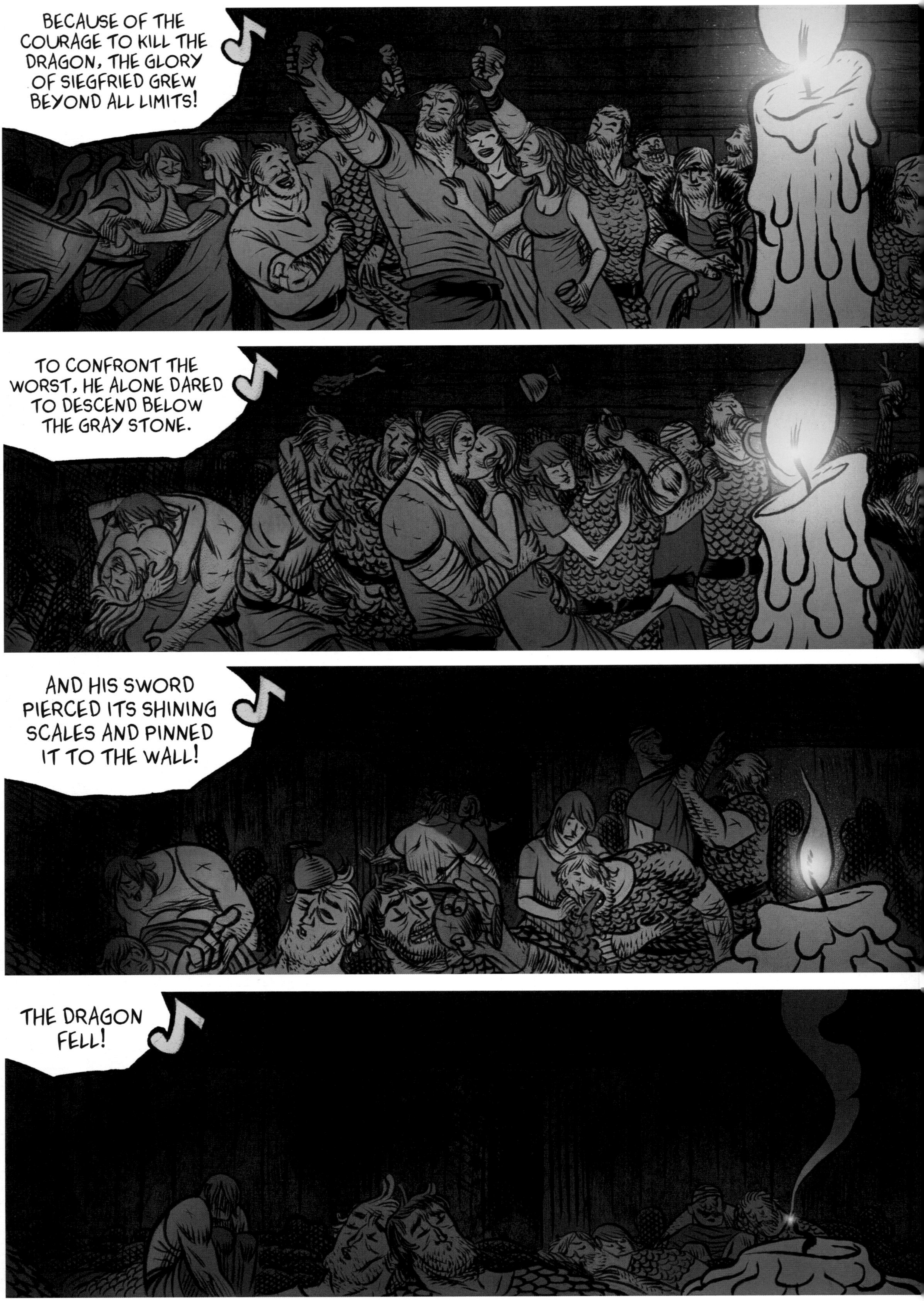
BECAUSE OF THE COURAGE TO KILL THE DRAGON, THE GLORY OF SIEGFRIED GREW BEYOND ALL LIMITS!
TO CONFRONT THE WORST, HE ALONE DARED TO DESCEND BELOW THE GRAY STONE.
AND HIS SWORD PIERCED ITS SHINING SCALES AND PINNED IT TO THE WALL!
THE DRAGON FELL!

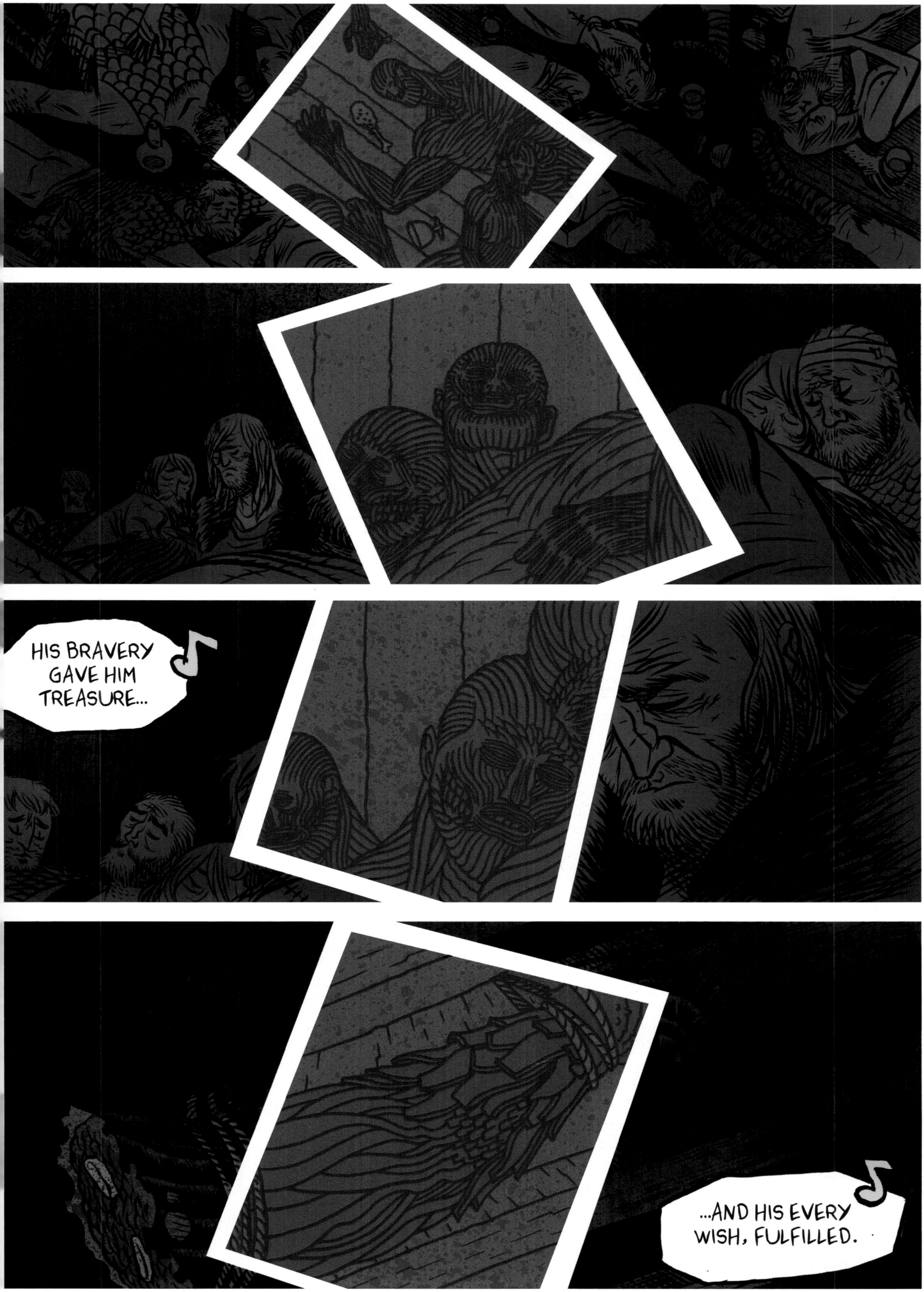
HIS BRAVERY GAVE HIM TREASURE...
...AND HIS EVERY WISH, FULFILLED.

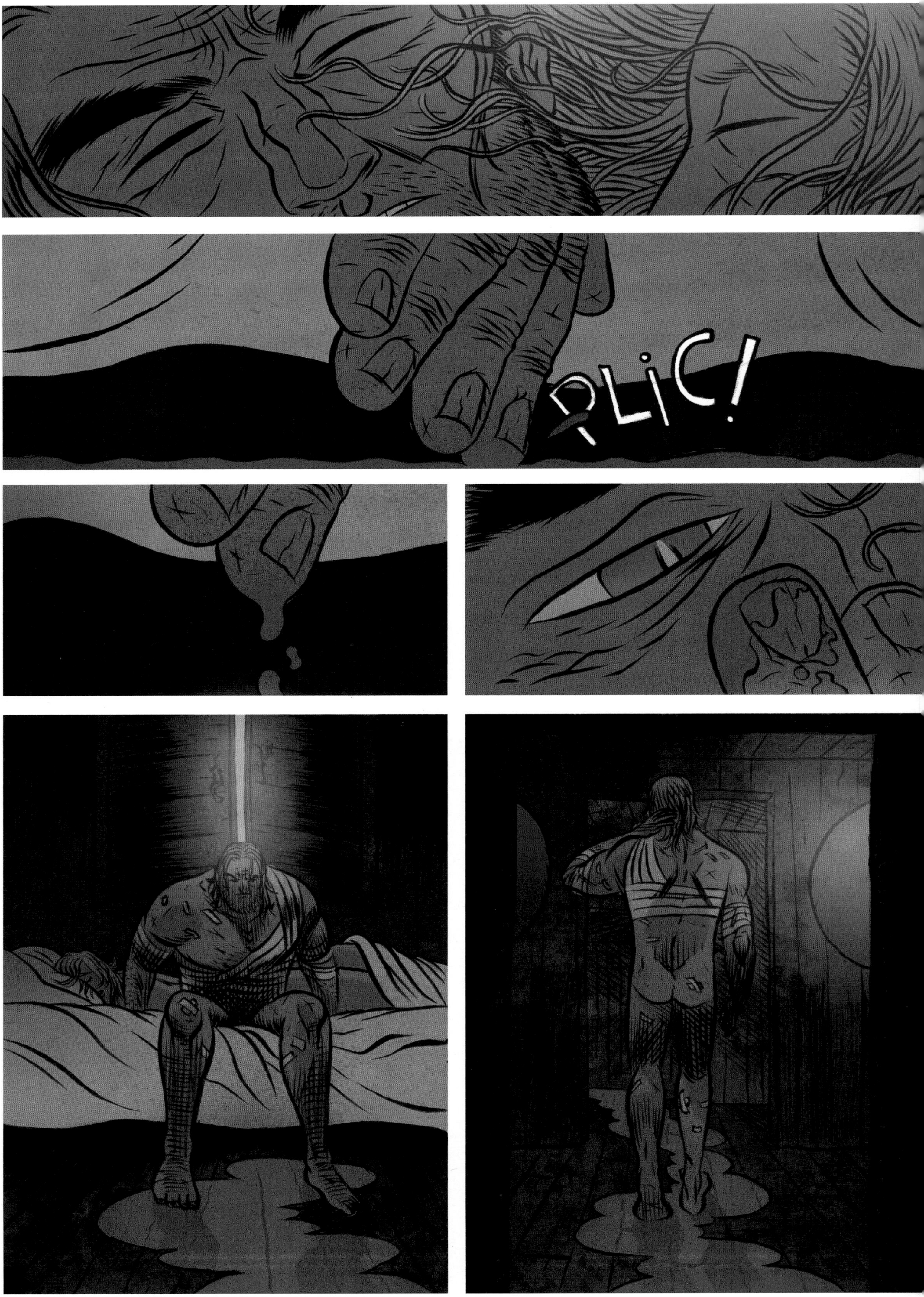
PLIC!

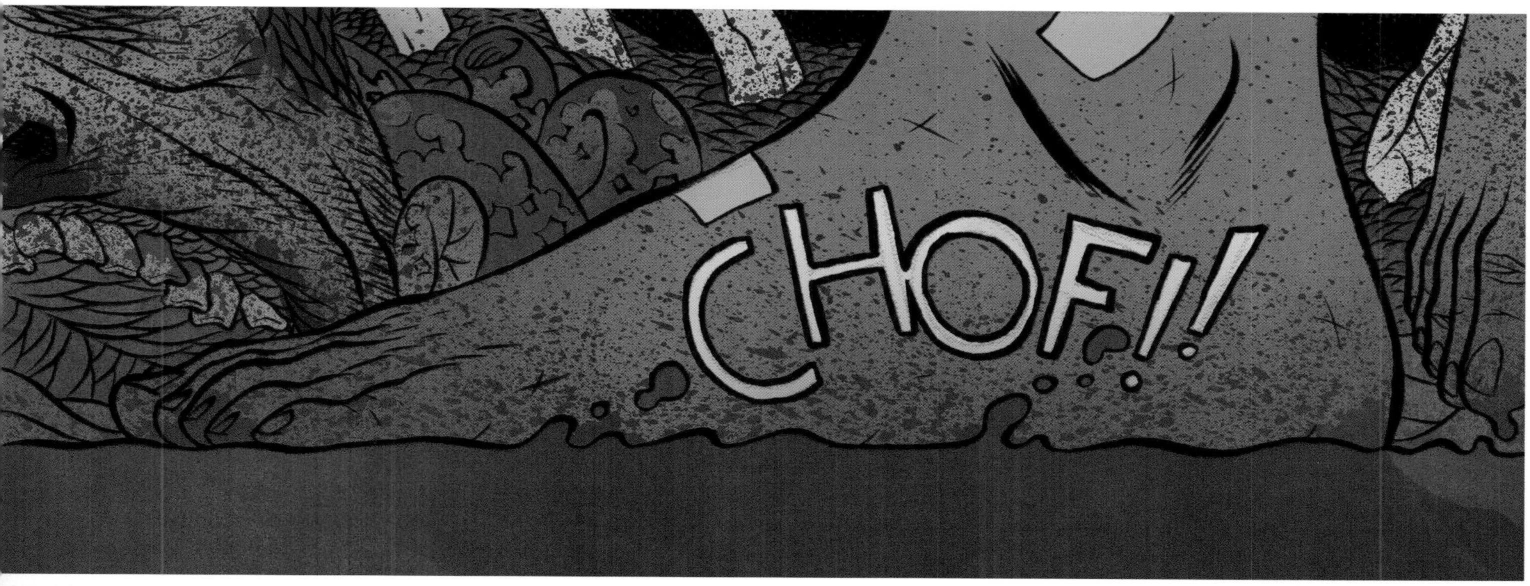
CHOF!!

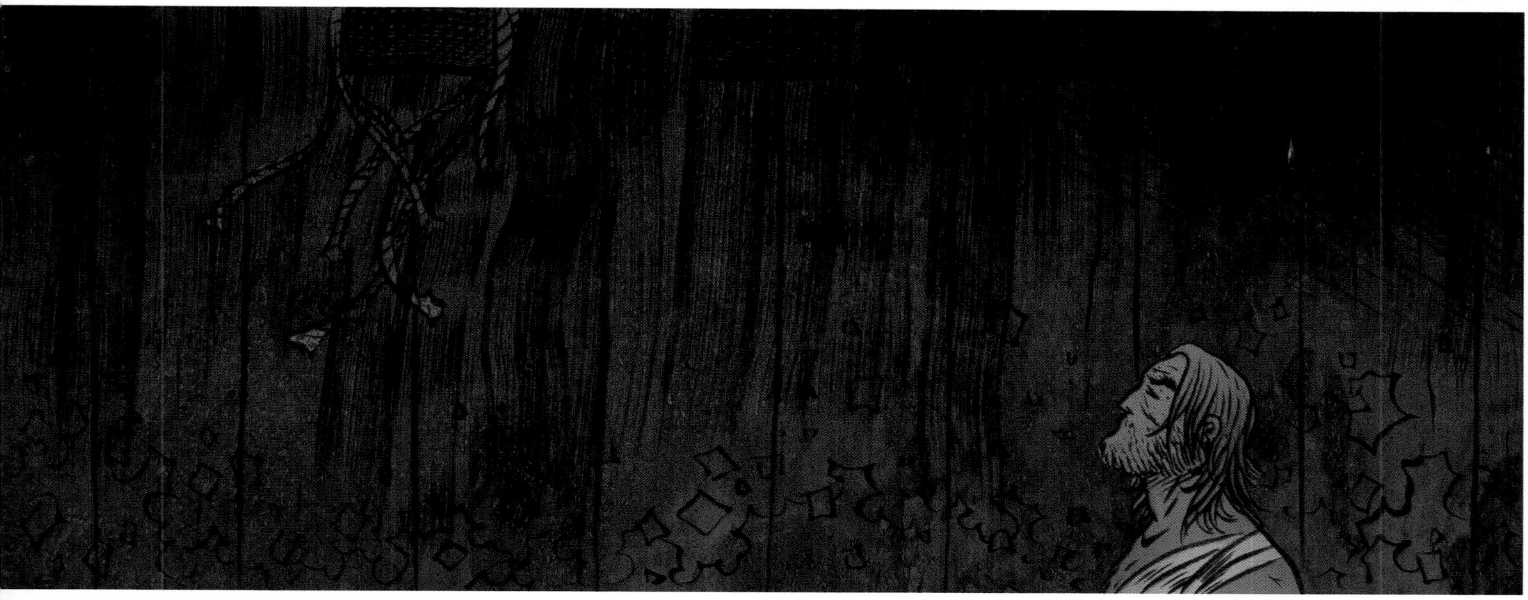

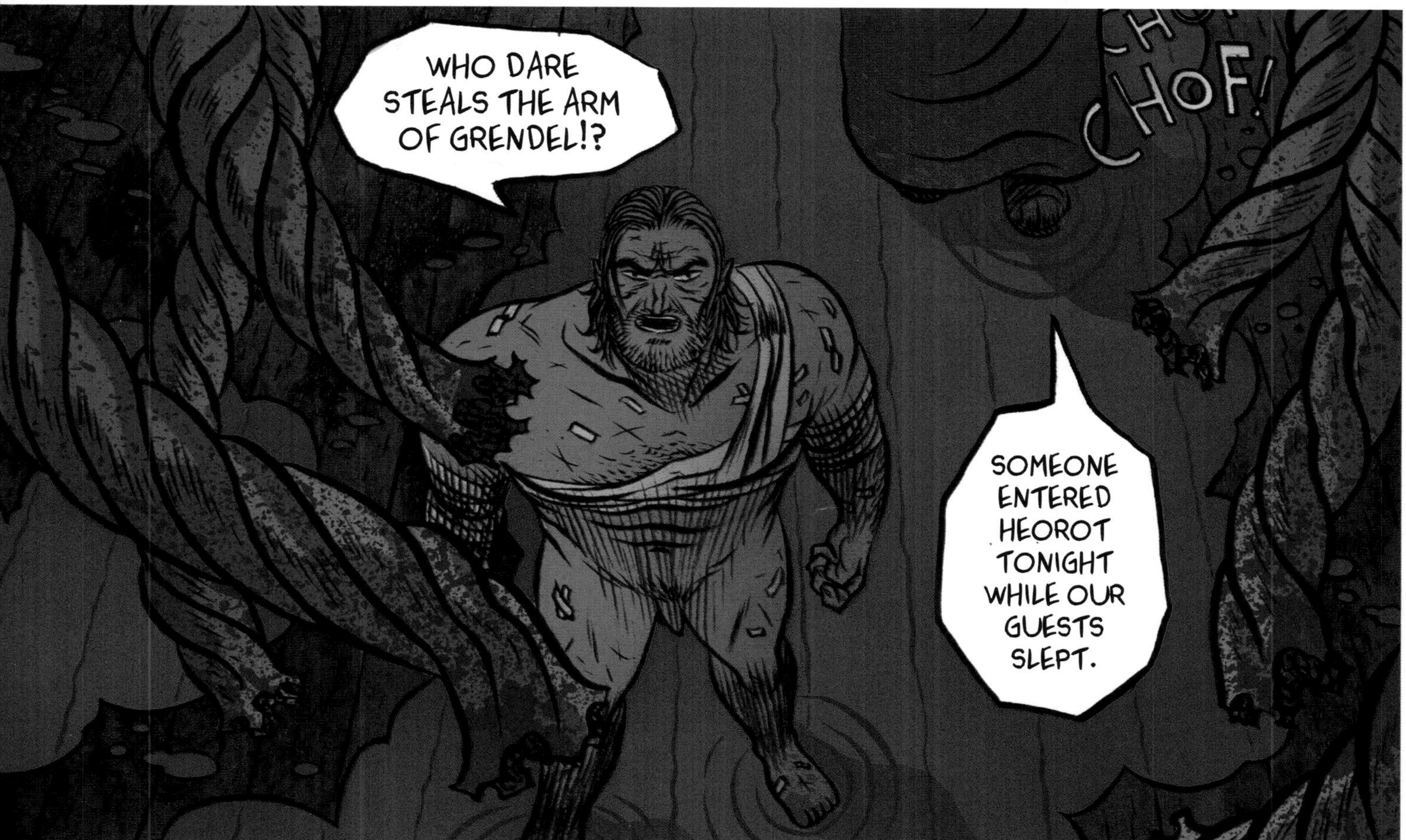
CHOF!
WHO DARE STEALS THE ARM OF GRENDEL!?
SOMEONE ENTERED HEOROT TONIGHT WHILE OUR GUESTS SLEPT.

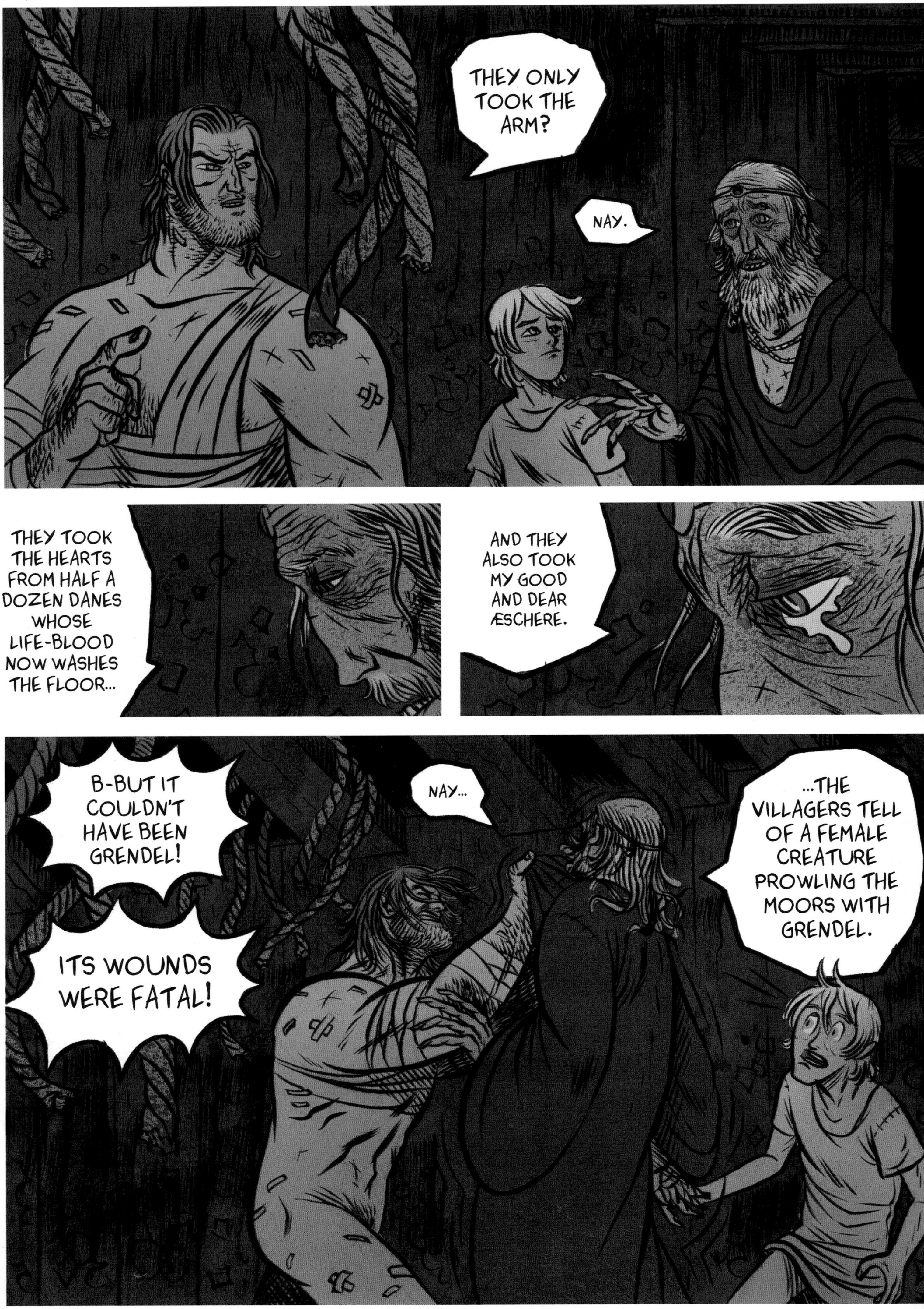
THEY ONLY TOOK THE ARM?
NAY.
THEY TOOK THE HEARTS FROM HALF A DOZEN DANES WHOSE LIFE-BLOOD NOW WASHES THE FLOOR...
AND THEY ALSO TOOK MY GOOD AND DEAR ÆSCHERE.
B-BUT IT COULDN'T HAVE BEEN GRENDEL!
ITS WOUNDS WERE FATAL!
NAY...
...THE VILLAGERS TELL OF A FEMALE CREATURE PROWLING THE MOORS WITH GRENDEL.

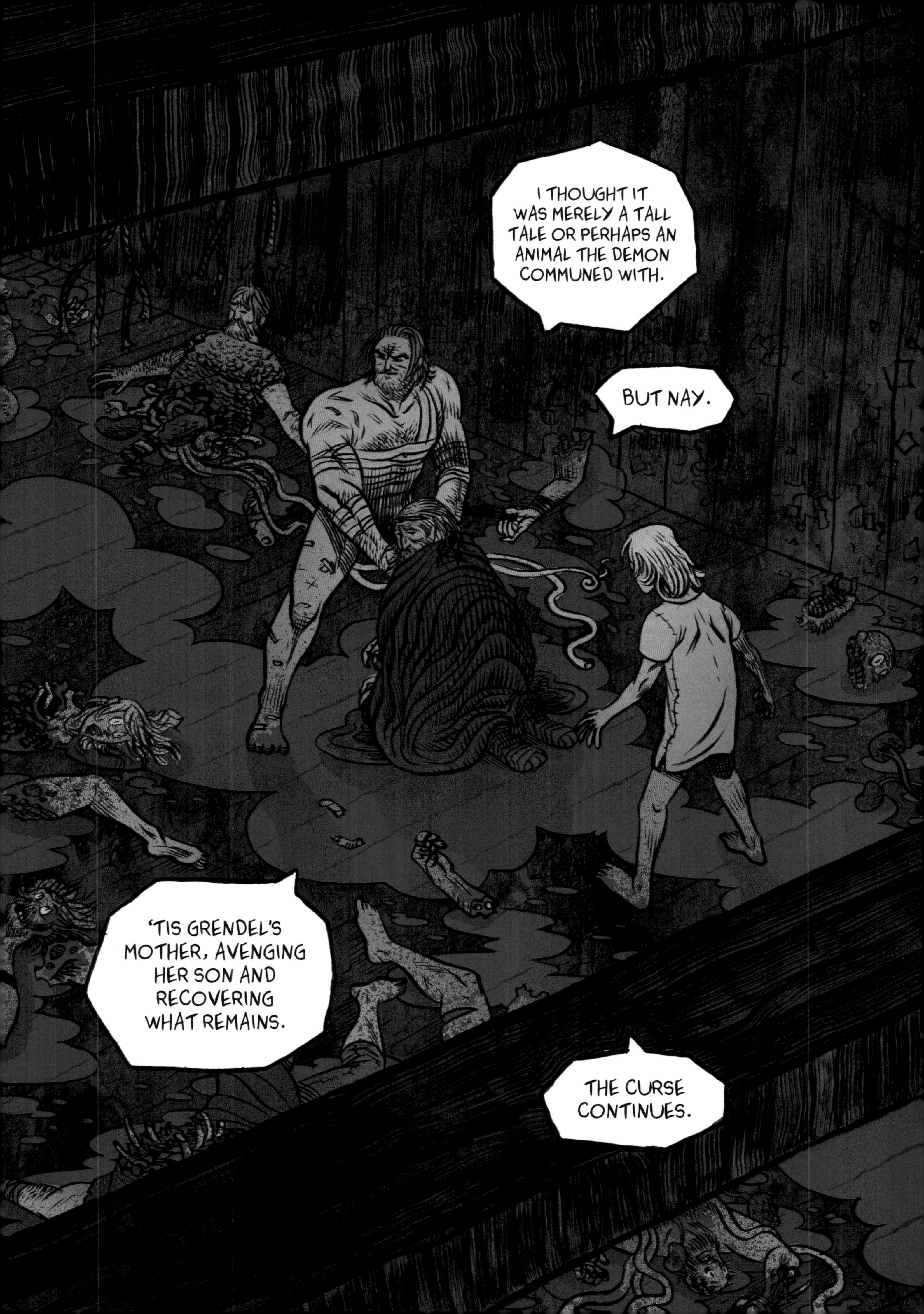
I THOUGHT IT WAS MERELY A TALL TALE OR PERHAPS AN ANIMAL THE DEMON COMMUNED WITH.
BUT NAY.
'TIS GRENDEL'S MOTHER, AVENGING HER SON AND RECOVERING WHAT REMAINS.
THE CURSE CONTINUES.

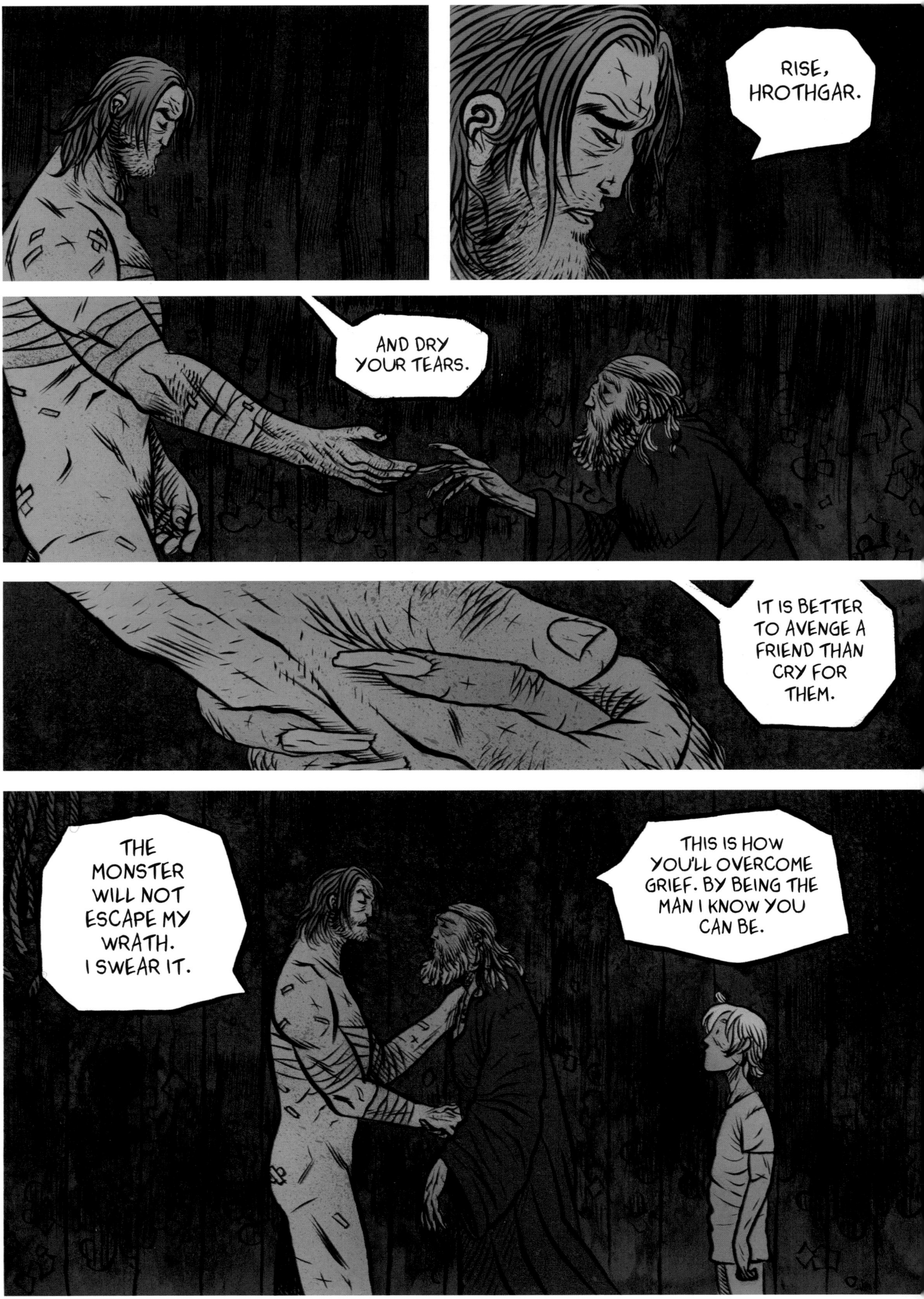
RISE, HROTHGAR.
AND DRY YOUR TEARS.
IT IS BETTER TO AVENGE A FRIEND THAN CRY FOR THEM.
THE MONSTER WILL NOT ESCAPE MY WRATH. I SWEAR IT.
THIS IS HOW YOU'LL OVERCOME GRIEF. BY BEING THE MAN I KNOW YOU CAN BE.

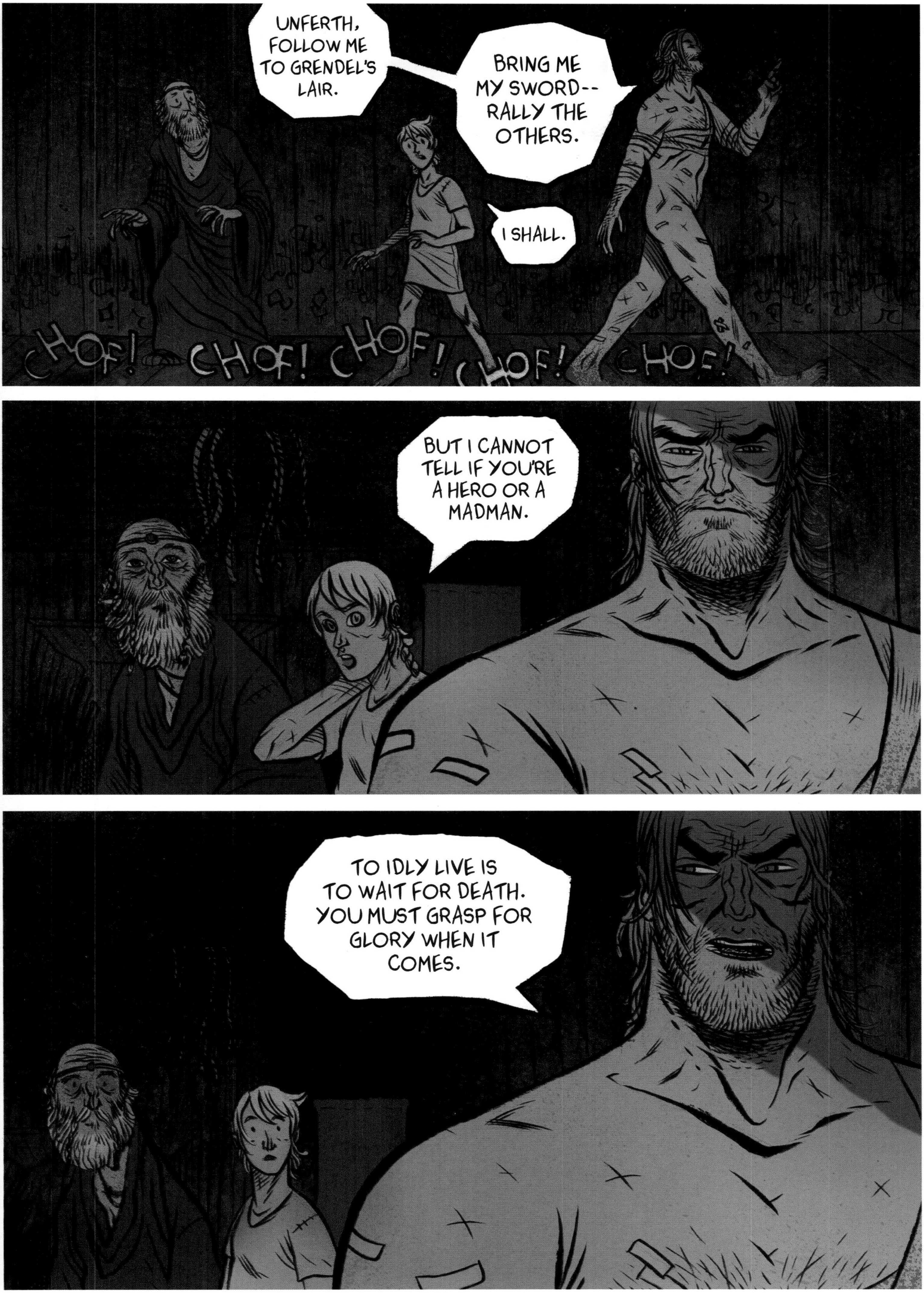
UNFERTH, FOLLOW ME TO GRENDEL'S LAIR.
BRING ME MY SWORD-- RALLY THE OTHERS.
I SHALL.
CHOF! CHOF! CHOF! CHOF! CHOF!
BUT I CANNOT TELL IF YOU'RE A HERO OR A MADMAN.
TO IDLY LIVE IS TO WAIT FOR DEATH. YOU MUST GRASP FOR GLORY WHEN IT COMES.

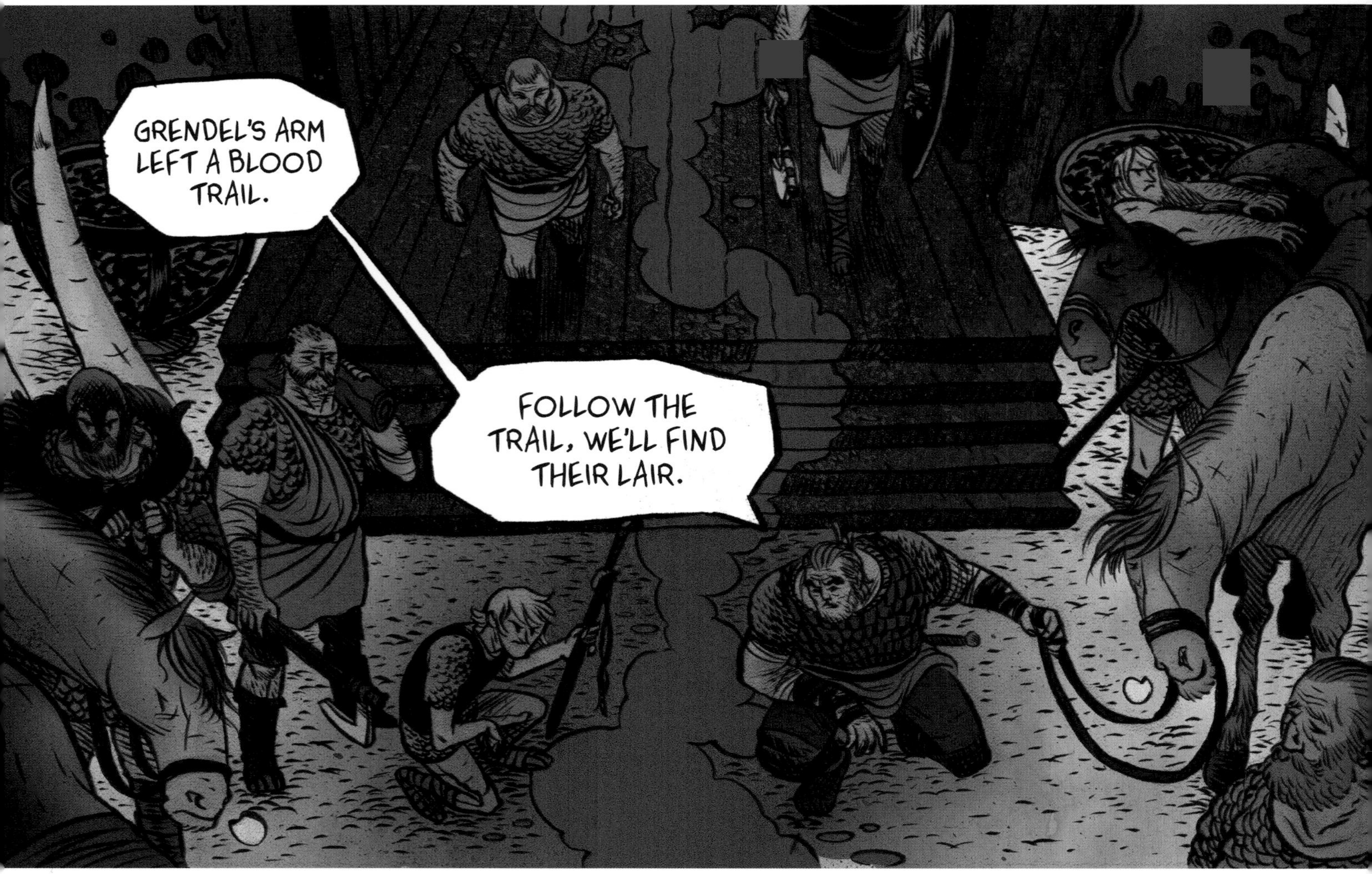
GRENDEL'S ARM LEFT A BLOOD TRAIL.
FOLLOW THE TRAIL, WE'LL FIND THEIR LAIR.
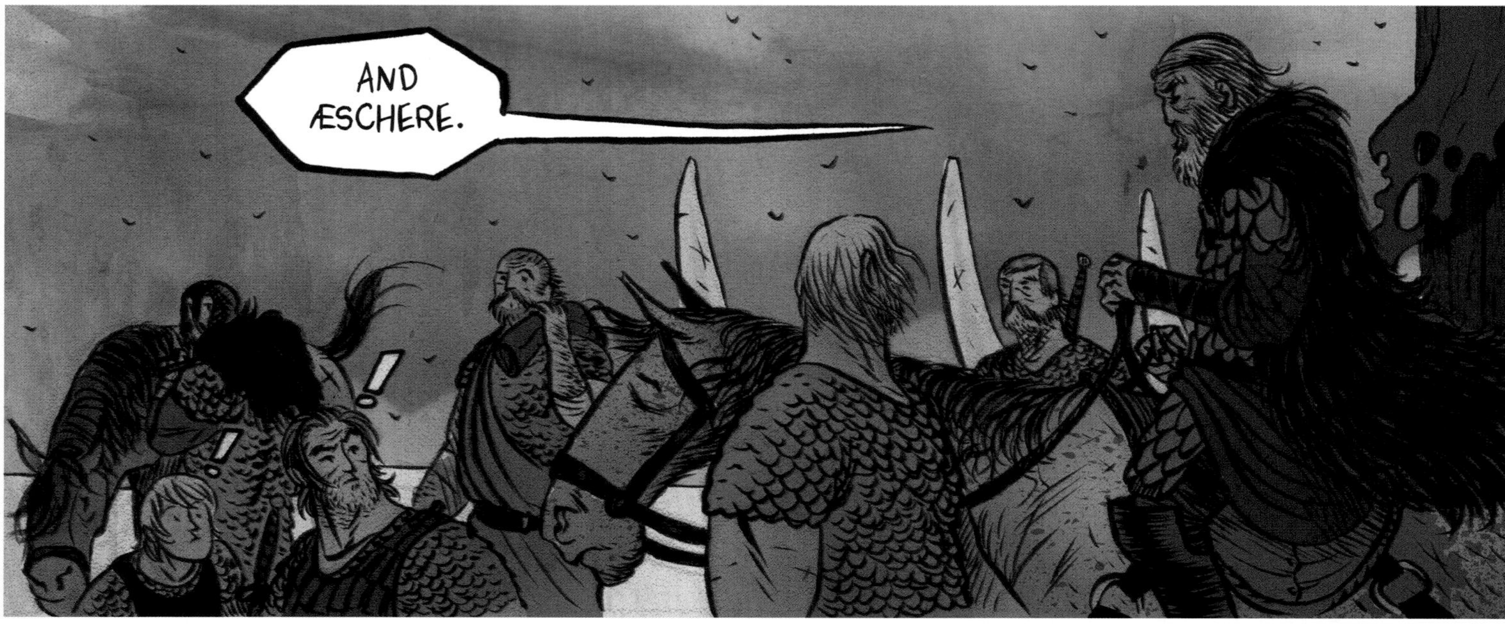
AND ÆSCHERE.
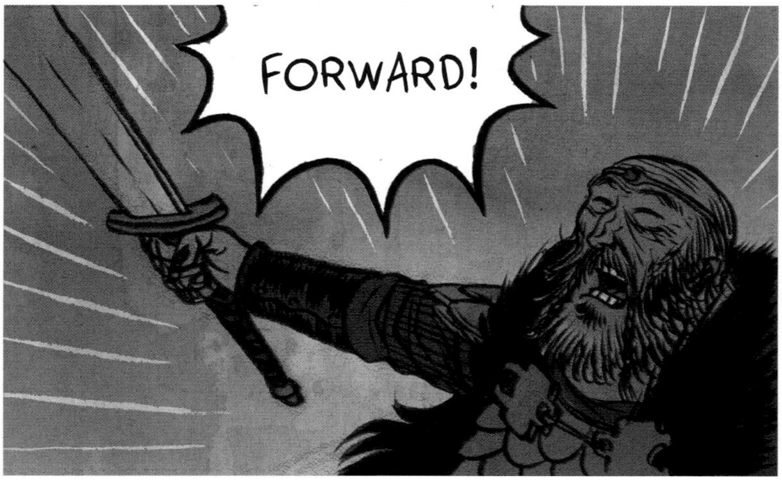
FORWARD!
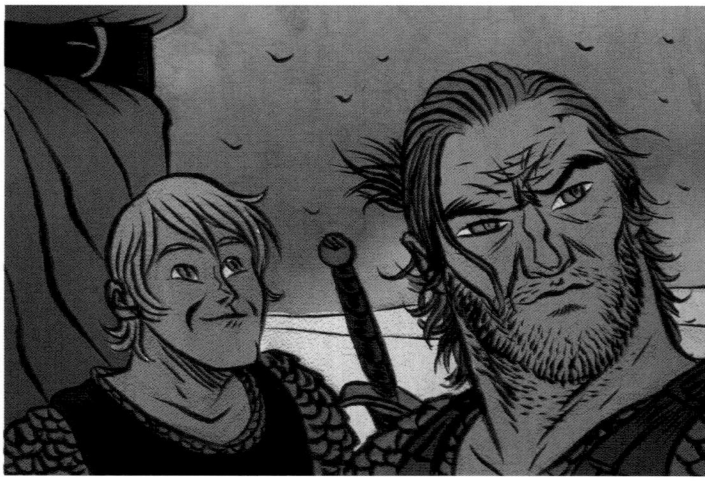

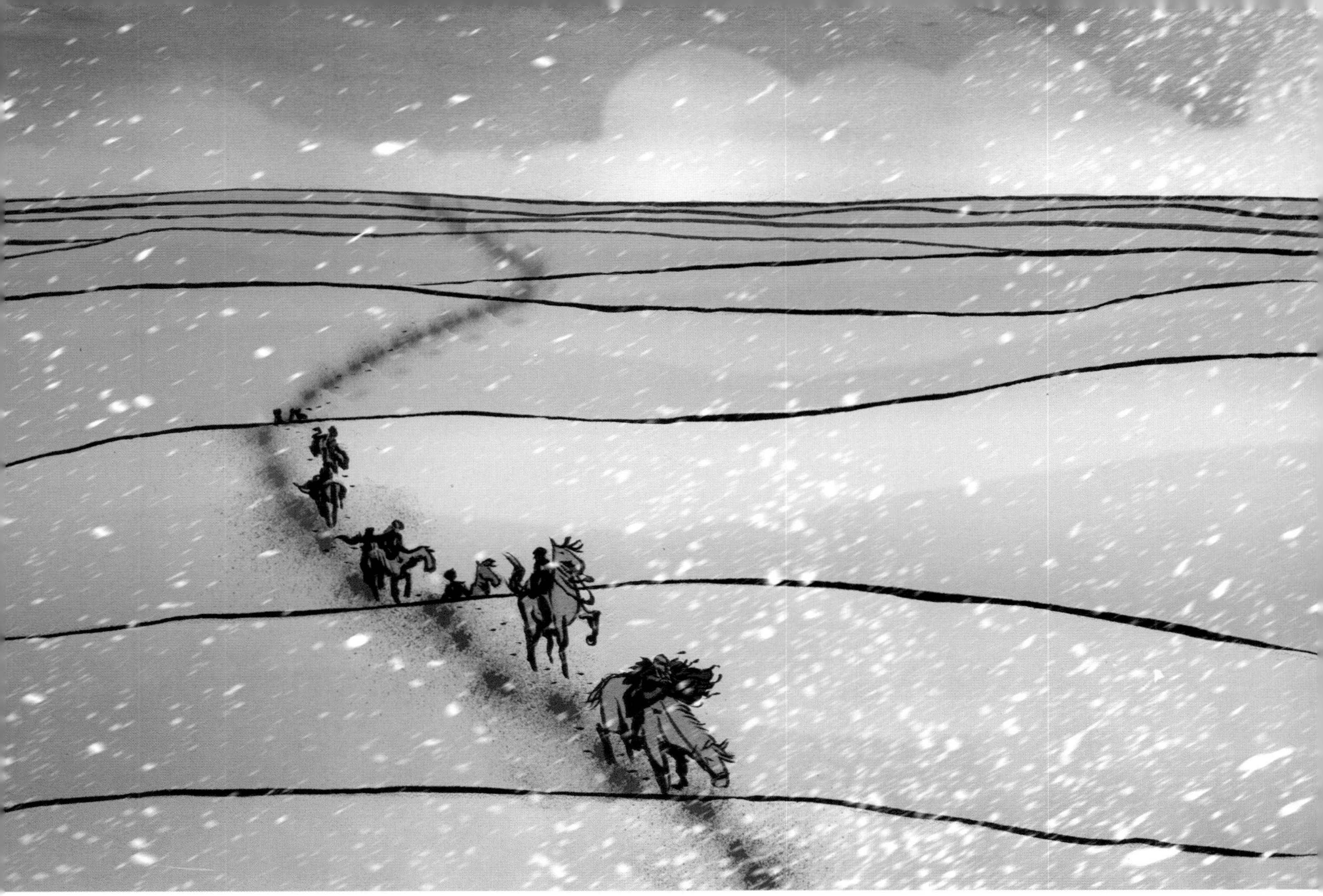

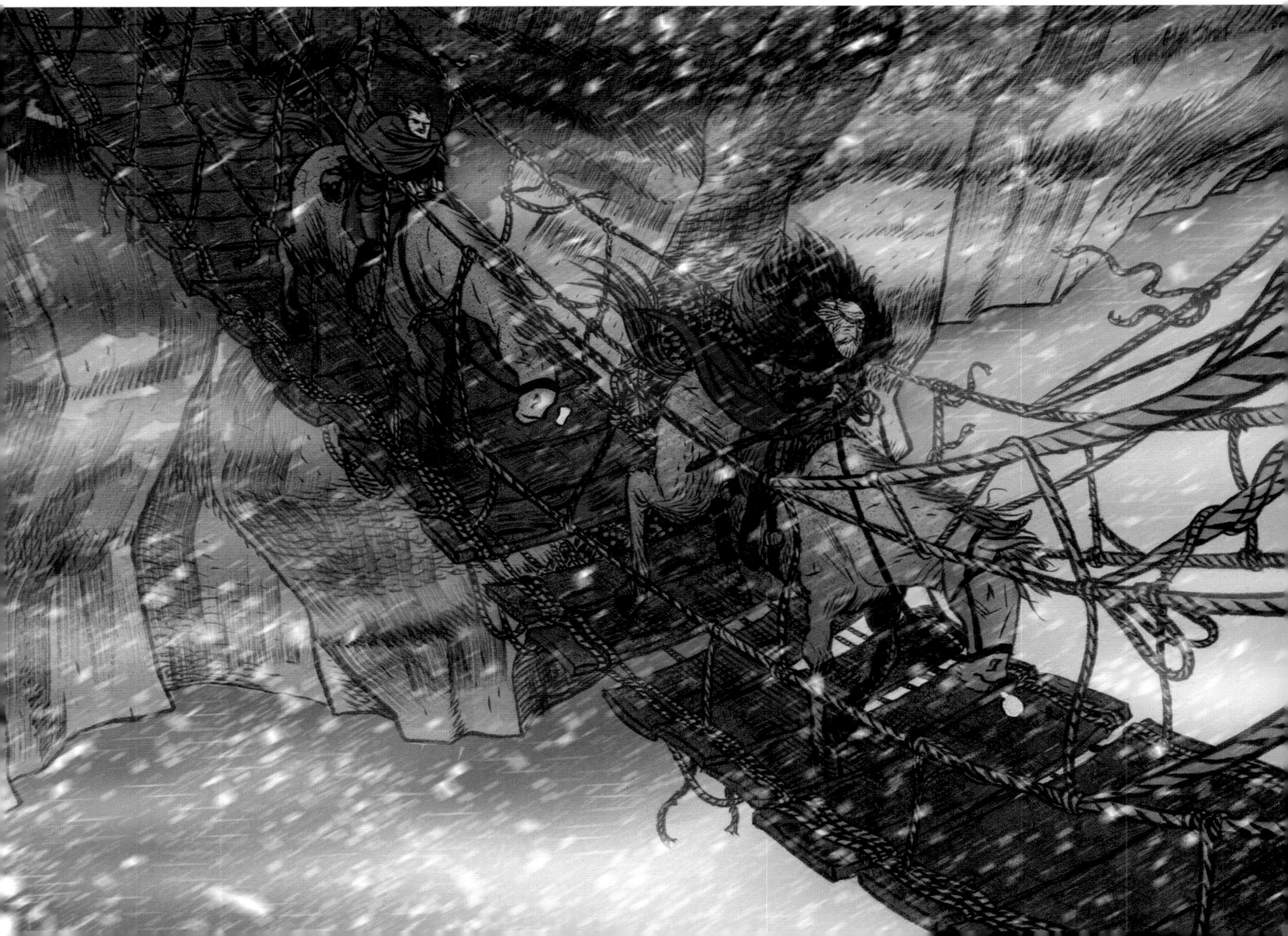

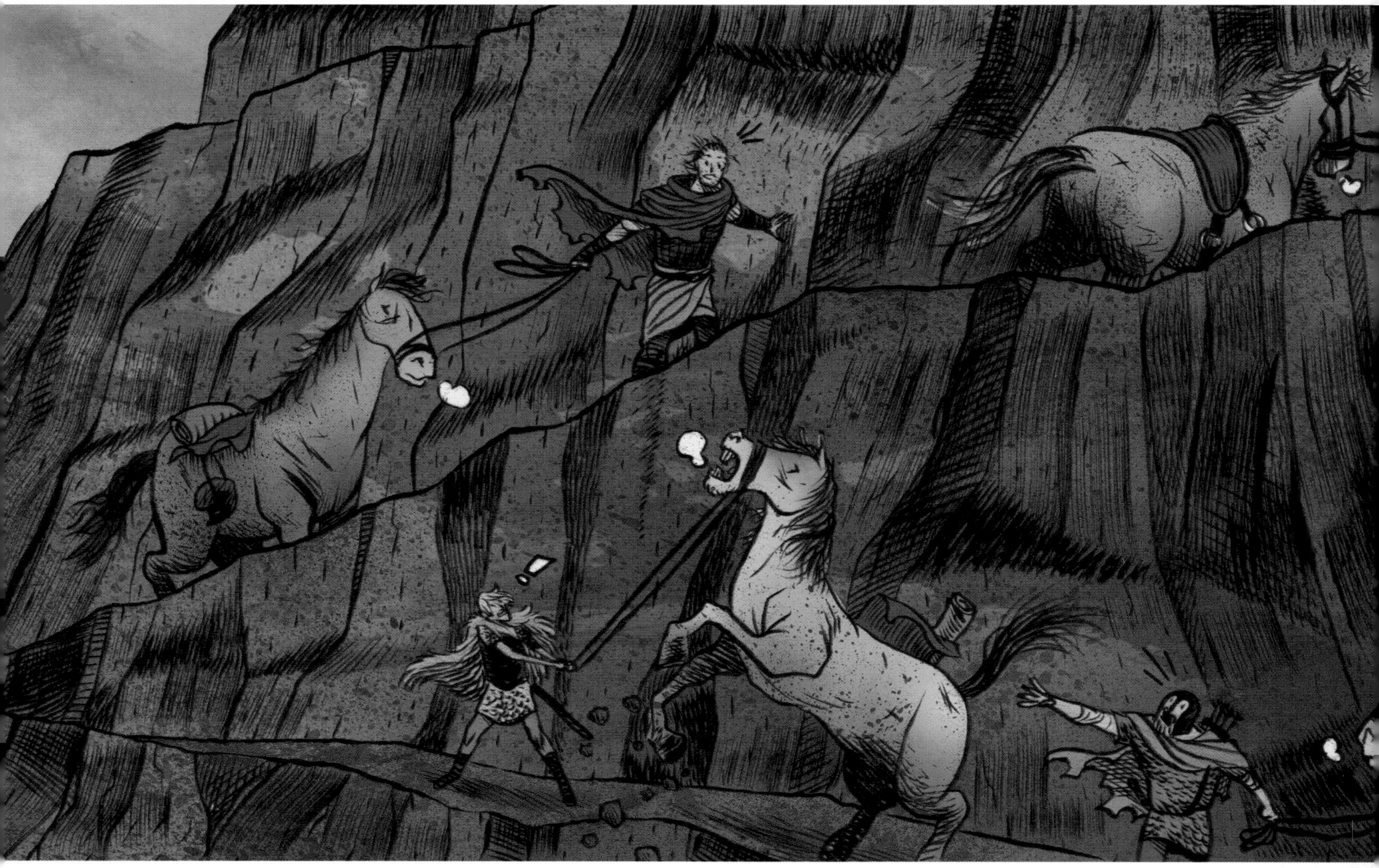
!

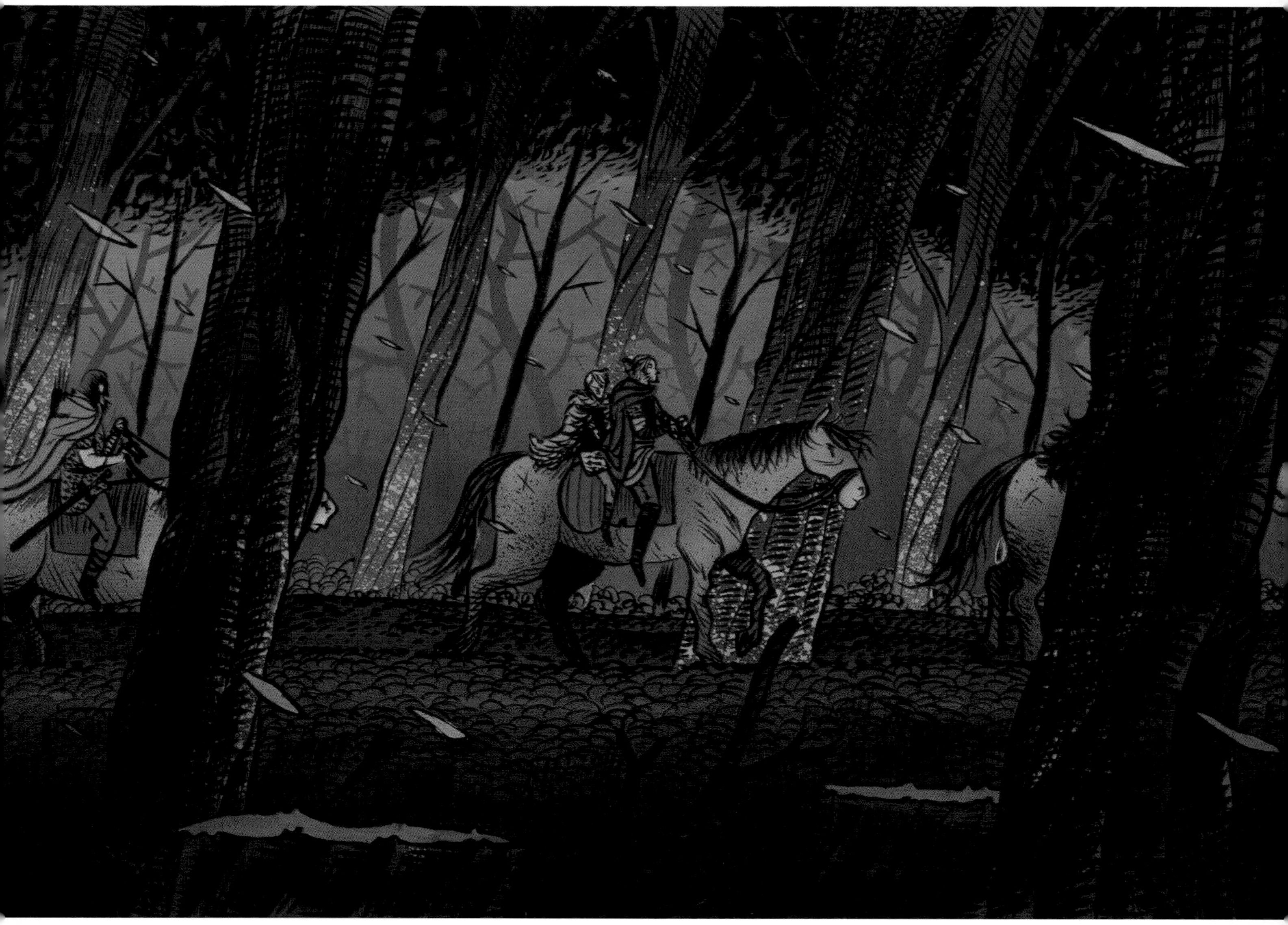

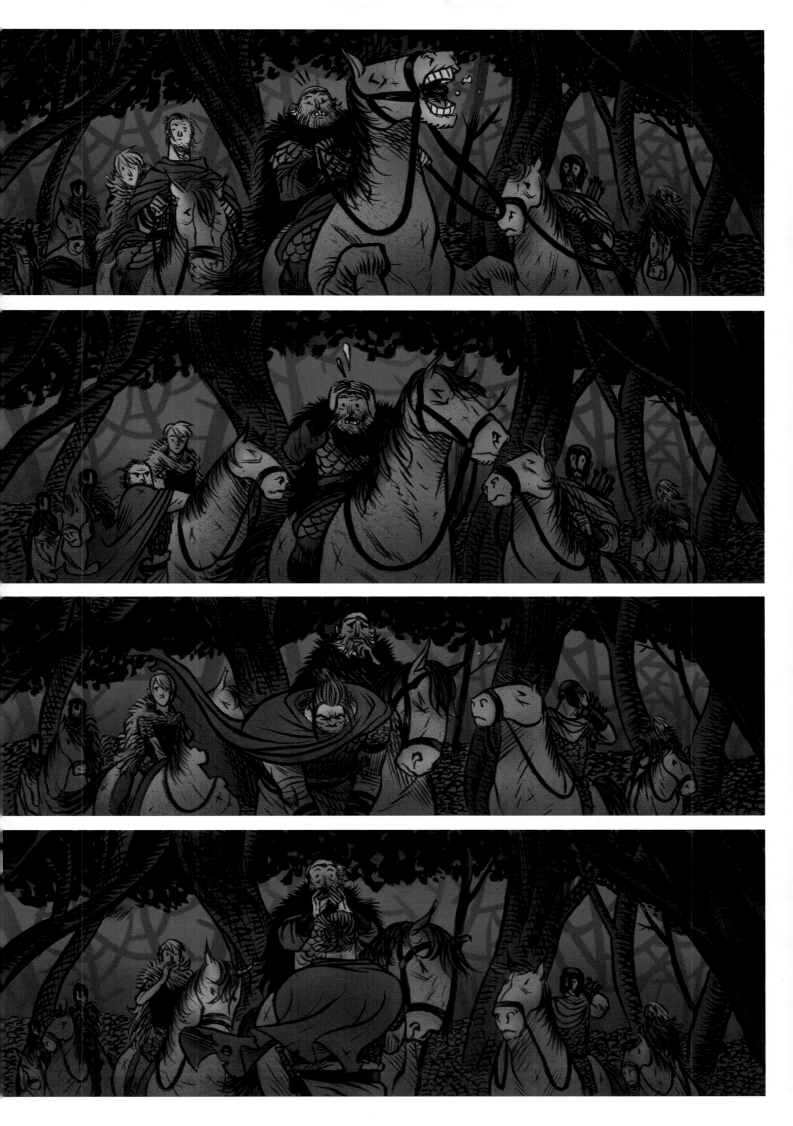

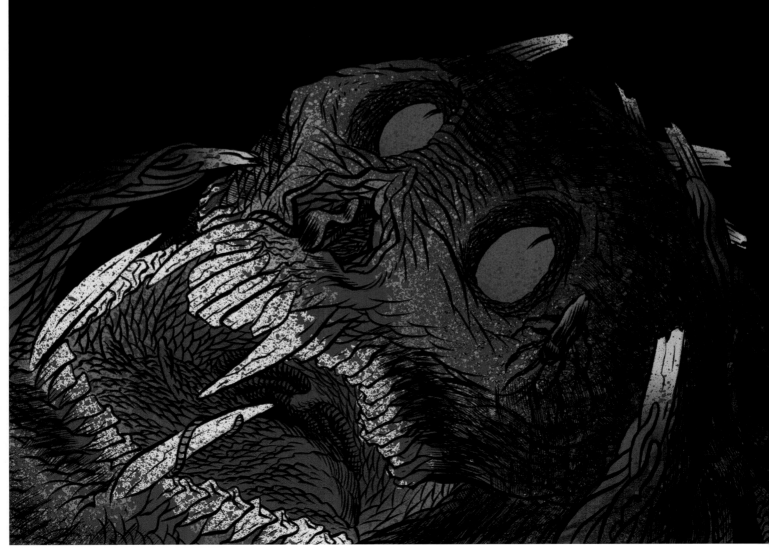

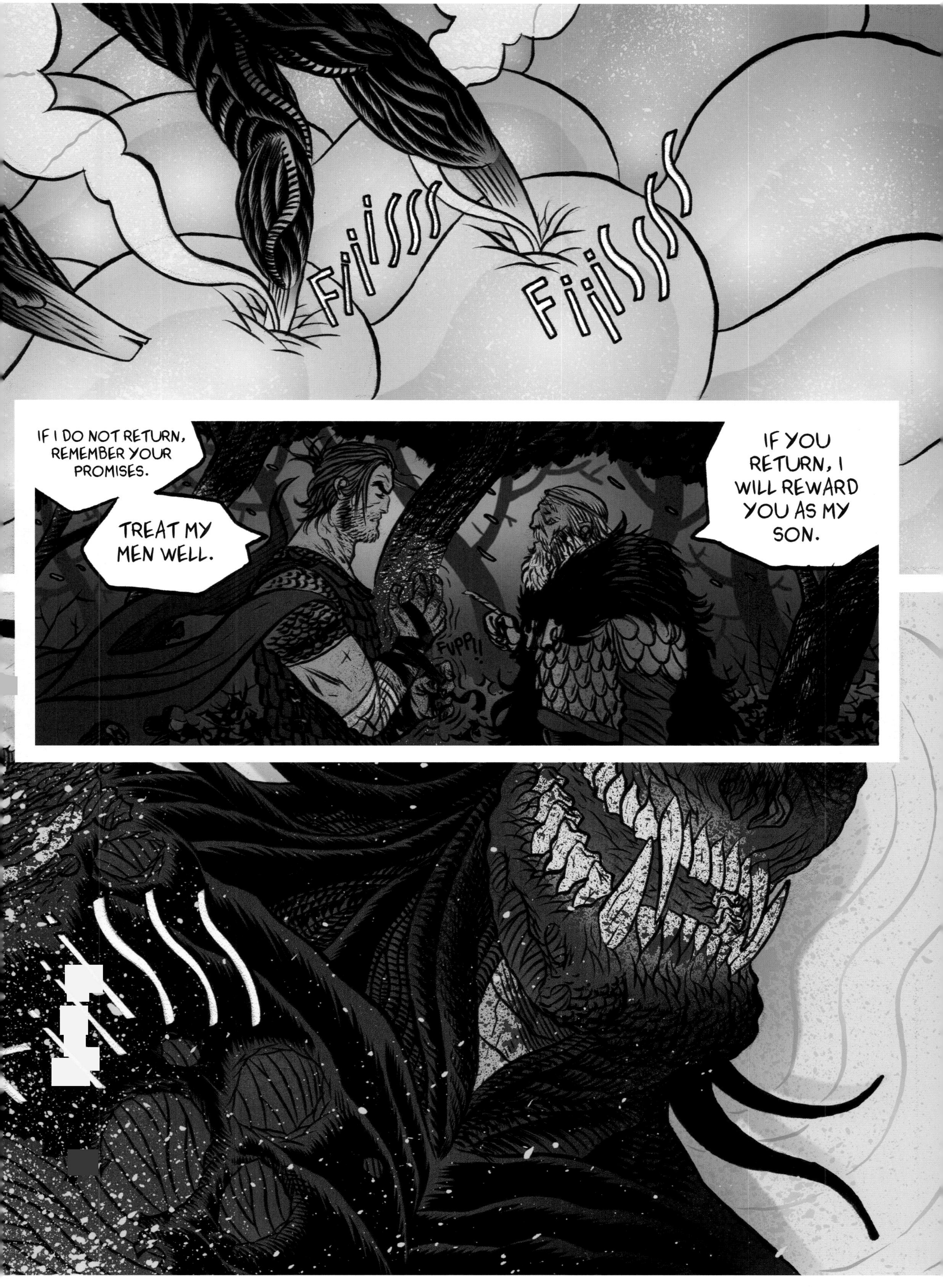
Fiisss
Fiiissss
IF I DO NOT RETURN, REMEMBER YOUR PROMISES.
TREAT MY MEN WELL.
IF YOU RETURN, I WILL REWARD YOU AS MY SON.
FUPP!!

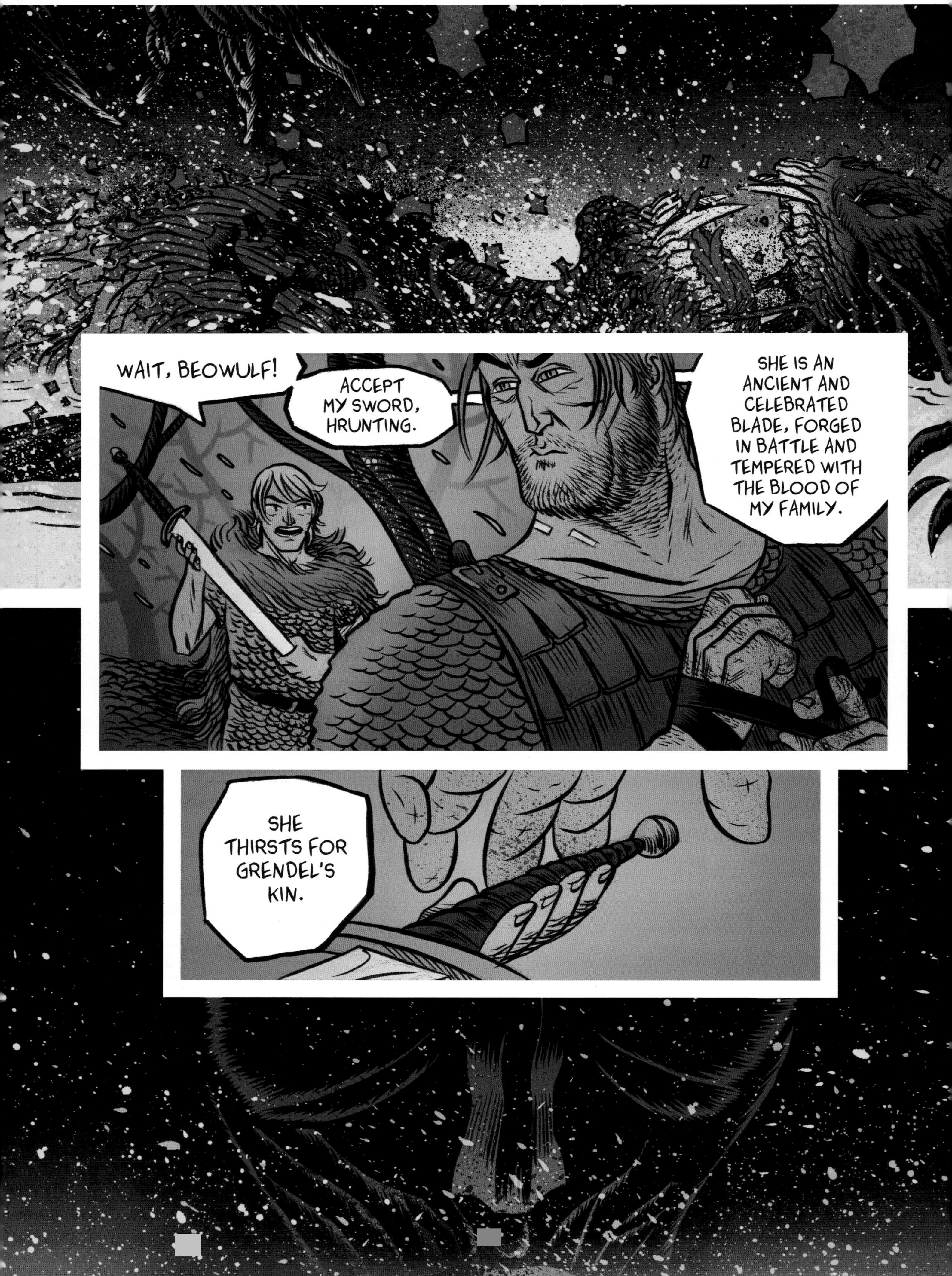
WAIT, BEOWULF!
ACCEPT MY SWORD, HRUNTING.
SHE IS AN ANCIENT AND CELEBRATED BLADE, FORGED IN BATTLE AND TEMPERED WITH THE BLOOD OF MY FAMILY.
SHE THIRSTS FOR GRENDEL'S KIN.

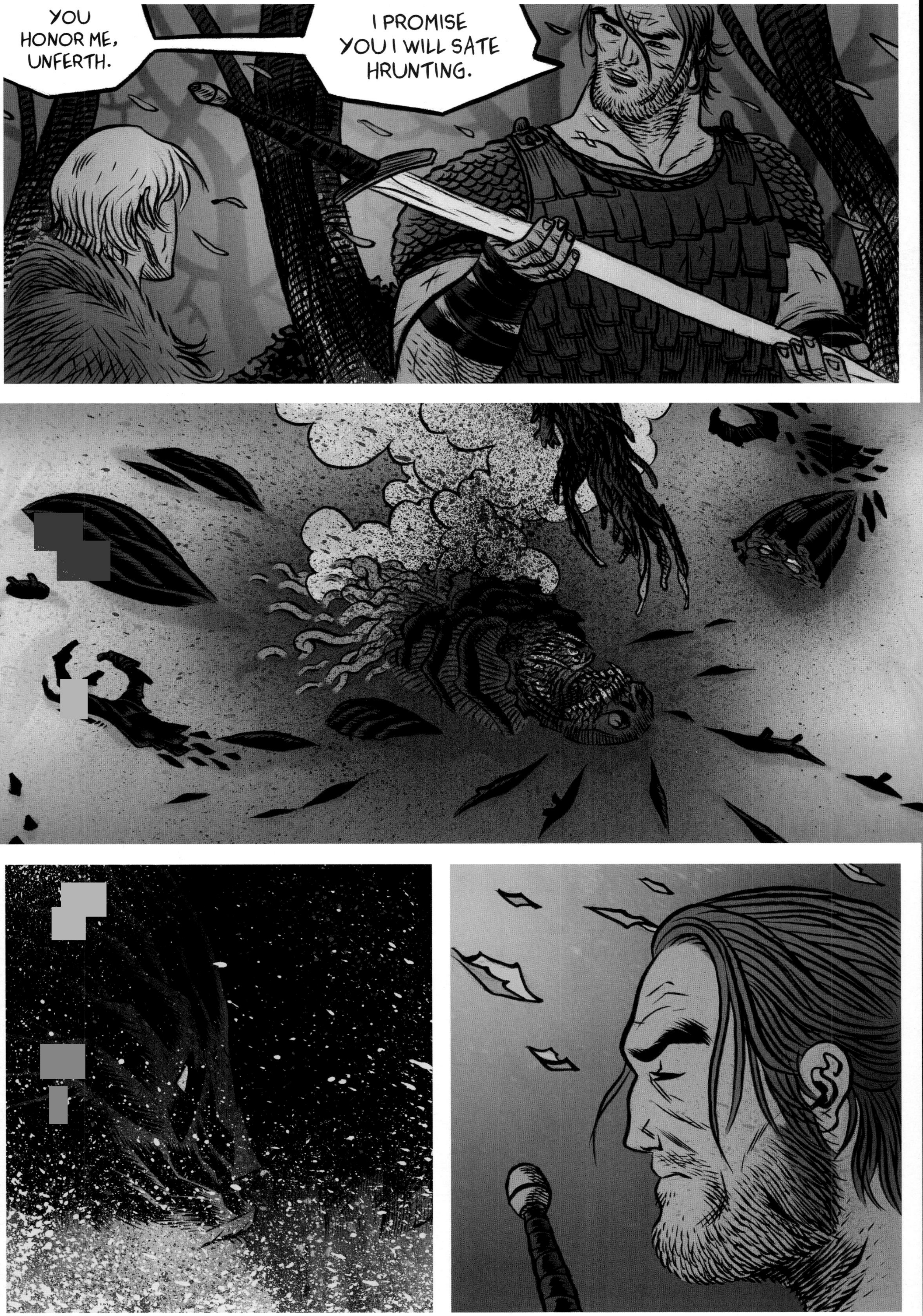
YOU HONOR ME, UNFERTH.
I PROMISE YOU I WILL SATE HRUNTING.

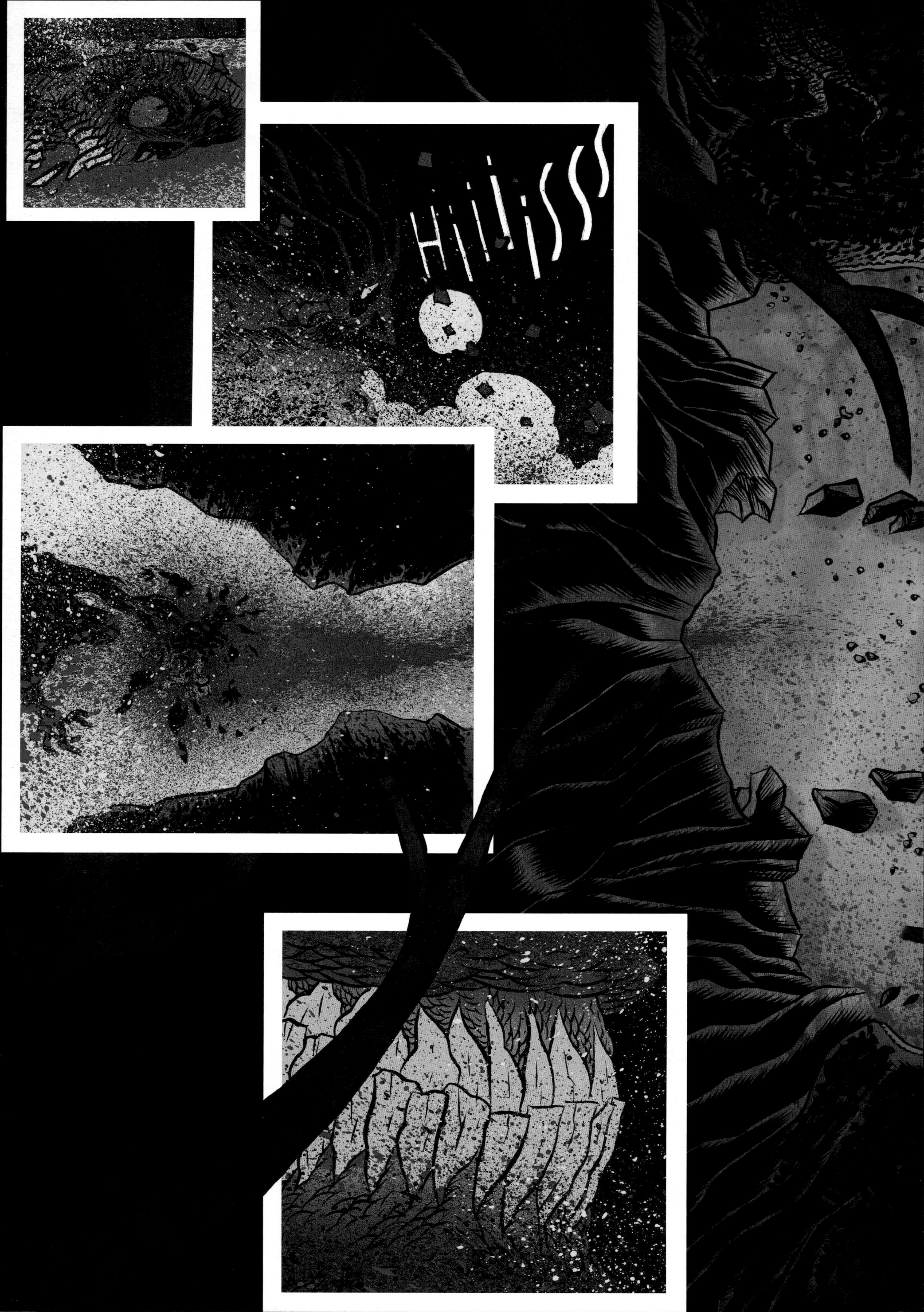
HIIISSS

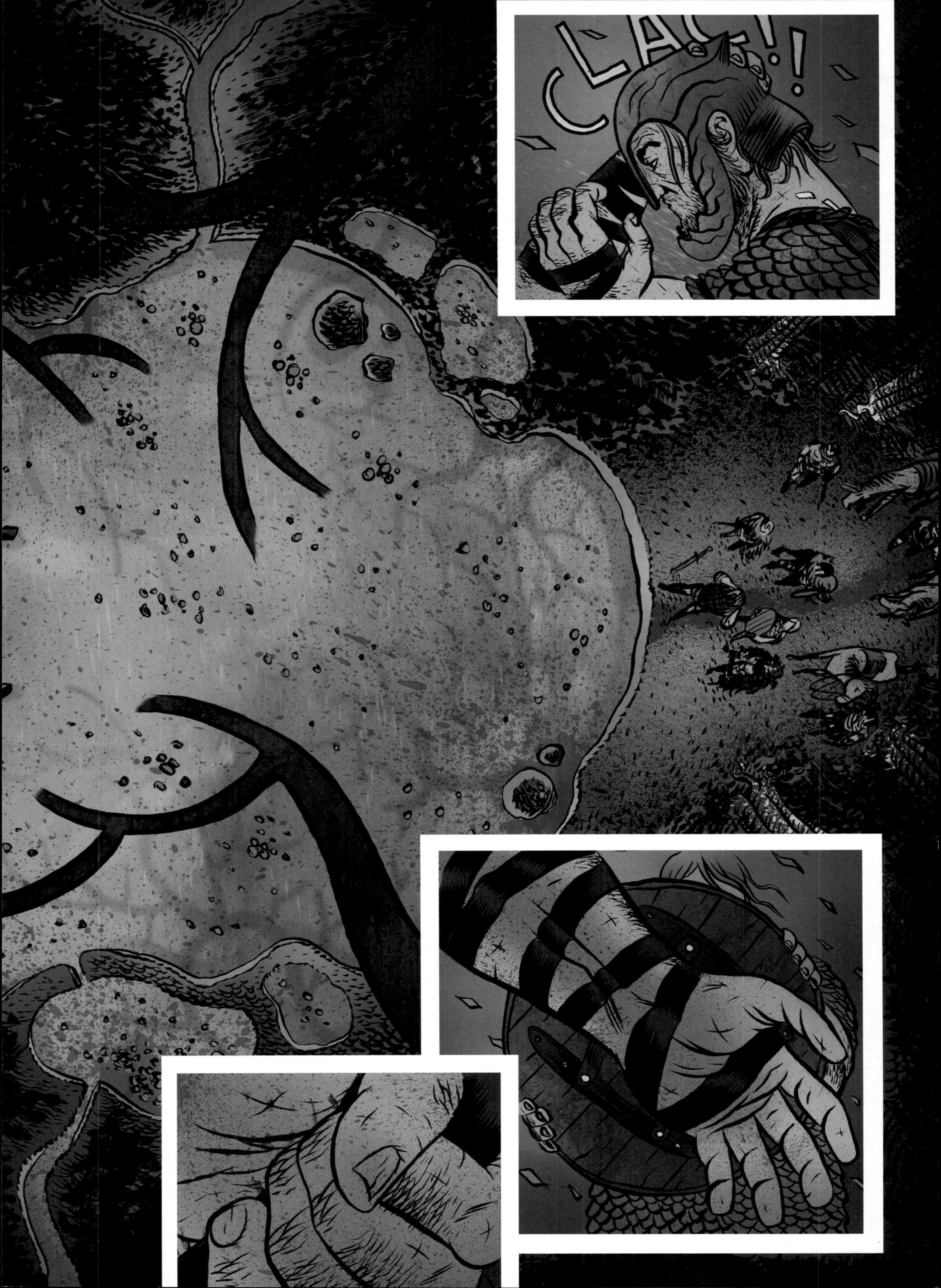
CLAC!!

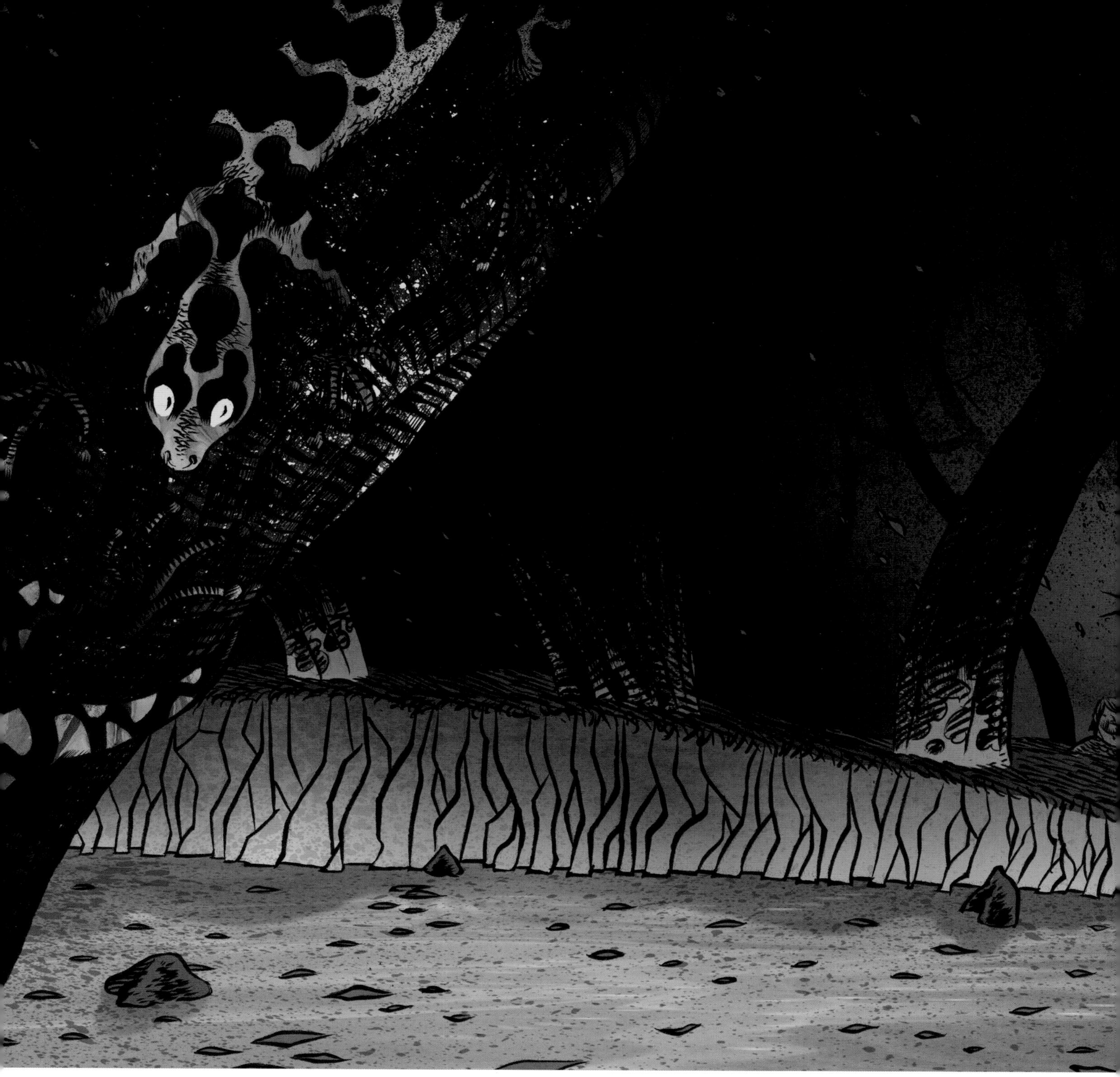

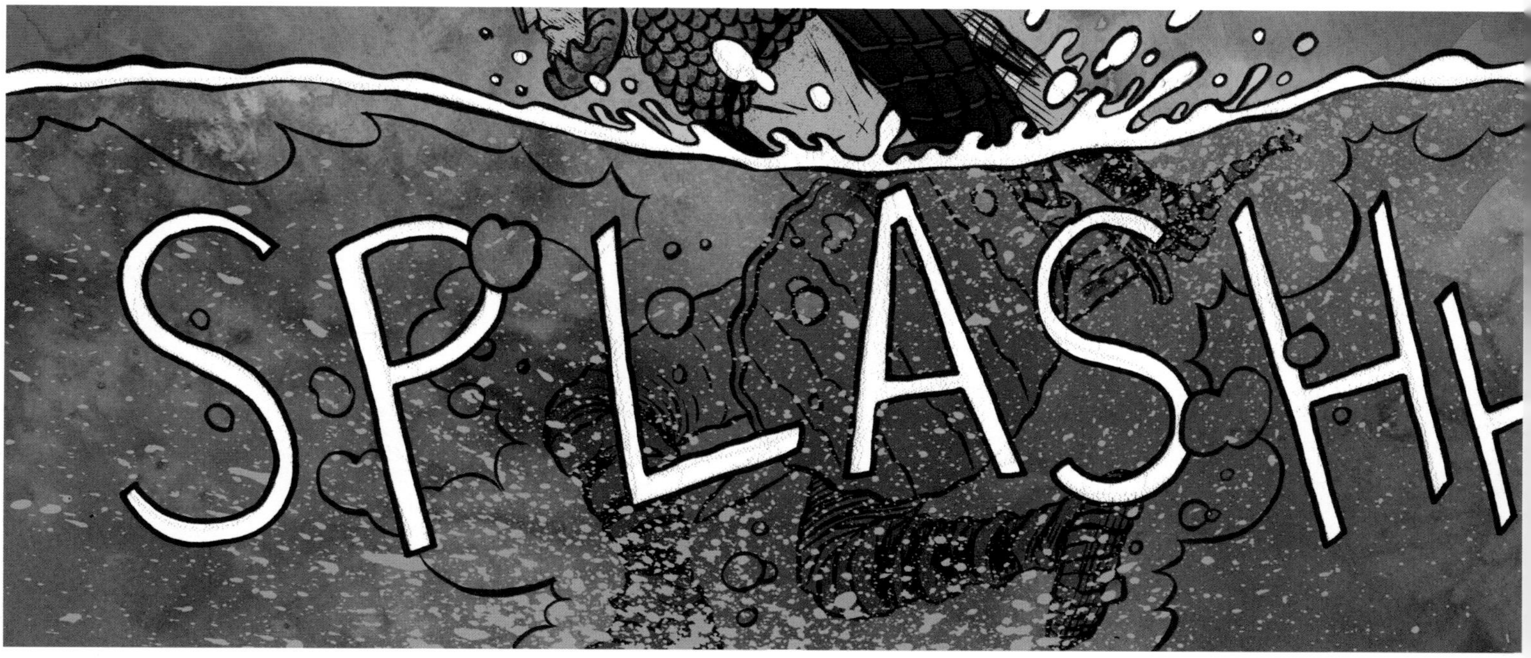
SPLASH

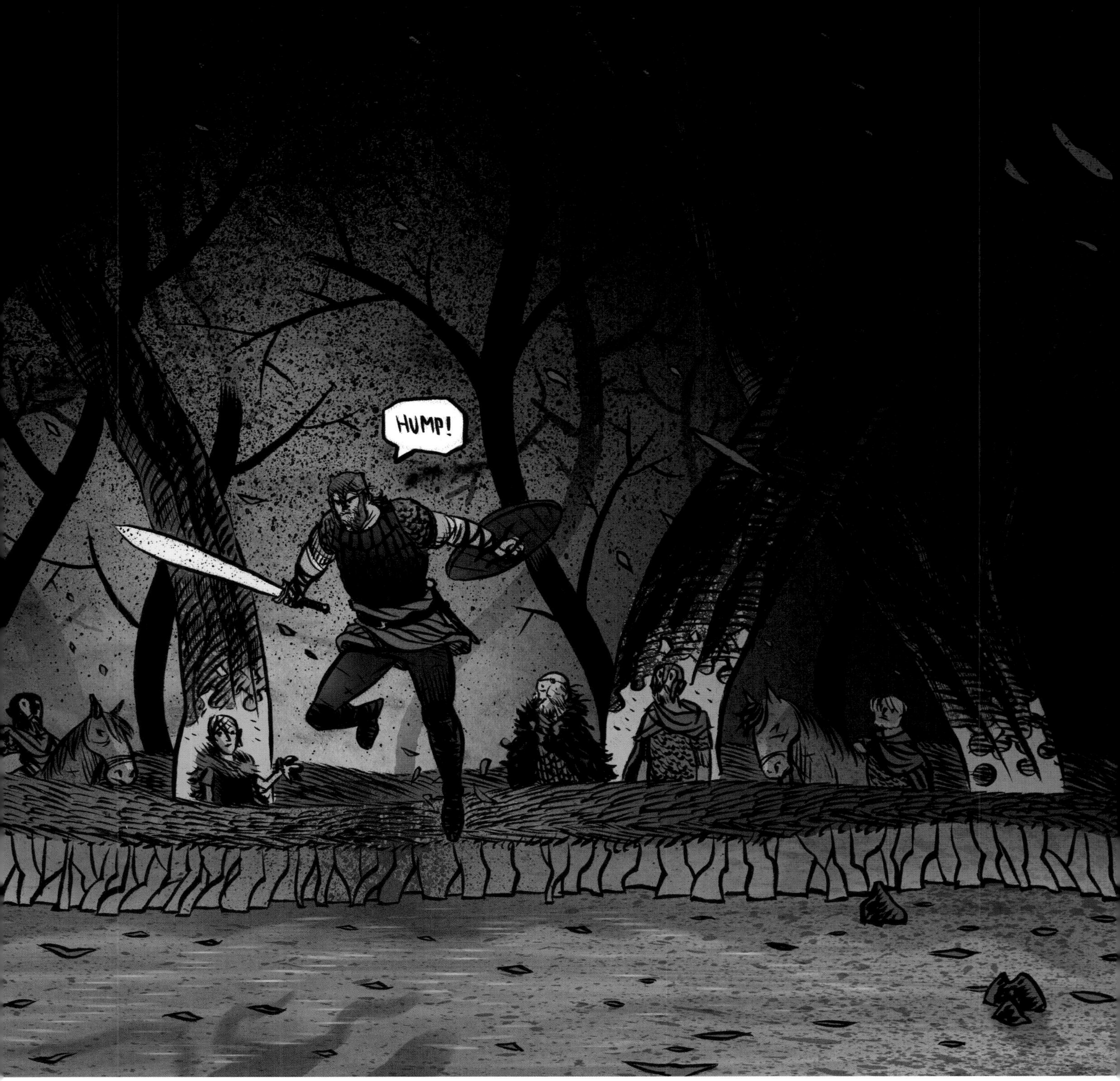
HUMP!

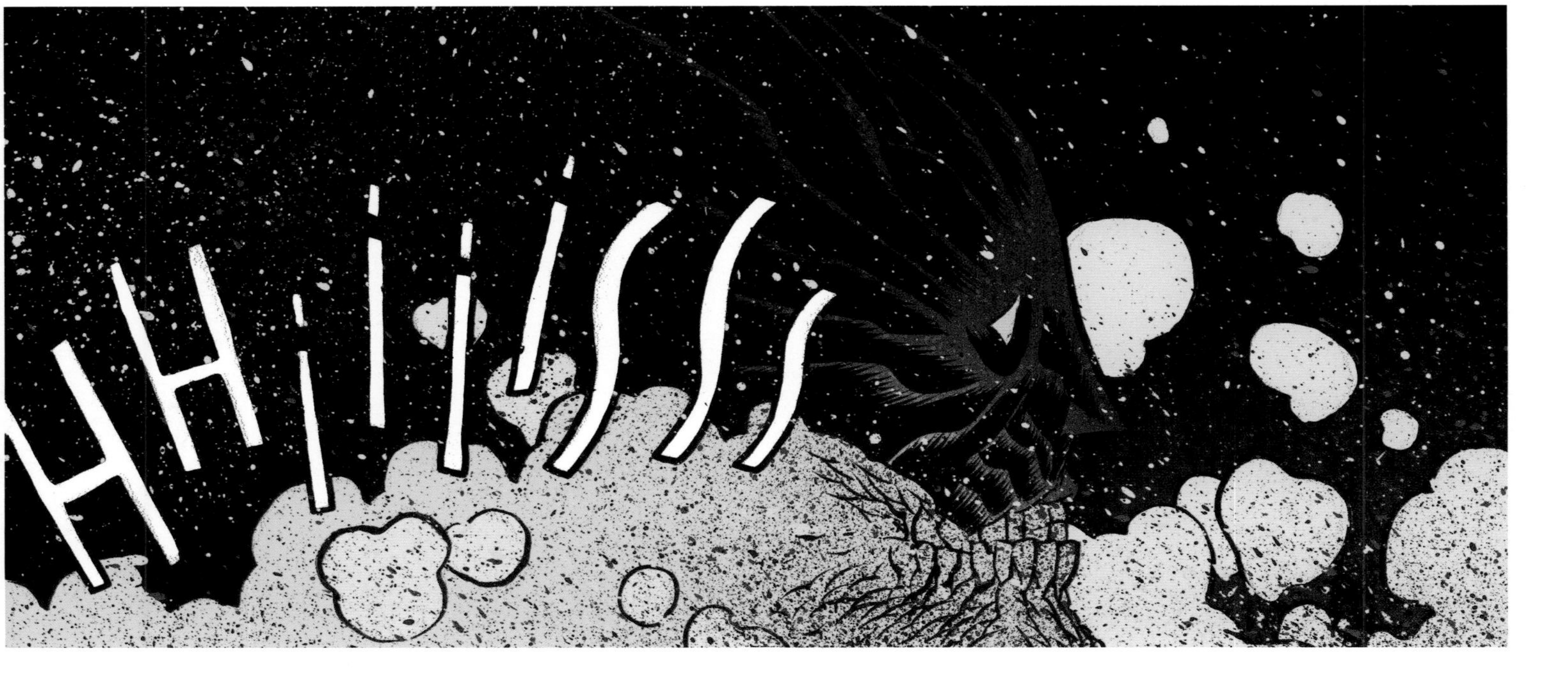
HHiiiSSSS

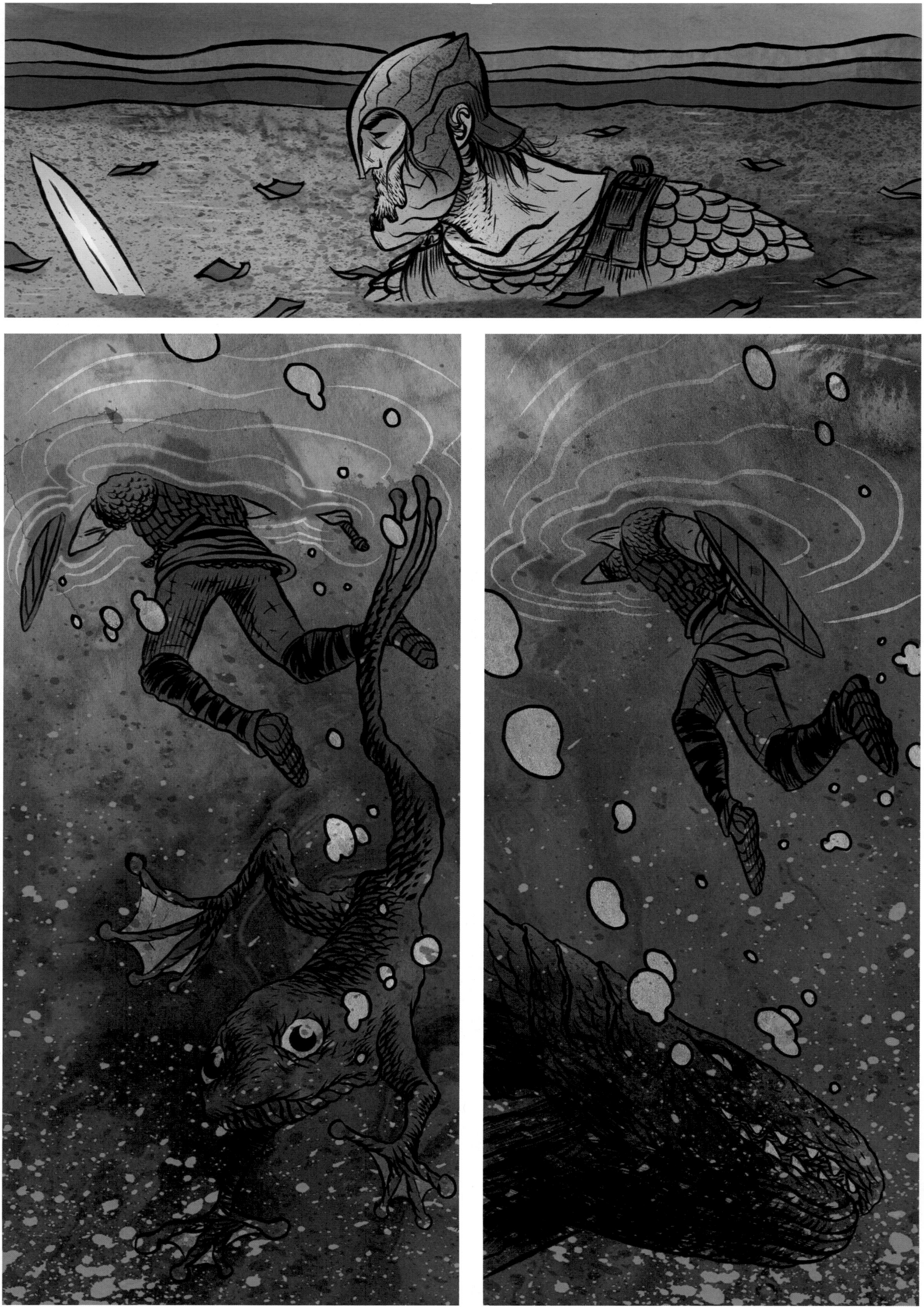

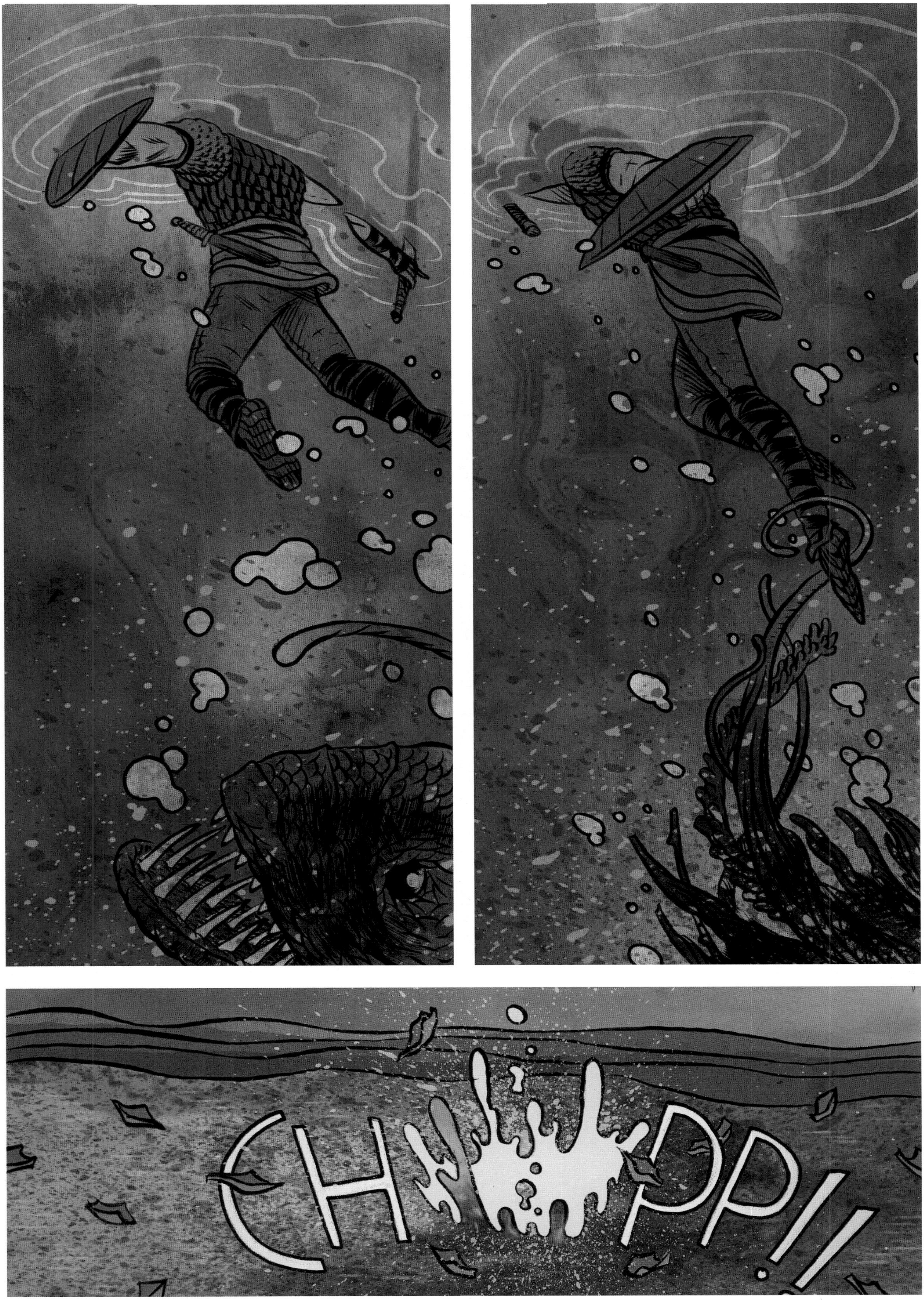
CH PP!!

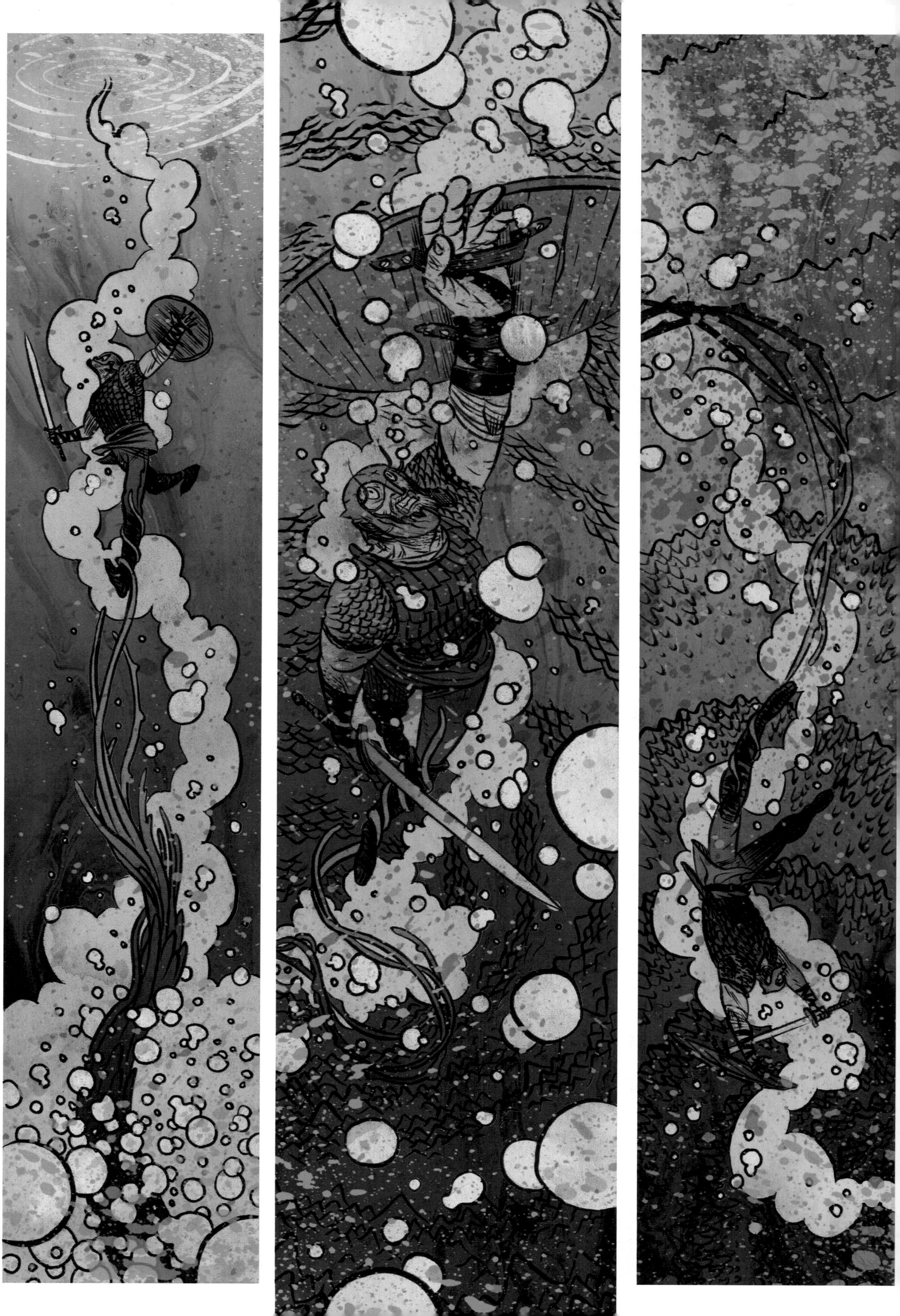

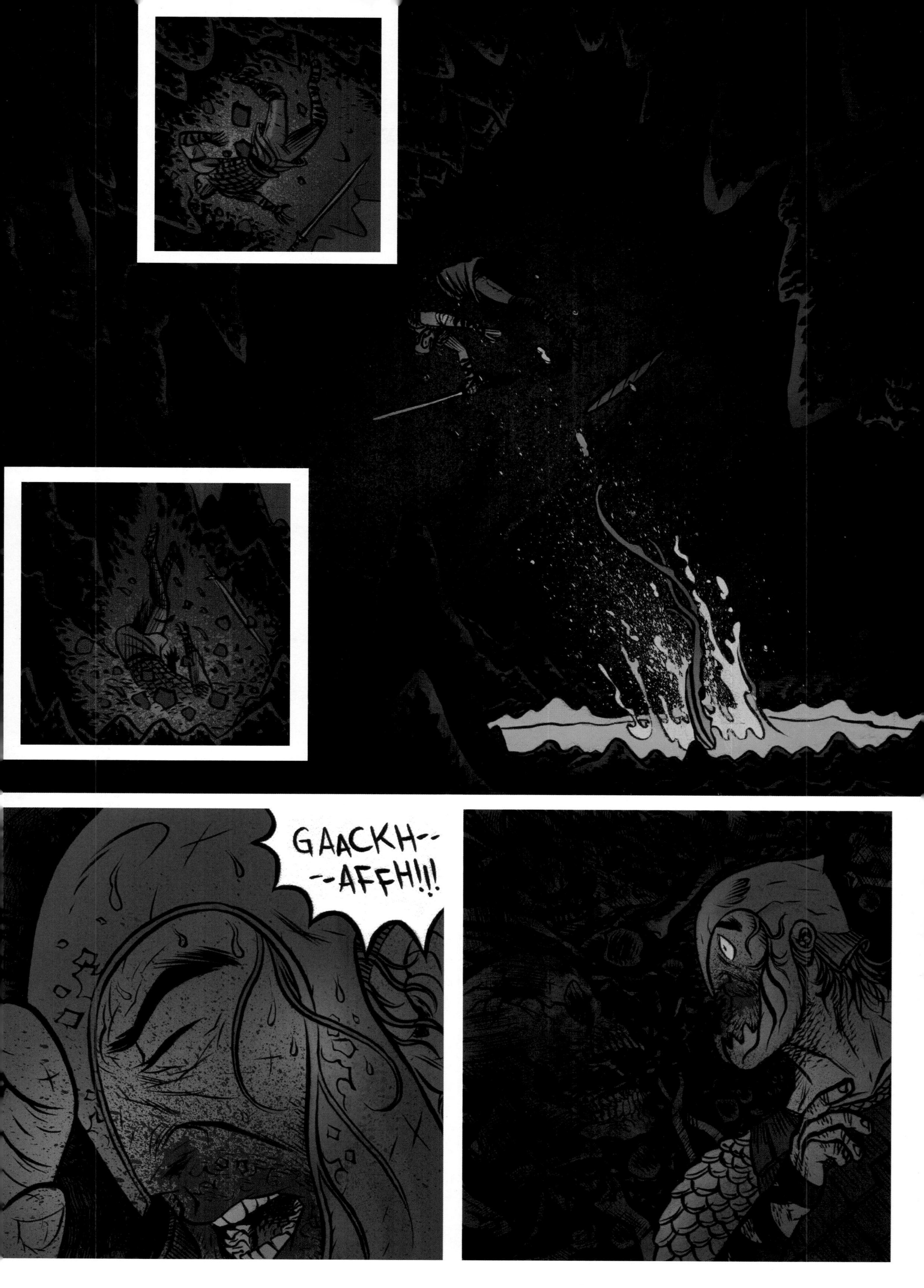
GAACKH--
--AFFH!!!

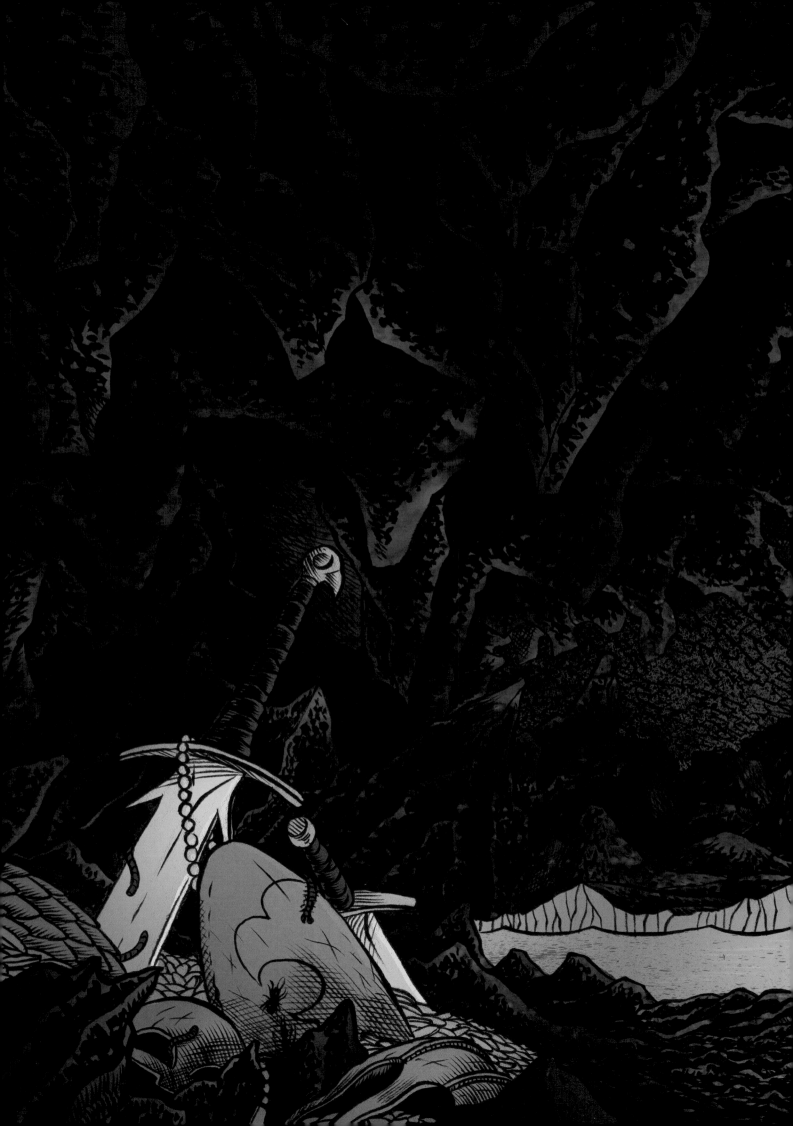

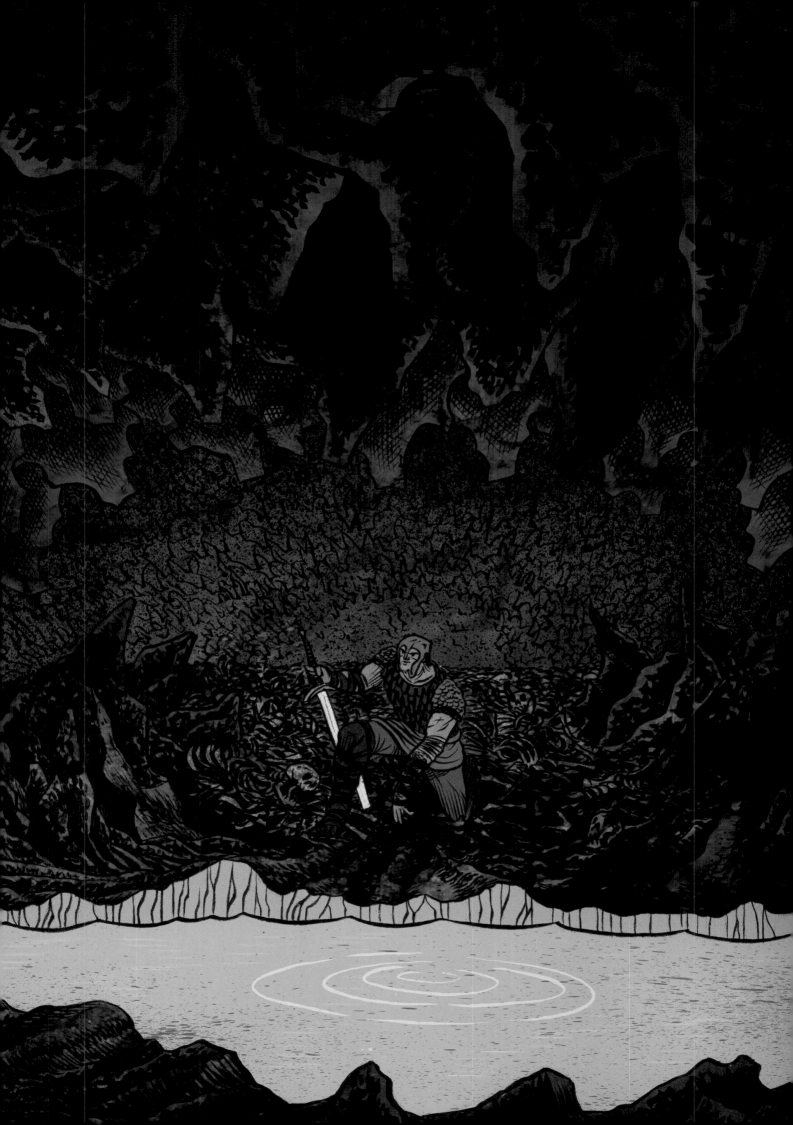

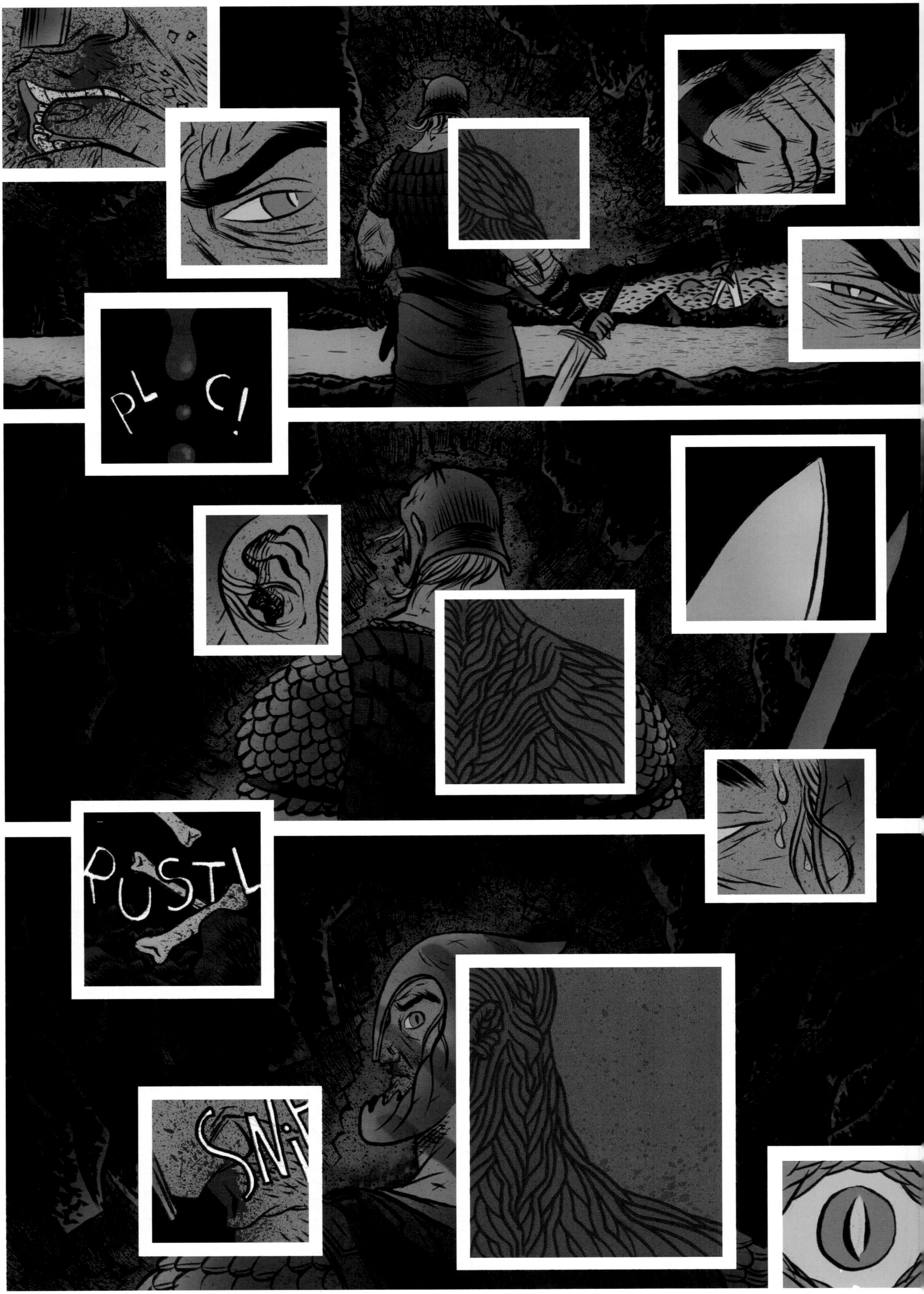
PL C!
RUSTL
SNi

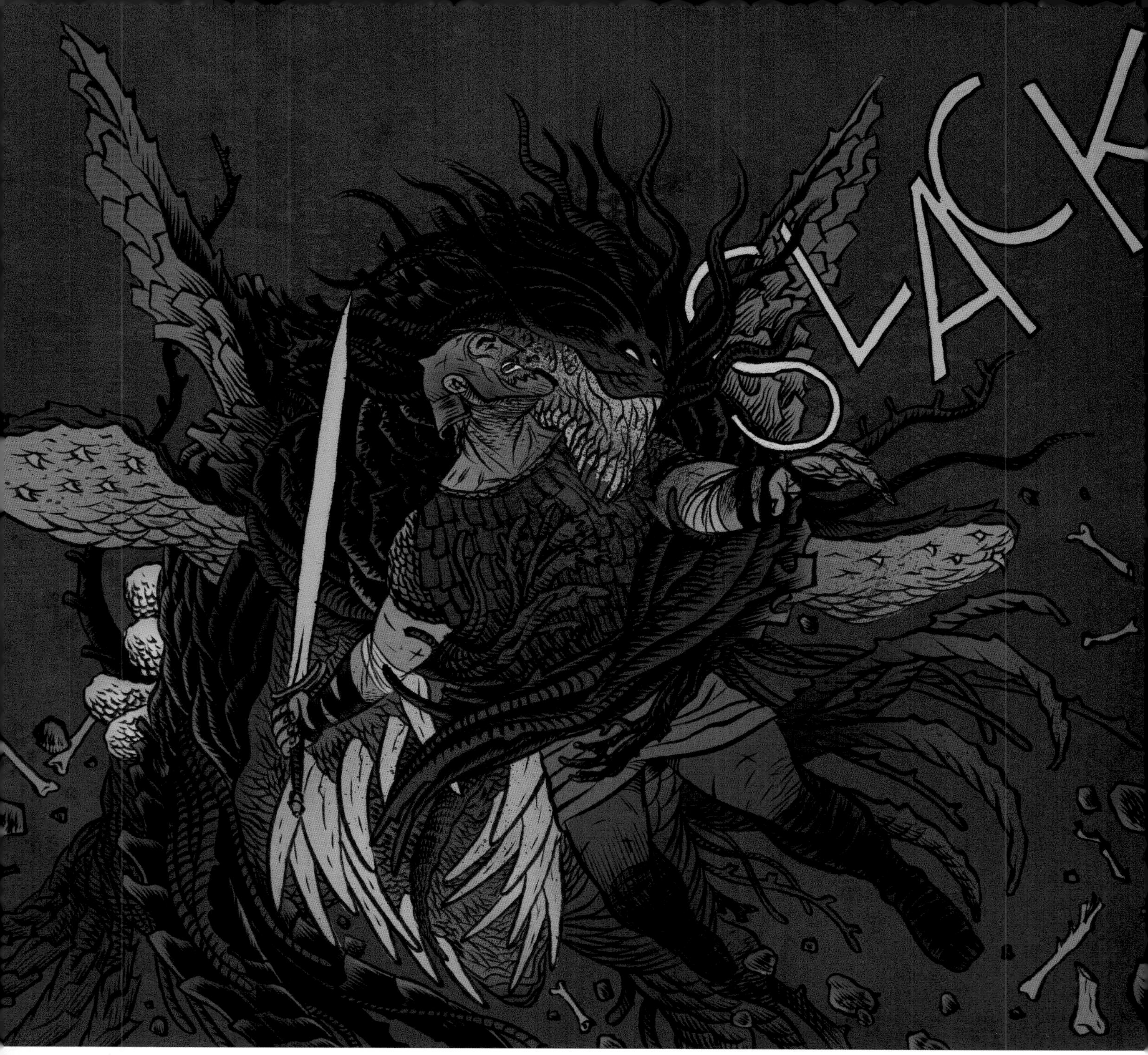
SLACK

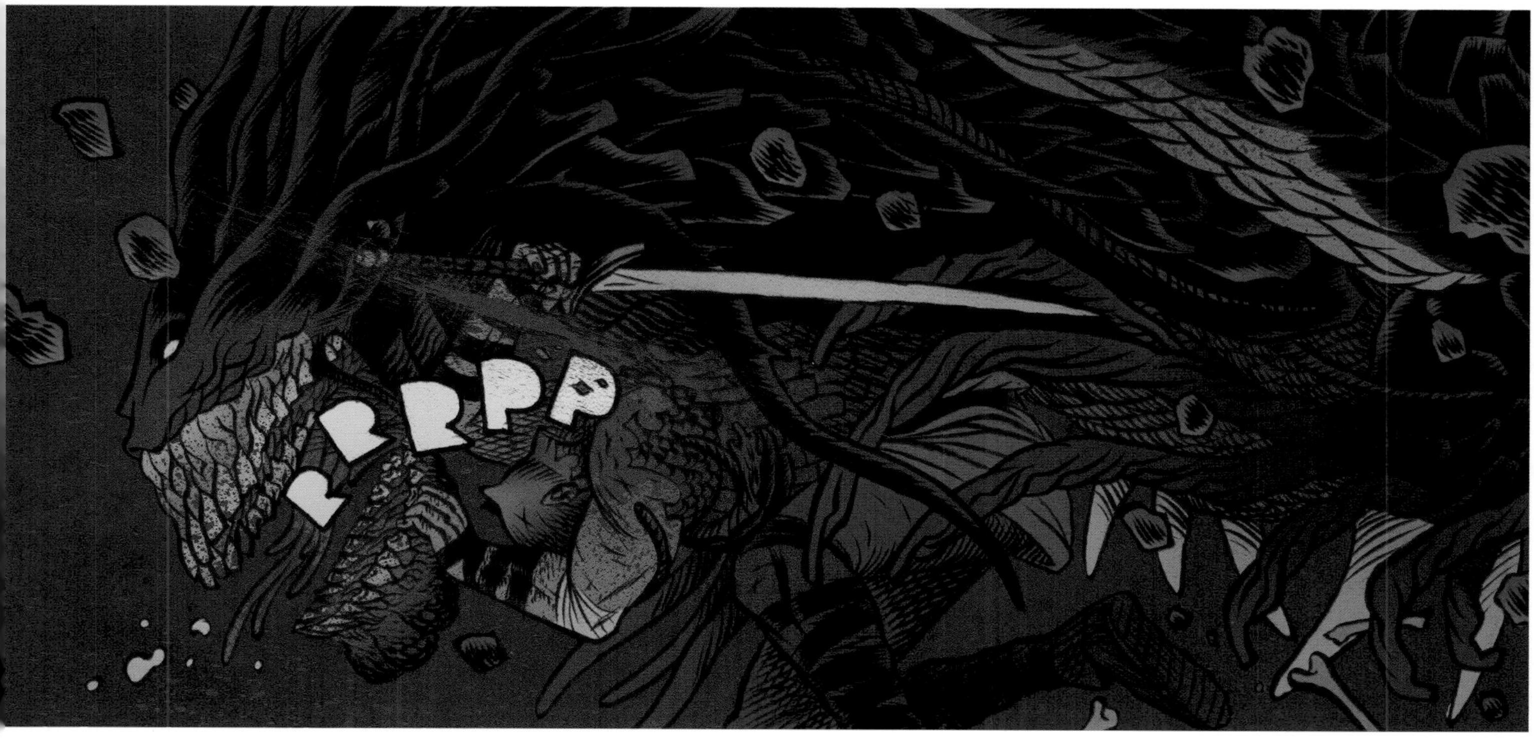
RRRPP

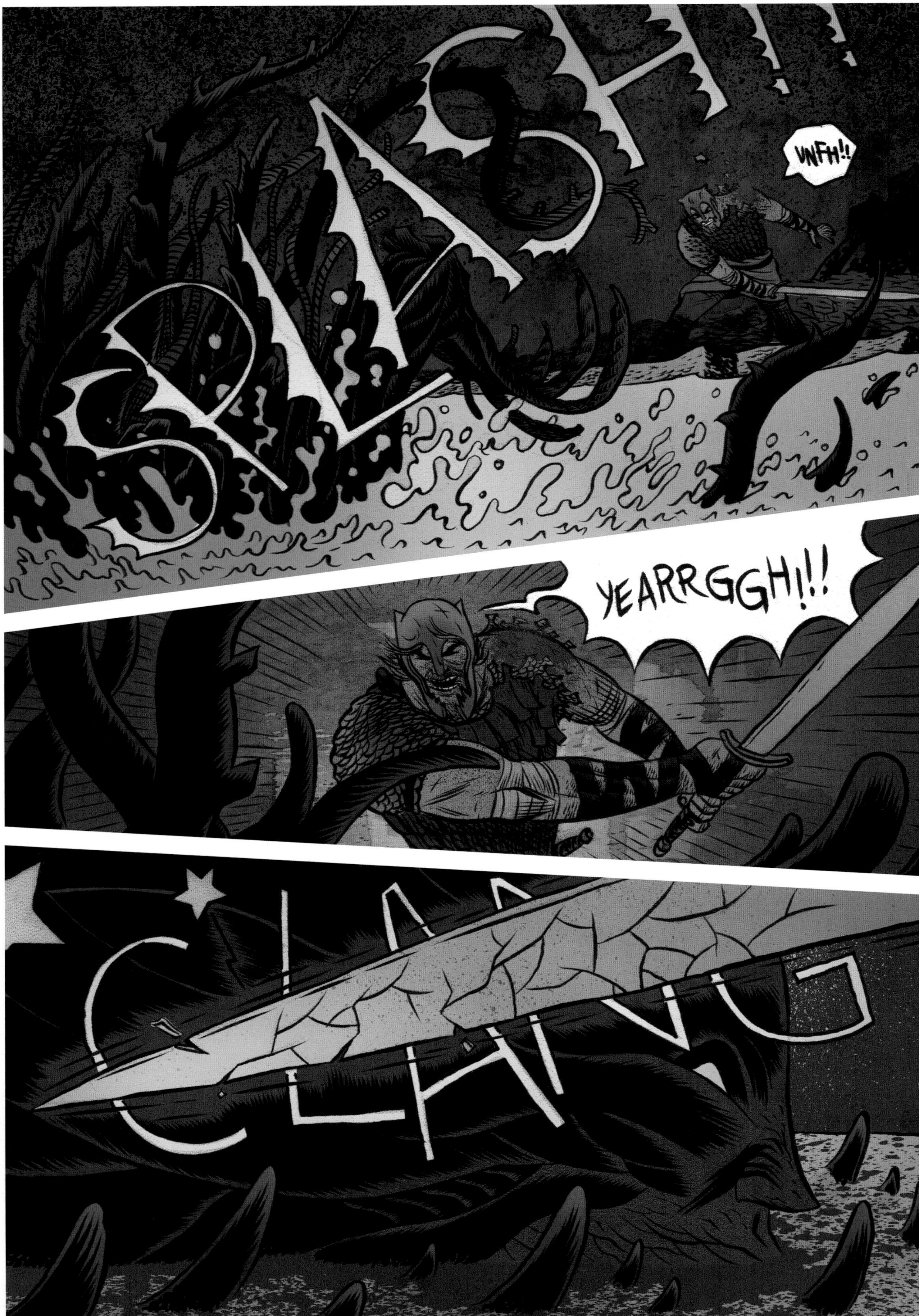
SPLASH!!
UNFH!!
YEARRGGH!!!
CLANG

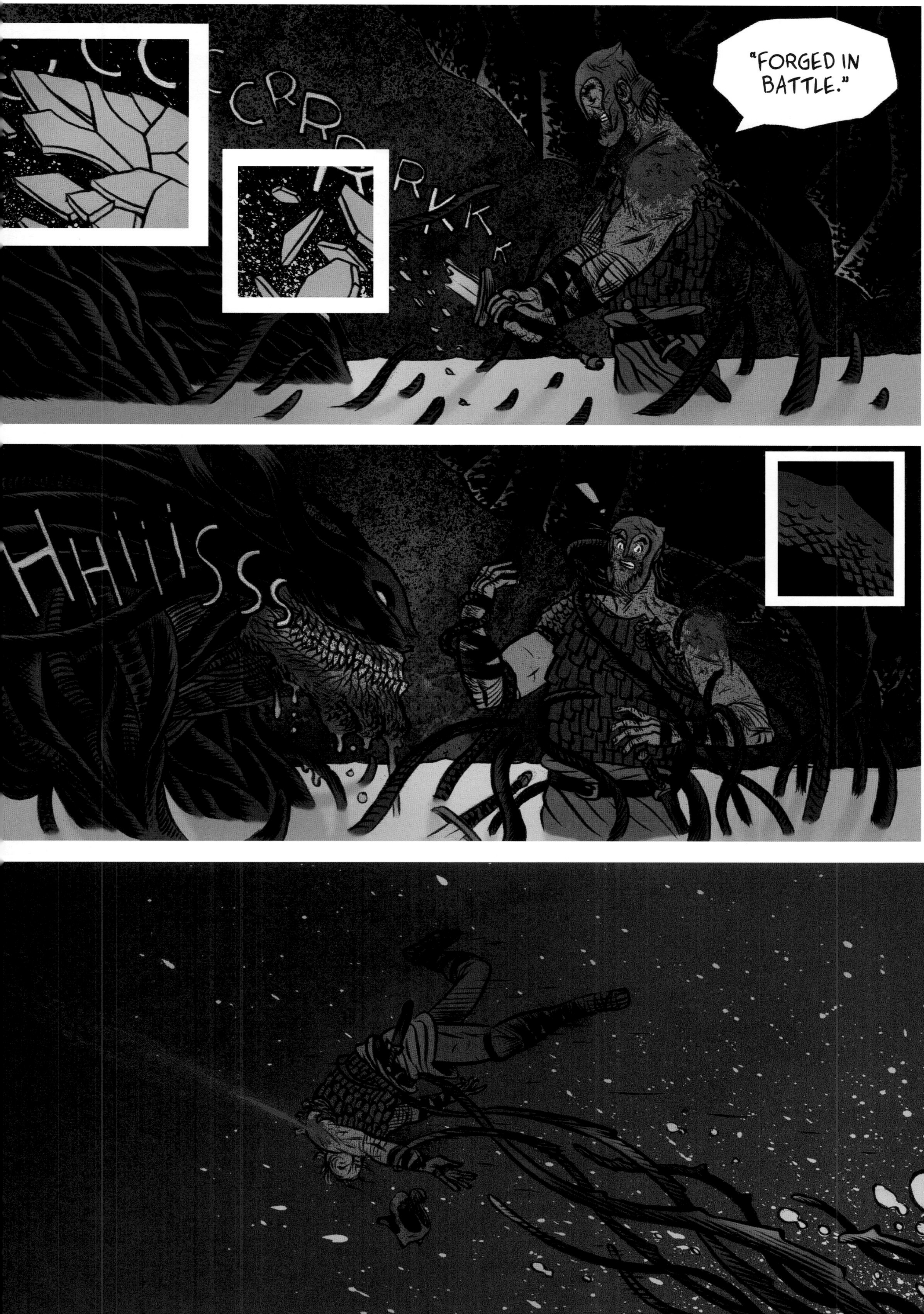
CCRRRRRVKKK
"FORGED IN BATTLE."
HHIIISSS

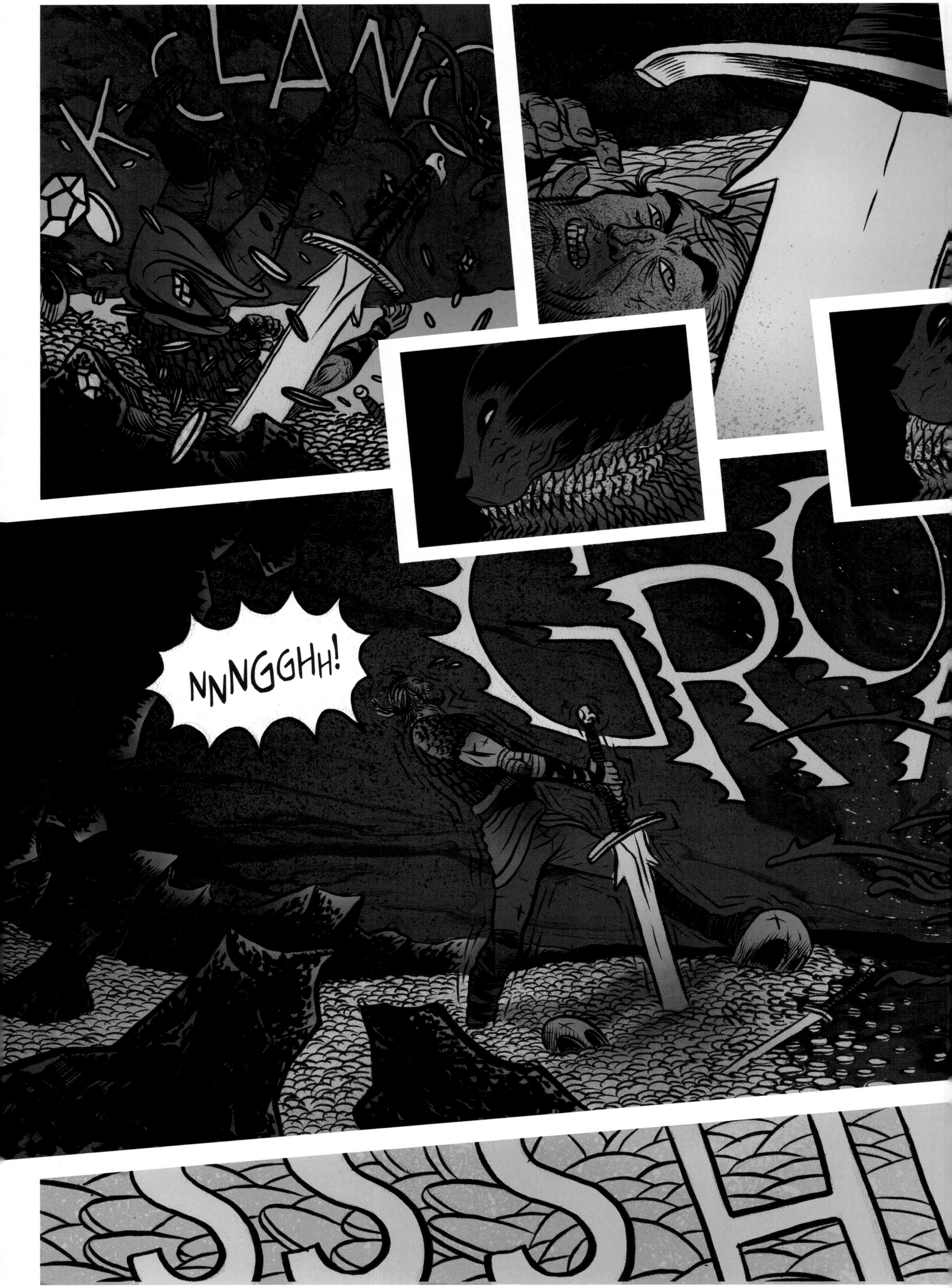
K-CLAN
NNNGGHH!
GRO
SSSH

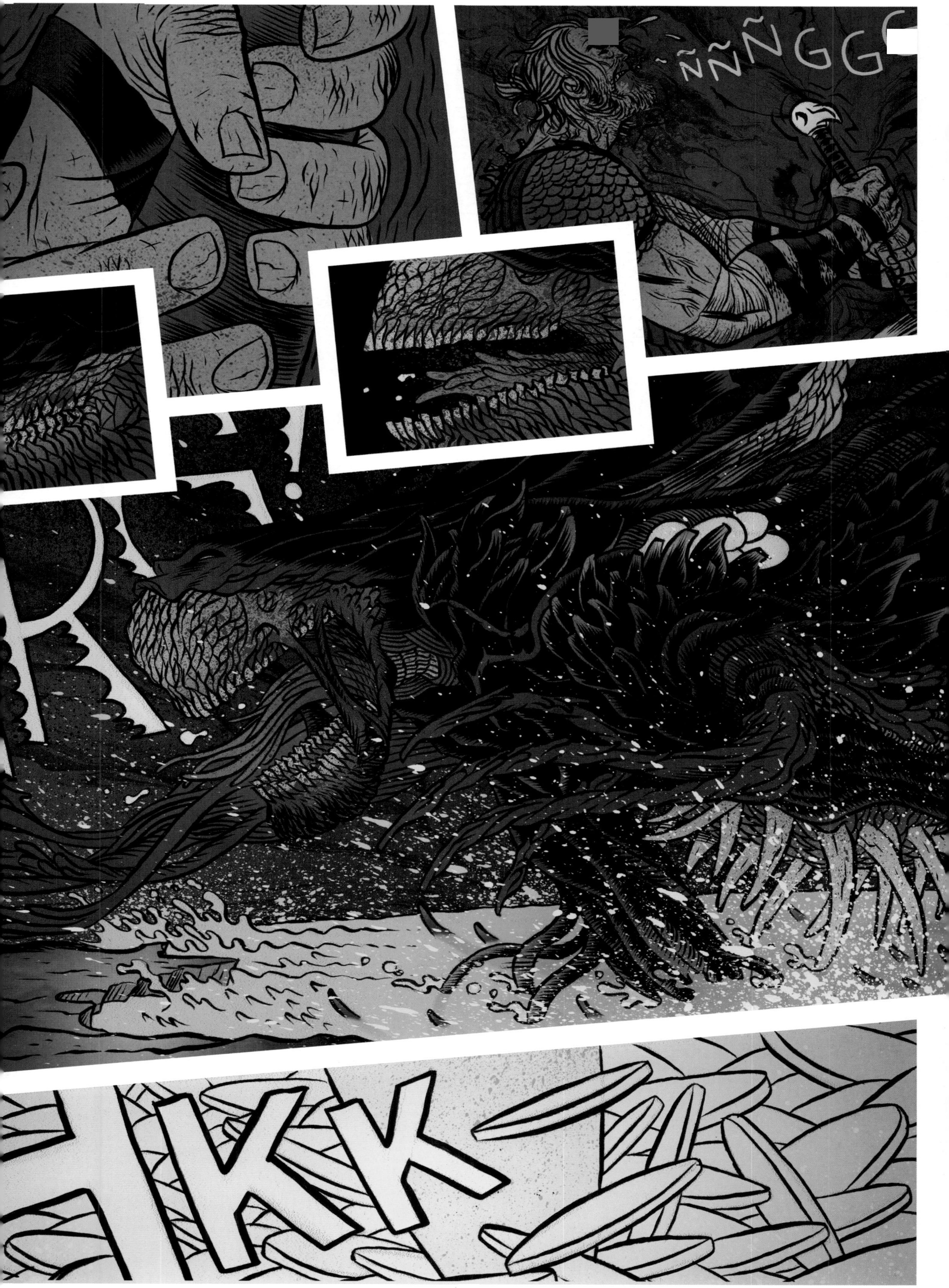
ÑÑÑGG
KK

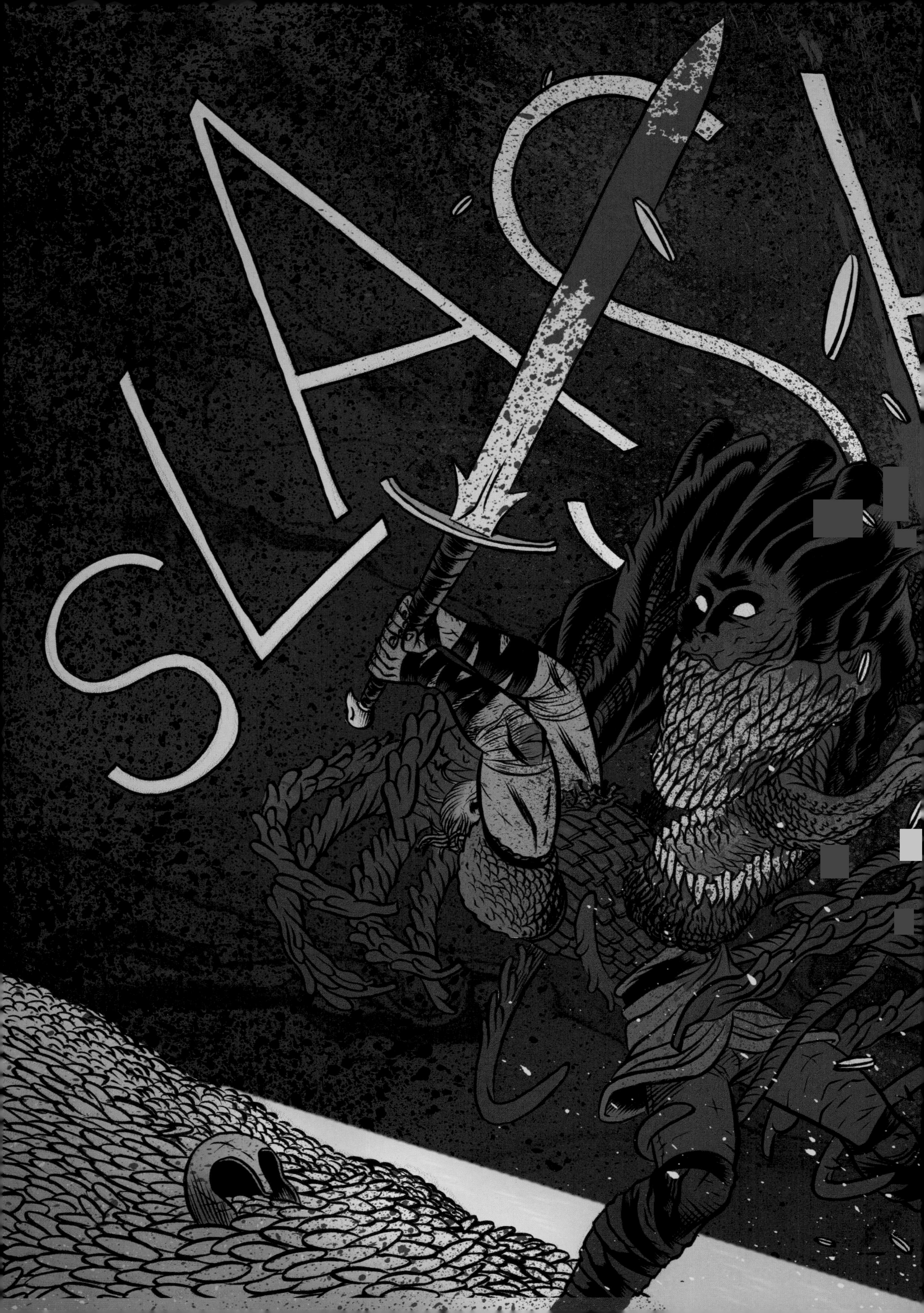
SLASH

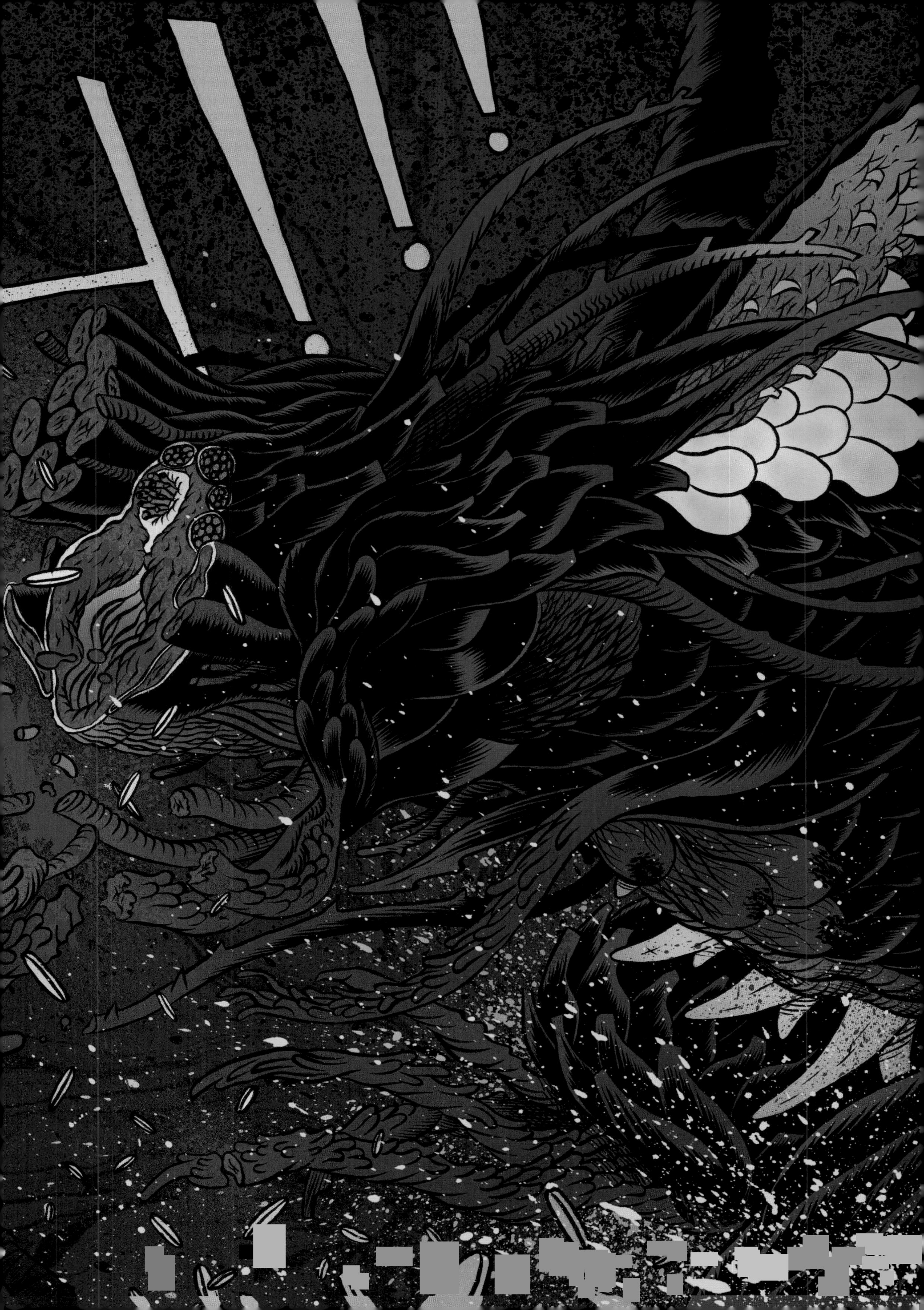
!!!!

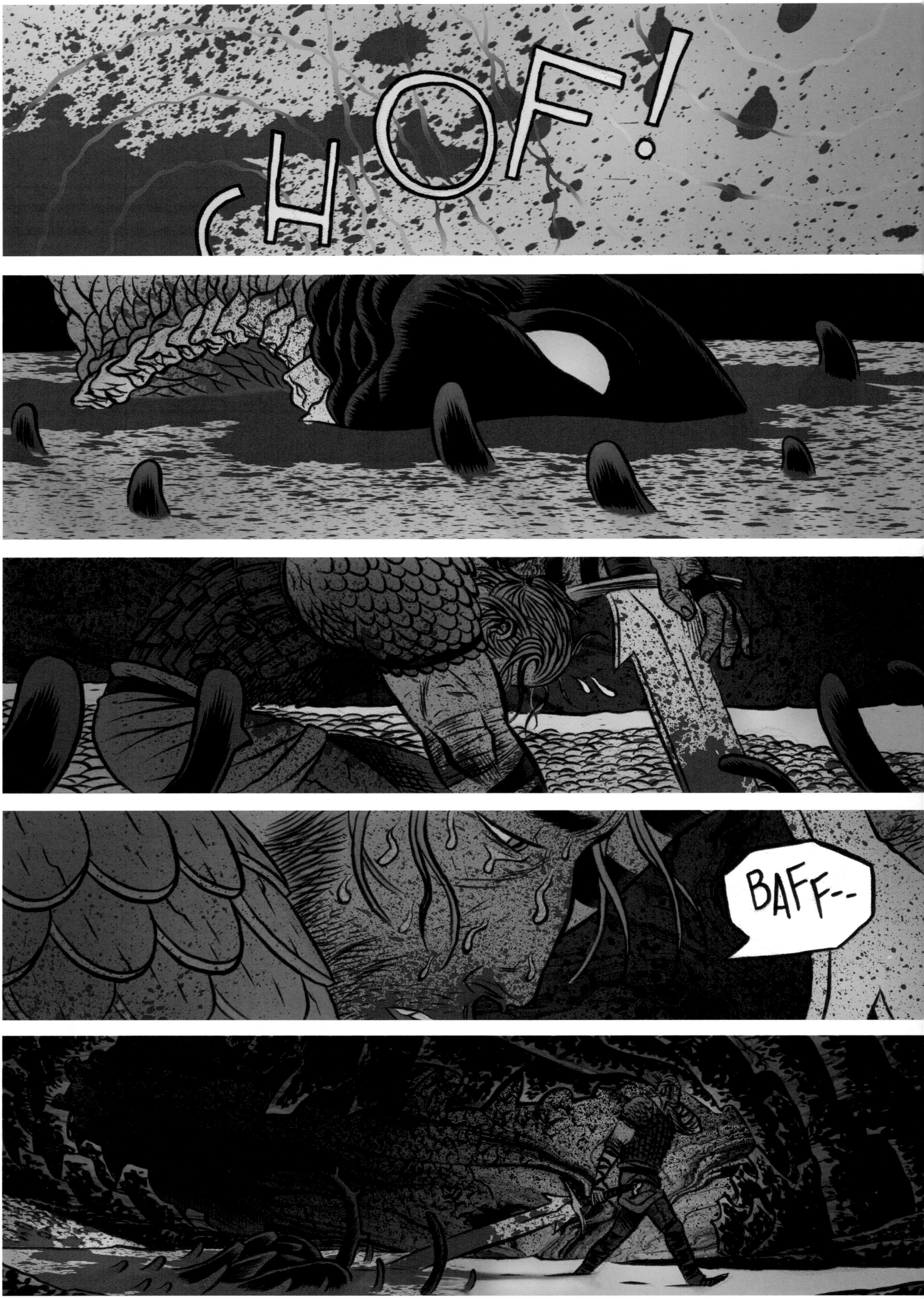
CHOF!
BAFF--

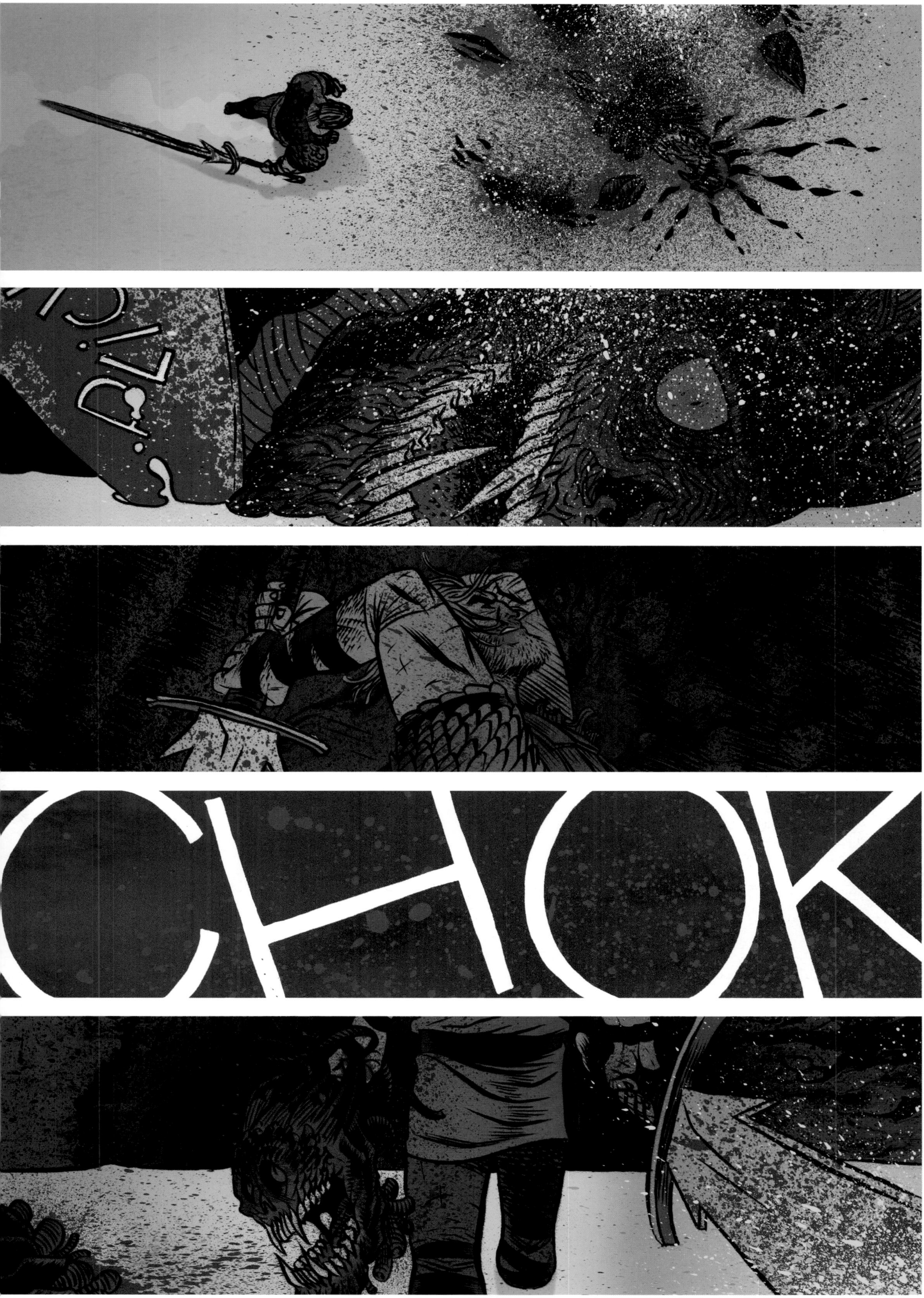
CHOK

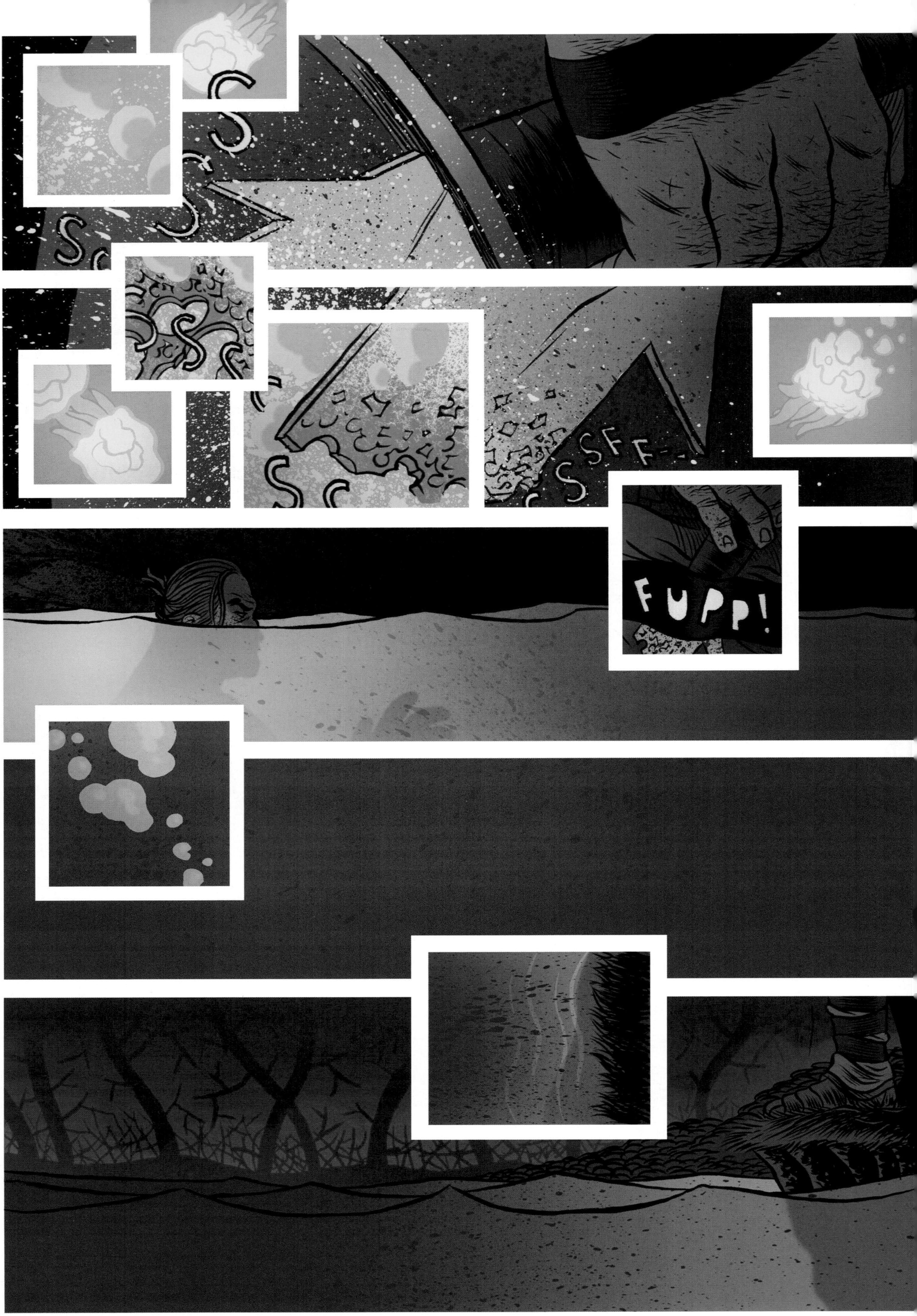
SSFF--
FUPP!

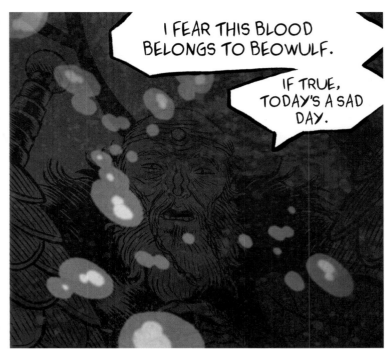

I FEAR THIS BLOOD BELONGS TO BEOWULF.

IF TRUE, TODAY'S A SAD DAY.

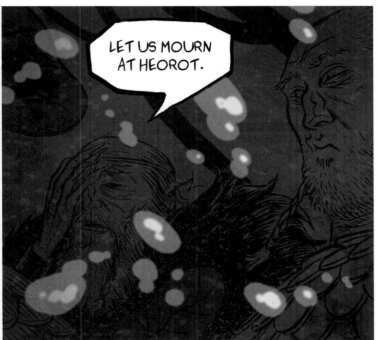

LET US MOURN AT HEOROT.

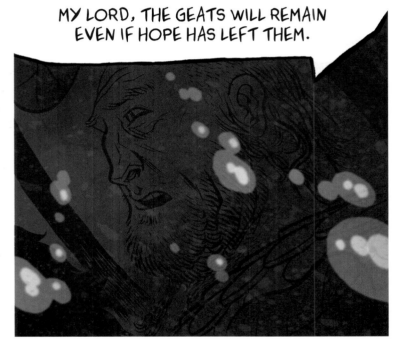

MY LORD, THE GEATS WILL REMAIN EVEN IF HOPE HAS LEFT THEM.

TODAY IS THE MOST FATEFUL DAY WITHIN TWELVE FATEFUL YEARS.

THE MONSTER YET LIVES AS ANOTHER HERO DIES IN VAIN.

BUT NOW ETERNAL GLORY'S HIS.

EVEN AS A SWAMP'S SLIME ENGULFS HIM.

GLORY IS FOR CHAMPIONS, NOT FODDER FOR AN EVIL RACE.

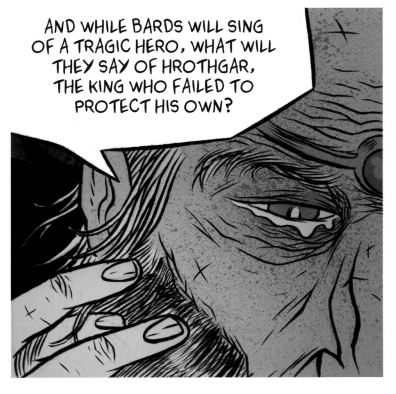

AND WHILE BARDS WILL SING OF A TRAGIC HERO, WHAT WILL THEY SAY OF HROTHGAR, THE KING WHO FAILED TO PROTECT HIS OWN?

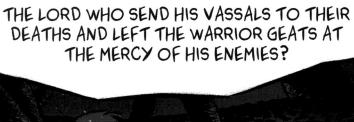

THE LORD WHO SEND HIS VASSALS TO THEIR DEATHS AND LEFT THE WARRIOR GEATS AT THE MERCY OF HIS ENEMIES?

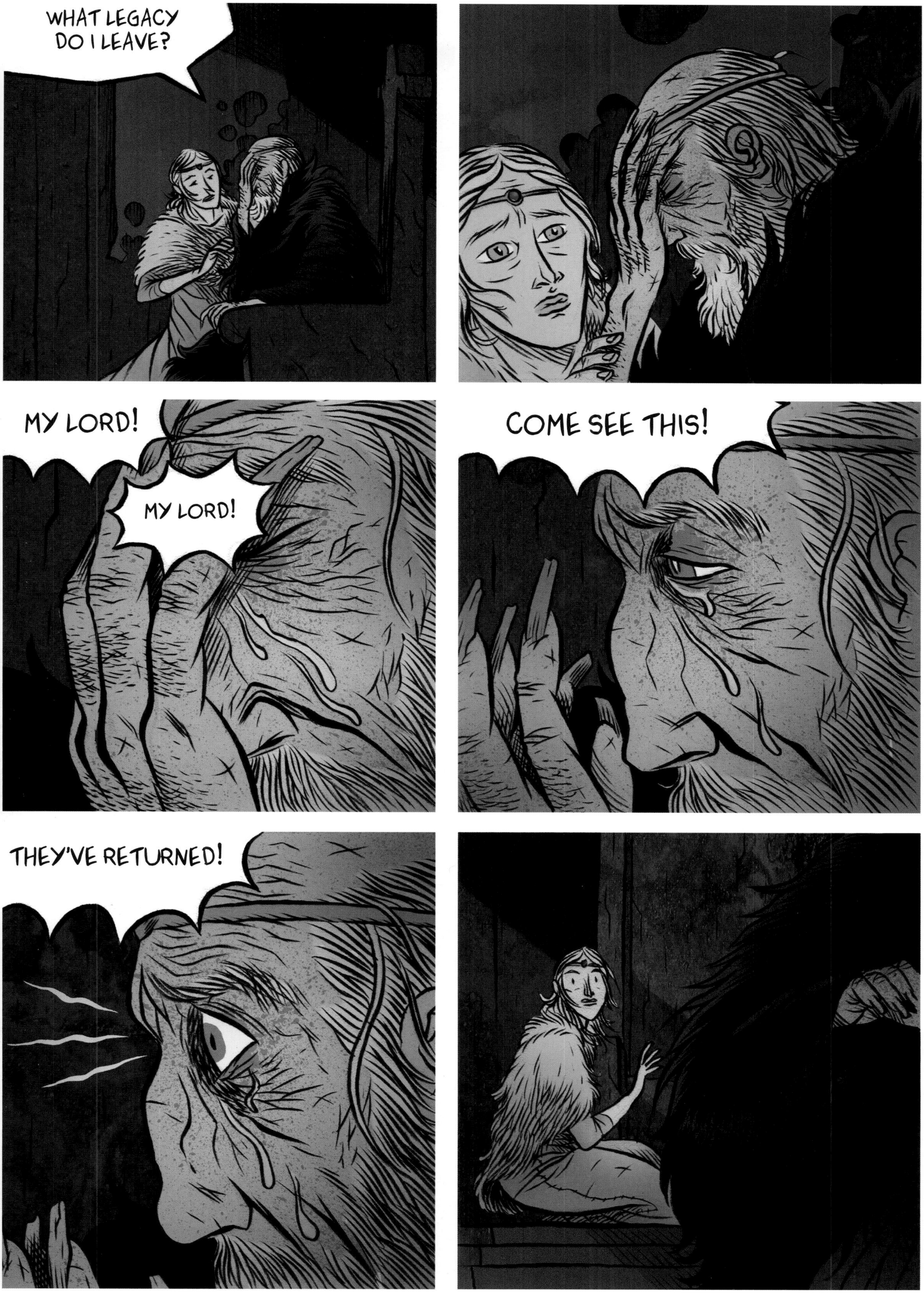
WHAT LEGACY DO I LEAVE?
MY LORD!
MY LORD!
COME SEE THIS!
THEY'VE RETURNED!

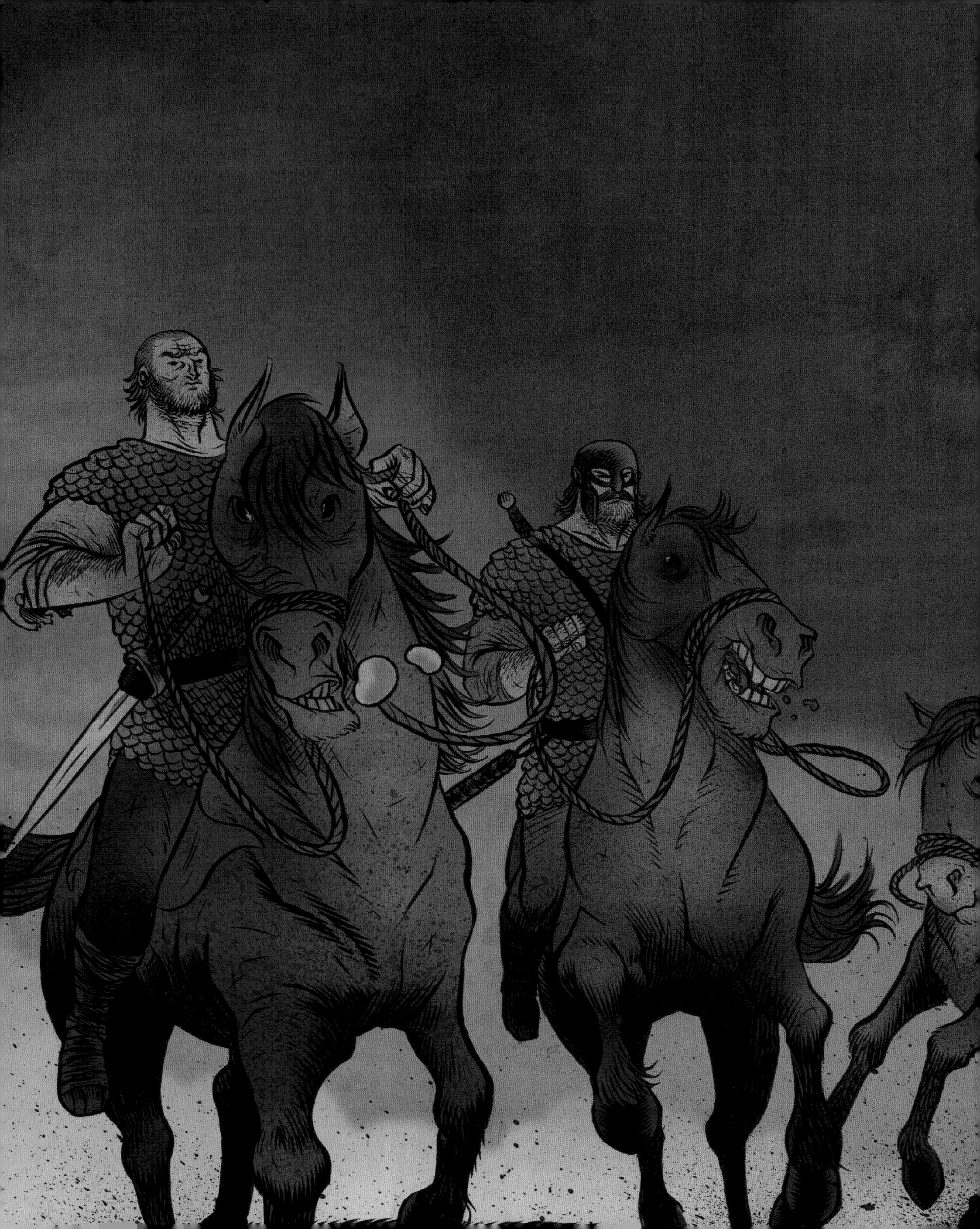

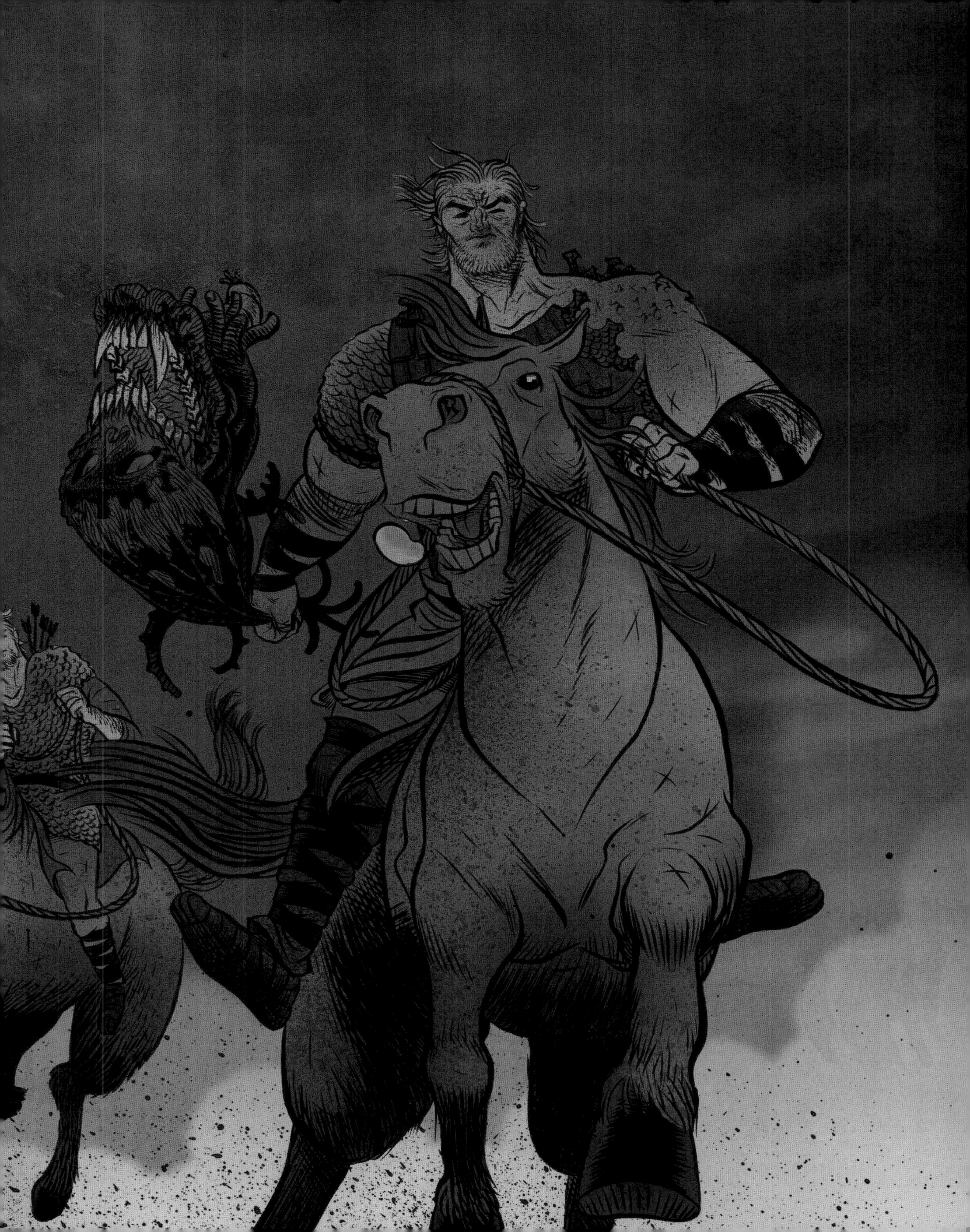

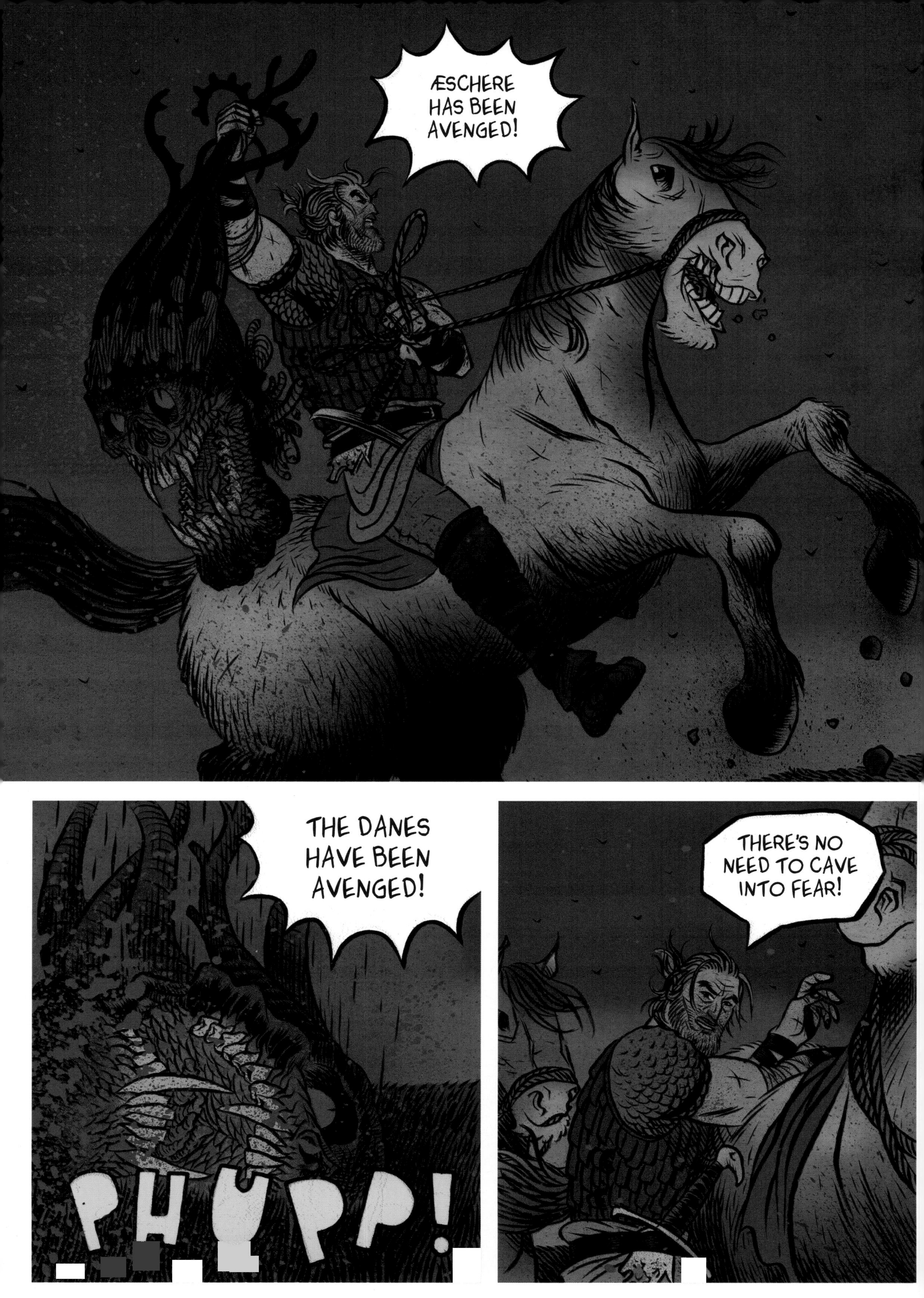
ÆSCHERE HAS BEEN AVENGED!
THE DANES HAVE BEEN AVENGED!
PHUPP!
THERE'S NO NEED TO CAVE INTO FEAR!

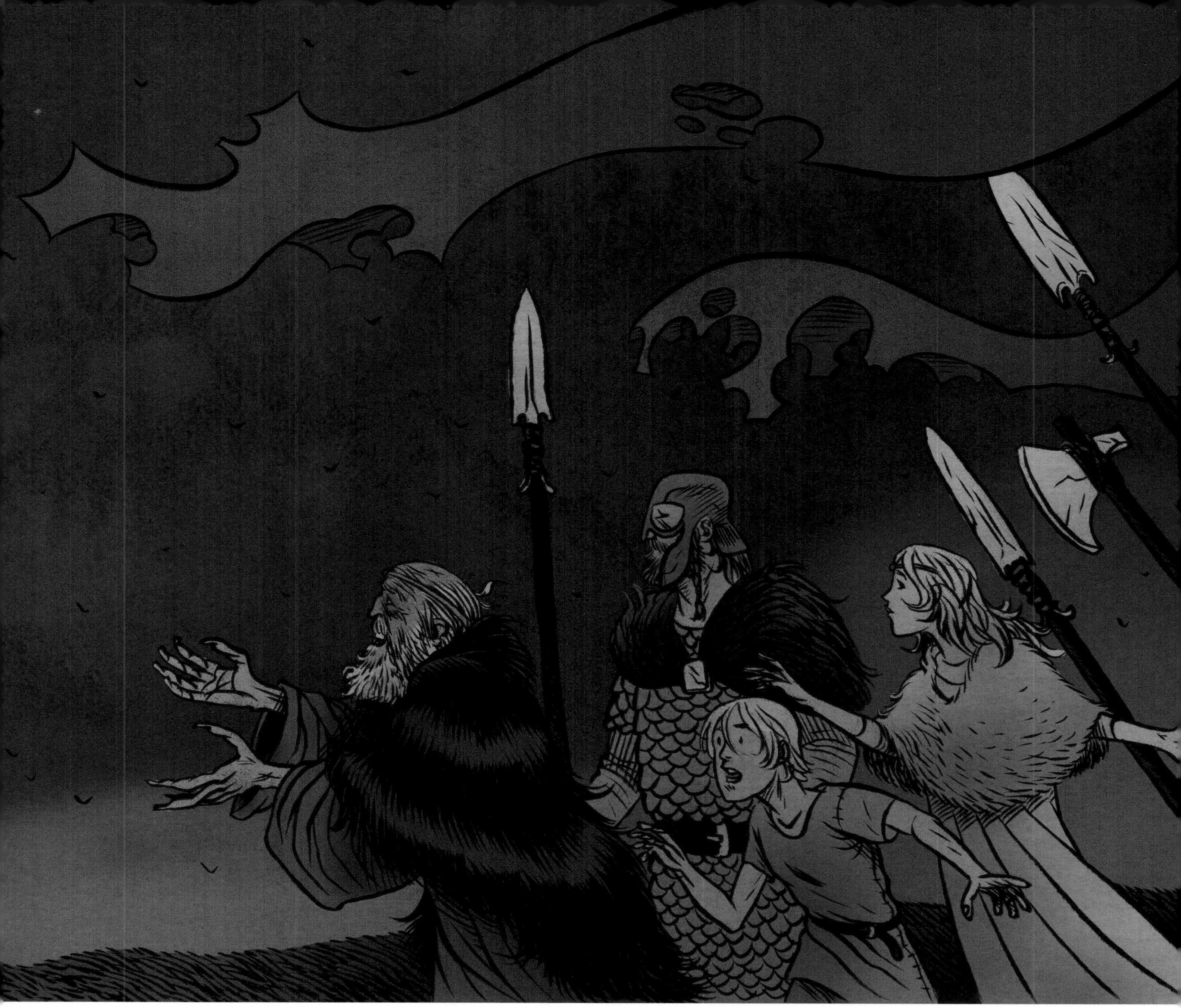

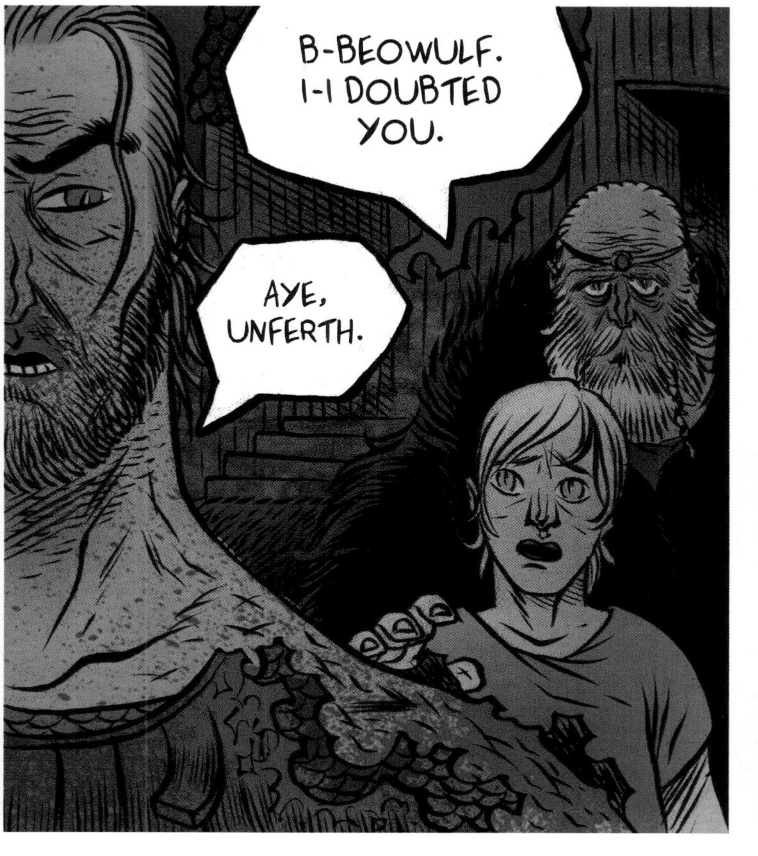
B-BEOWULF. I-I DOUBTED YOU.
AYE, UNFERTH.

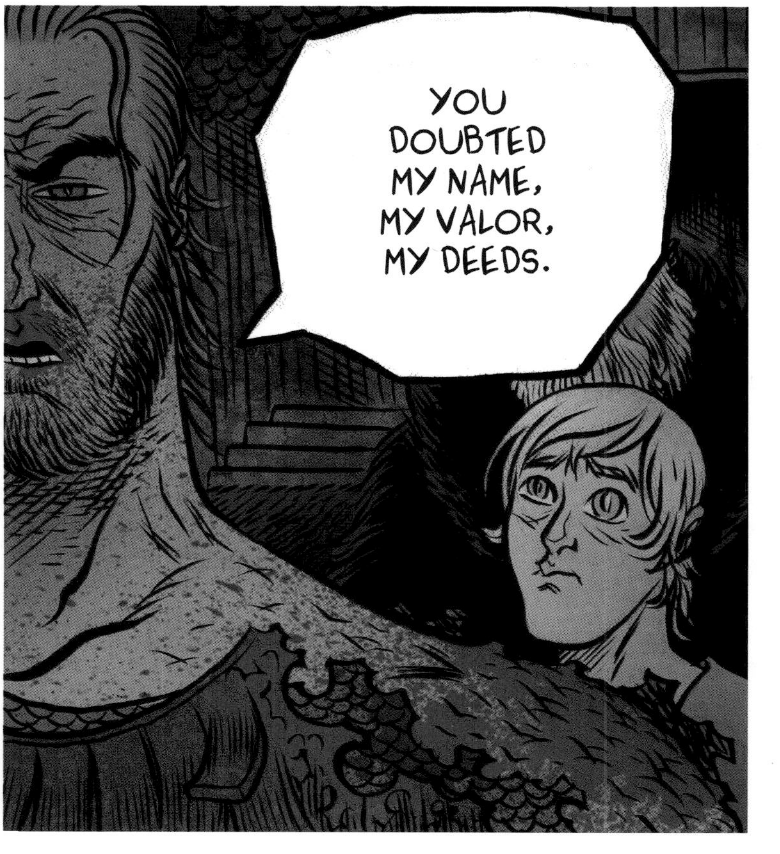
YOU DOUBTED MY NAME, MY VALOR, MY DEEDS.

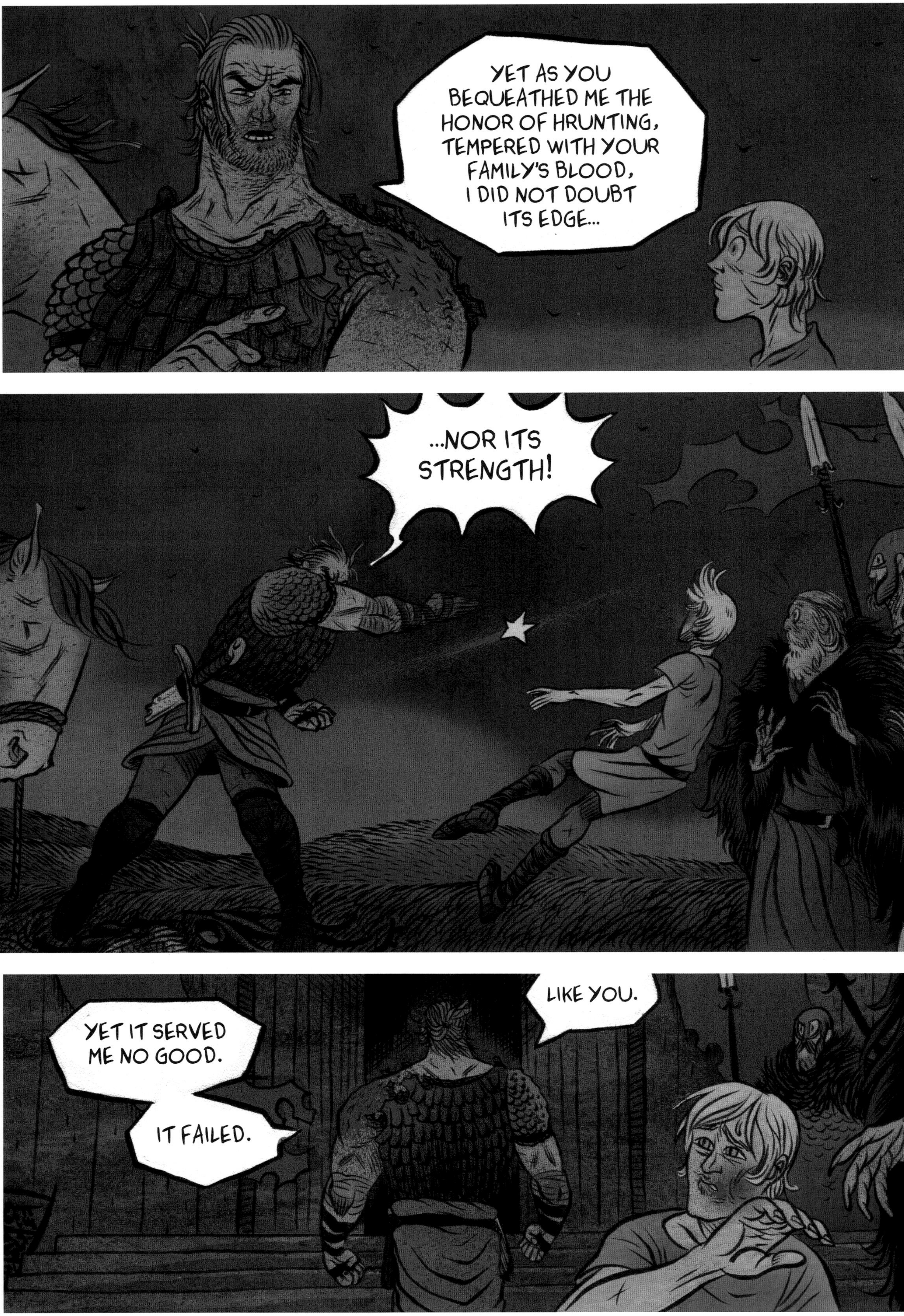

YET AS YOU BEQUEATHED ME THE HONOR OF HRUNTING, TEMPERED WITH YOUR FAMILY'S BLOOD, I DID NOT DOUBT ITS EDGE...
...NOR ITS STRENGTH!
YET IT SERVED ME NO GOOD.
IT FAILED.
LIKE YOU.

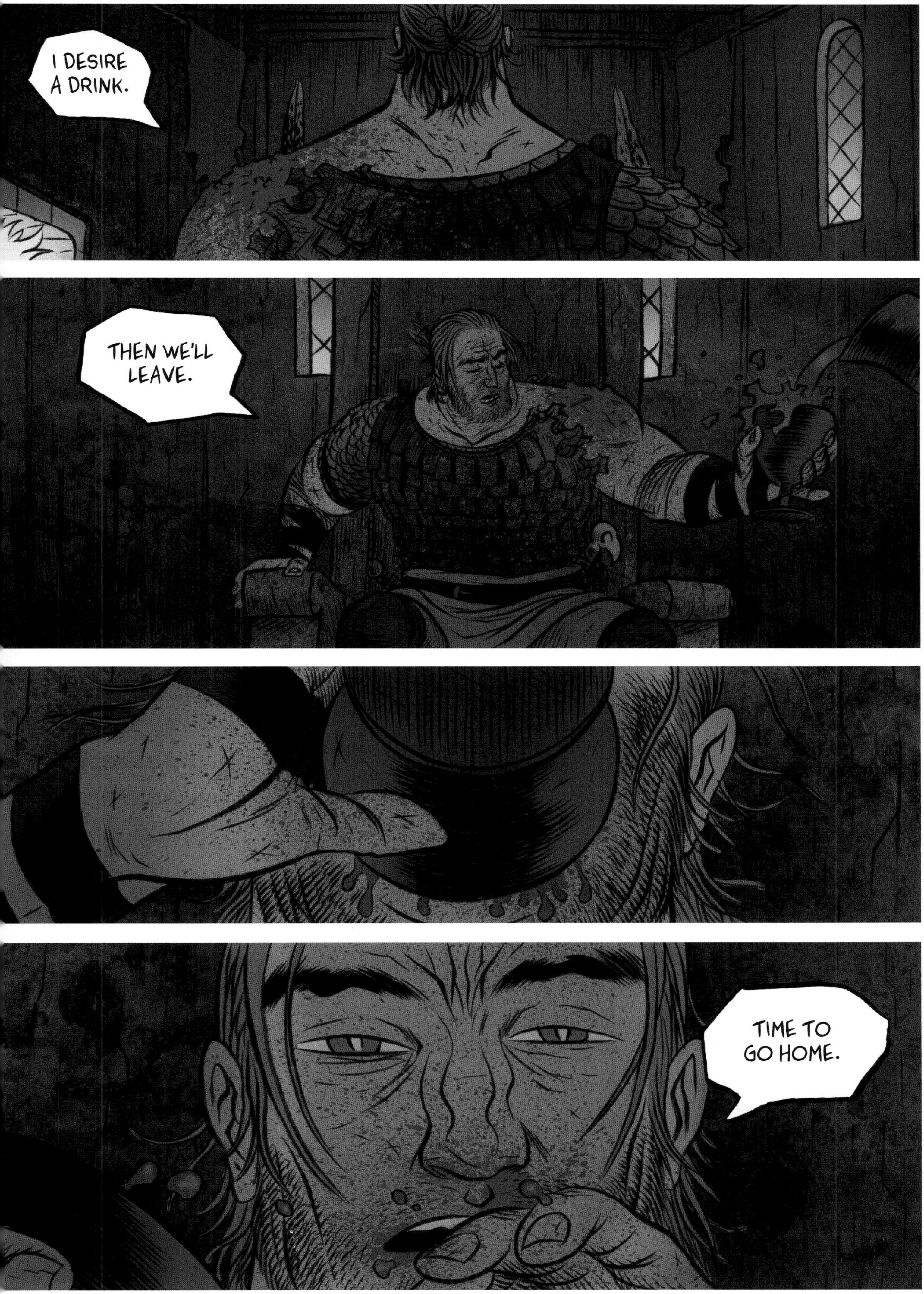
I DESIRE A DRINK.
THEN WE'LL LEAVE.
TIME TO GO HOME.

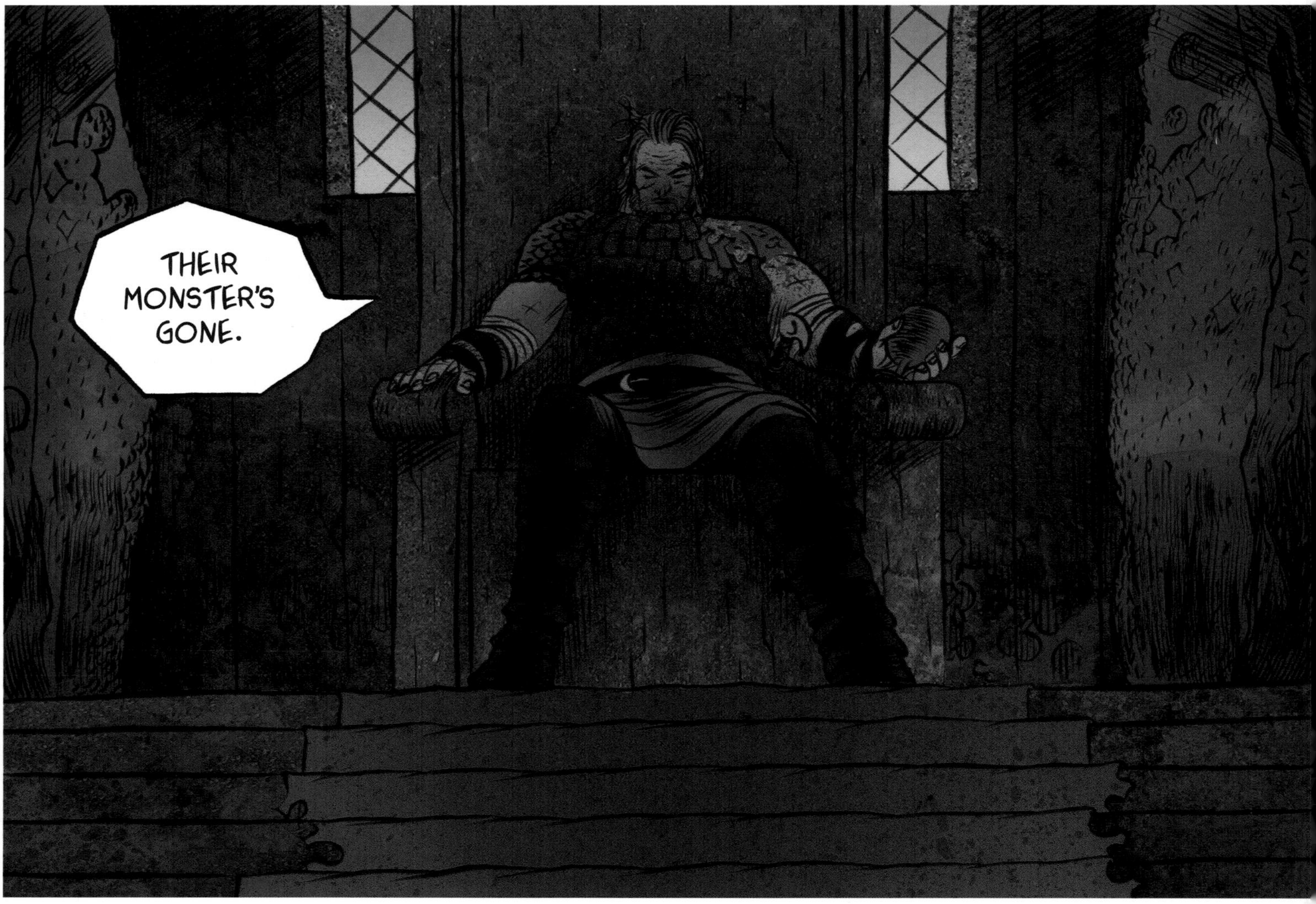
THEIR MONSTER'S GONE.

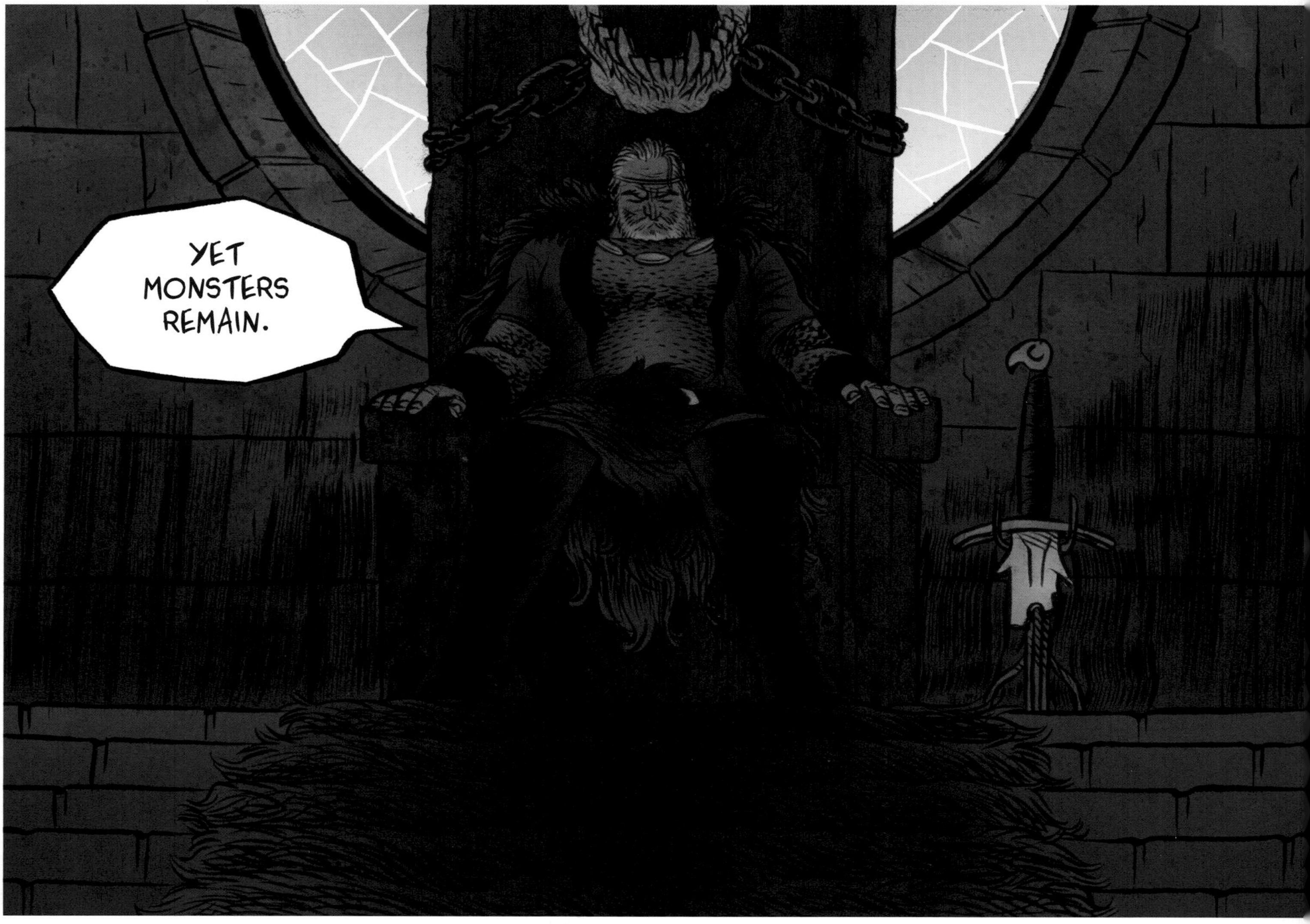
YET MONSTERS REMAIN.

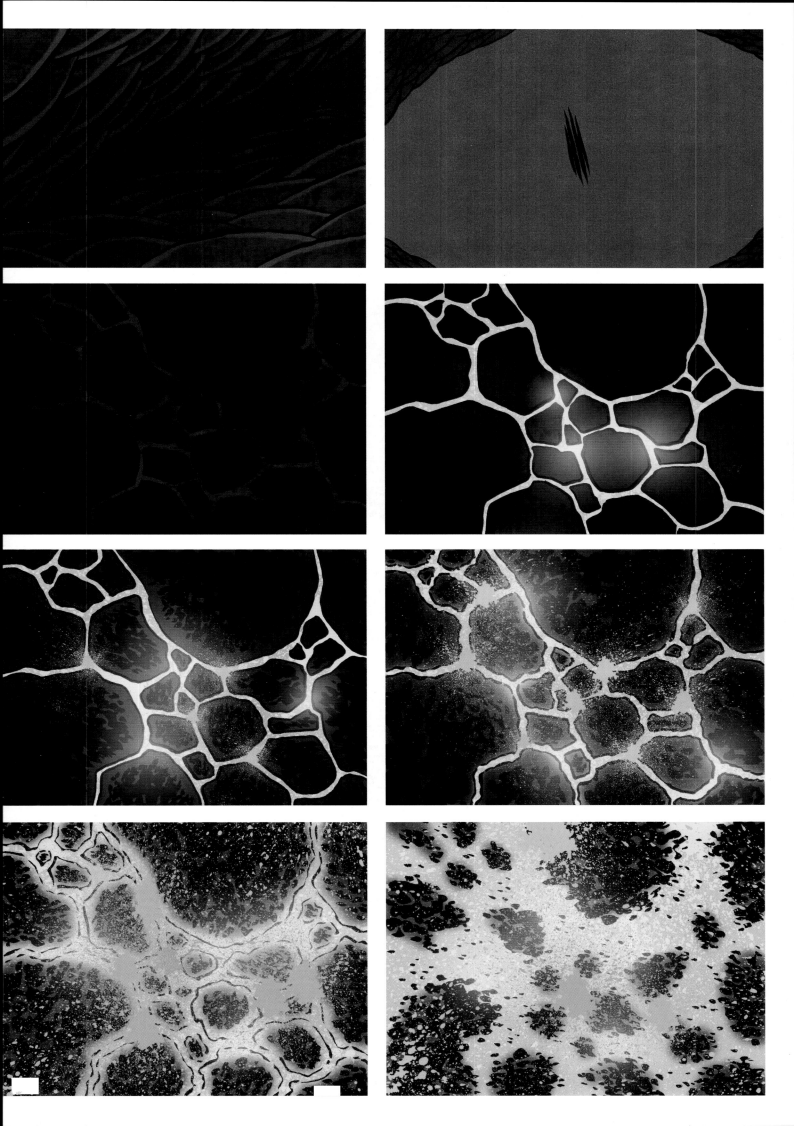

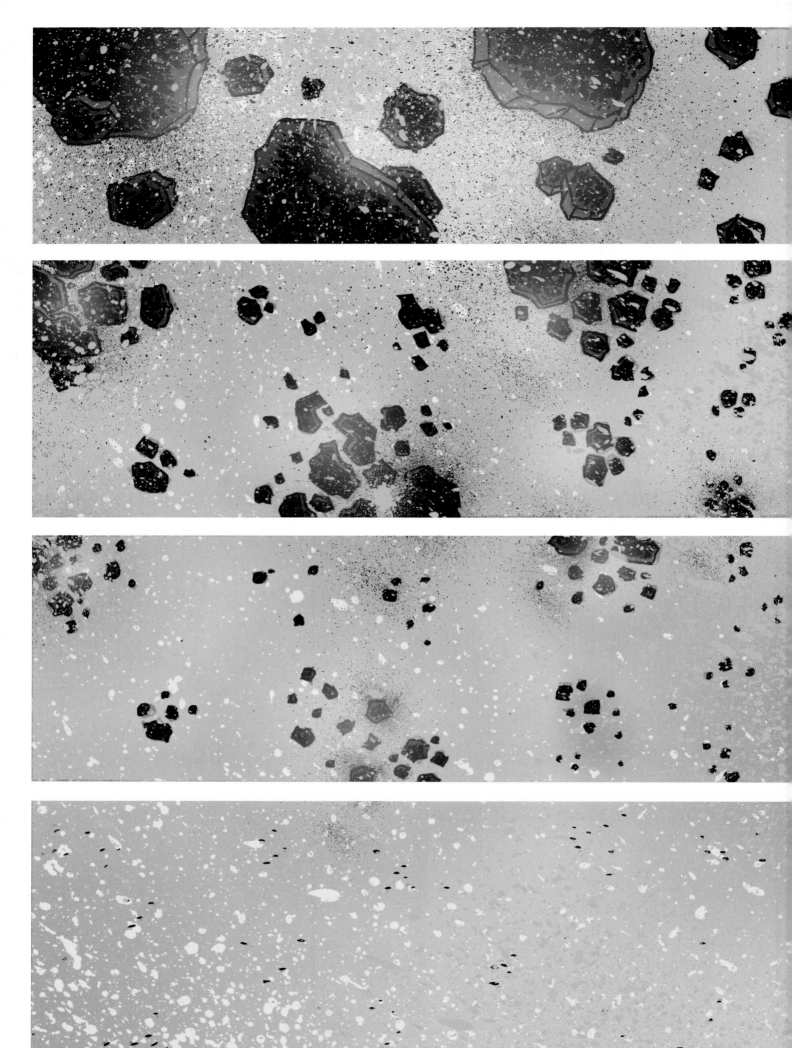

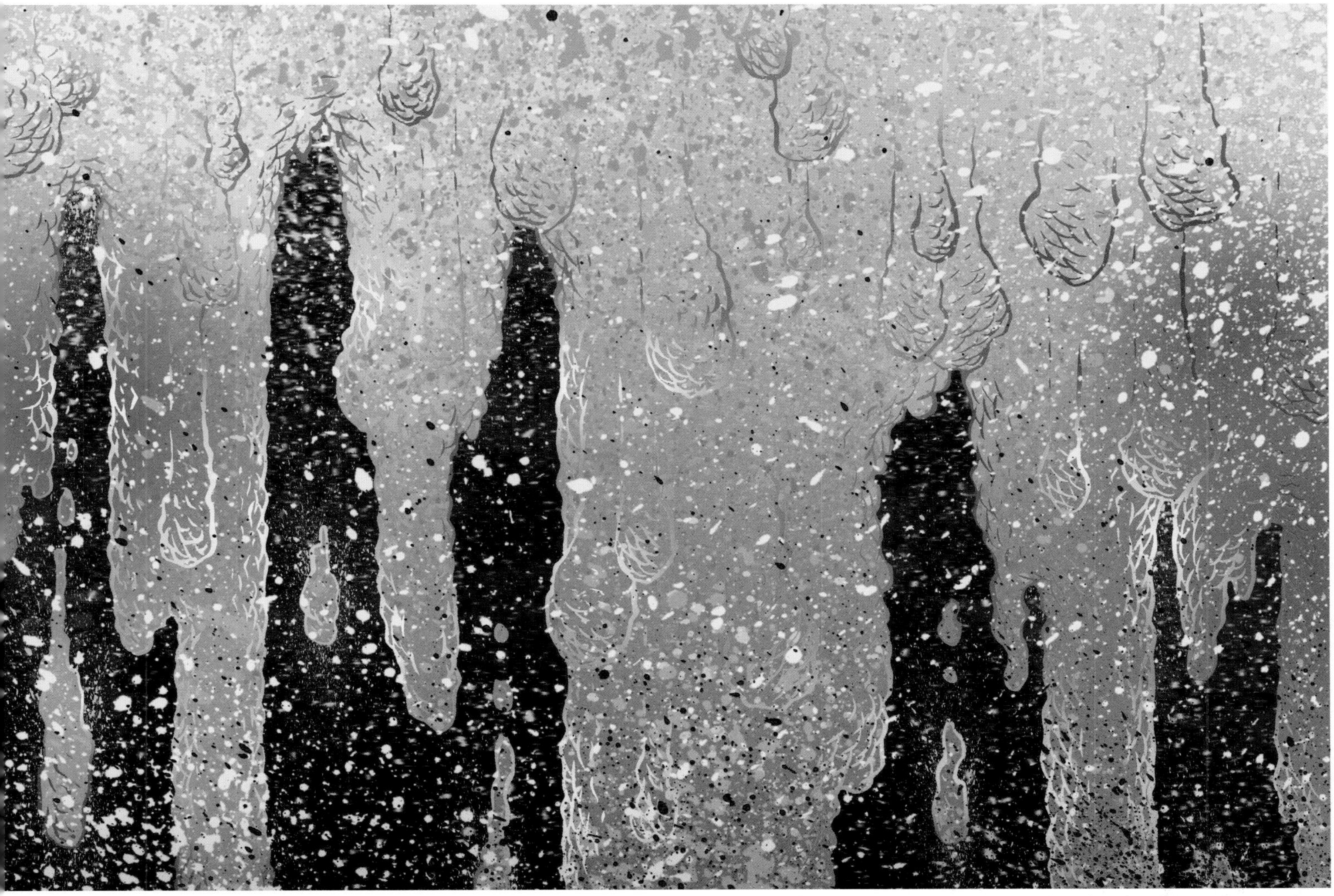
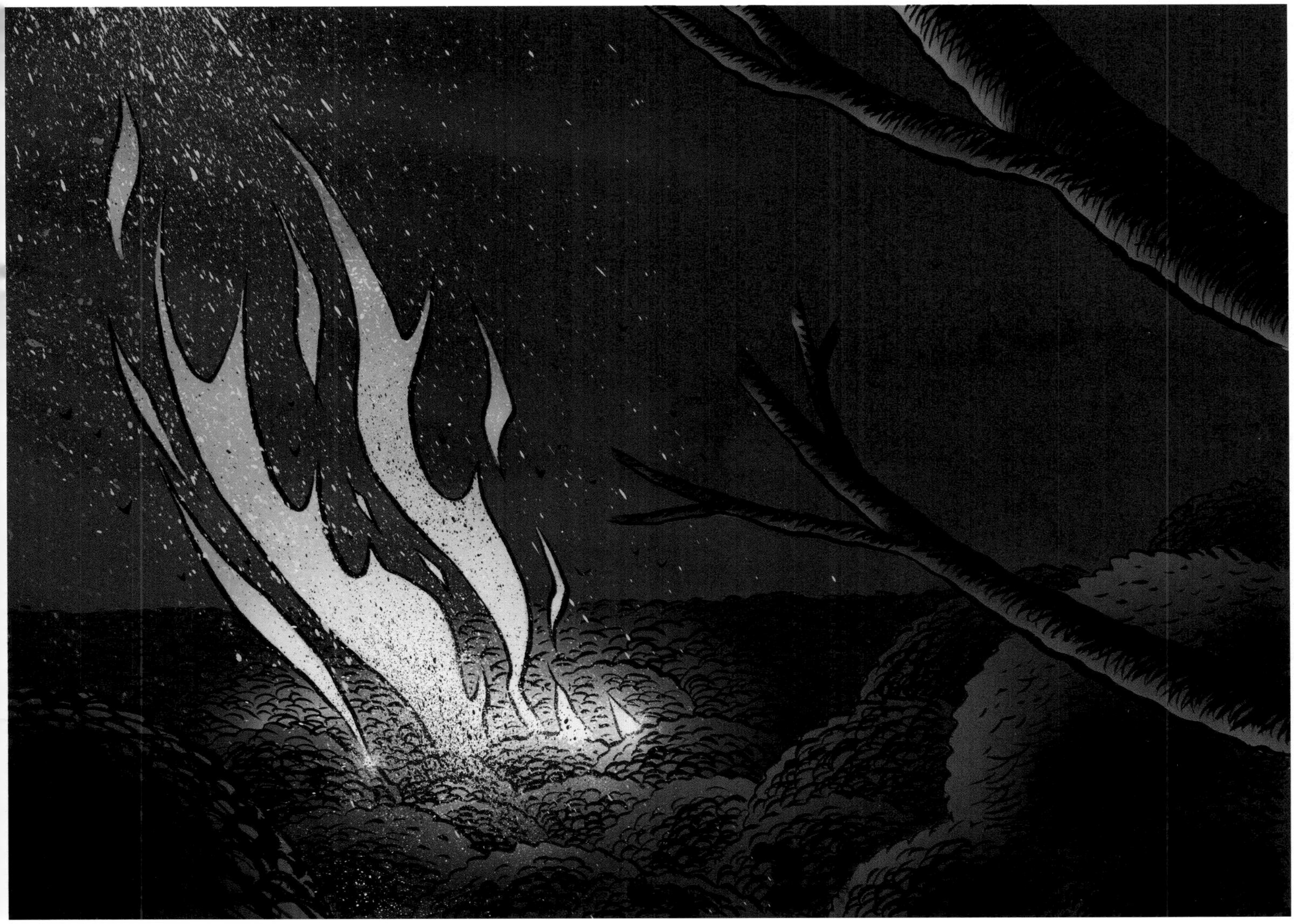

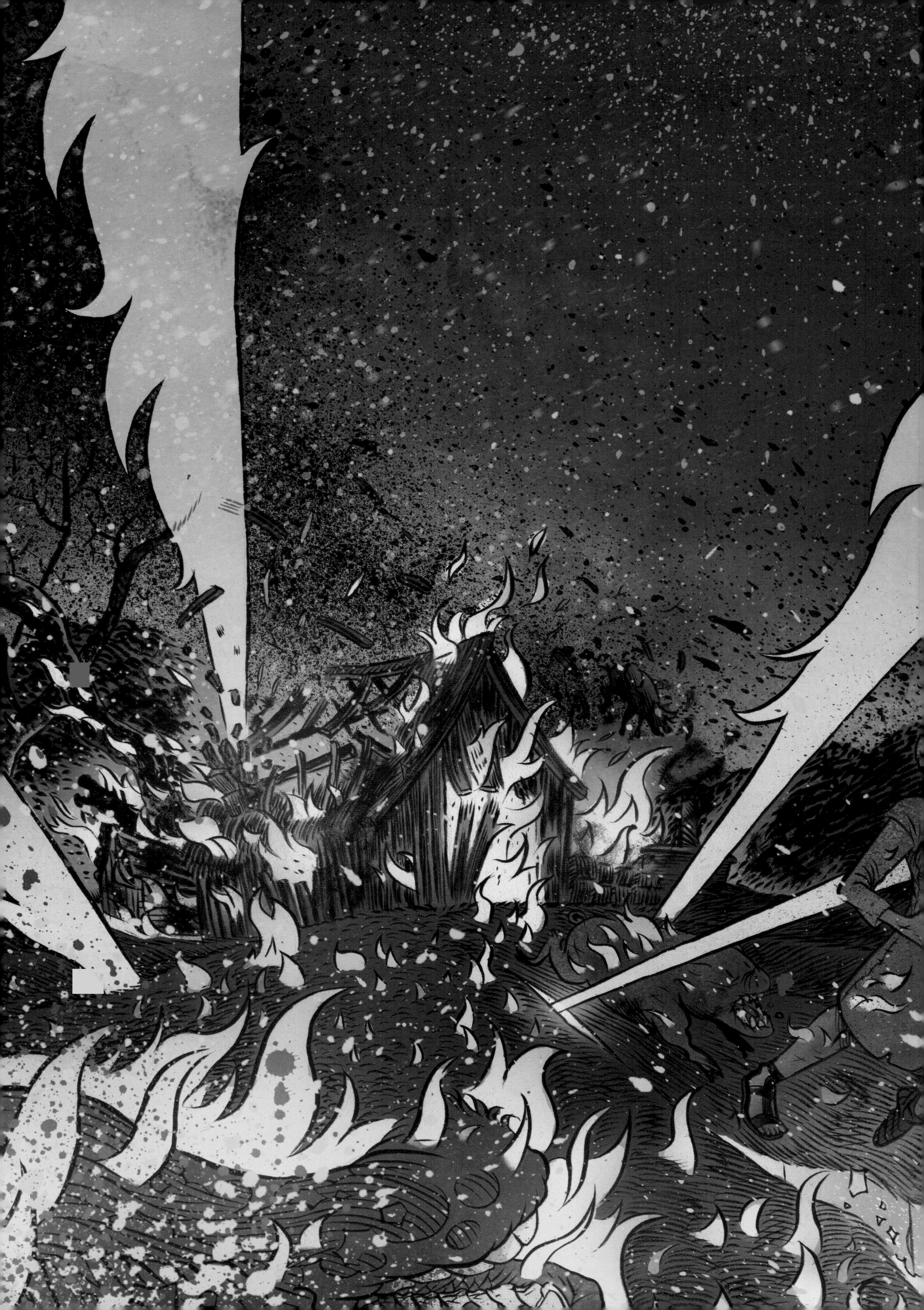

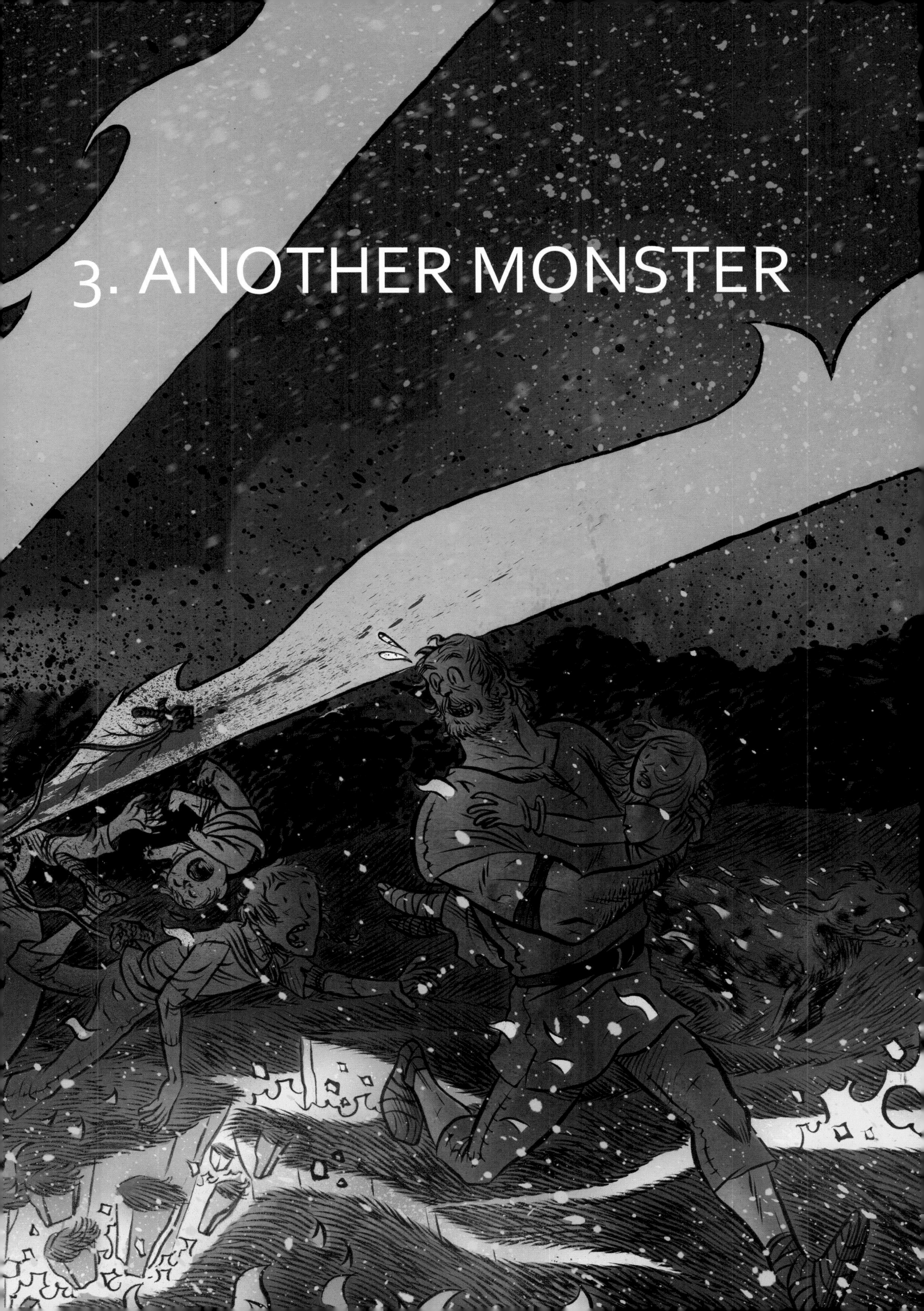
3. ANOTHER MONSTER

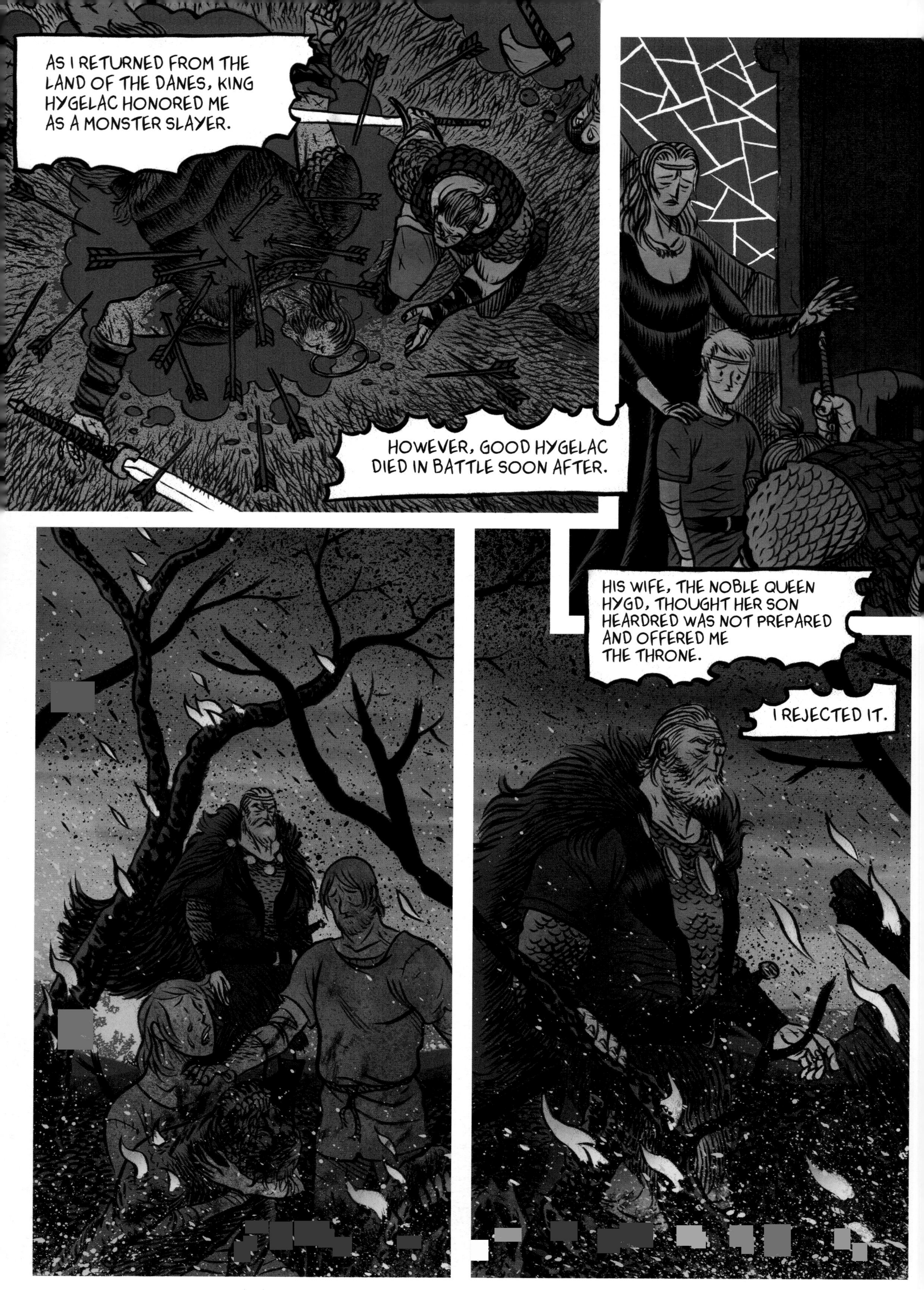
AS I RETURNED FROM THE LAND OF THE DANES, KING HYGELAC HONORED ME AS A MONSTER SLAYER.
HOWEVER, GOOD HYGELAC DIED IN BATTLE SOON AFTER.
HIS WIFE, THE NOBLE QUEEN HYGD, THOUGHT HER SON HEARDRED WAS NOT PREPARED AND OFFERED ME THE THRONE.
I REJECTED IT.

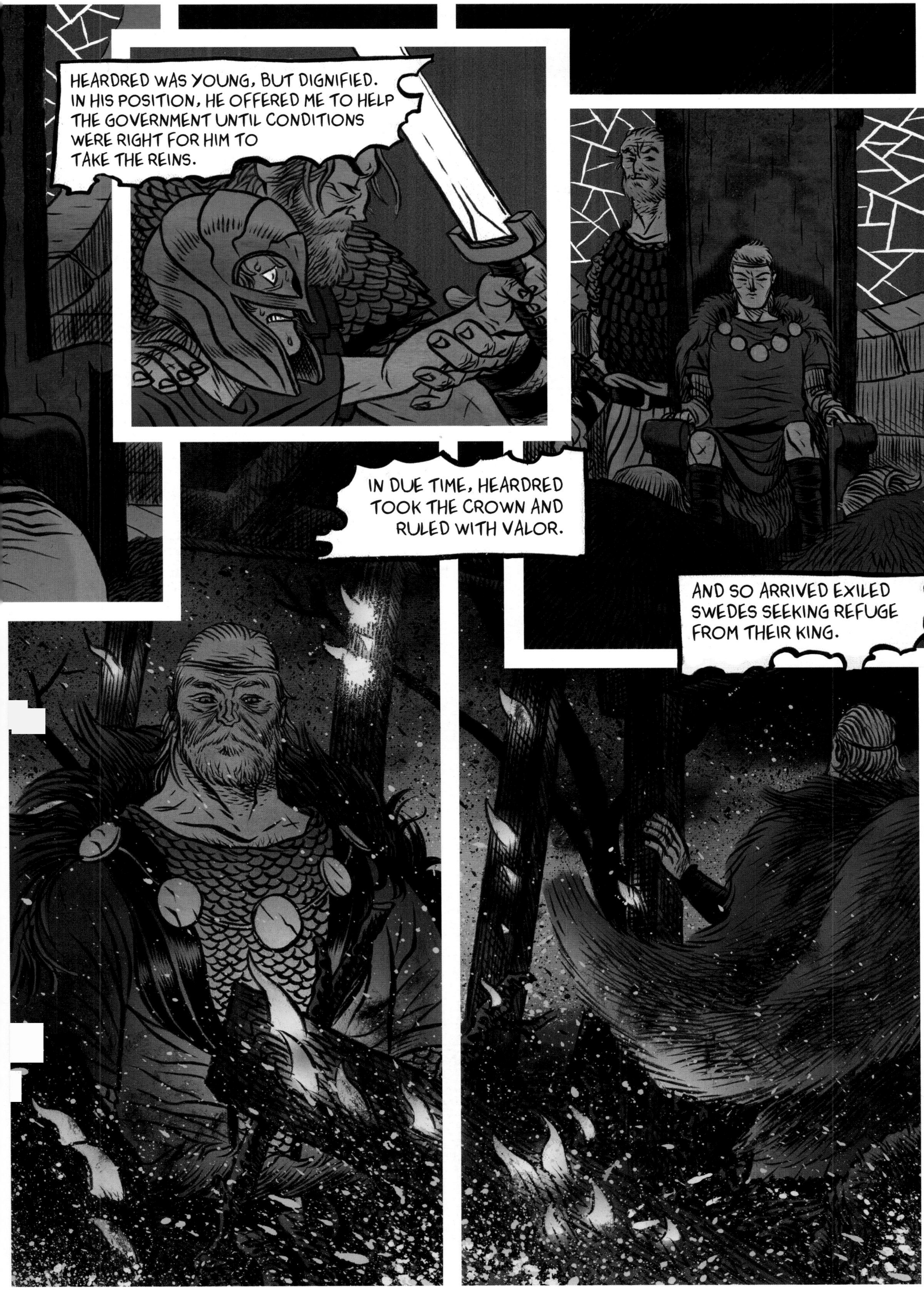
HEARDRED WAS YOUNG, BUT DIGNIFIED. IN HIS POSITION, HE OFFERED ME TO HELP THE GOVERNMENT UNTIL CONDITIONS WERE RIGHT FOR HIM TO TAKE THE REINS.
IN DUE TIME, HEARDRED TOOK THE CROWN AND RULED WITH VALOR.
AND SO ARRIVED EXILED SWEDES SEEKING REFUGE FROM THEIR KING.

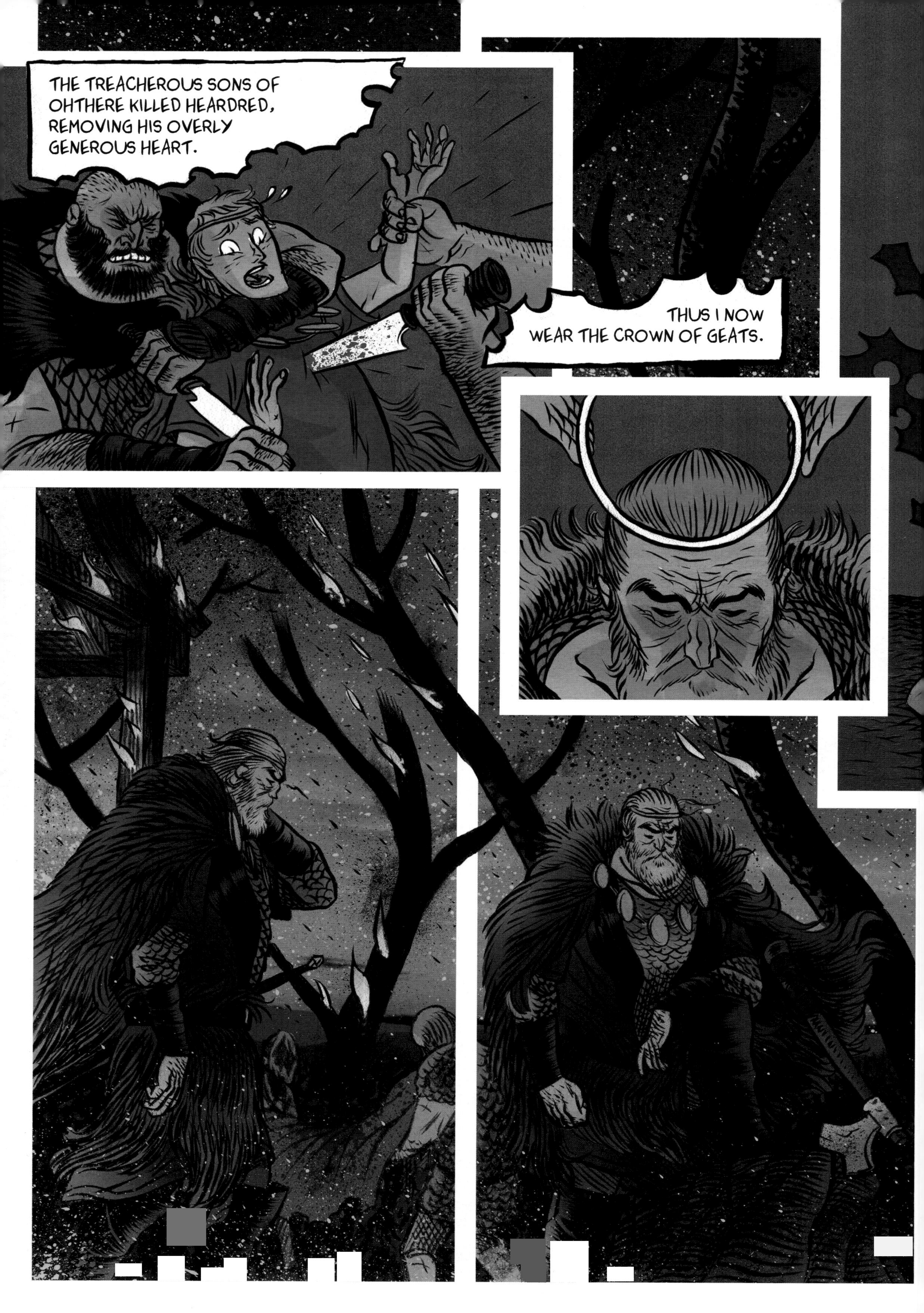
THE TREACHEROUS SONS OF OHTHERE KILLED HEARDRED, REMOVING HIS OVERLY GENEROUS HEART.
THUS I NOW WEAR THE CROWN OF GEATS.

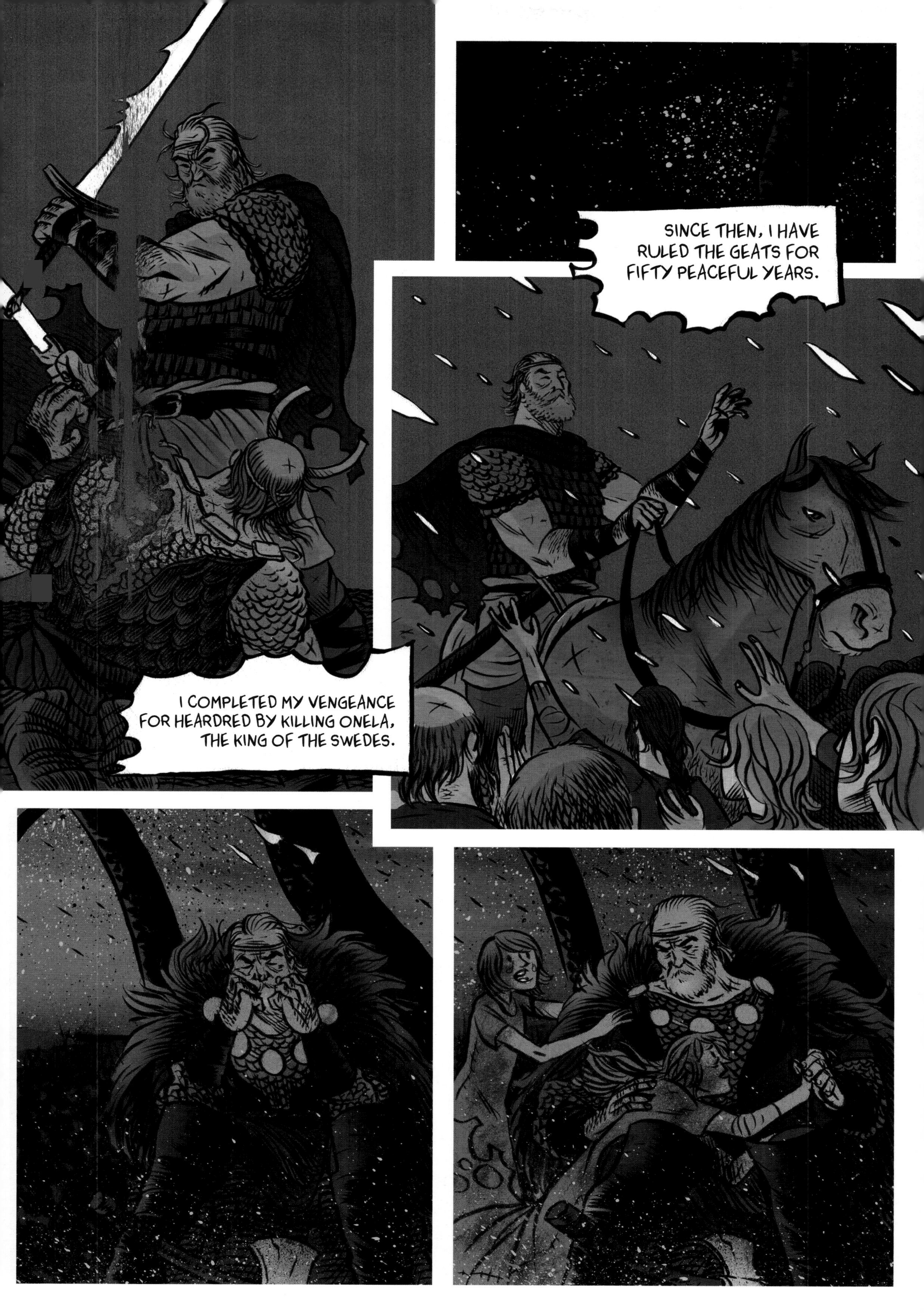
I COMPLETED MY VENGEANCE FOR HEARDRED BY KILLING ONELA, THE KING OF THE SWEDES.
SINCE THEN, I HAVE RULED THE GEATS FOR FIFTY PEACEFUL YEARS.

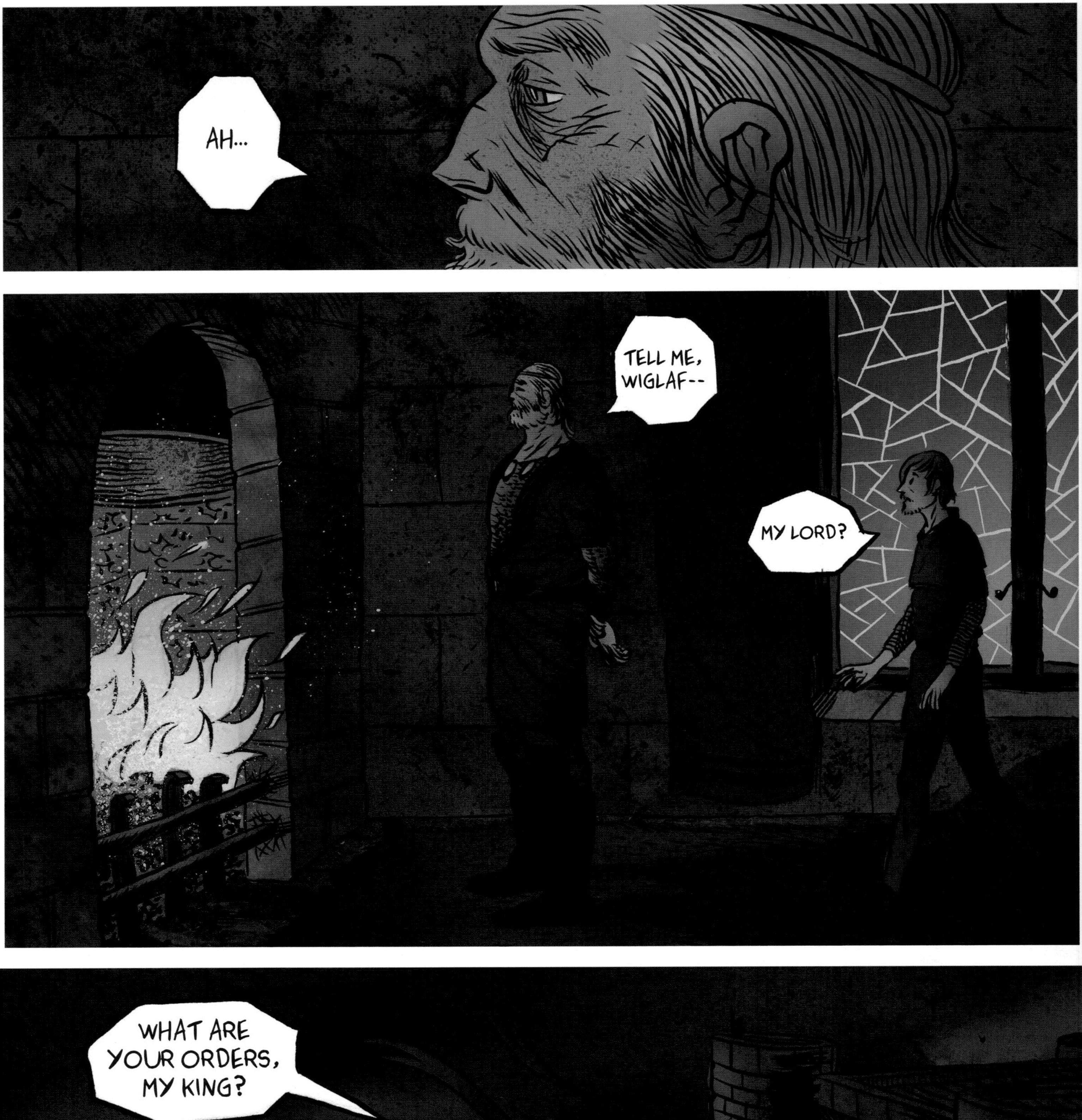
AH...
TELL ME, WIGLAF--
MY LORD?
WHAT ARE YOUR ORDERS, MY KING?

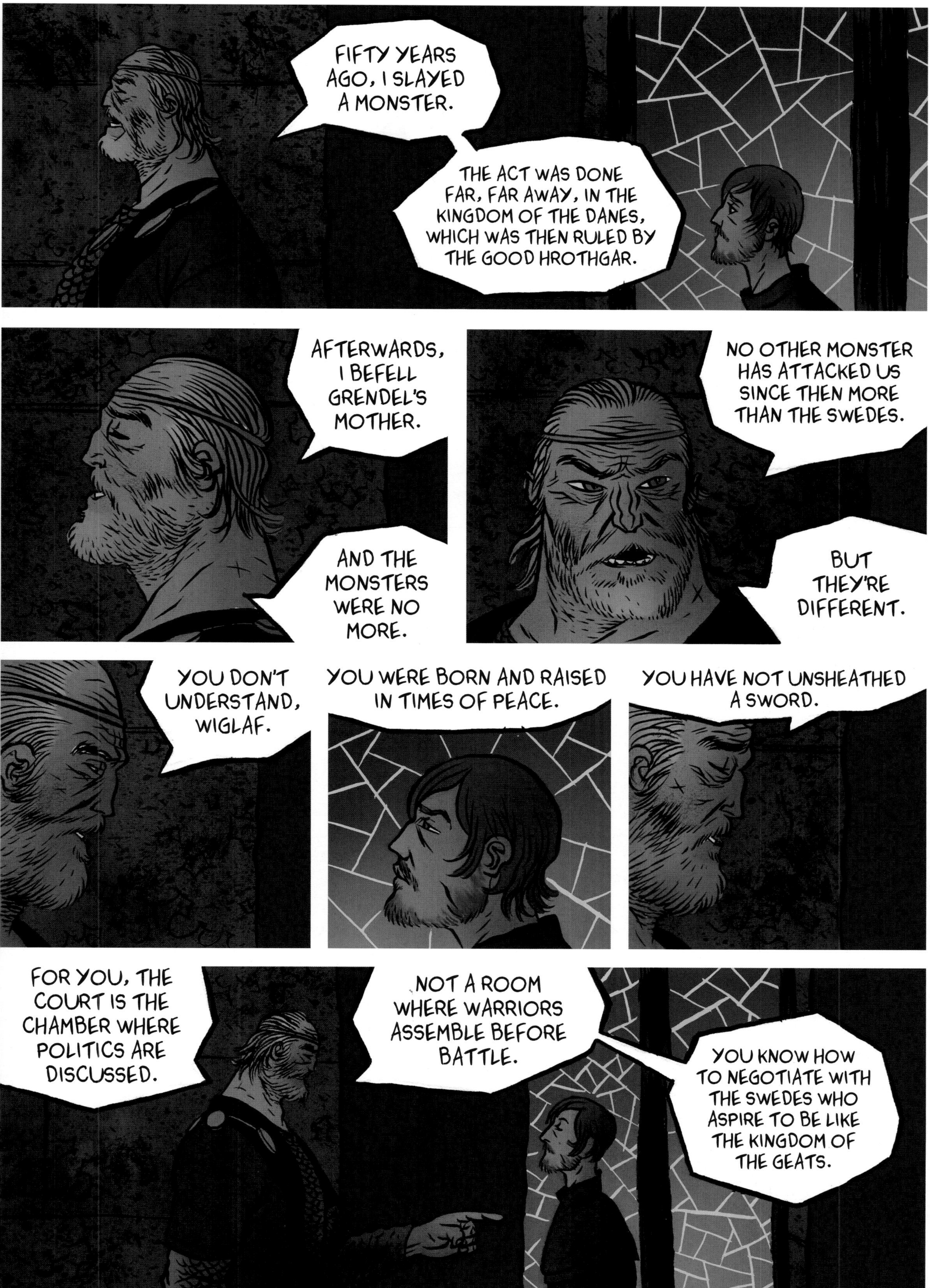
FIFTY YEARS AGO, I SLAYED A MONSTER.
THE ACT WAS DONE FAR, FAR AWAY, IN THE KINGDOM OF THE DANES, WHICH WAS THEN RULED BY THE GOOD HROTHGAR.
AFTERWARDS, I BEFELL GRENDEL'S MOTHER.
AND THE MONSTERS WERE NO MORE.
NO OTHER MONSTER HAS ATTACKED US SINCE THEN MORE THAN THE SWEDES.
BUT THEY'RE DIFFERENT.
YOU DON'T UNDERSTAND, WIGLAF.
YOU WERE BORN AND RAISED IN TIMES OF PEACE.
YOU HAVE NOT UNSHEATHED A SWORD.
FOR YOU, THE COURT IS THE CHAMBER WHERE POLITICS ARE DISCUSSED.
NOT A ROOM WHERE WARRIORS ASSEMBLE BEFORE BATTLE.
YOU KNOW HOW TO NEGOTIATE WITH THE SWEDES WHO ASPIRE TO BE LIKE THE KINGDOM OF THE GEATS.

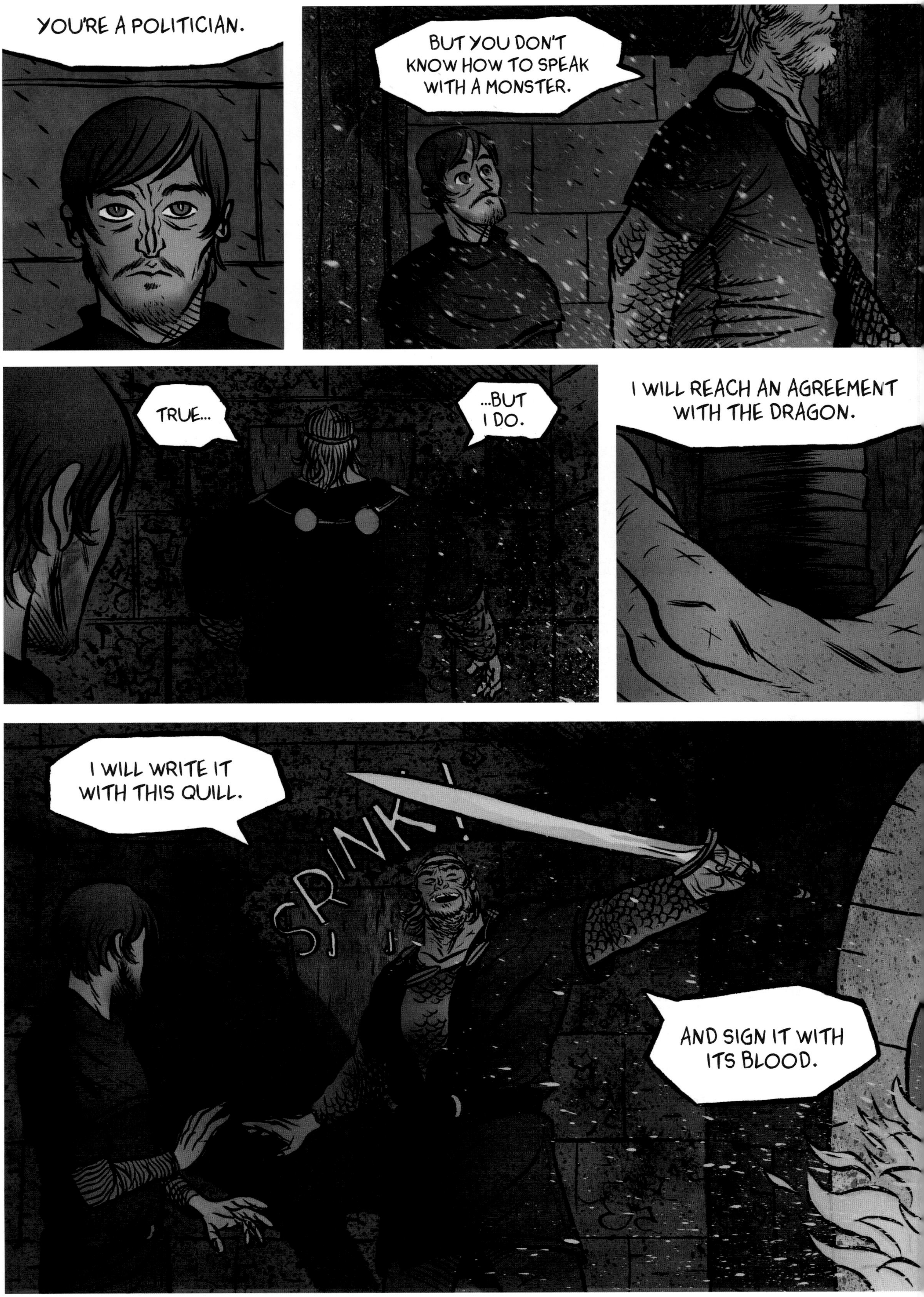
YOU'RE A POLITICIAN.
BUT YOU DON'T KNOW HOW TO SPEAK WITH A MONSTER.
TRUE...
...BUT I DO.
I WILL REACH AN AGREEMENT WITH THE DRAGON.
I WILL WRITE IT WITH THIS QUILL.
SRINK!
AND SIGN IT WITH ITS BLOOD.

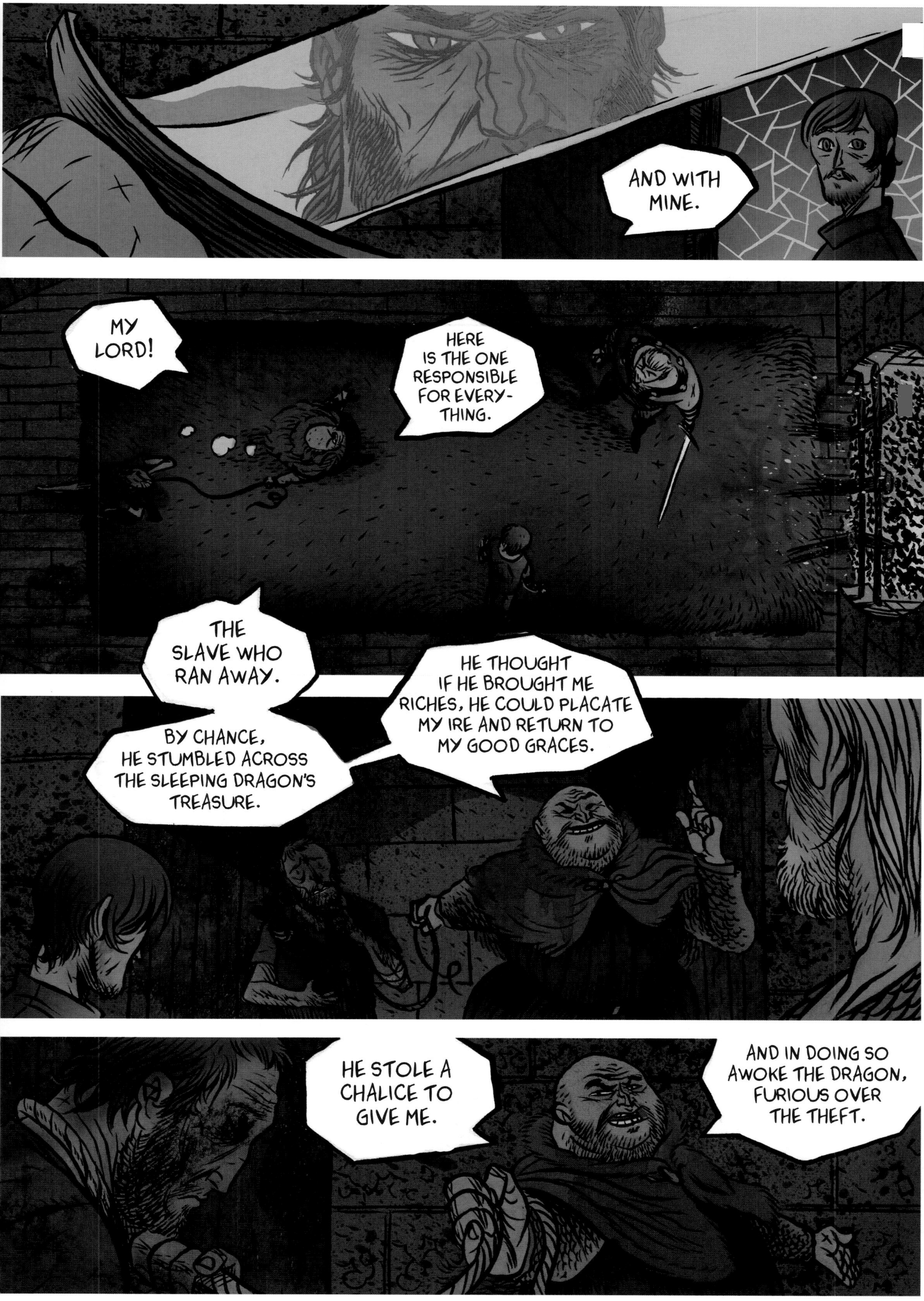
AND WITH MINE.
MY LORD!
HERE IS THE ONE RESPONSIBLE FOR EVERY-THING.
THE SLAVE WHO RAN AWAY.
BY CHANCE, HE STUMBLED ACROSS THE SLEEPING DRAGON'S TREASURE.
HE THOUGHT IF HE BROUGHT ME RICHES, HE COULD PLACATE MY IRE AND RETURN TO MY GOOD GRACES.
HE STOLE A CHALICE TO GIVE ME.
AND IN DOING SO AWOKE THE DRAGON, FURIOUS OVER THE THEFT.

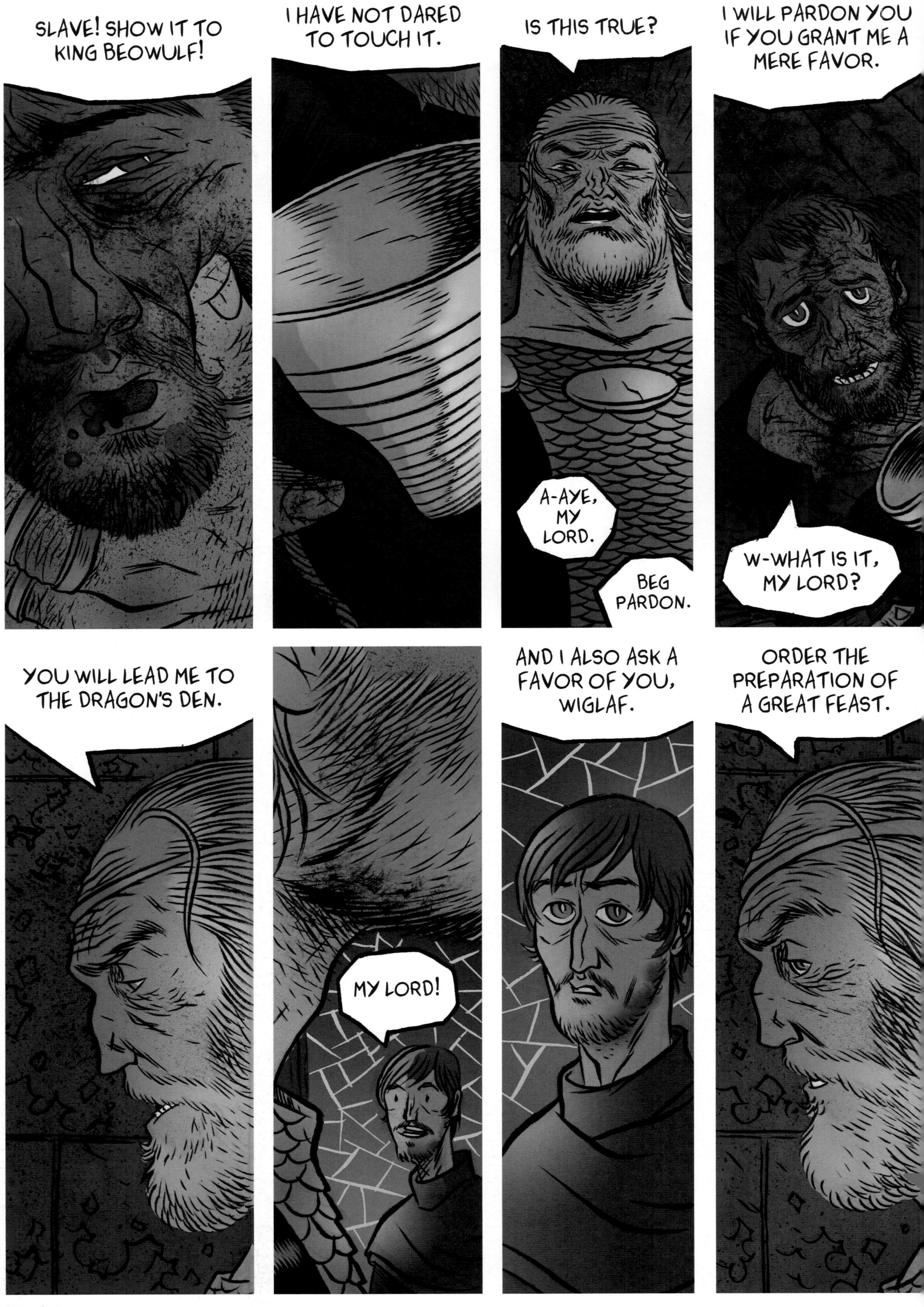
SLAVE! SHOW IT TO KING BEOWULF!
I HAVE NOT DARED TO TOUCH IT.
IS THIS TRUE?
A-AYE, MY LORD.
BEG PARDON.
I WILL PARDON YOU IF YOU GRANT ME A MERE FAVOR.
W-WHAT IS IT, MY LORD?
YOU WILL LEAD ME TO THE DRAGON'S DEN.
MY LORD!
AND I ALSO ASK A FAVOR OF YOU, WIGLAF.
ORDER THE PREPARATION OF A GREAT FEAST.

I HUNGER!

AH, THIS IS EXTRAORDINARY, WIGLAF!

IT'S BEEN YEARS SINCE I ATE SOMETHING SO DELICIOUS!

YET YOU HAVEN'T TOUCHED YOUR PLATE.

I DON'T HAVE AN APPETITE, MY LORD.

MY LORD...

...I MUST INFORM YOU.

THE DRAGON LAID WASTE TO YOUR FAMILY'S ESTATE.

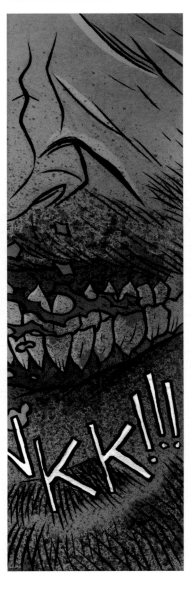

GNNNKK!!!!

ASSEMBLE MY HONOR GUARD.

FIND MY SHIELD.

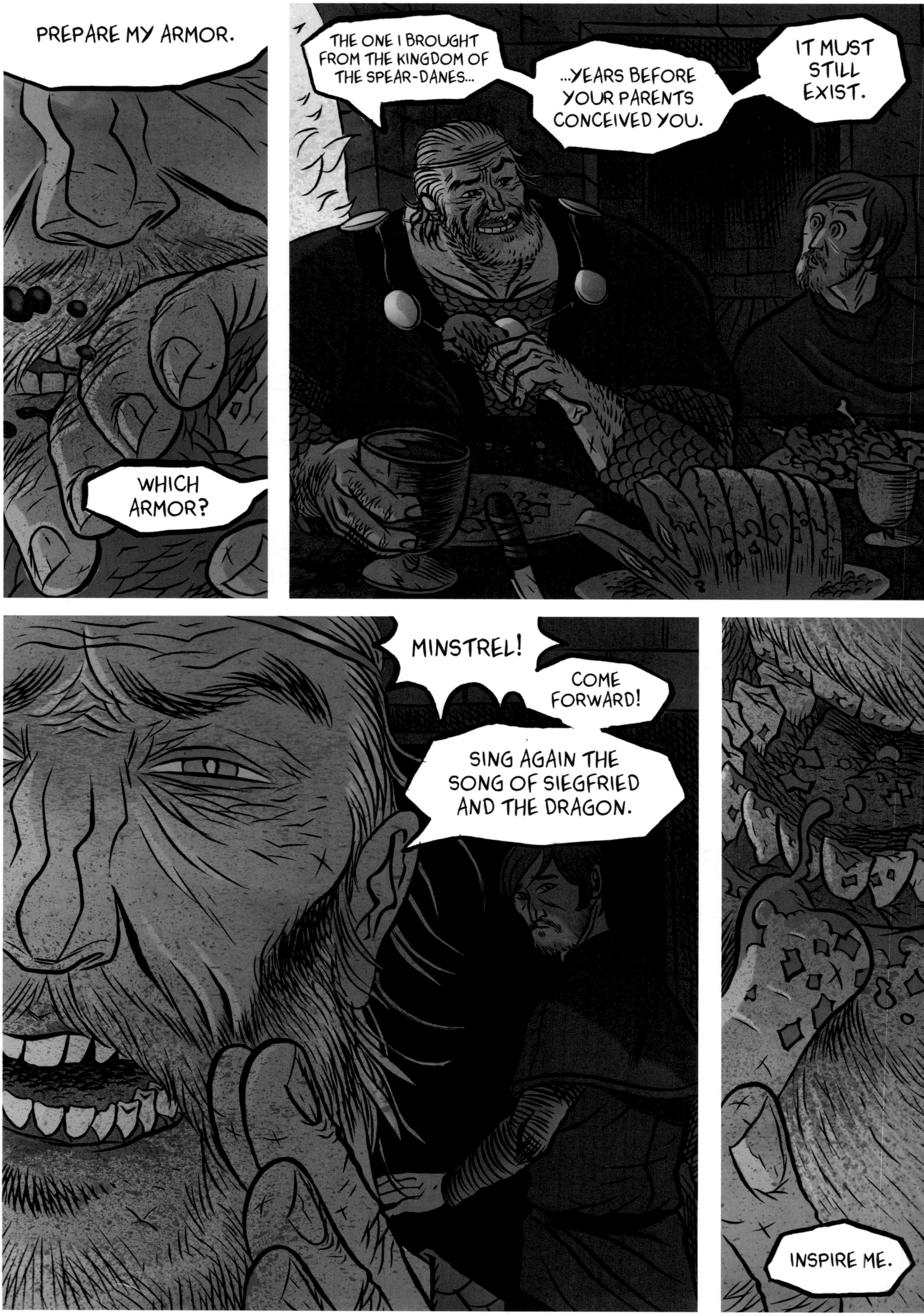
PREPARE MY ARMOR.
WHICH ARMOR?
THE ONE I BROUGHT FROM THE KINGDOM OF THE SPEAR-DANES...
...YEARS BEFORE YOUR PARENTS CONCEIVED YOU.
IT MUST STILL EXIST.
MINSTREL!
COME FORWARD!
SING AGAIN THE SONG OF SIEGFRIED AND THE DRAGON.
INSPIRE ME.

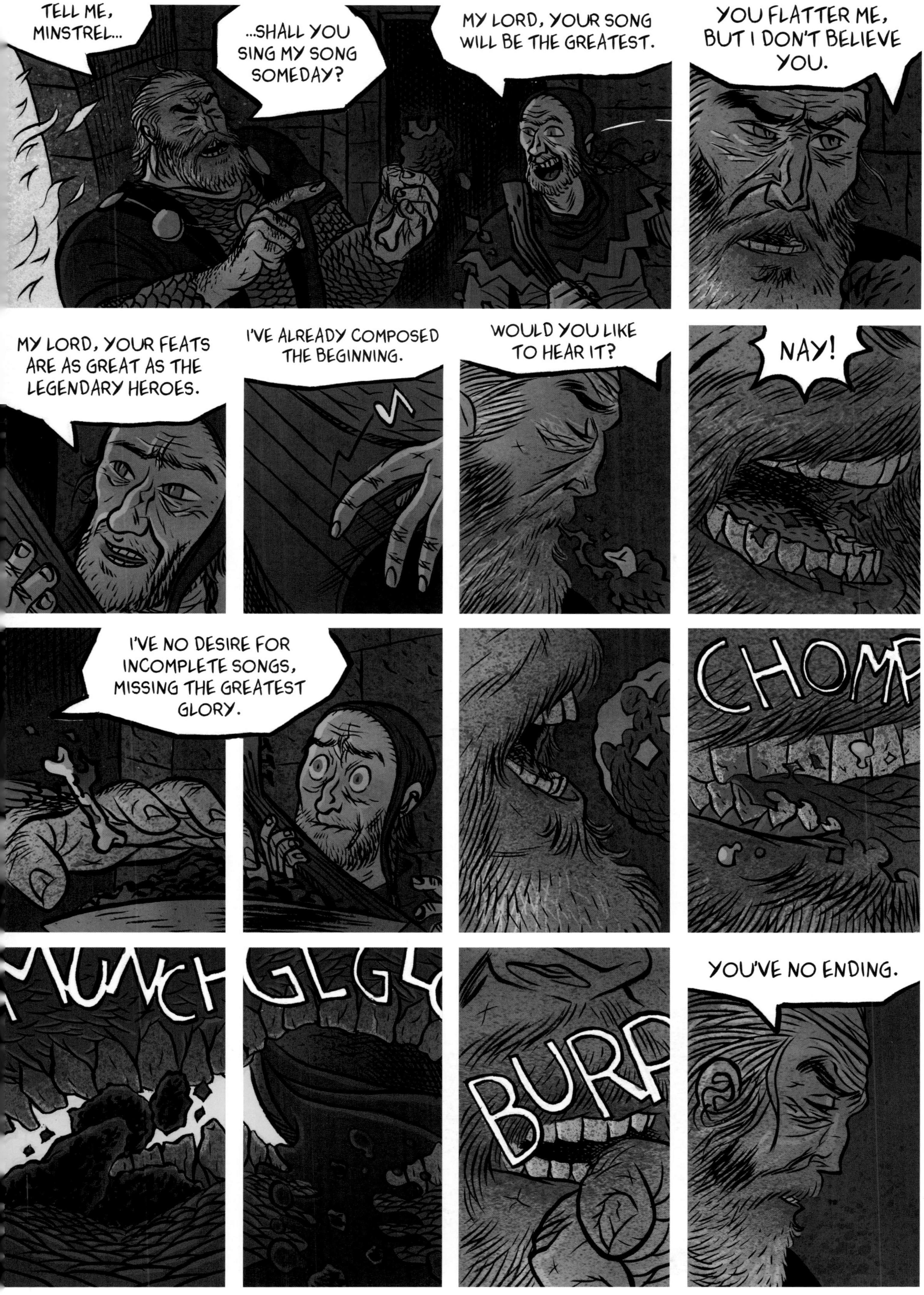
TELL ME, MINSTREL...
...SHALL YOU SING MY SONG SOMEDAY?
MY LORD, YOUR SONG WILL BE THE GREATEST.
YOU FLATTER ME, BUT I DON'T BELIEVE YOU.
MY LORD, YOUR FEATS ARE AS GREAT AS THE LEGENDARY HEROES.
I'VE ALREADY COMPOSED THE BEGINNING.
WOULD YOU LIKE TO HEAR IT?
NAY!
I'VE NO DESIRE FOR INCOMPLETE SONGS, MISSING THE GREATEST GLORY.
CHOMP
MUNCH
GLGLG
BURP
YOU'VE NO ENDING.

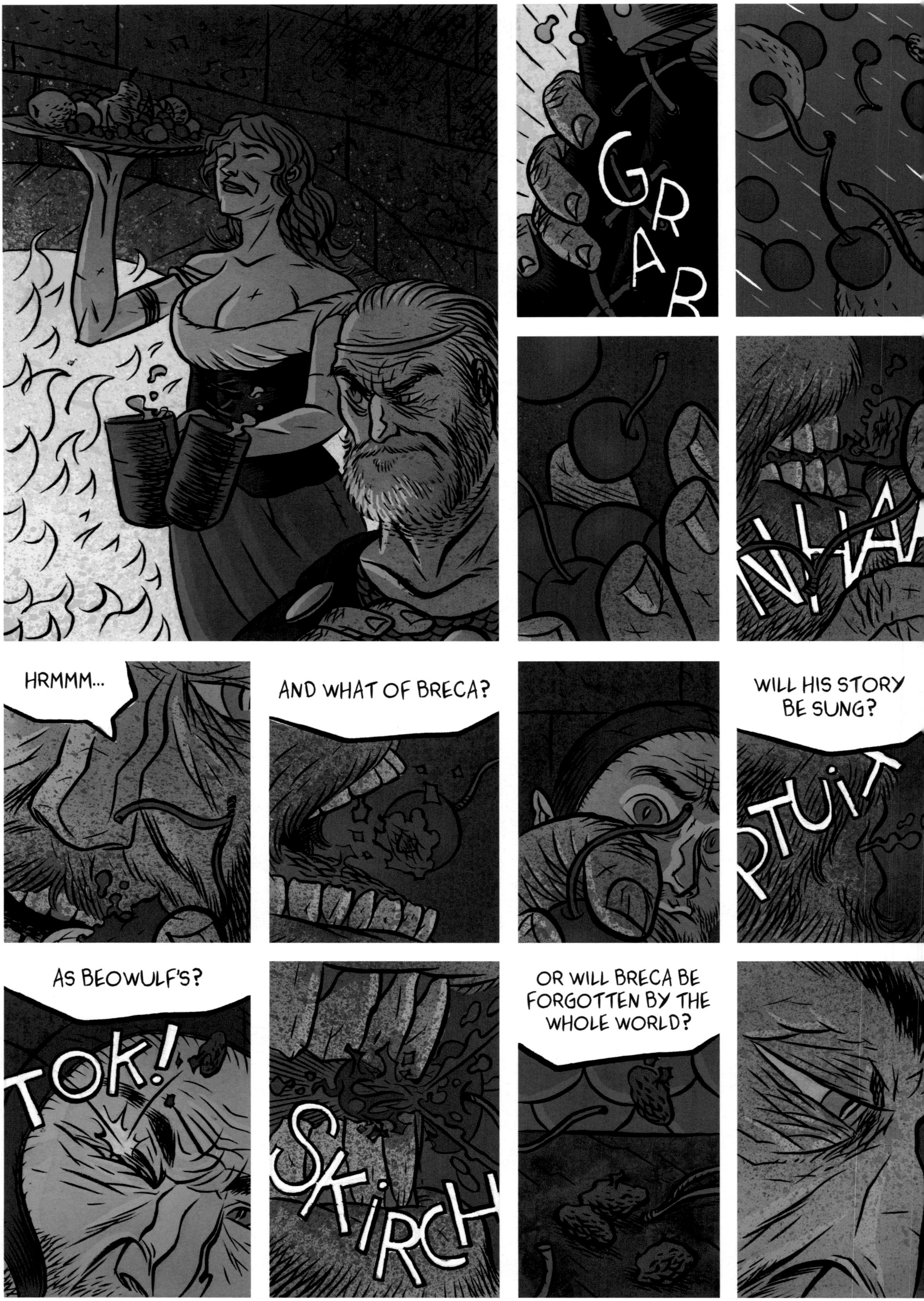
GRAR
NHAA
HRMMM...
AND WHAT OF BRECA?
WILL HIS STORY BE SUNG?
PTUIT
AS BEOWULF'S?
TOK!
SKIRCH
OR WILL BRECA BE FORGOTTEN BY THE WHOLE WORLD?

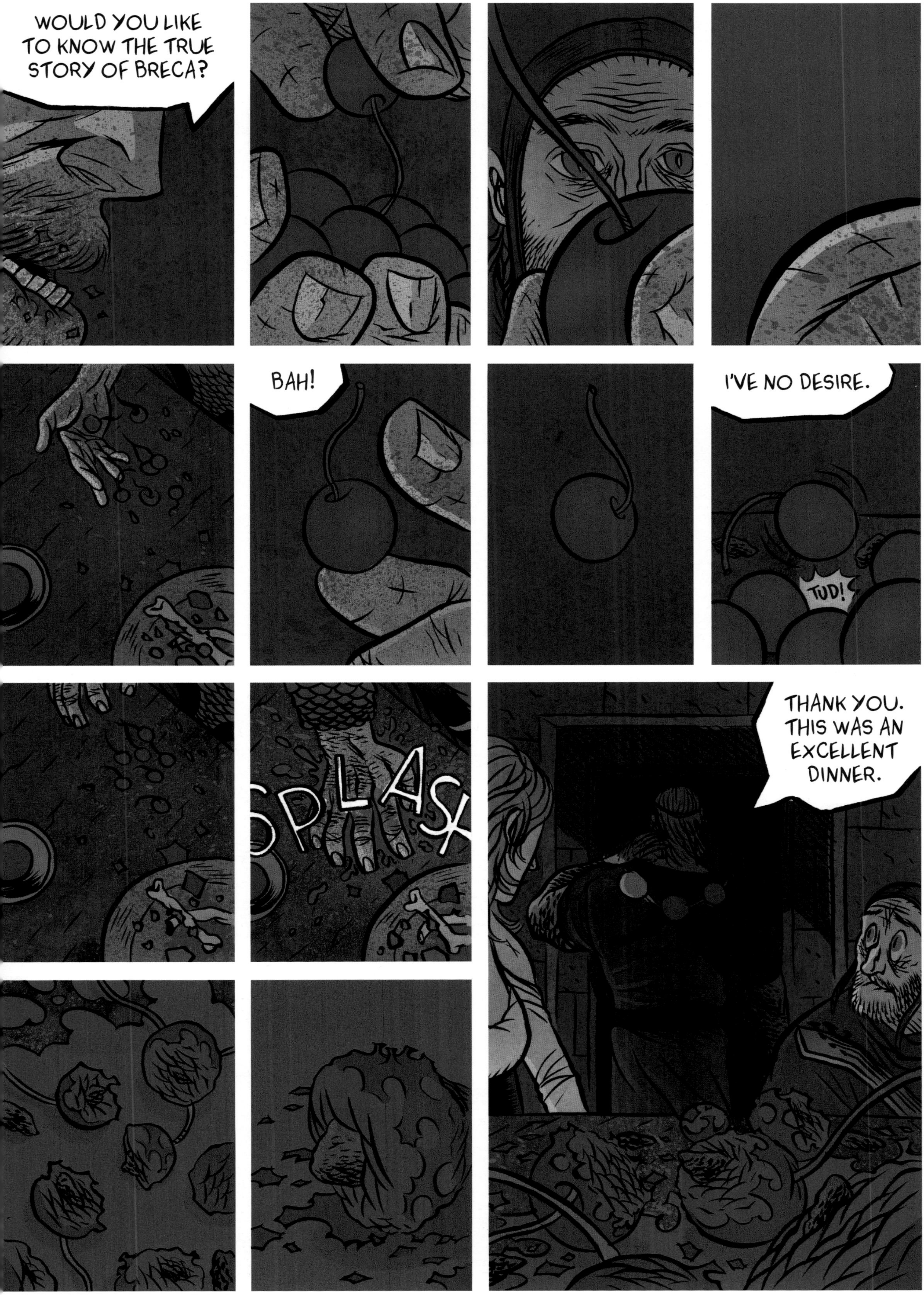
WOULD YOU LIKE TO KNOW THE TRUE STORY OF BRECA?
BAH!
I'VE NO DESIRE.
TUD!
SPLASH
THANK YOU. THIS WAS AN EXCELLENT DINNER.

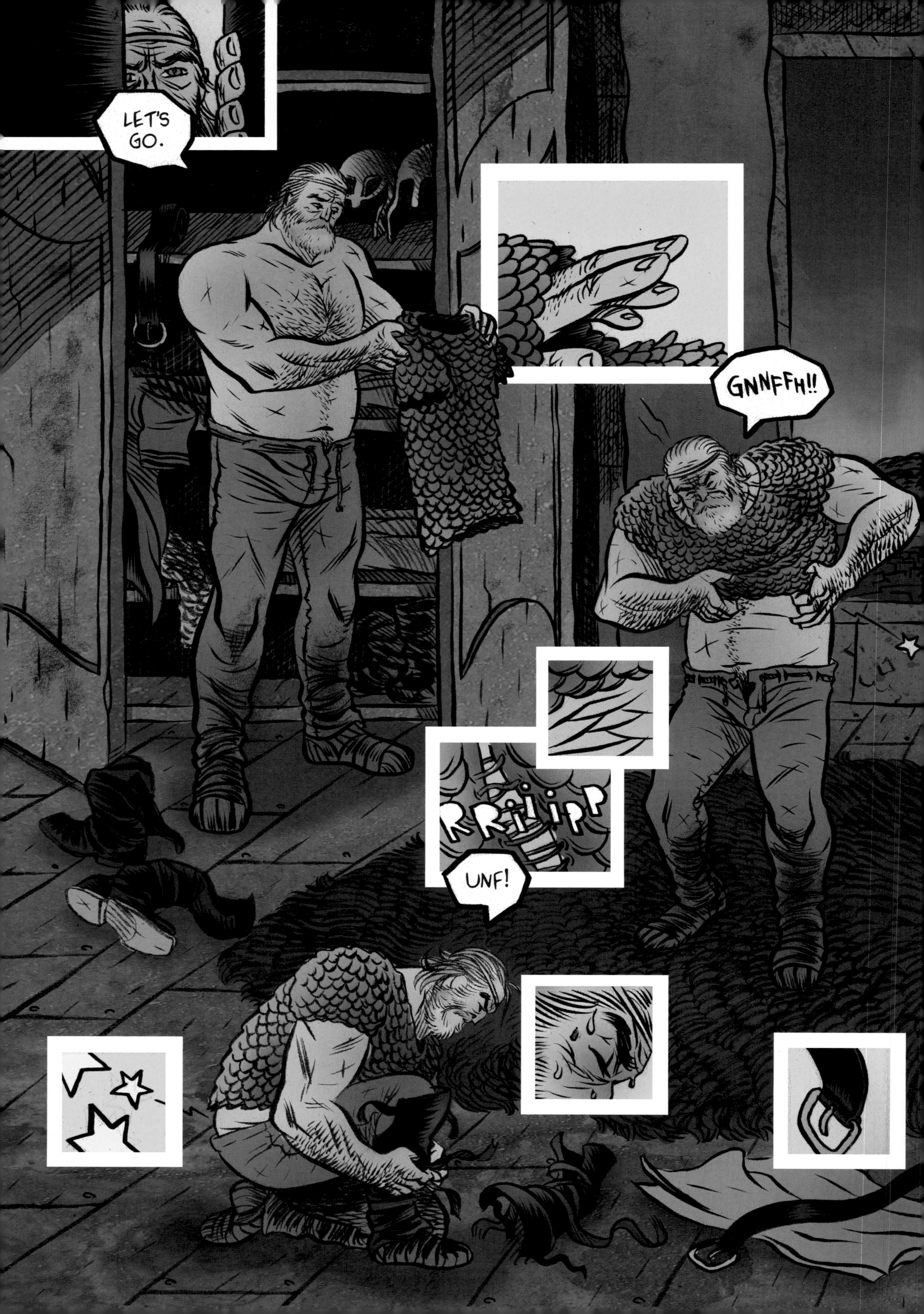
LET'S GO.
GNNFFH!!
RRRIIPP
UNF!

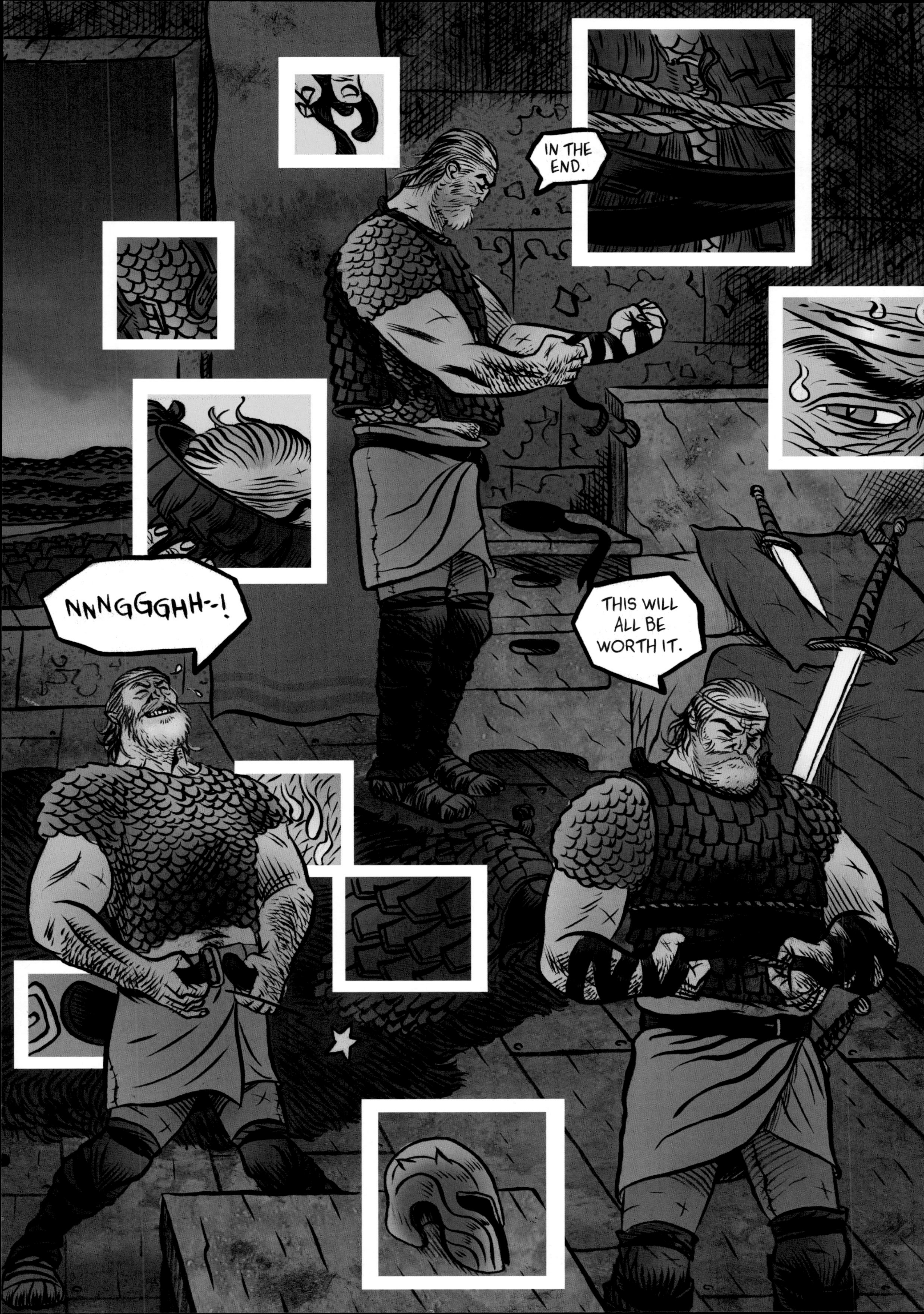
IN THE END.
NNNGGGHH--!
THIS WILL ALL BE WORTH IT.

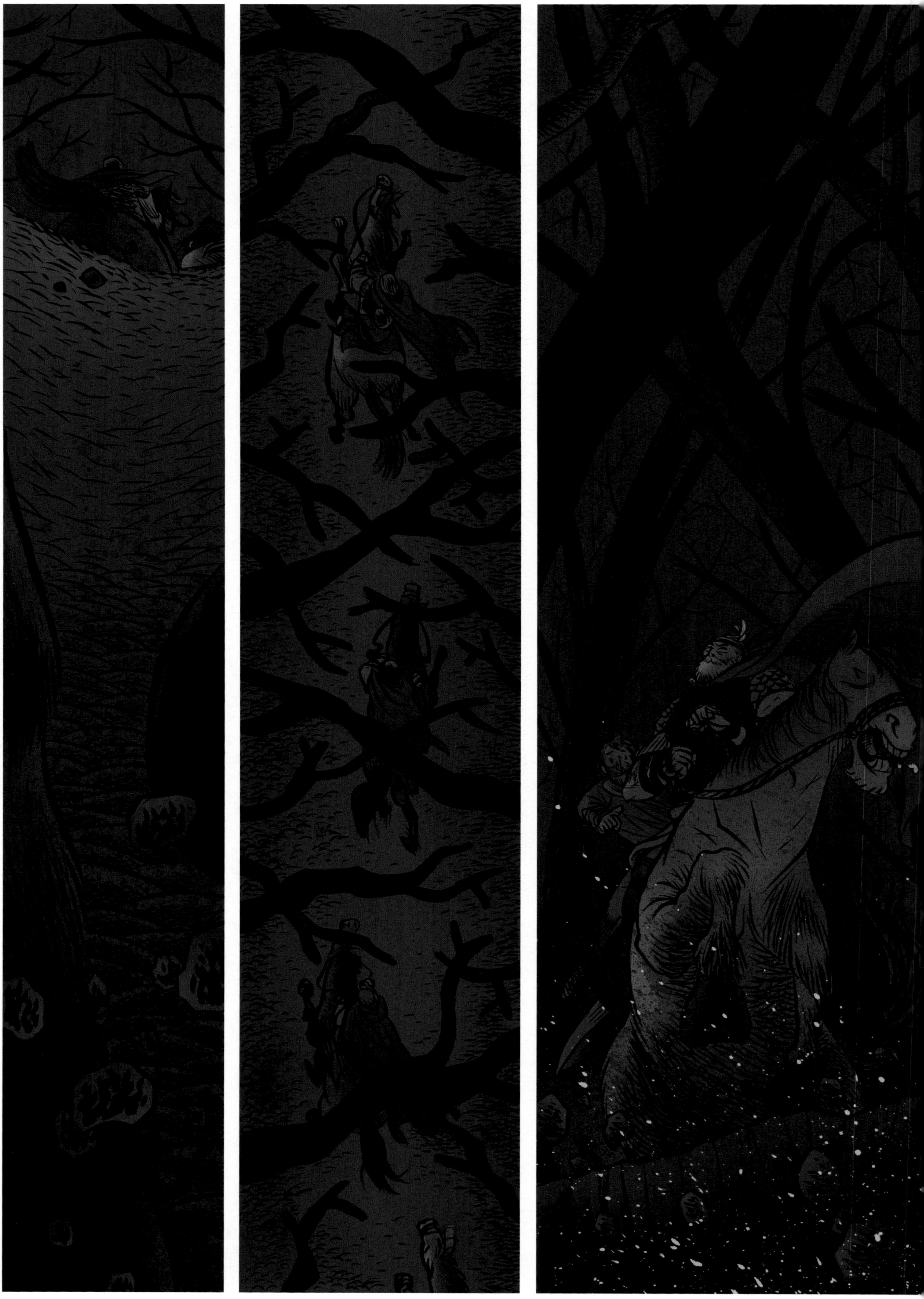

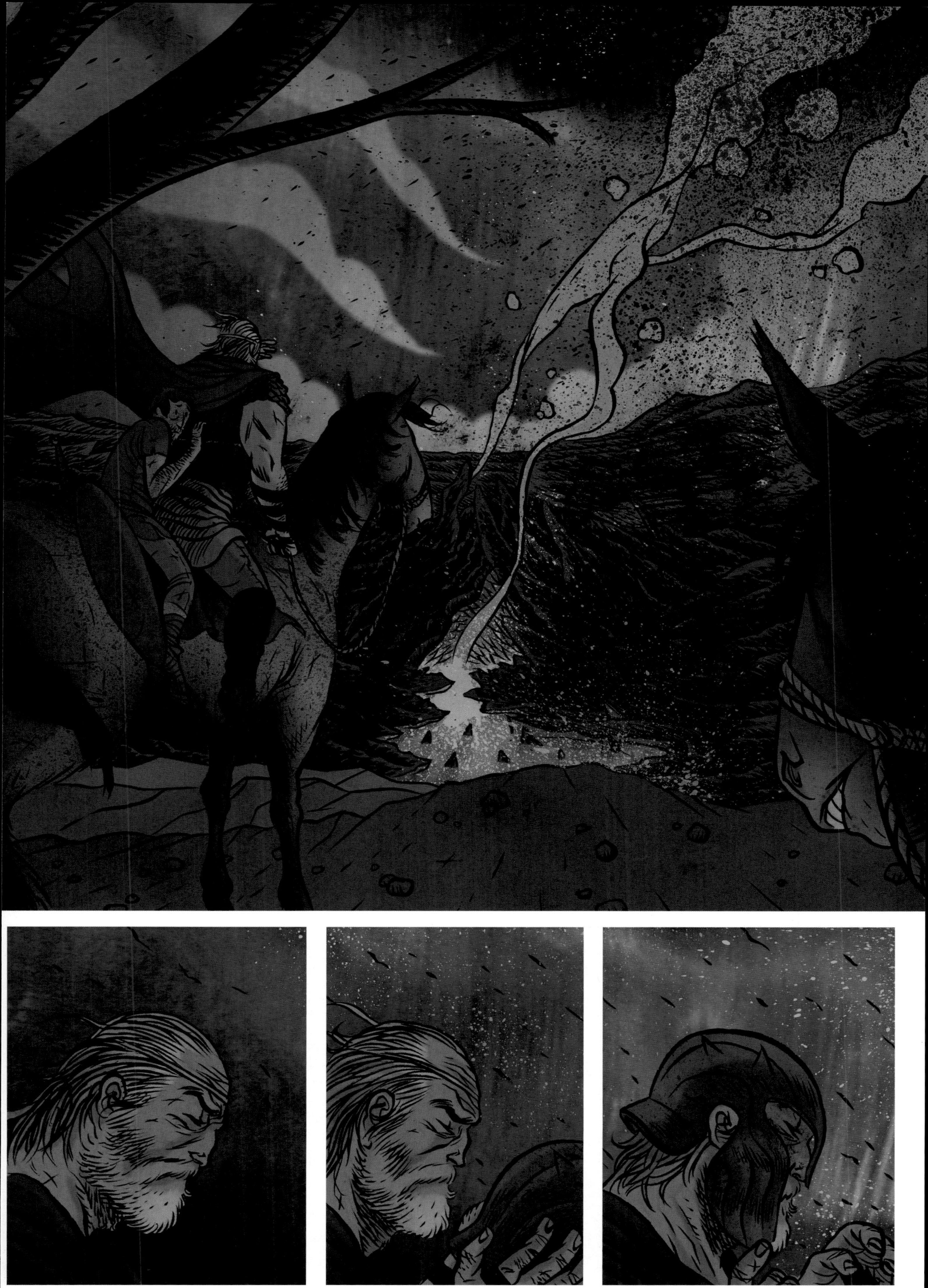

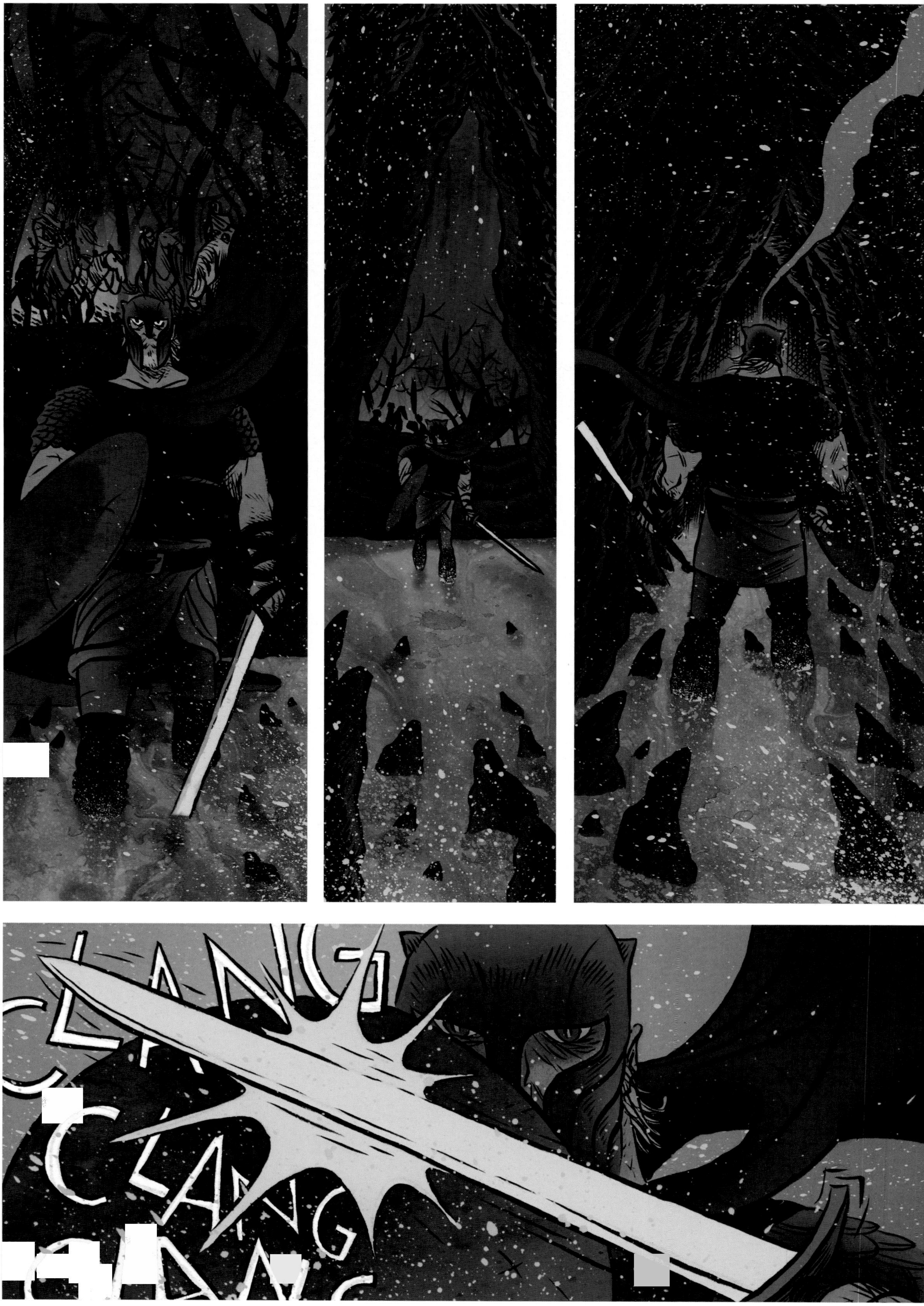
CLANG
CLANG

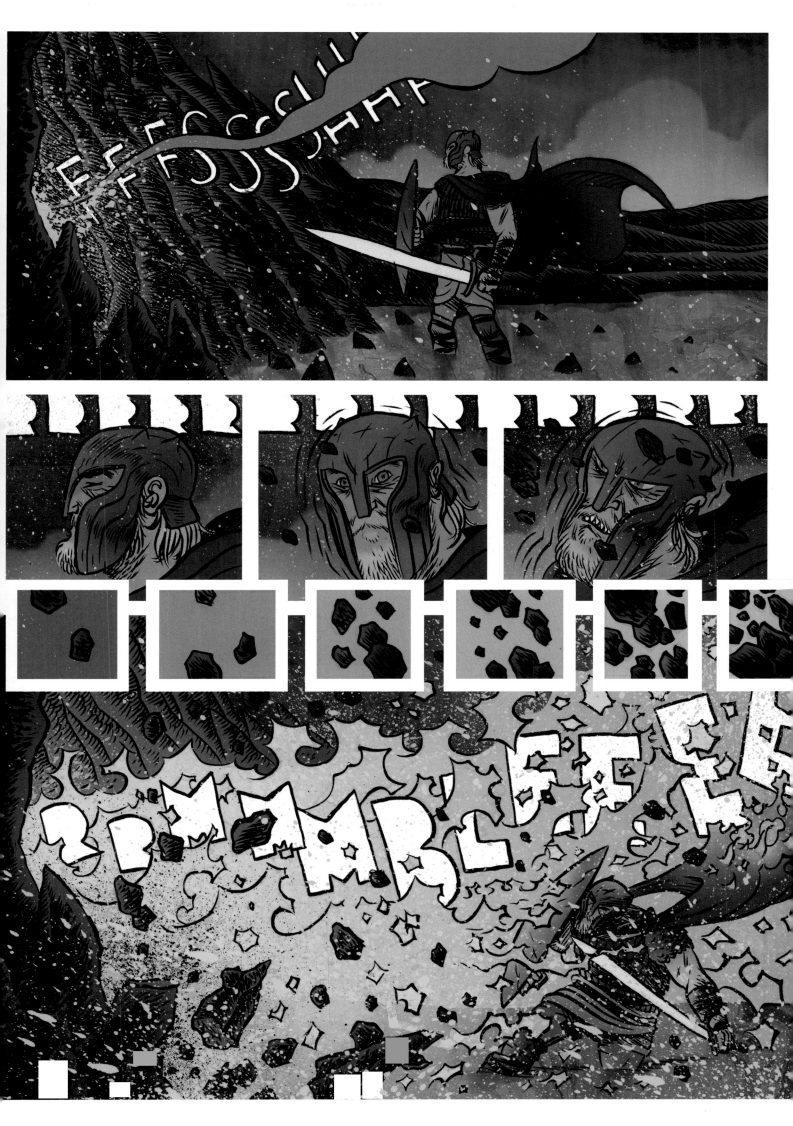

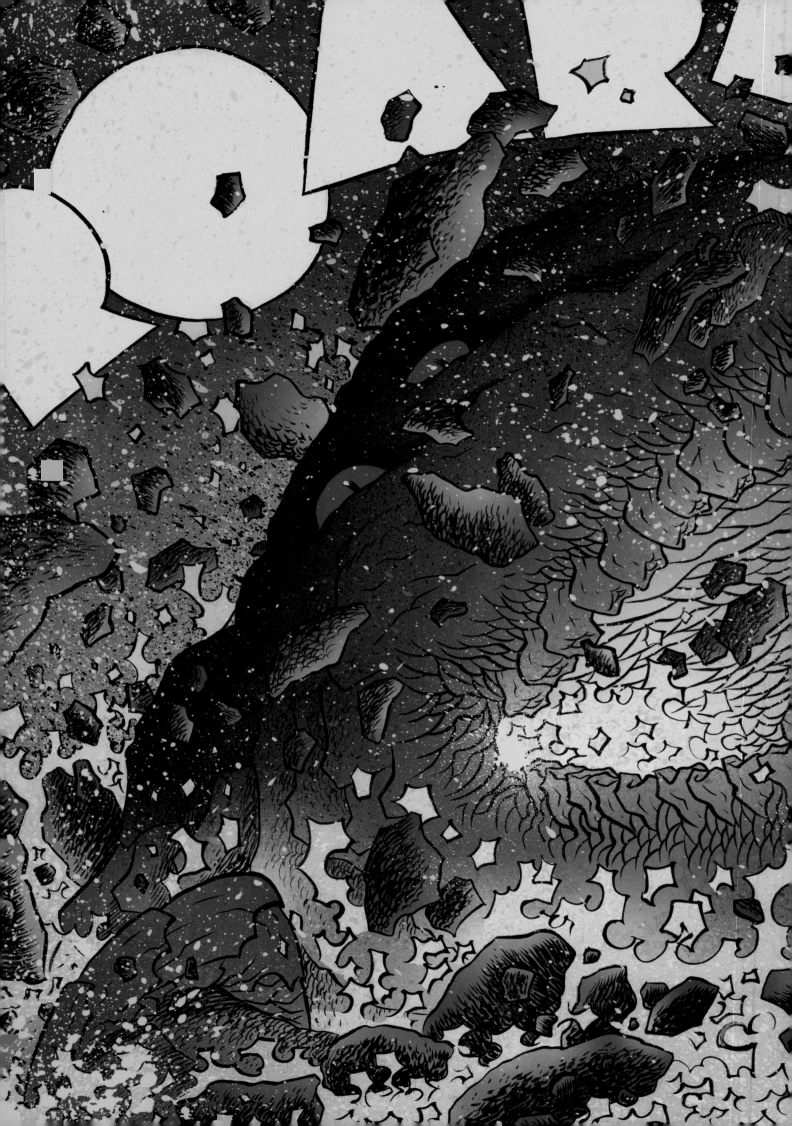

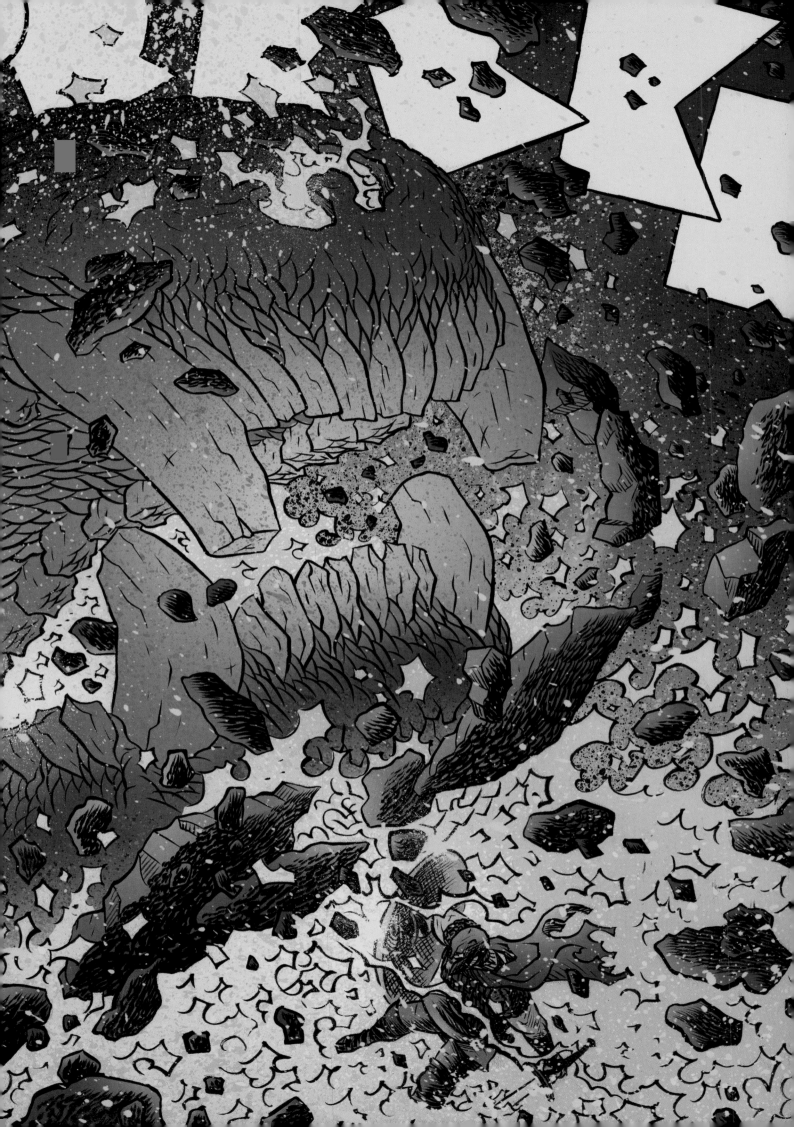

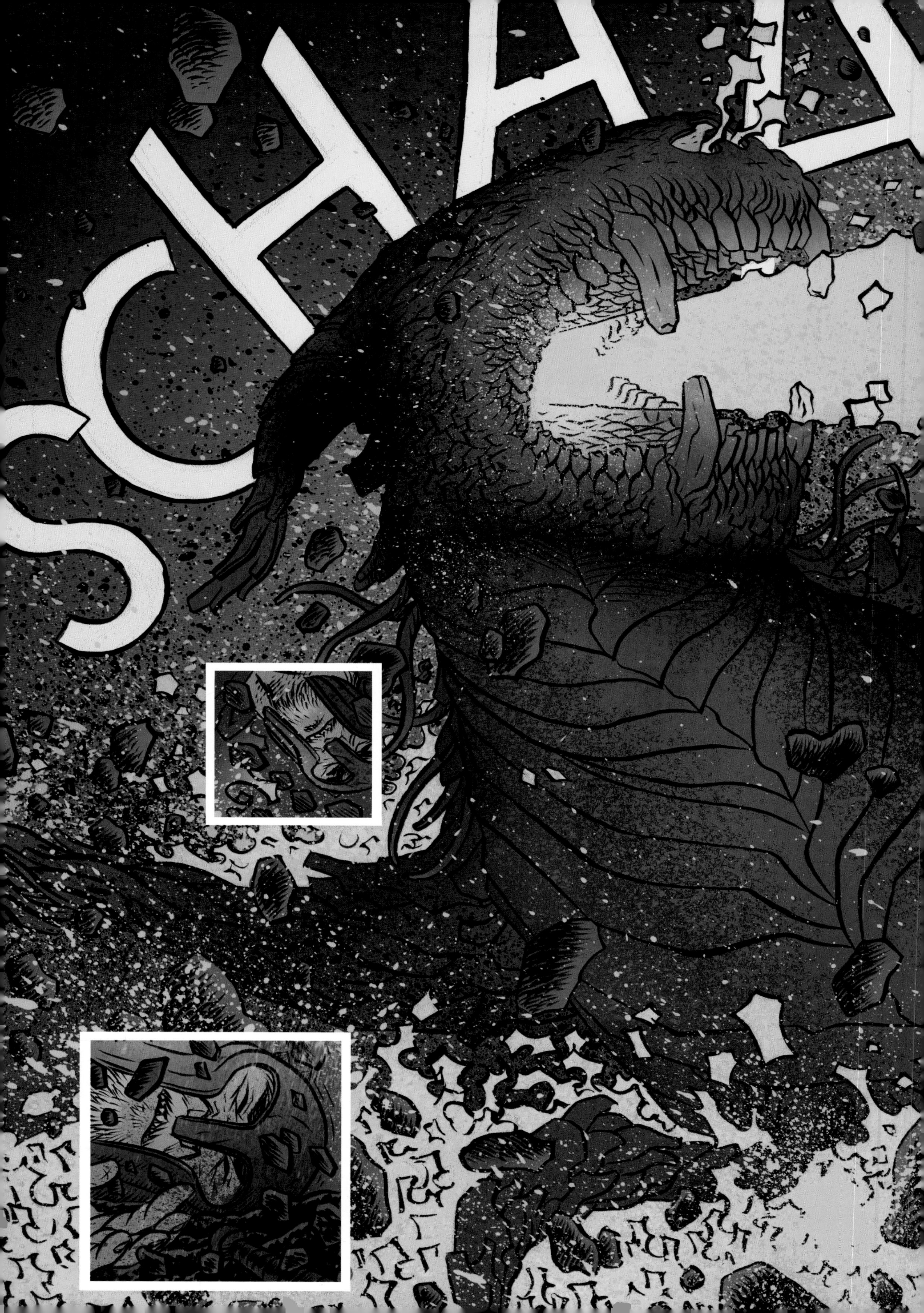
SCHA

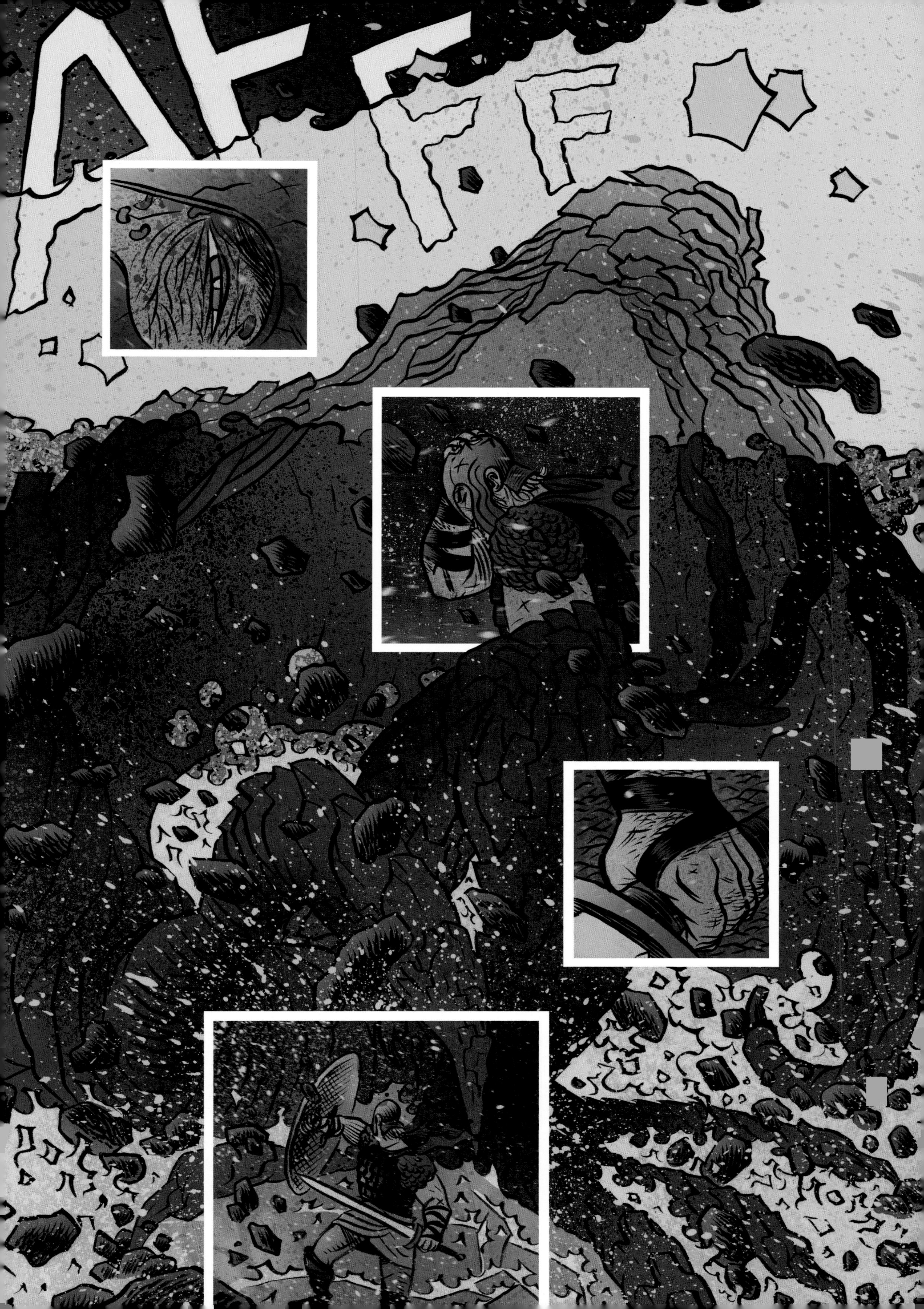
AFFF

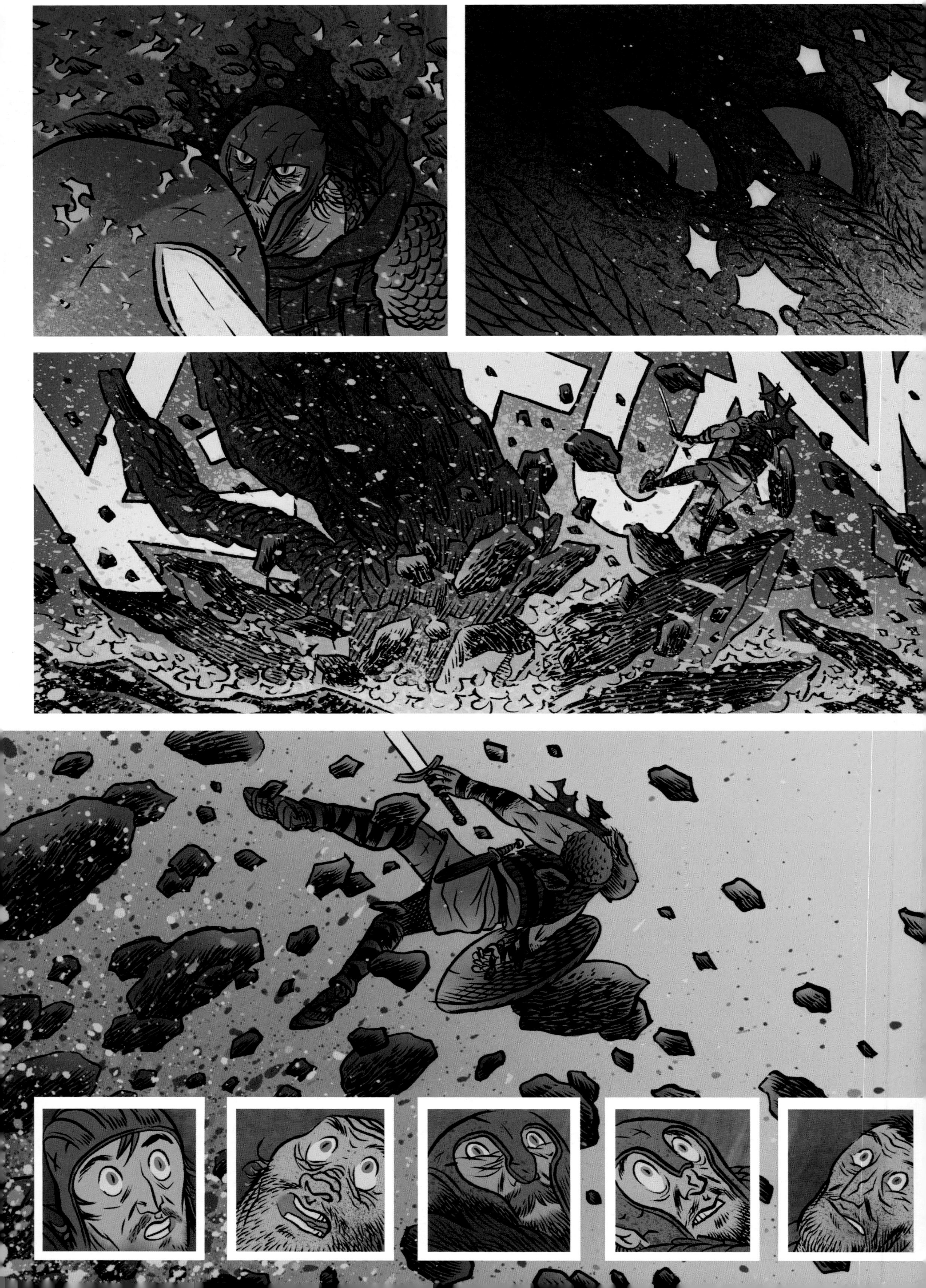

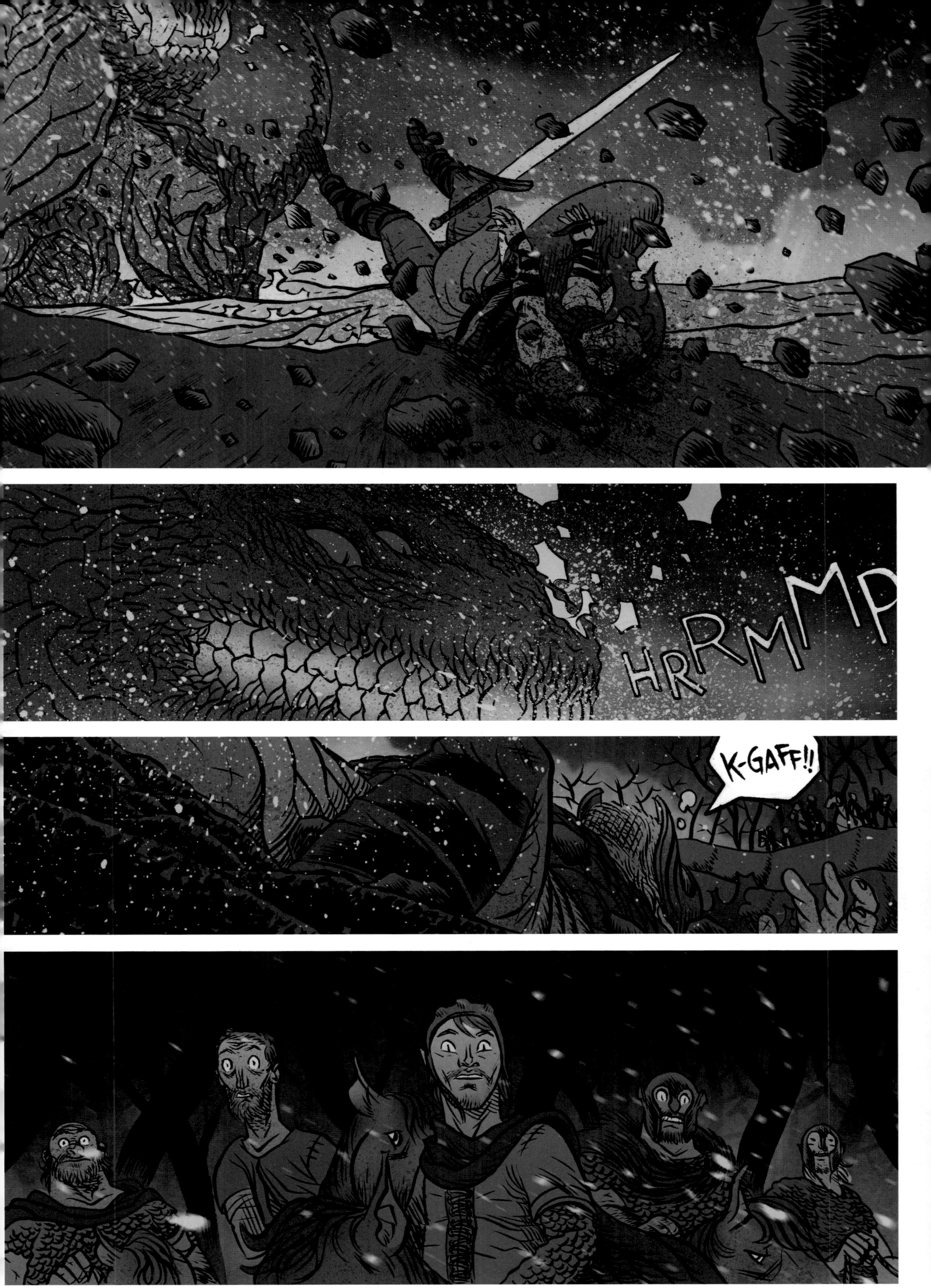
HRRMMP
K-GAFF!!

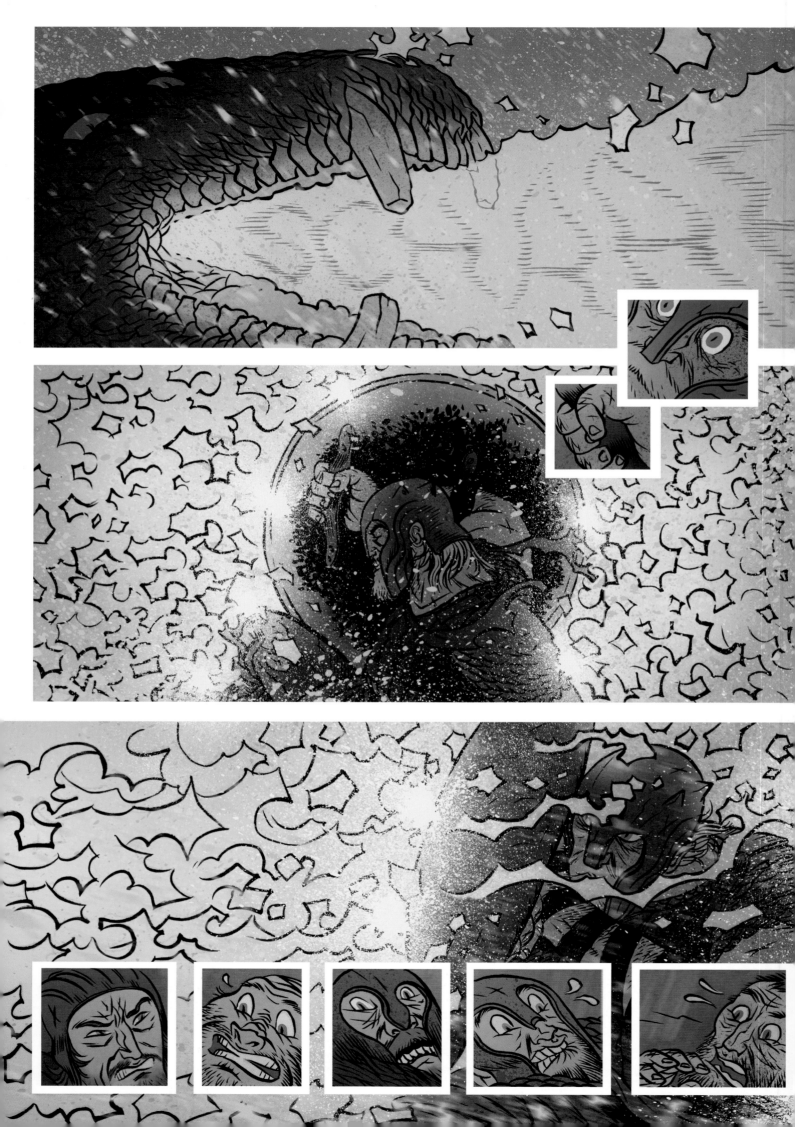

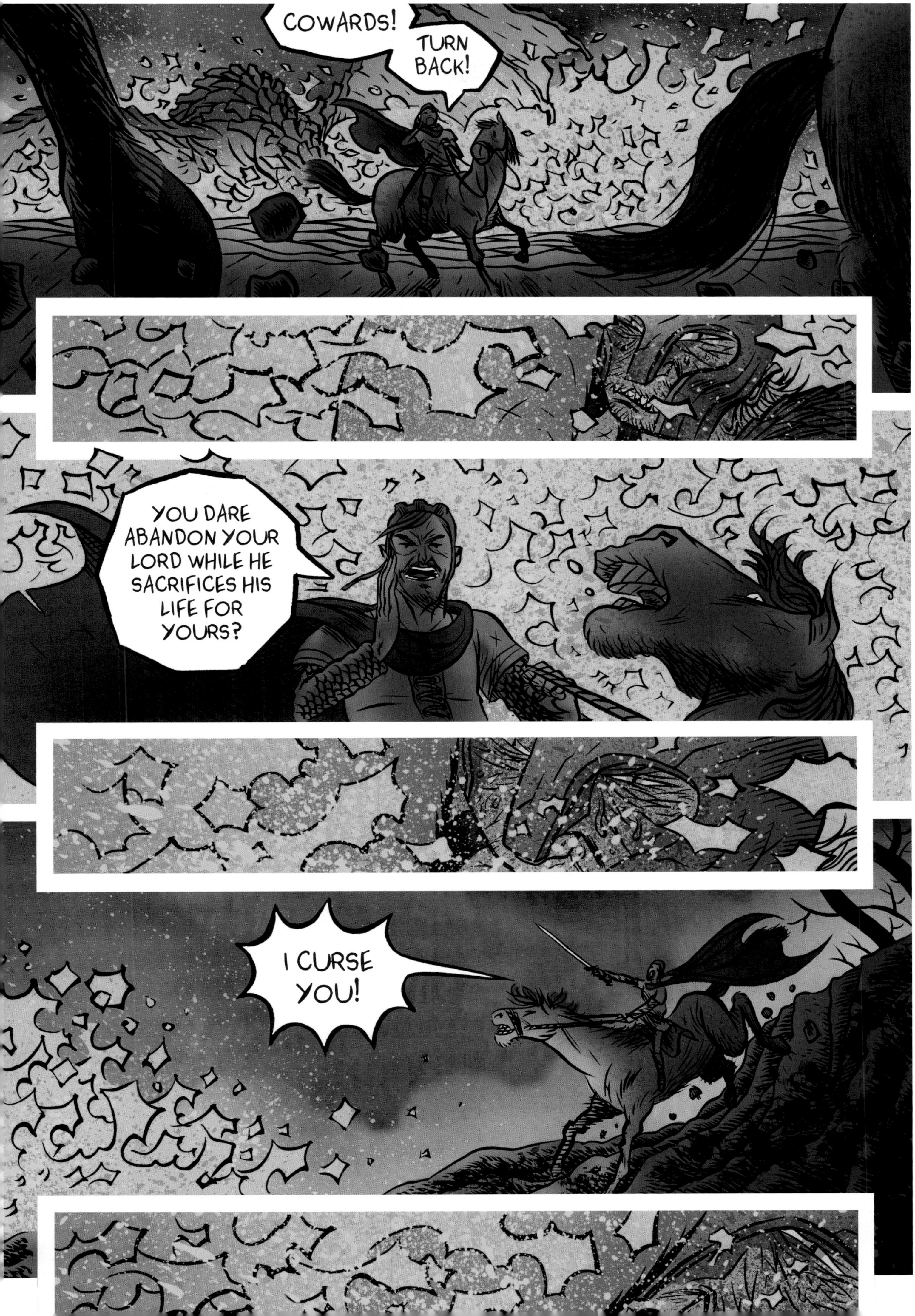
COWARDS!
TURN BACK!
YOU DARE ABANDON YOUR LORD WHILE HE SACRIFICES HIS LIFE FOR YOURS?
I CURSE YOU!

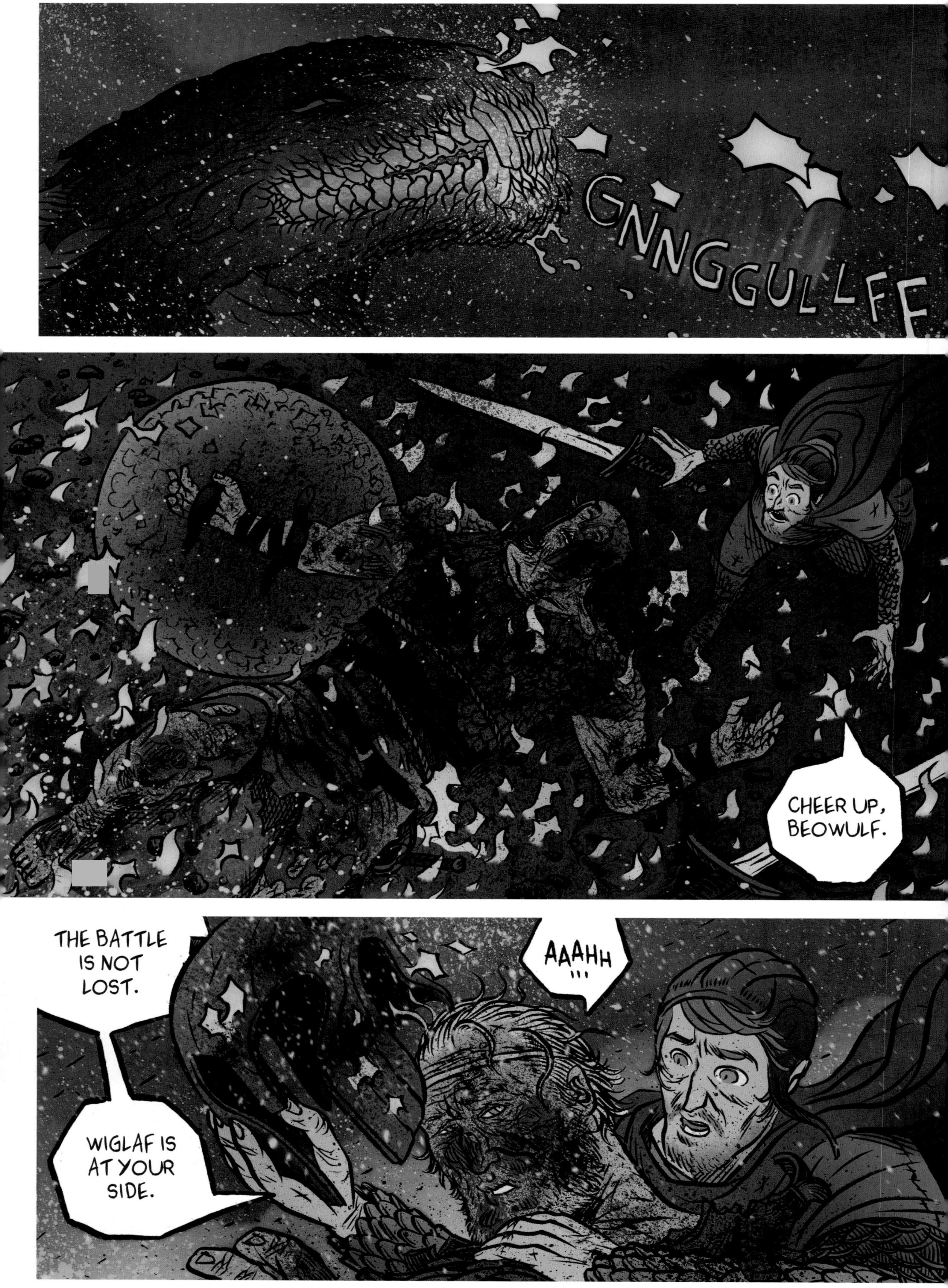
GNNGGULLFE
CHEER UP, BEOWULF.
THE BATTLE IS NOT LOST.
AAAHH !!!
WIGLAF IS AT YOUR SIDE.

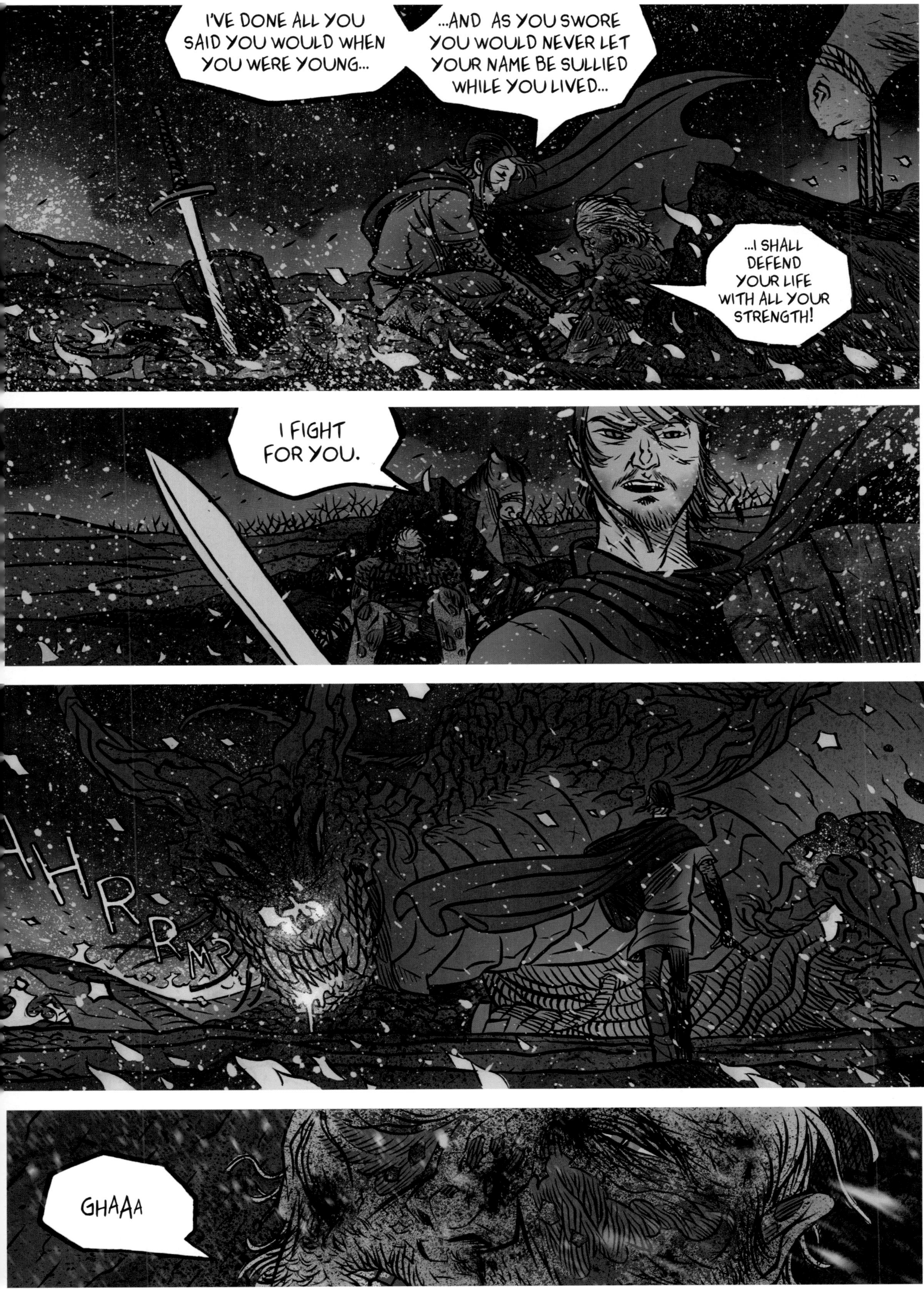
I'VE DONE ALL YOU SAID YOU WOULD WHEN YOU WERE YOUNG...
...AND AS YOU SWORE YOU WOULD NEVER LET YOUR NAME BE SULLIED WHILE YOU LIVED...
...I SHALL DEFEND YOUR LIFE WITH ALL YOUR STRENGTH!
I FIGHT FOR YOU.
HRRRM
GHAAA

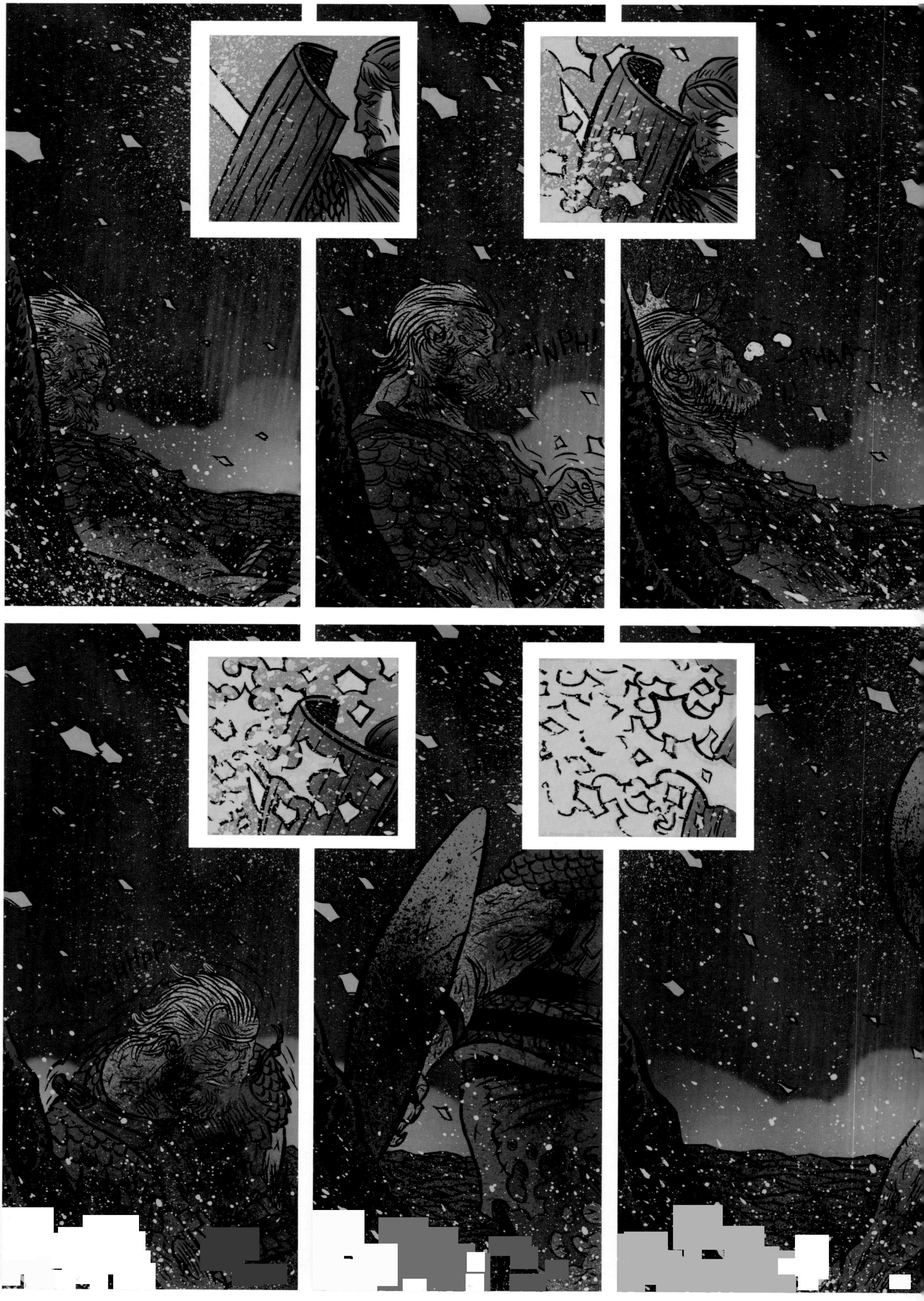
NPH
PHAA
HHPP

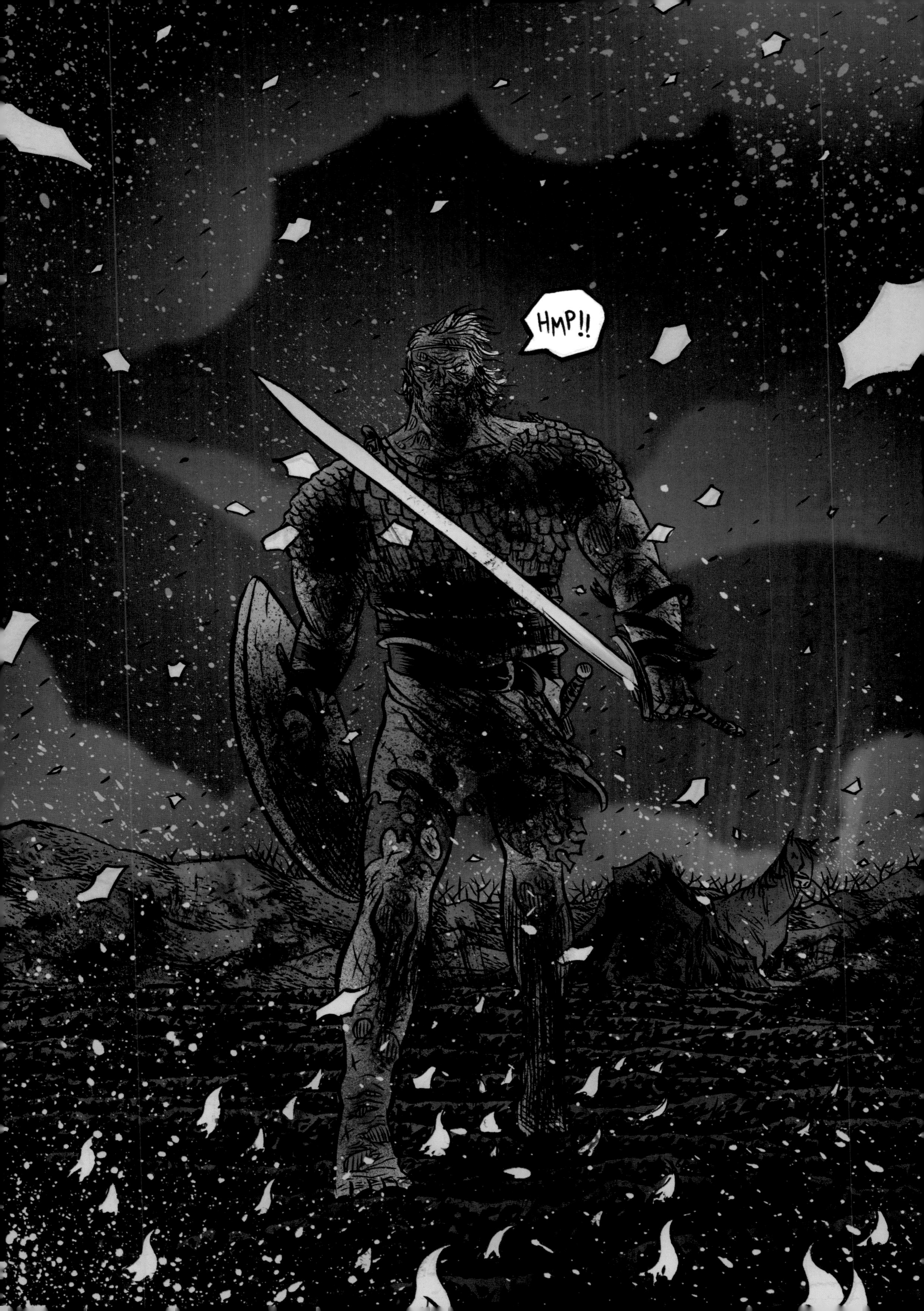
HMP!!

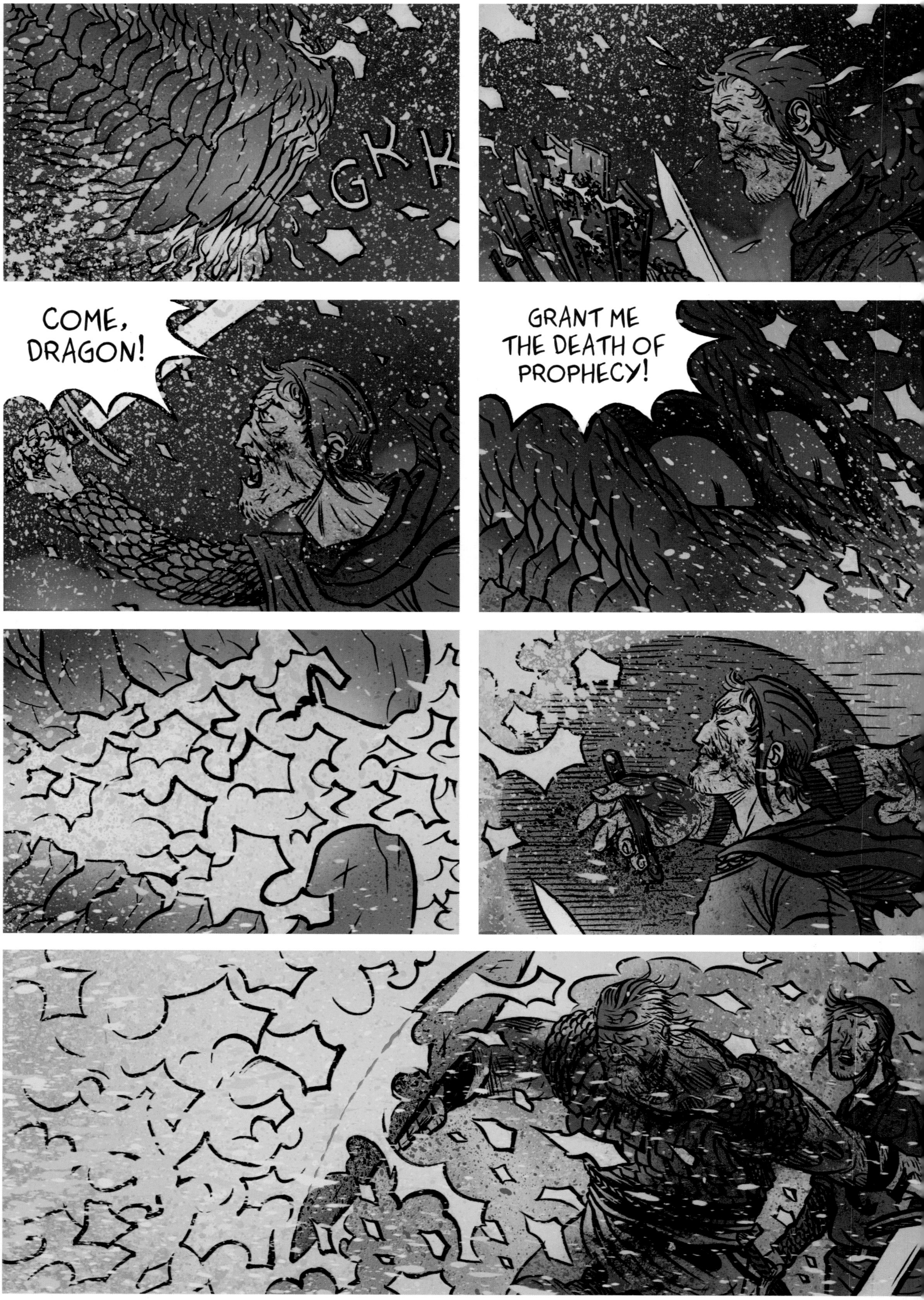
GKK
COME, DRAGON!
GRANT ME THE DEATH OF PROPHECY!

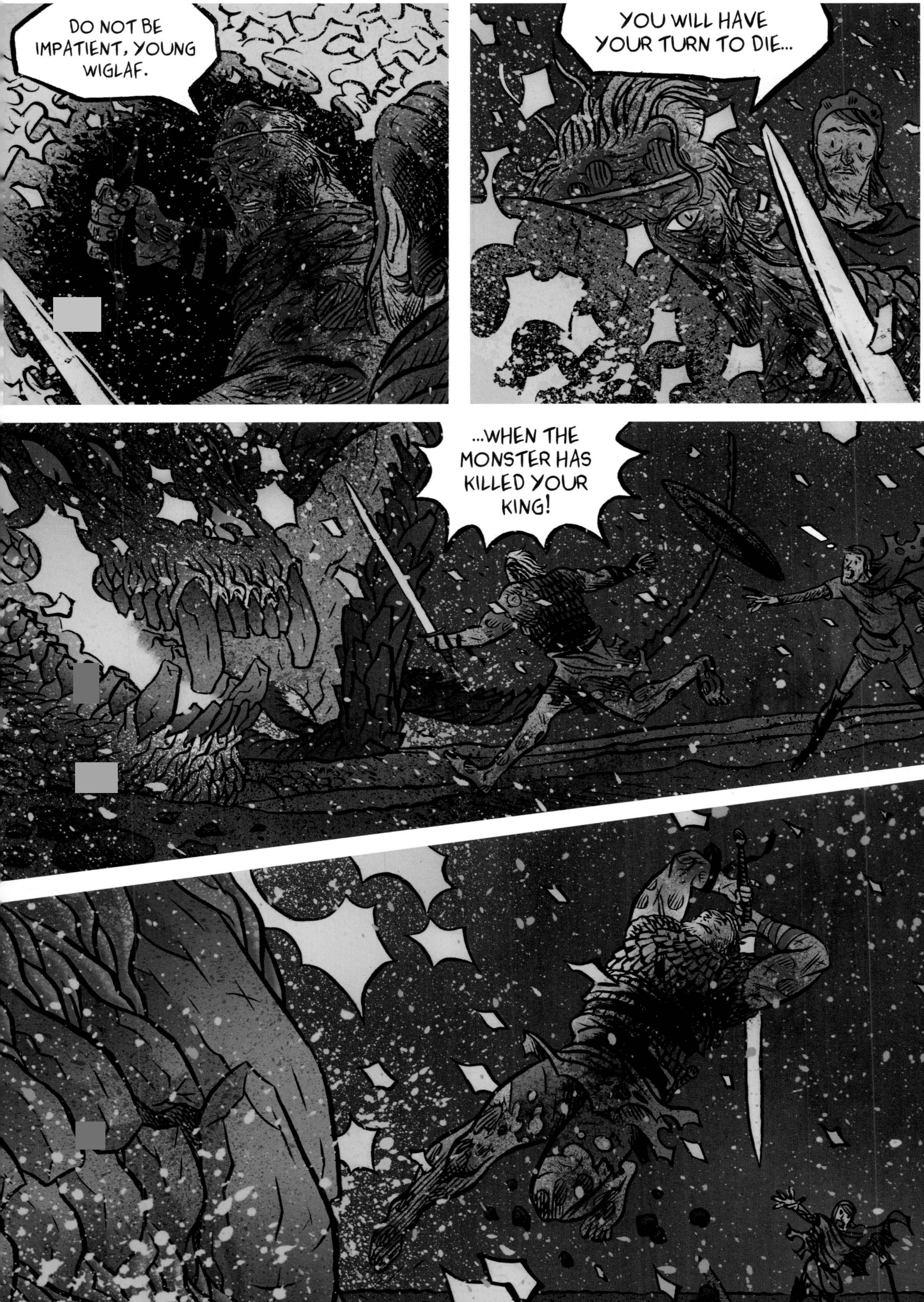
DO NOT BE IMPATIENT, YOUNG WIGLAF.
YOU WILL HAVE YOUR TURN TO DIE...
...WHEN THE MONSTER HAS KILLED YOUR KING!

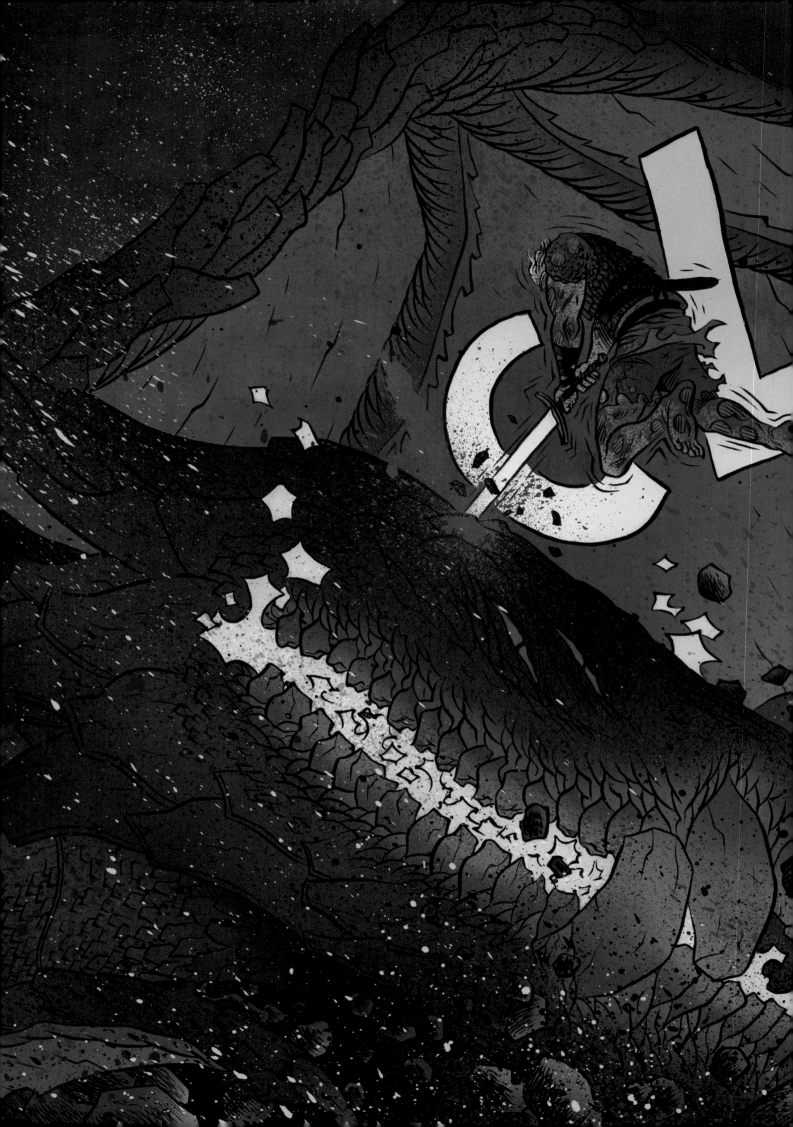

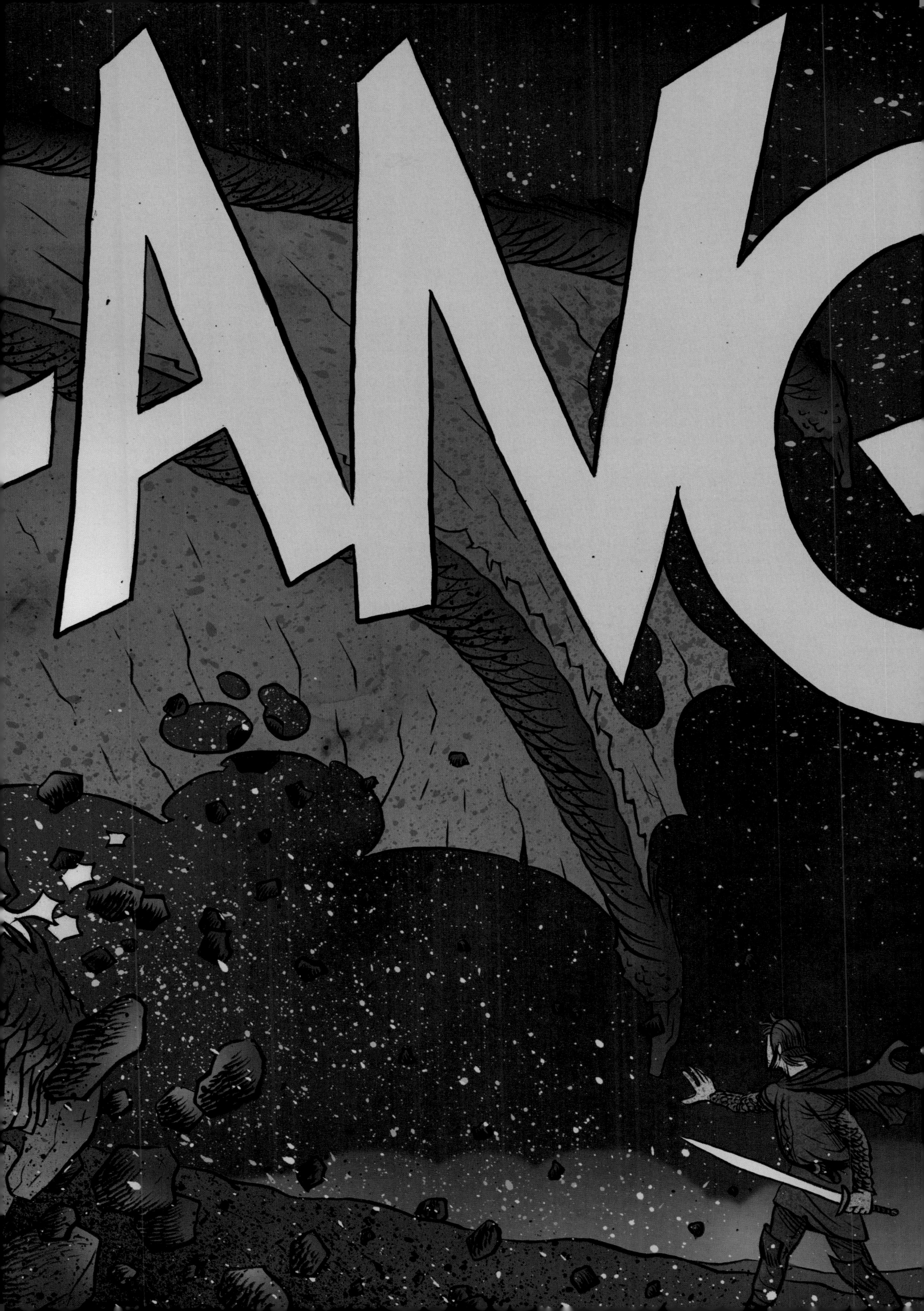
ANG

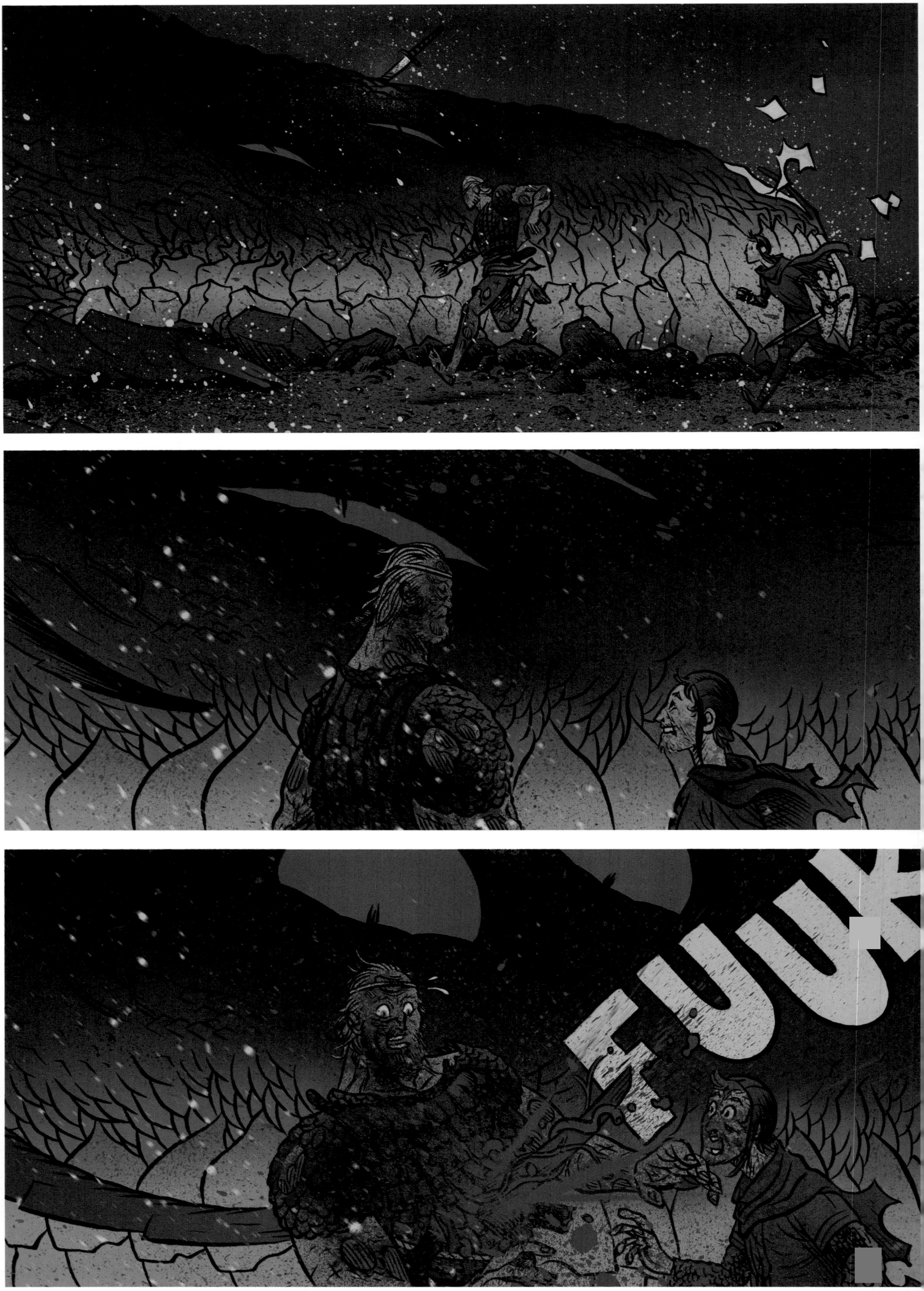
FUU

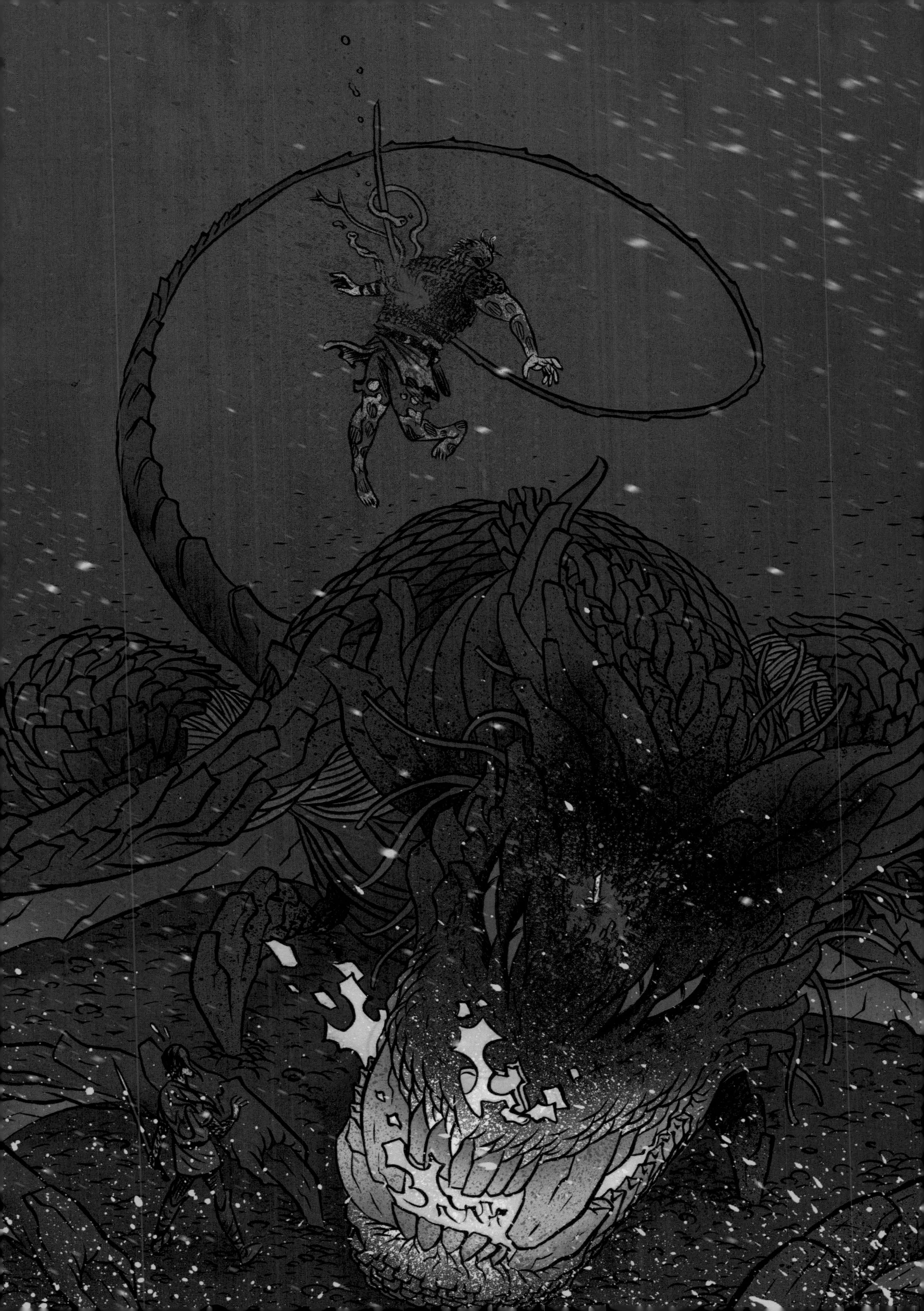

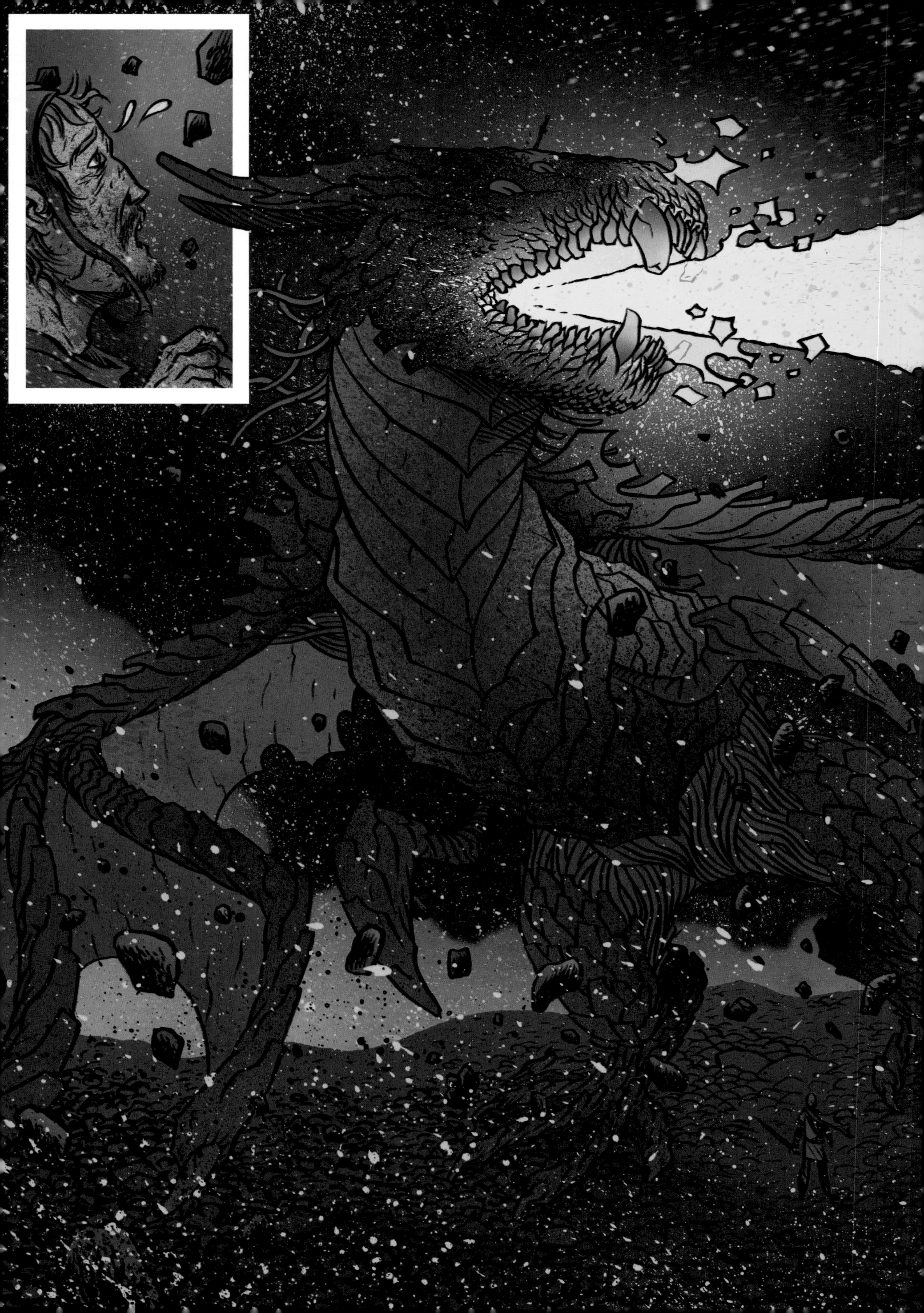

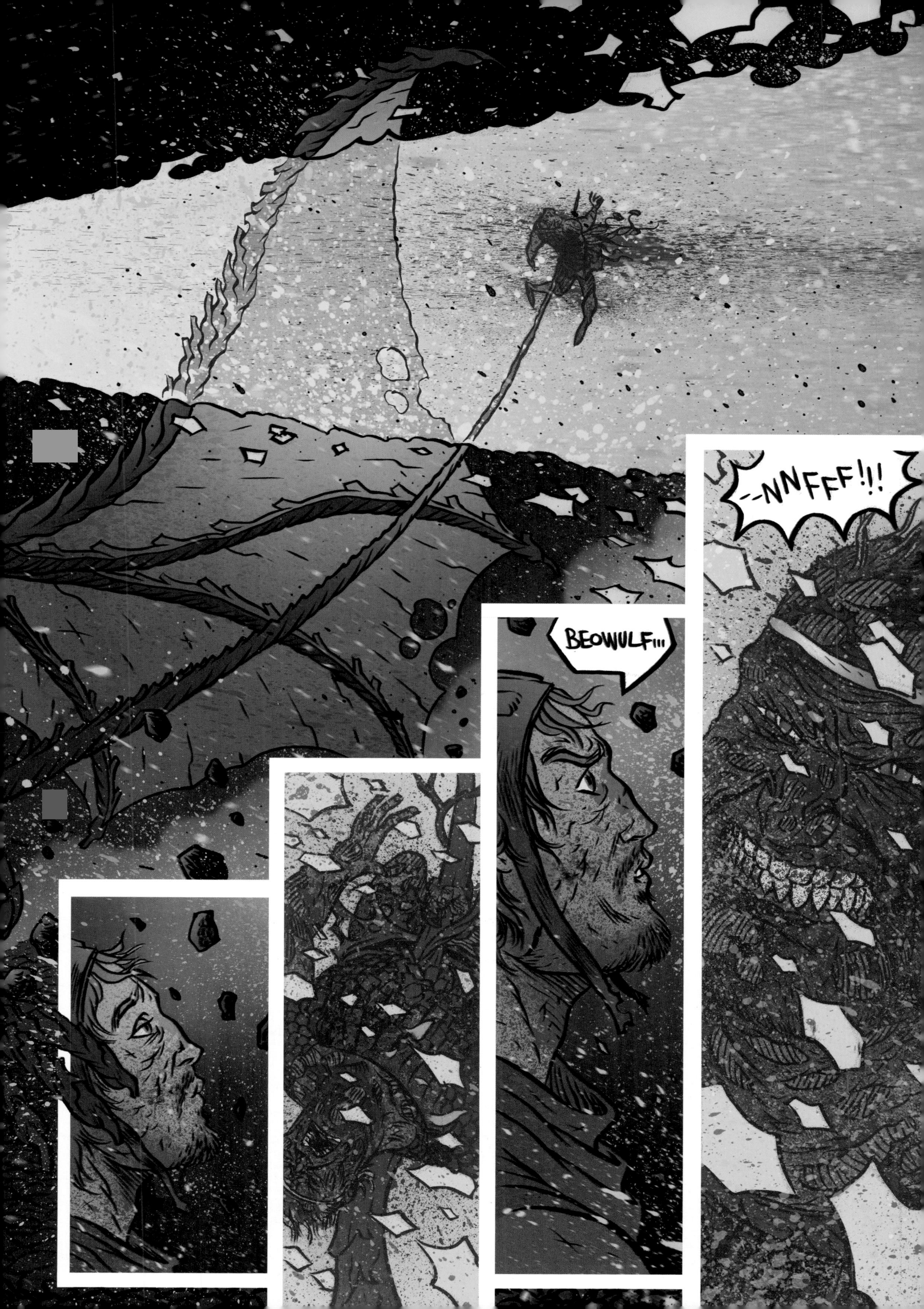
BEOWULF!!!
--NNFFF!!!

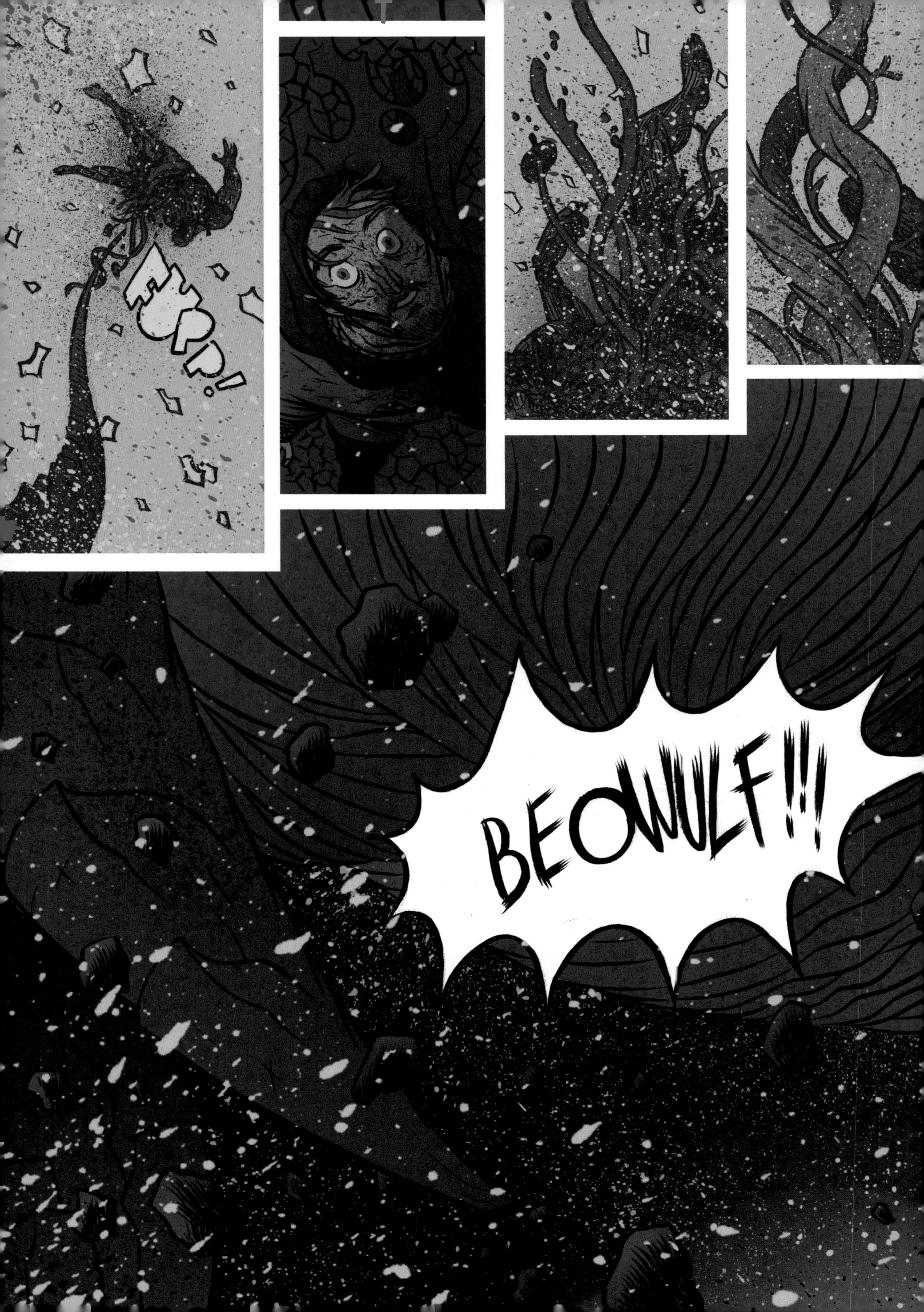
FURP!
BEOWULF!!!

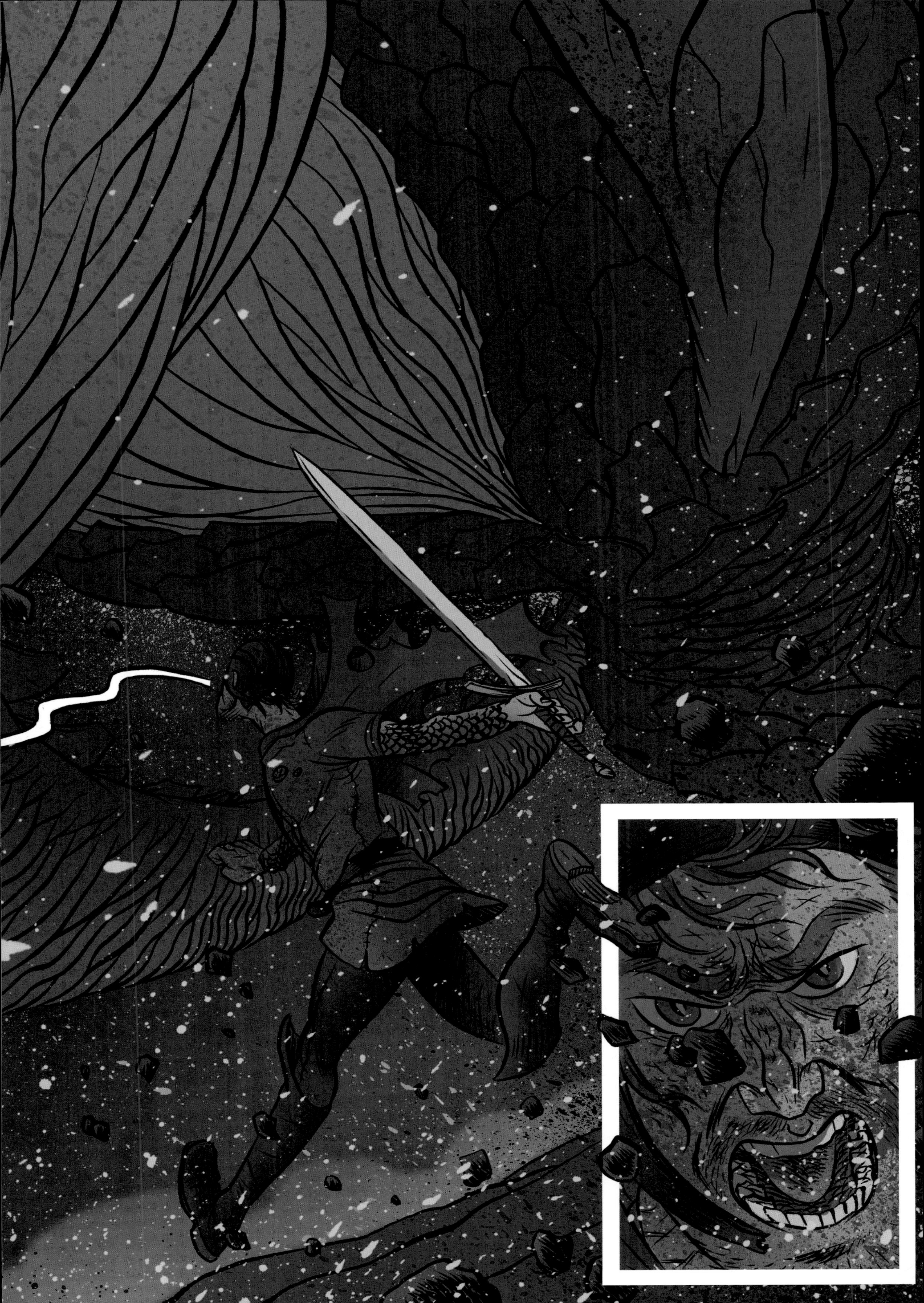

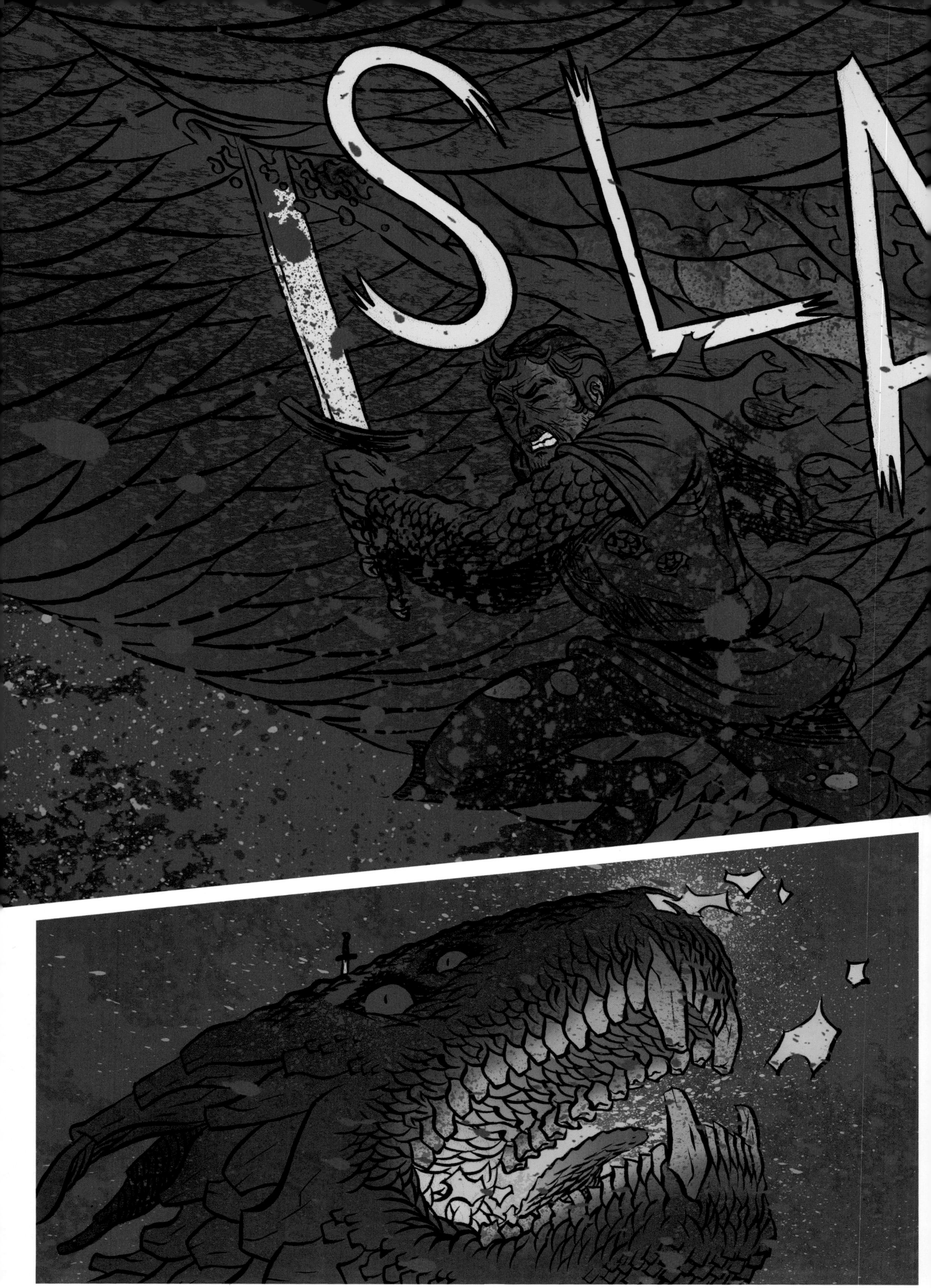
SLA

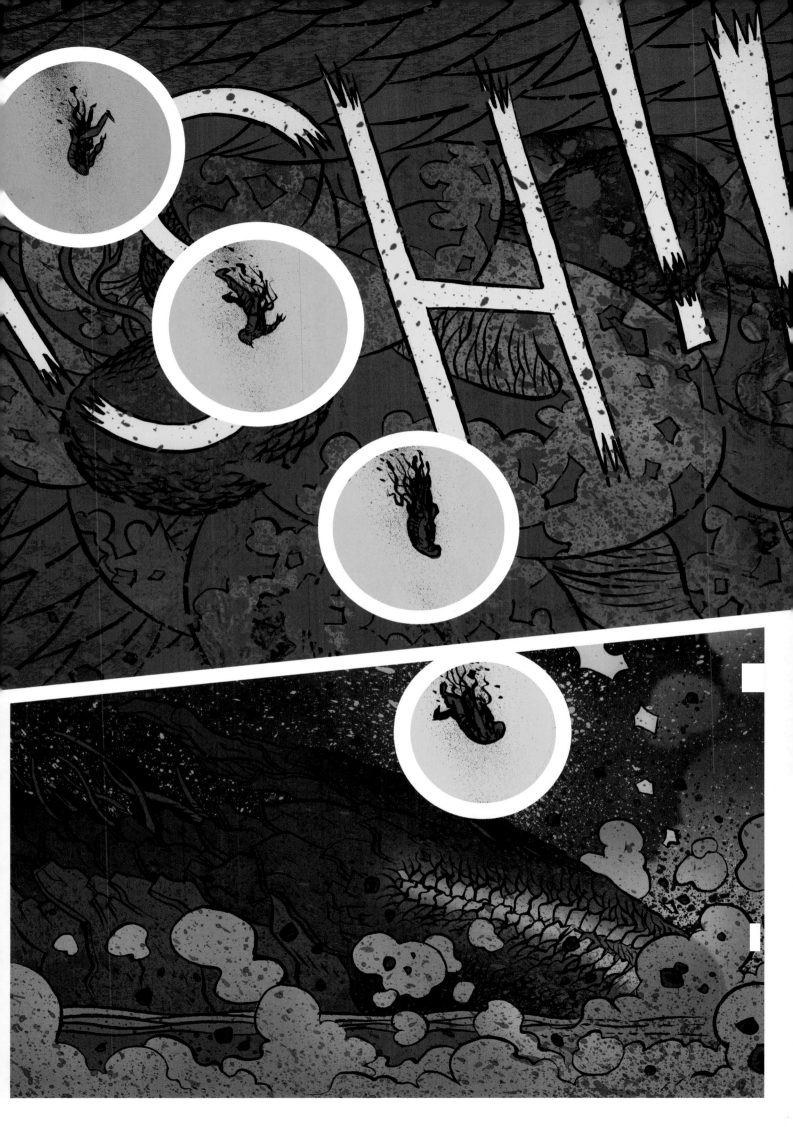

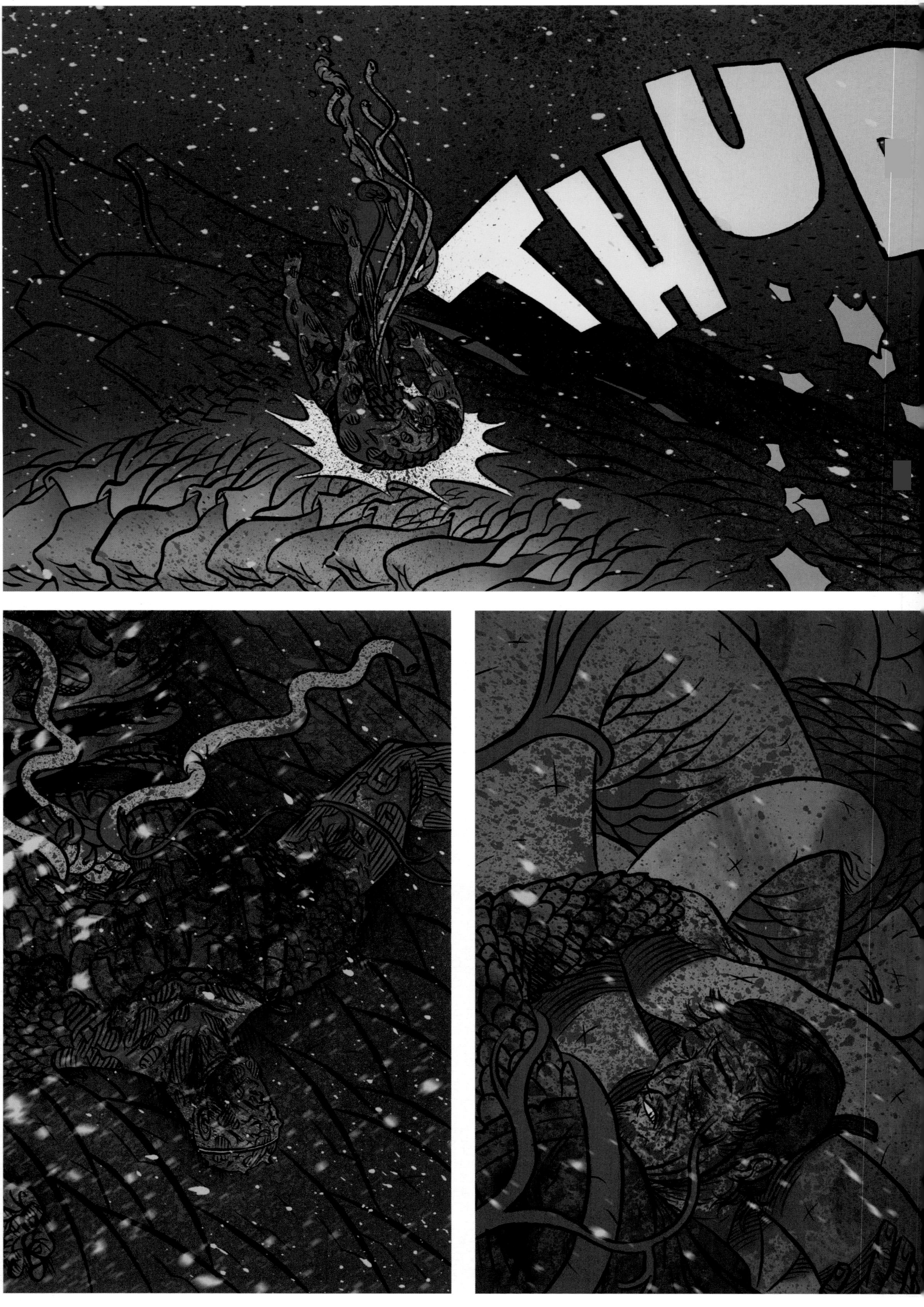
THU

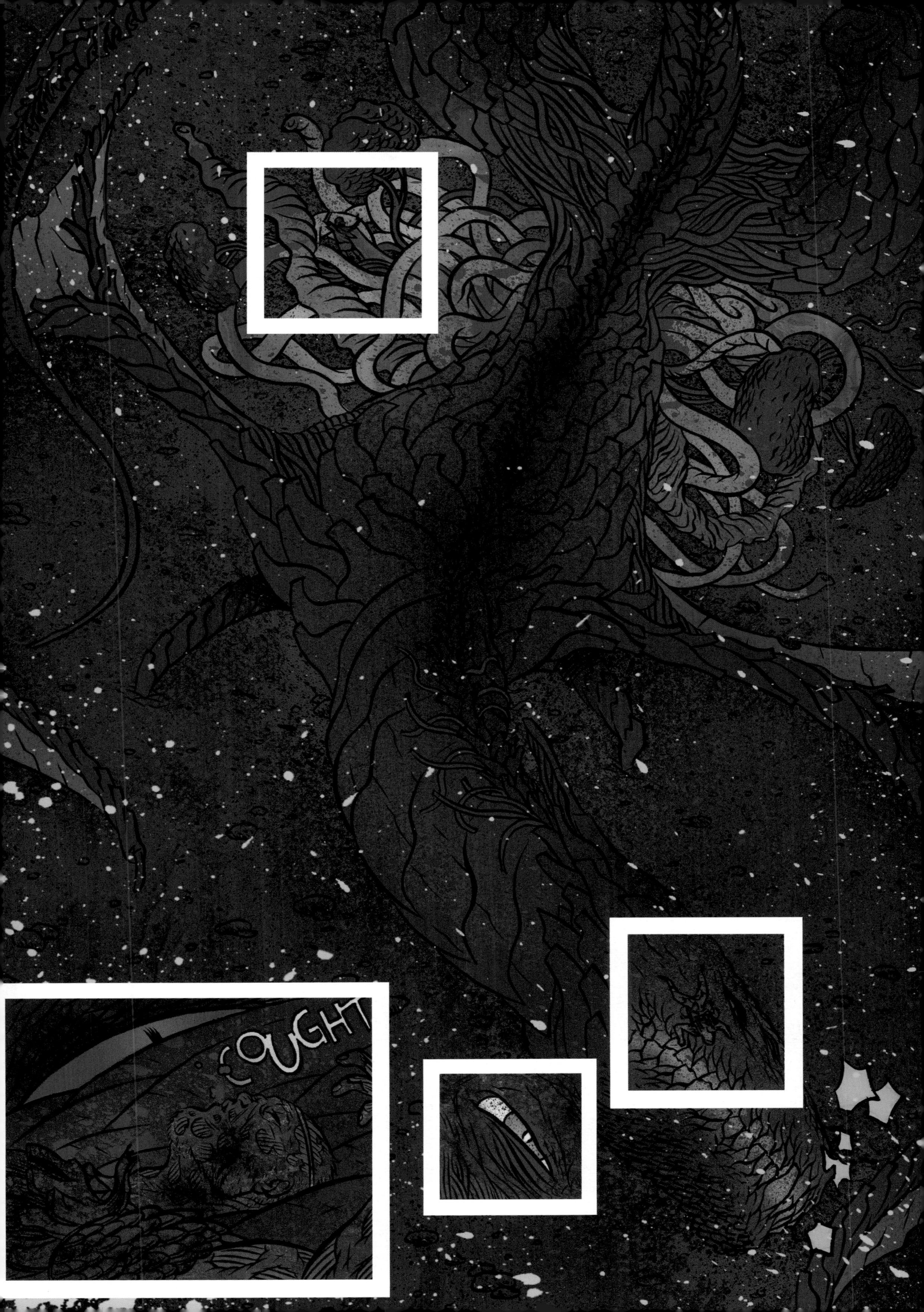
COUGH

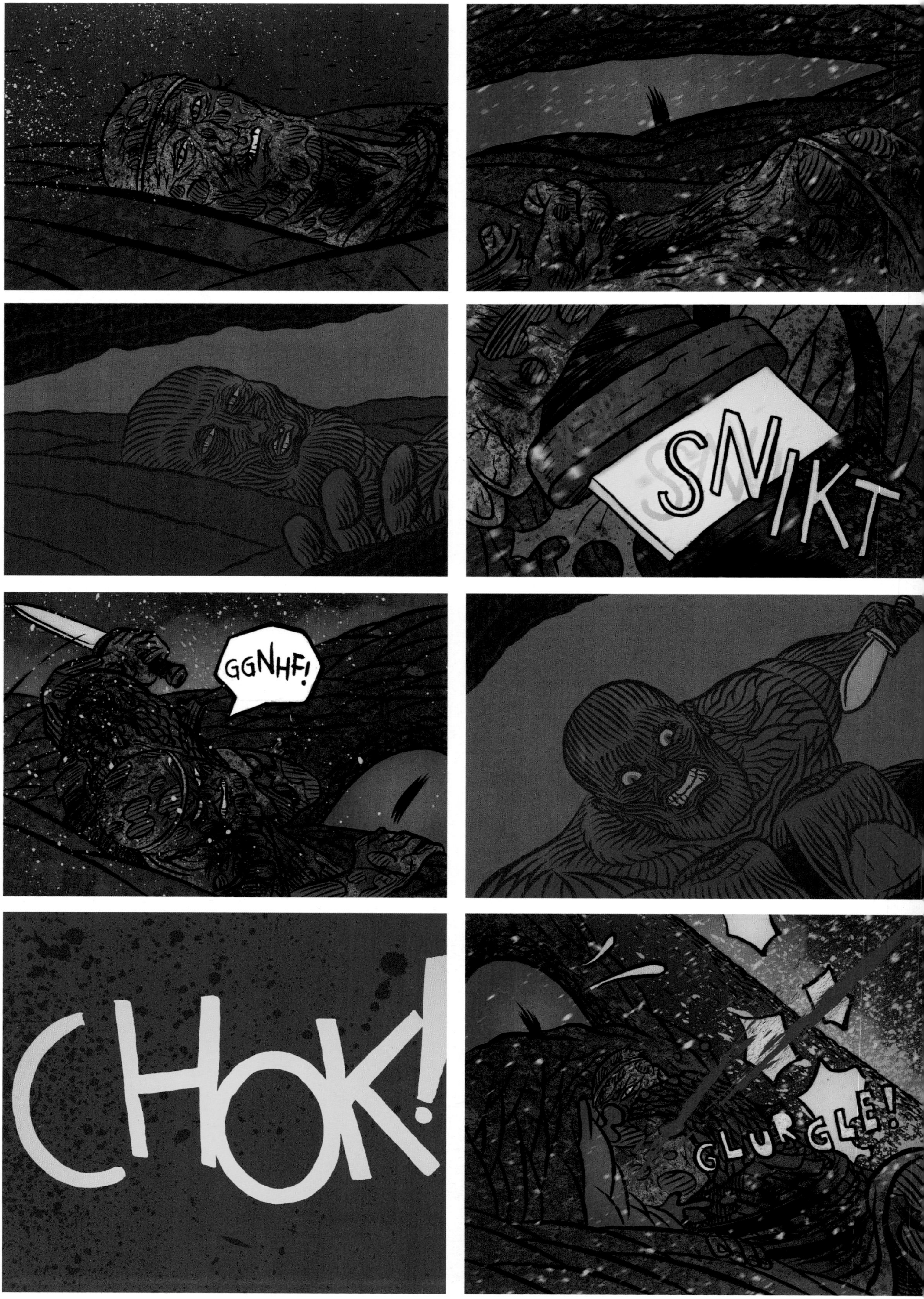
SNIKT
GGNHF!
CHOK!
GLURGLE!

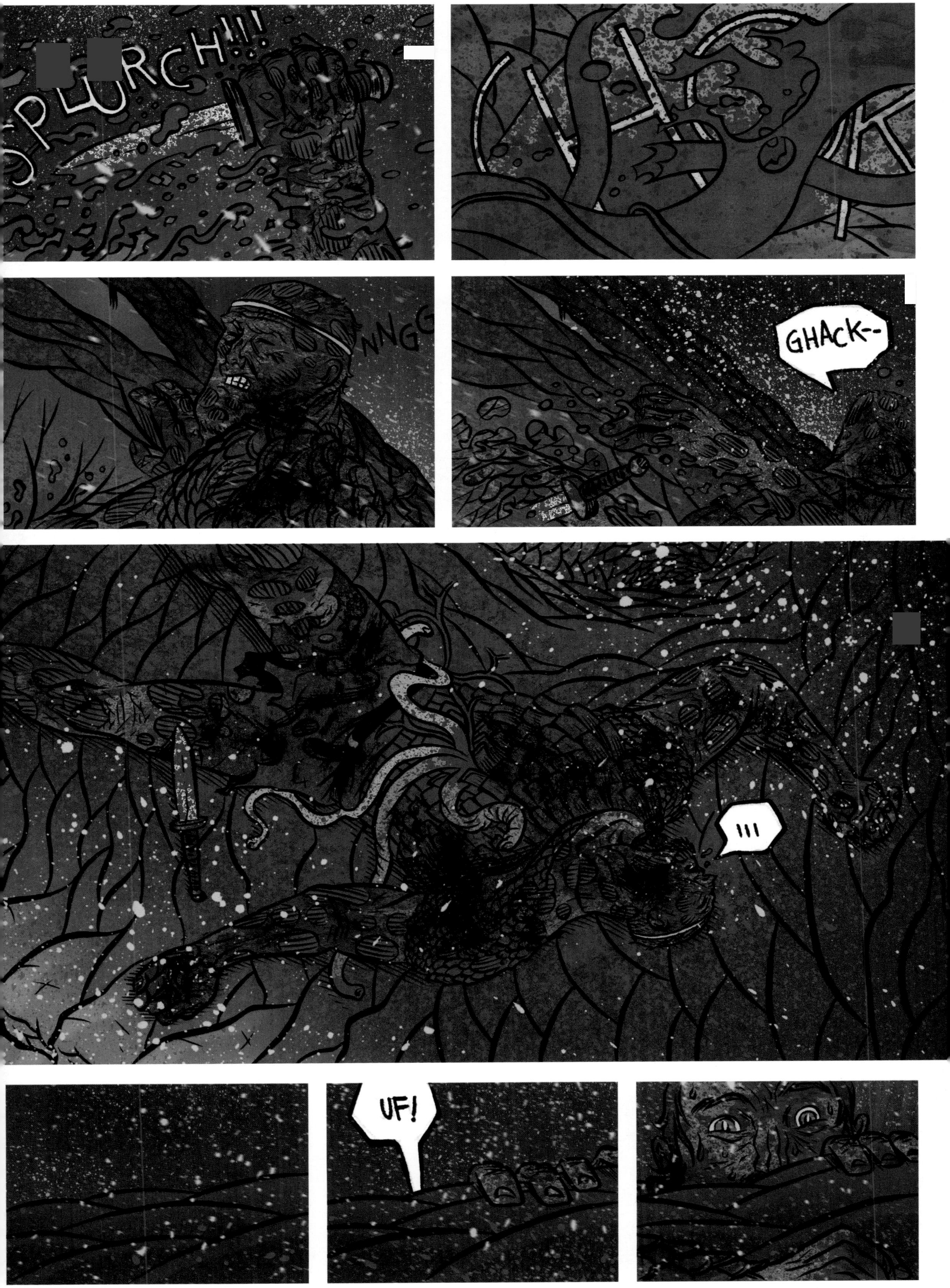
SPLURCH!!!
NNGG
GHACK--
!!!
UF!

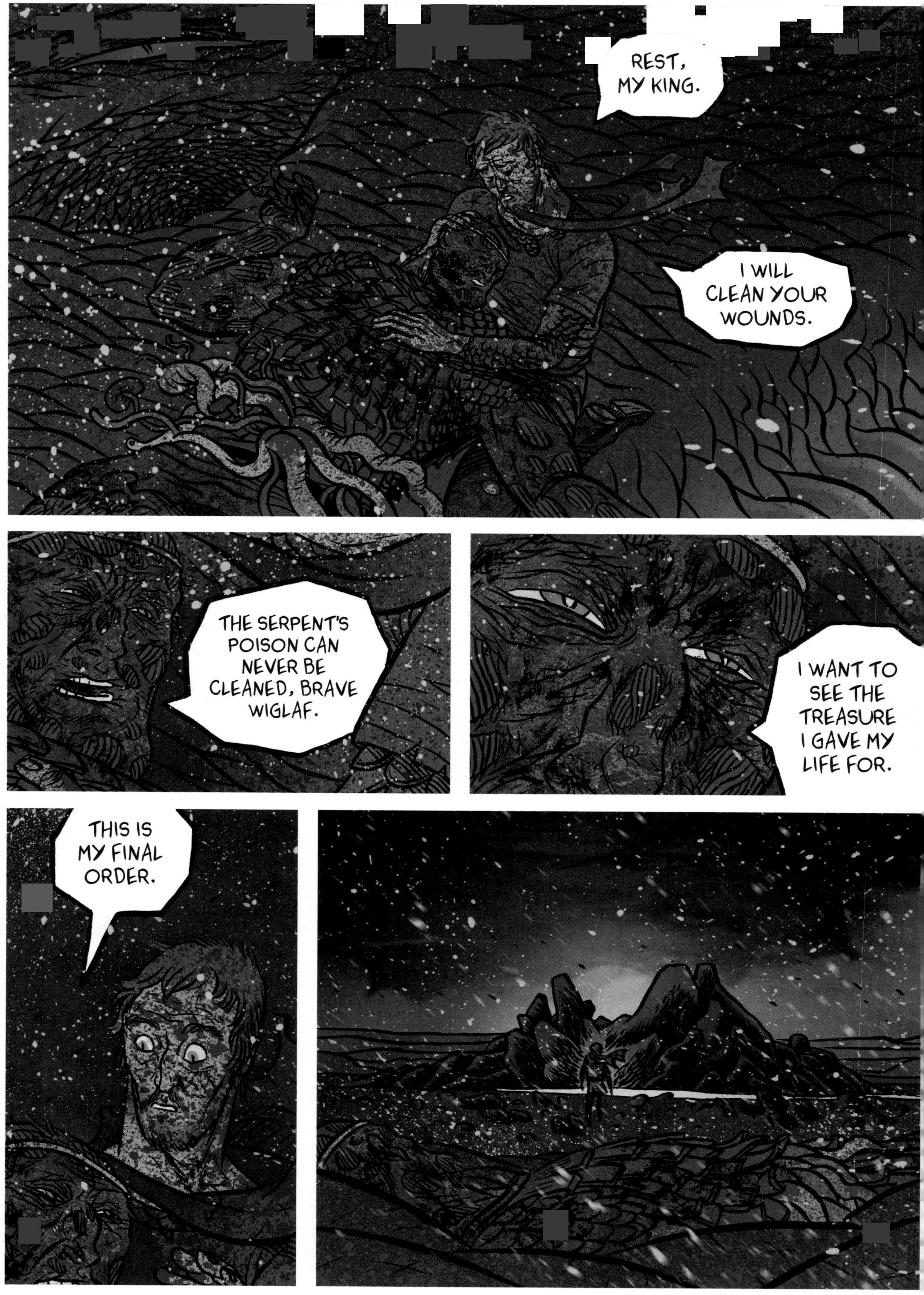
REST, MY KING.
I WILL CLEAN YOUR WOUNDS.
THE SERPENT'S POISON CAN NEVER BE CLEANED, BRAVE WIGLAF.
I WANT TO SEE THE TREASURE I GAVE MY LIFE FOR.
THIS IS MY FINAL ORDER.

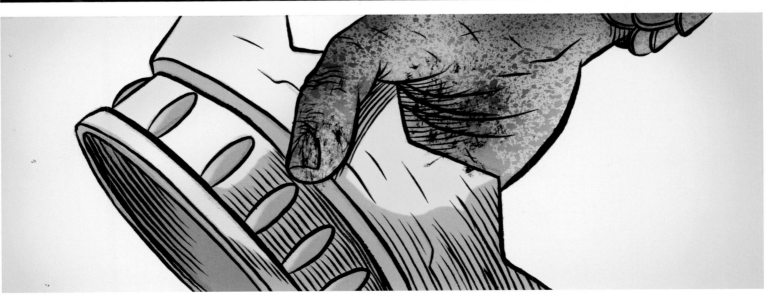

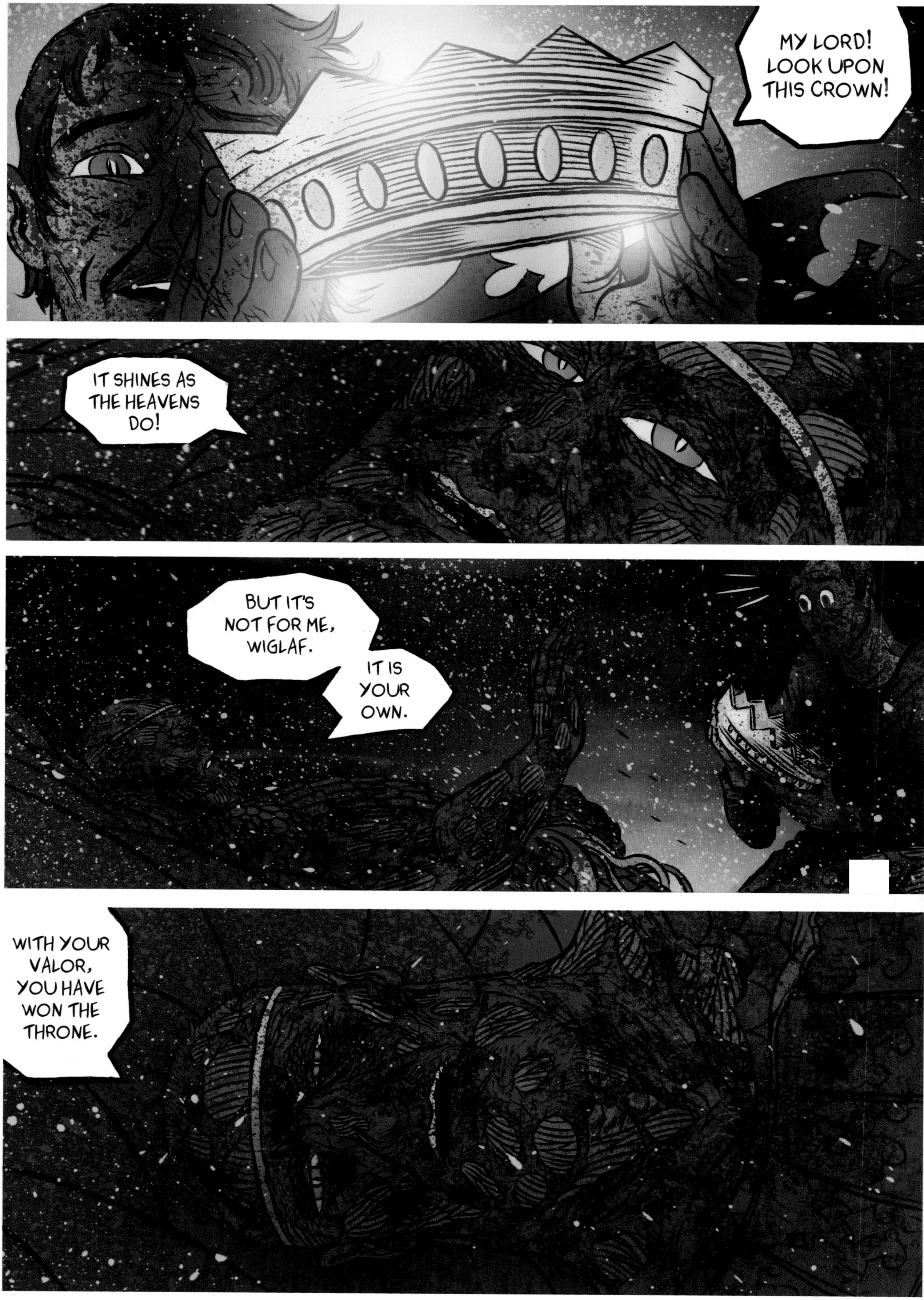
MY LORD! LOOK UPON THIS CROWN!
IT SHINES AS THE HEAVENS DO!
BUT IT'S NOT FOR ME, WIGLAF.
IT IS YOUR OWN.
WITH YOUR VALOR, YOU HAVE WON THE THRONE.

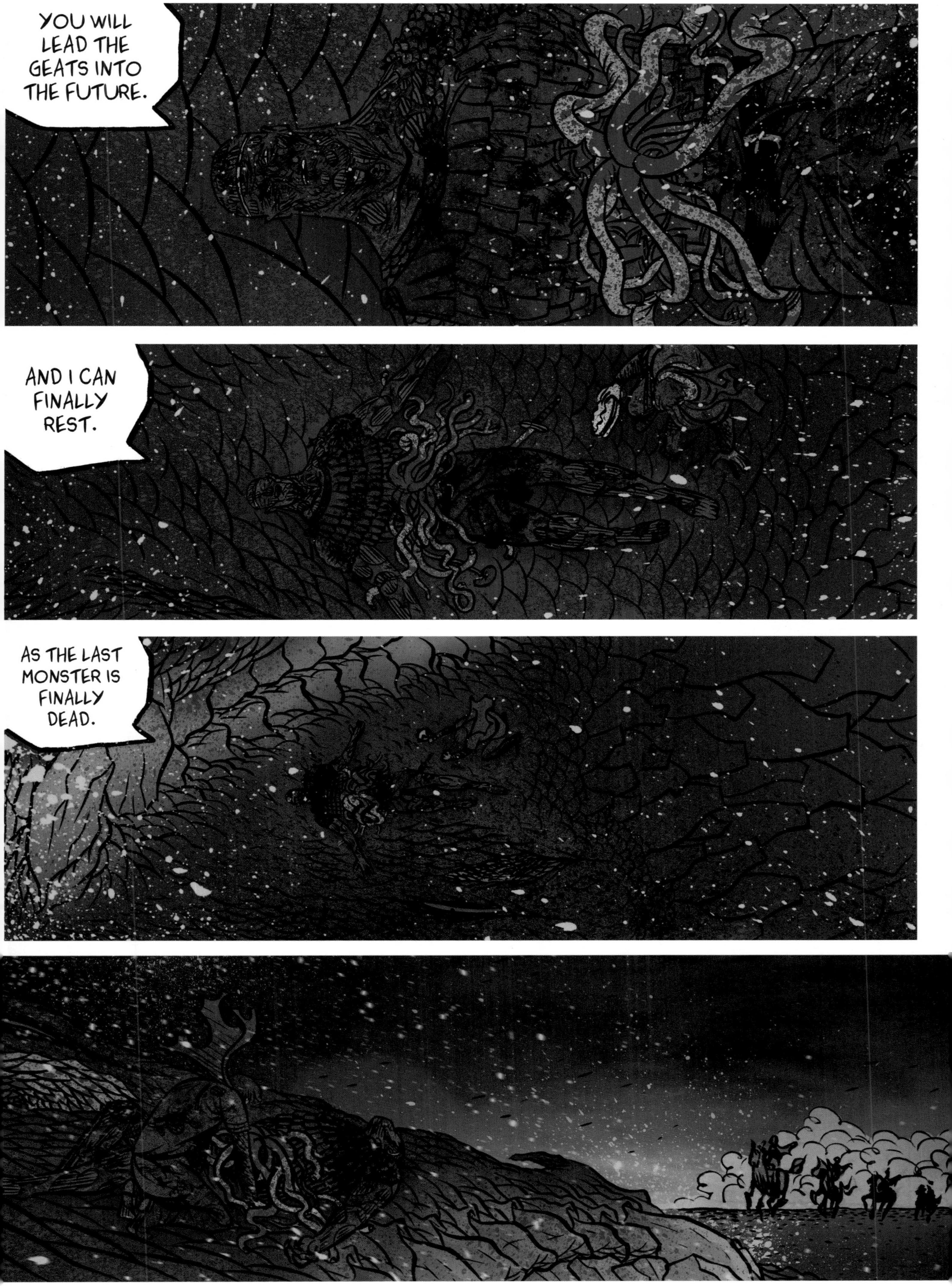
YOU WILL LEAD THE GEATS INTO THE FUTURE.
AND I CAN FINALLY REST.
AS THE LAST MONSTER IS FINALLY DEAD.

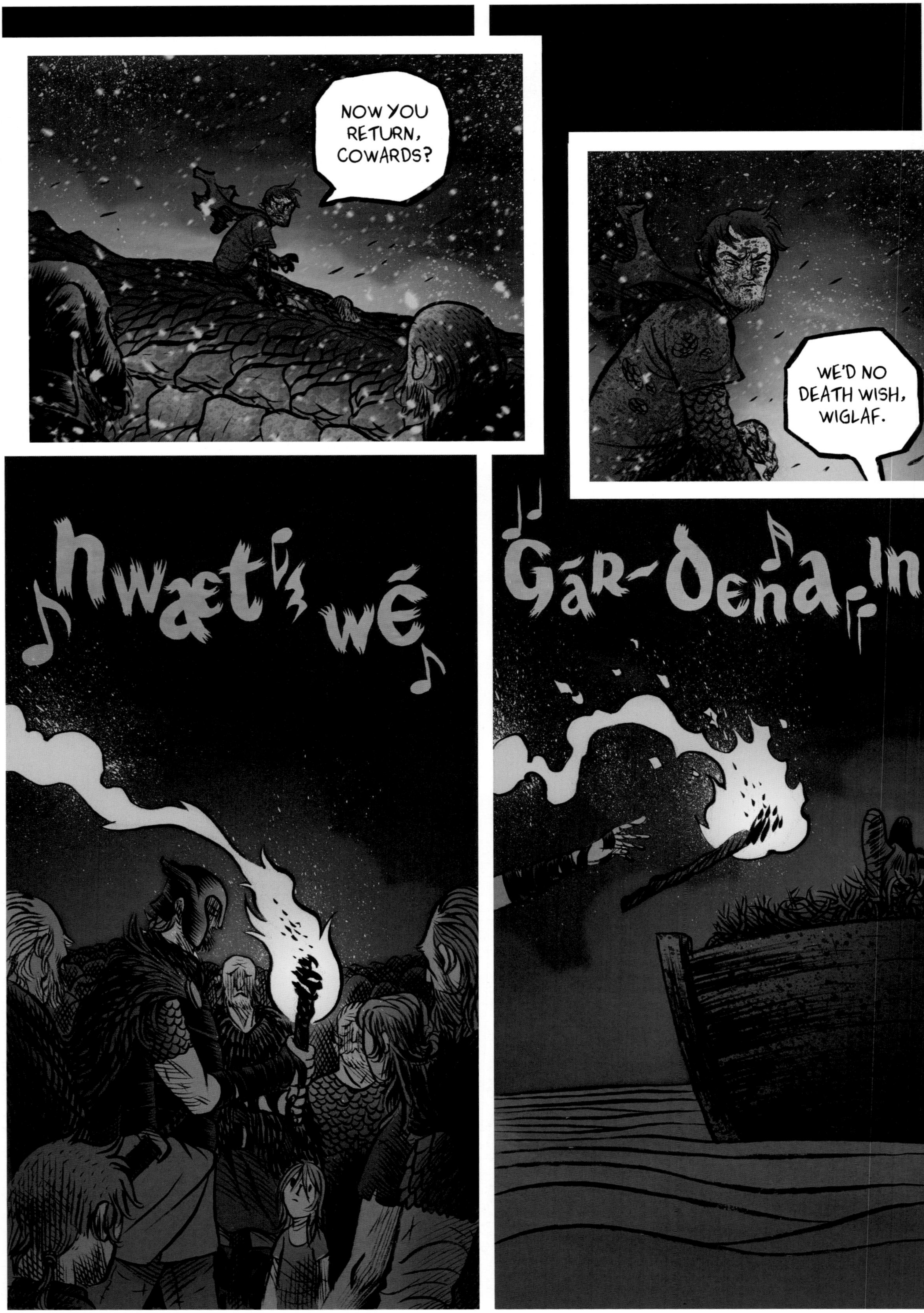
NOW YOU RETURN, COWARDS?
WE'D NO DEATH WISH, WIGLAF.
hwæt wé
Gār-Dena in

A TRUE WARRIOR PREFERS DEATH OVER A LIFE OF SHAME!

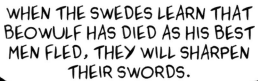

WHEN THE SWEDES LEARN THAT BEOWULF HAS DIED AS HIS BEST MEN FLED, THEY WILL SHARPEN THEIR SWORDS.

GEÁR-DA GUM

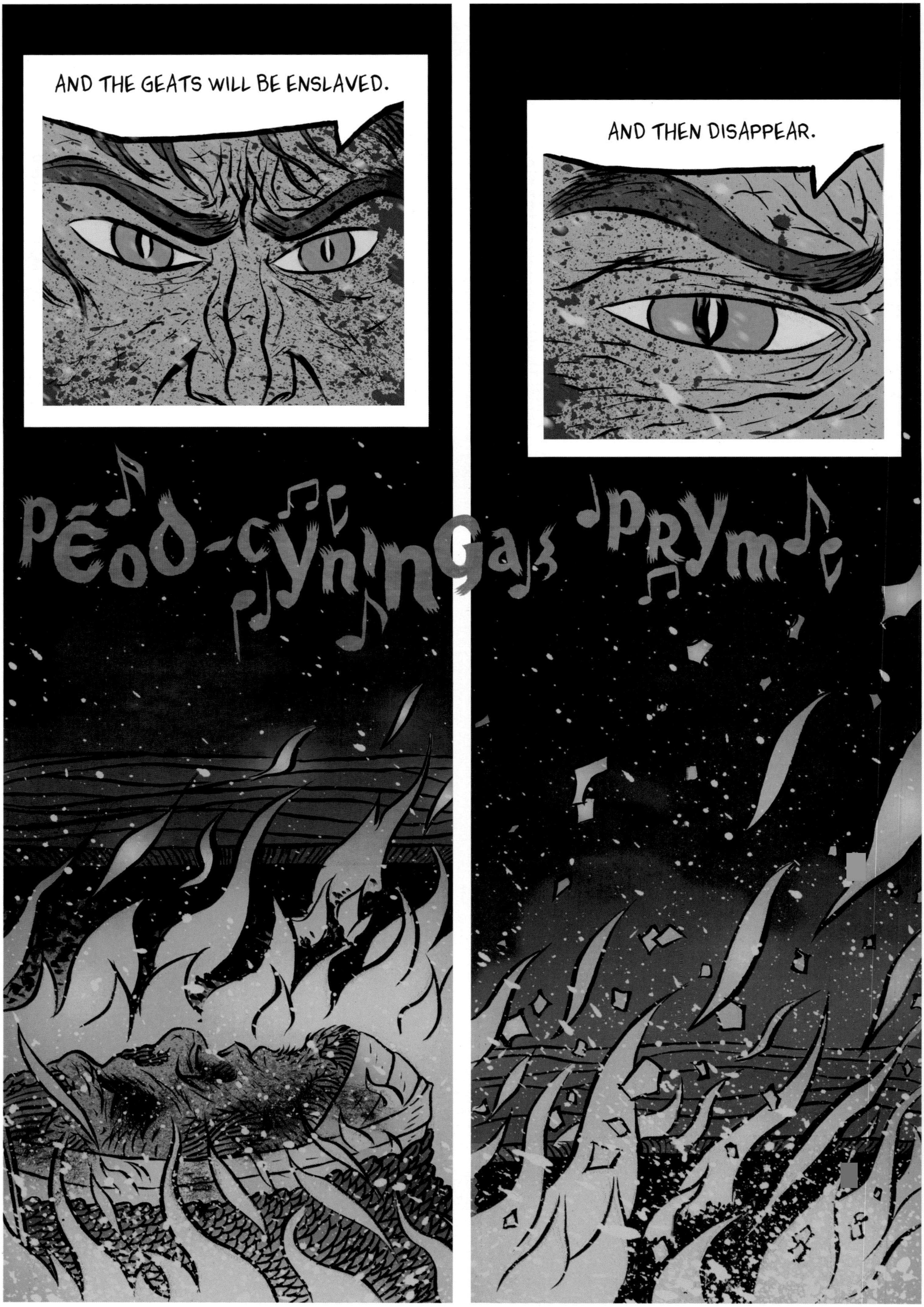
AND THE GEATS WILL BE ENSLAVED.
AND THEN DISAPPEAR.
Þēod-cyningas þrym

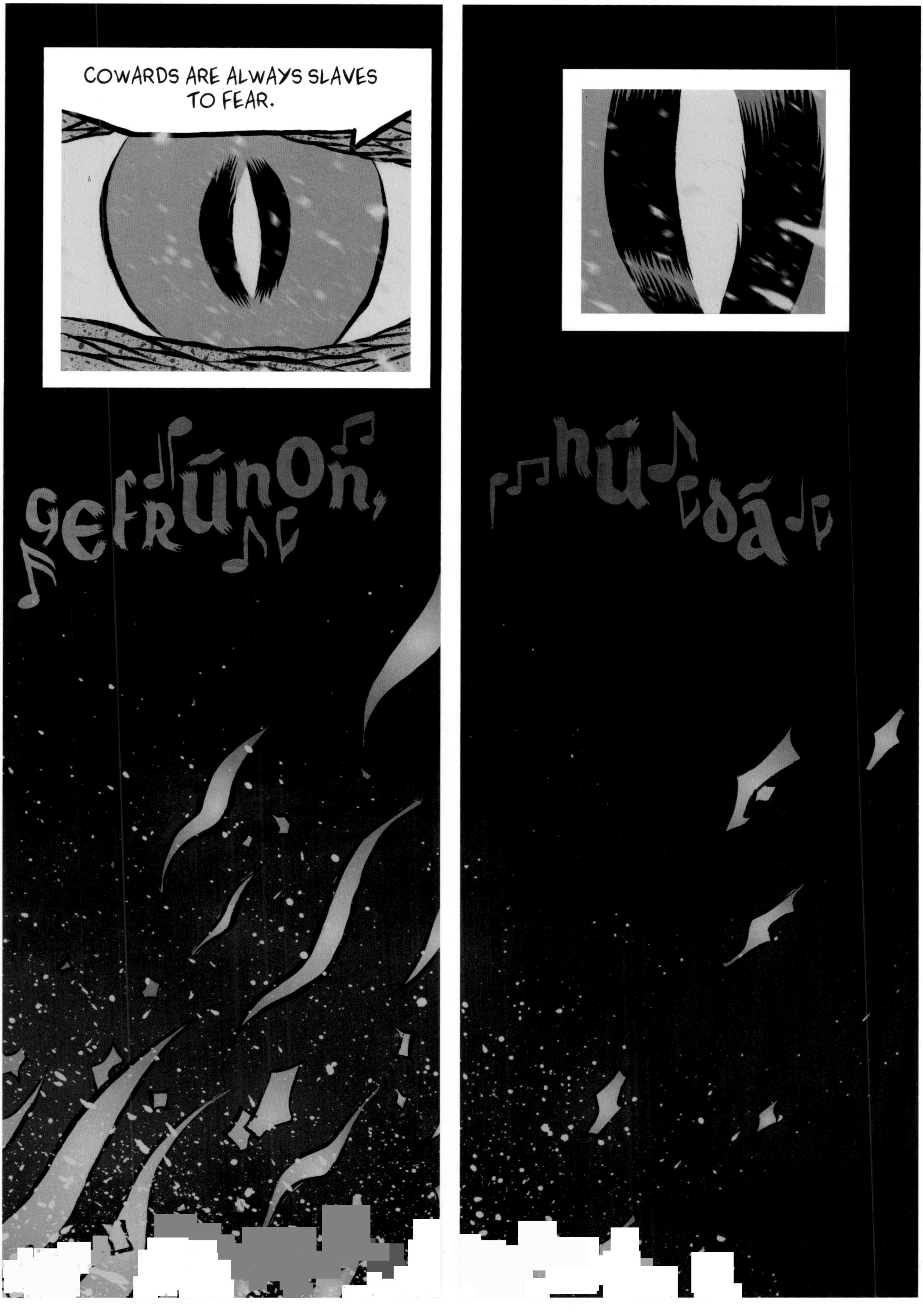
COWARDS ARE ALWAYS SLAVES TO FEAR.
gefrūnon,
hū ðā

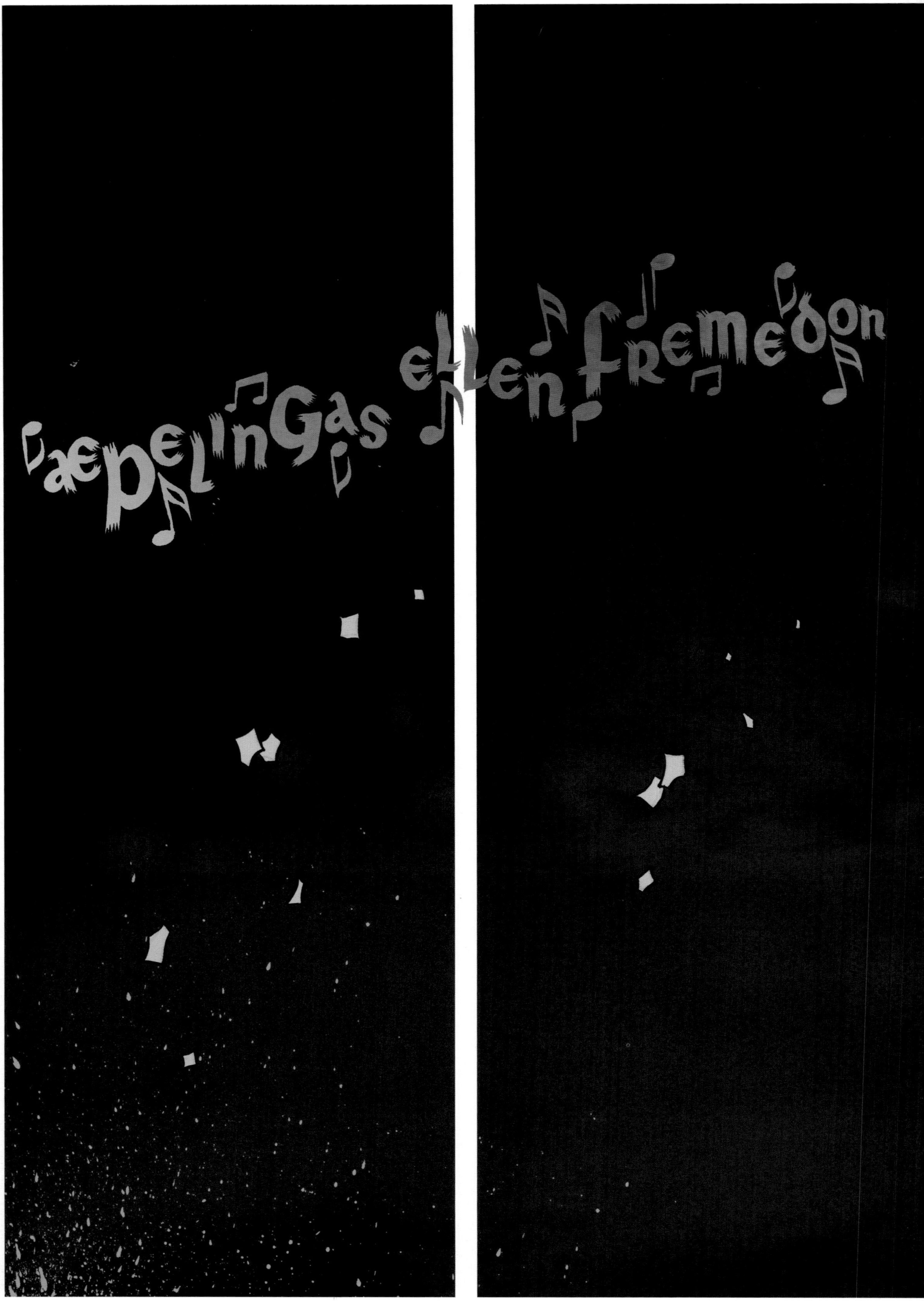
æpelingas ellen fremedon

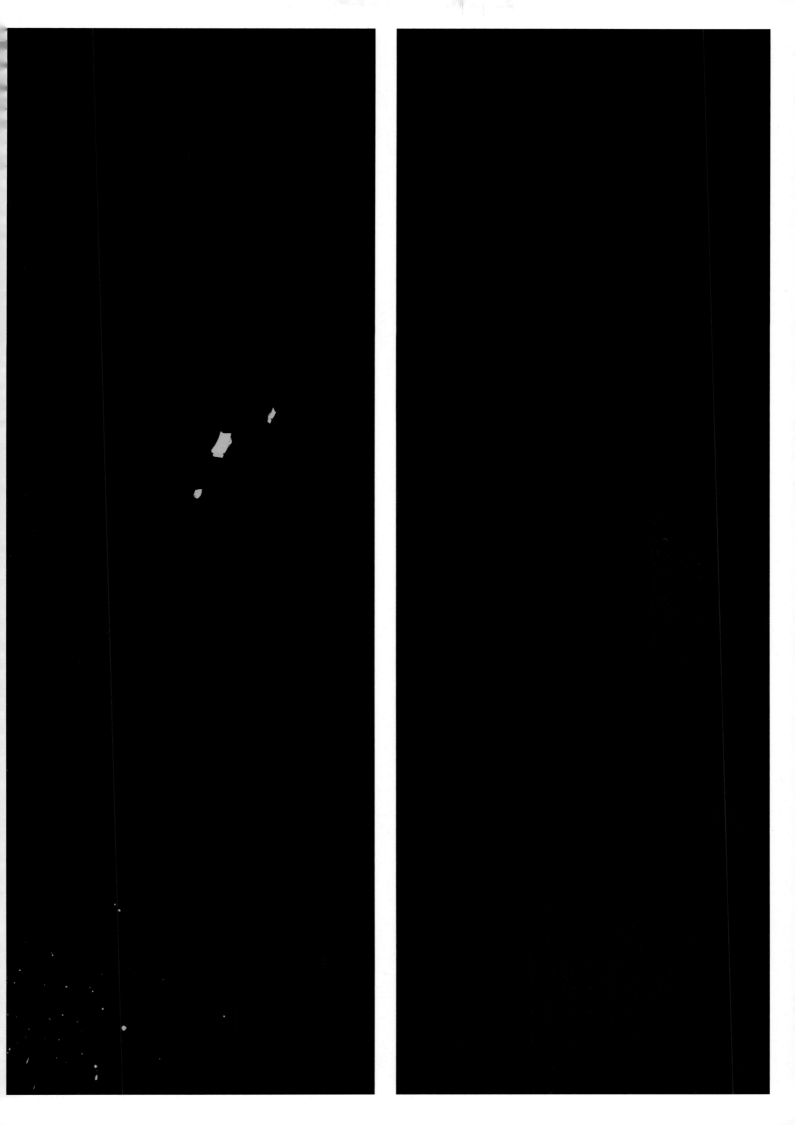

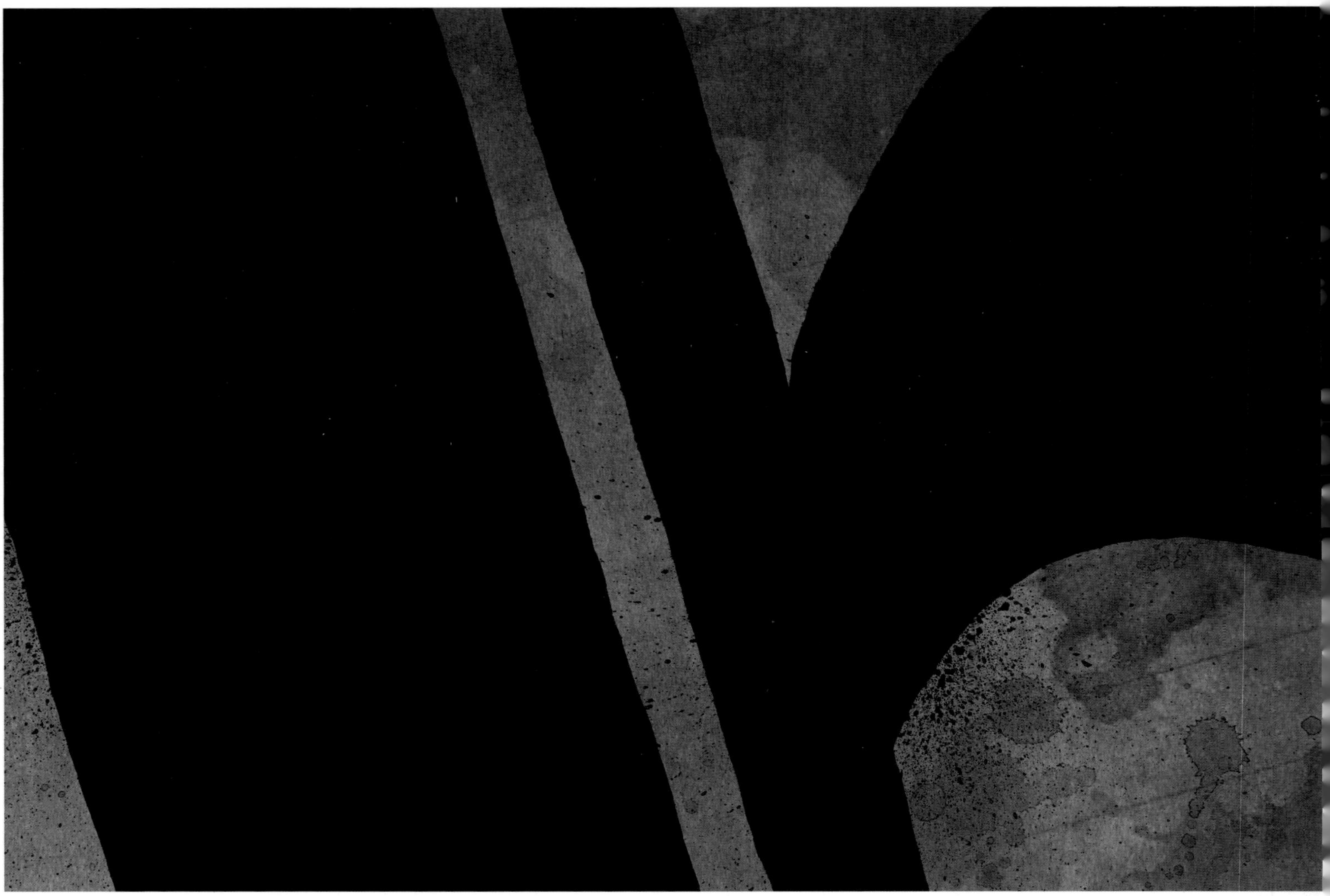

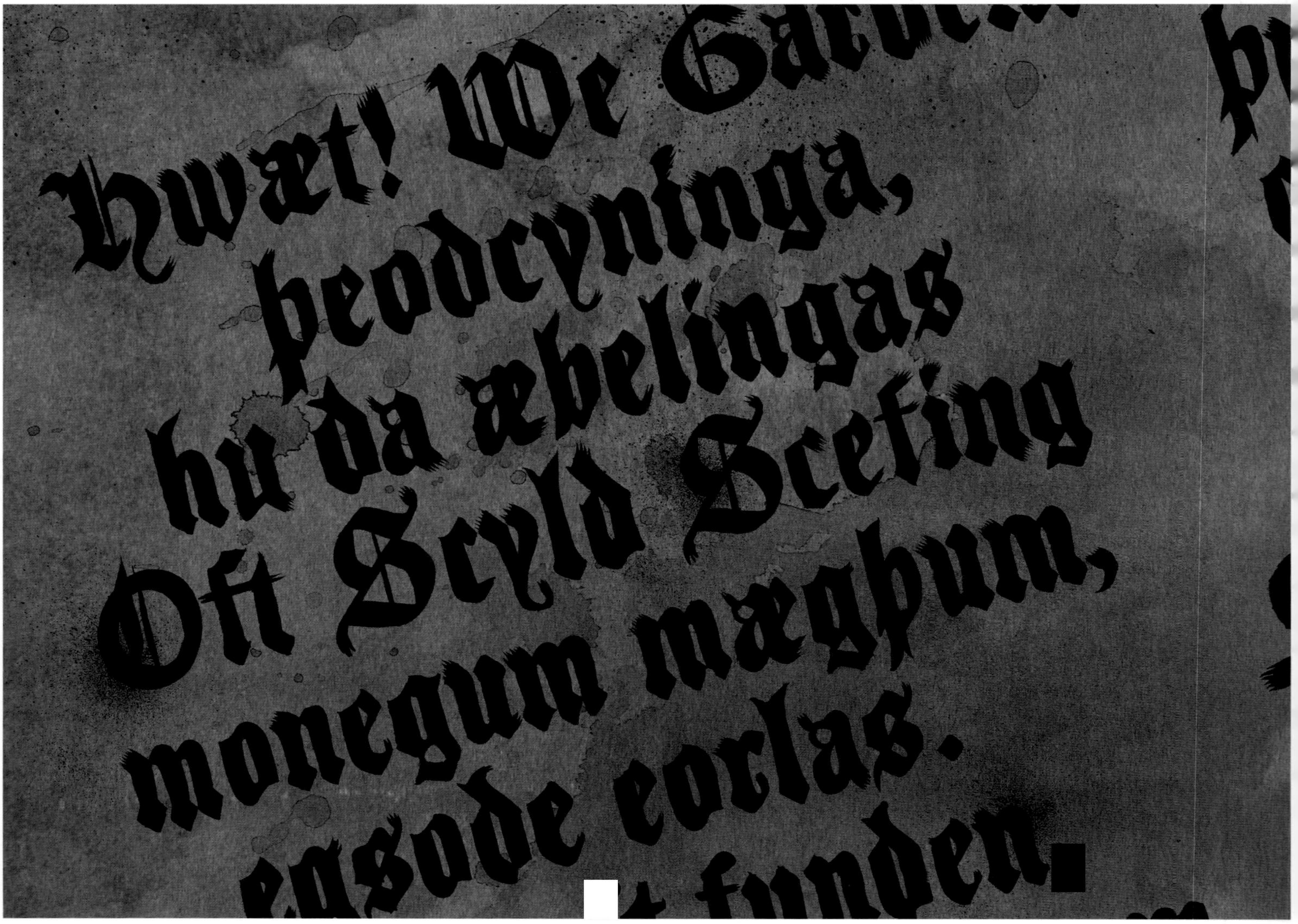
Hwæt! We
þeodcyninga,
hu ða æþelingas
Oft Scyld Scefing
monegum mægþum,
egsode eorlas.
funden.

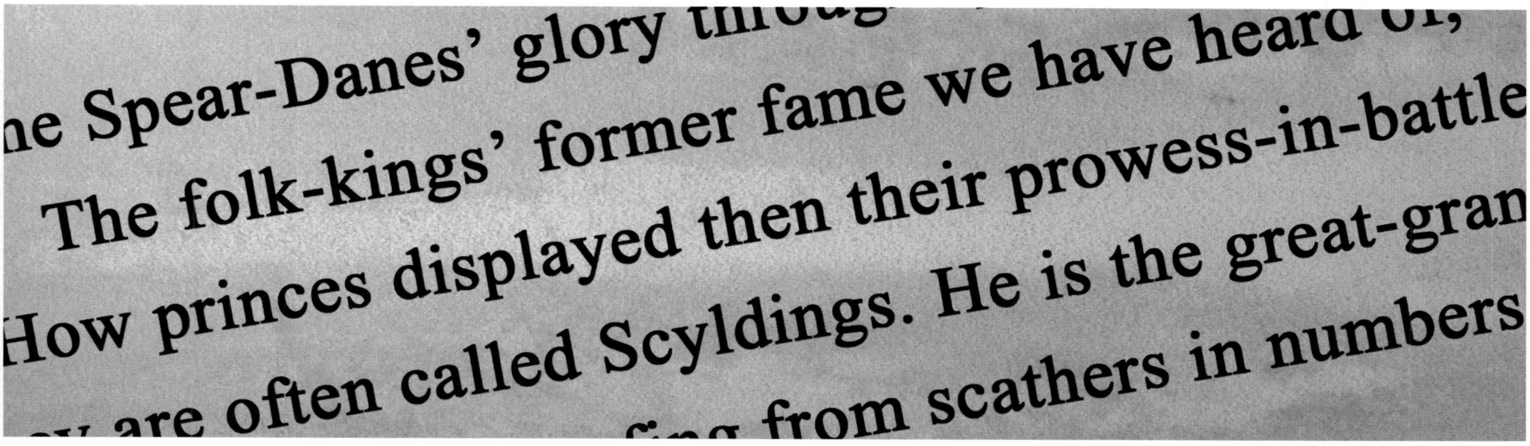
Spear-Danes' glory
The folk-kings' former fame we have heard
How princes displayed then their prowess-in-battle
are often called Scyldings. He is the great-
from scathers in numbers
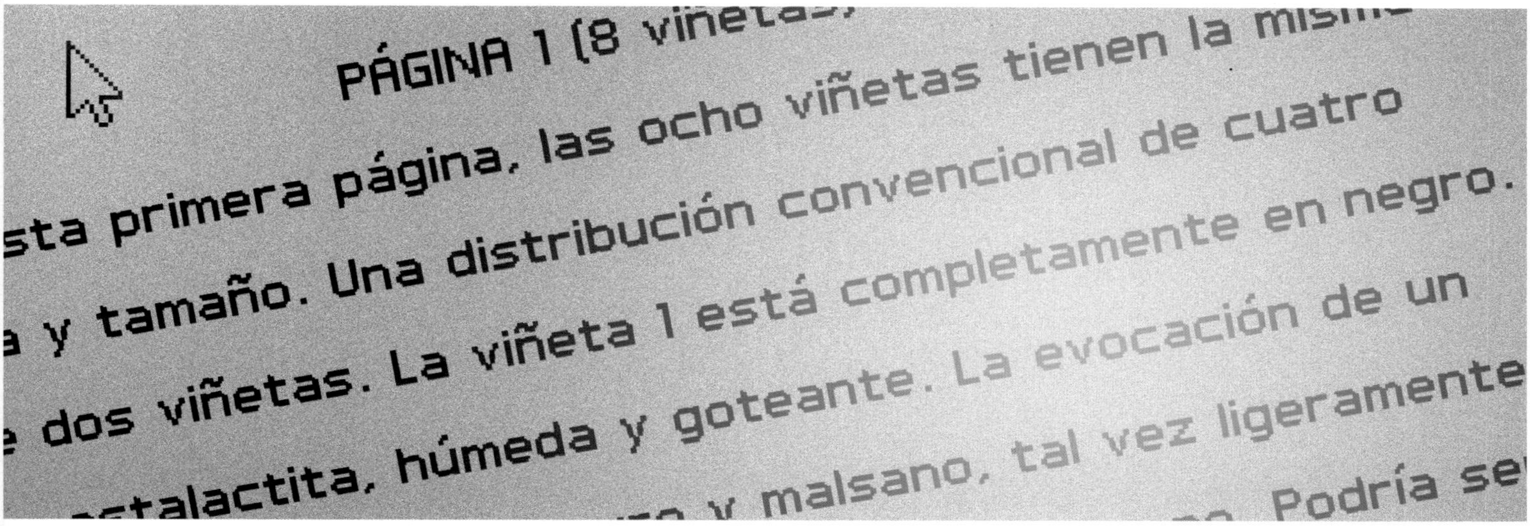
PÁGINA 1
primera página, las ocho viñetas tienen la
y tamaño. Una distribución convencional de cuatro
dos viñetas. La viñeta 1 está completamente en negro.
stalactita, húmeda y goteante. La evocación de un
y malsano, tal vez ligeramente
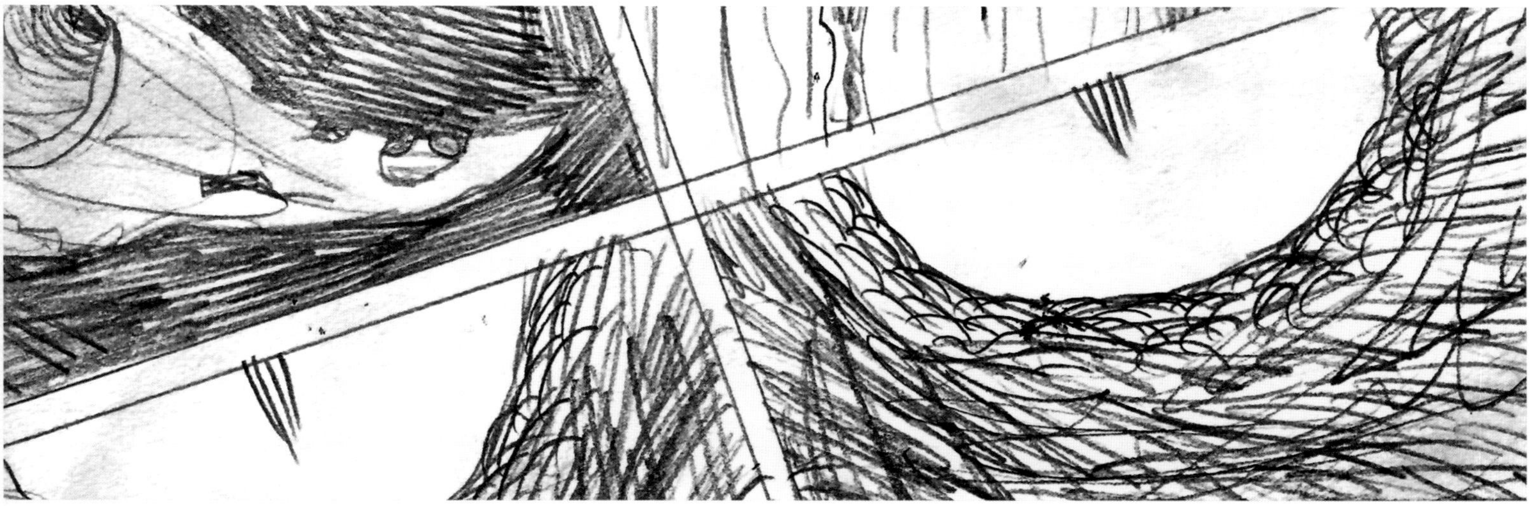
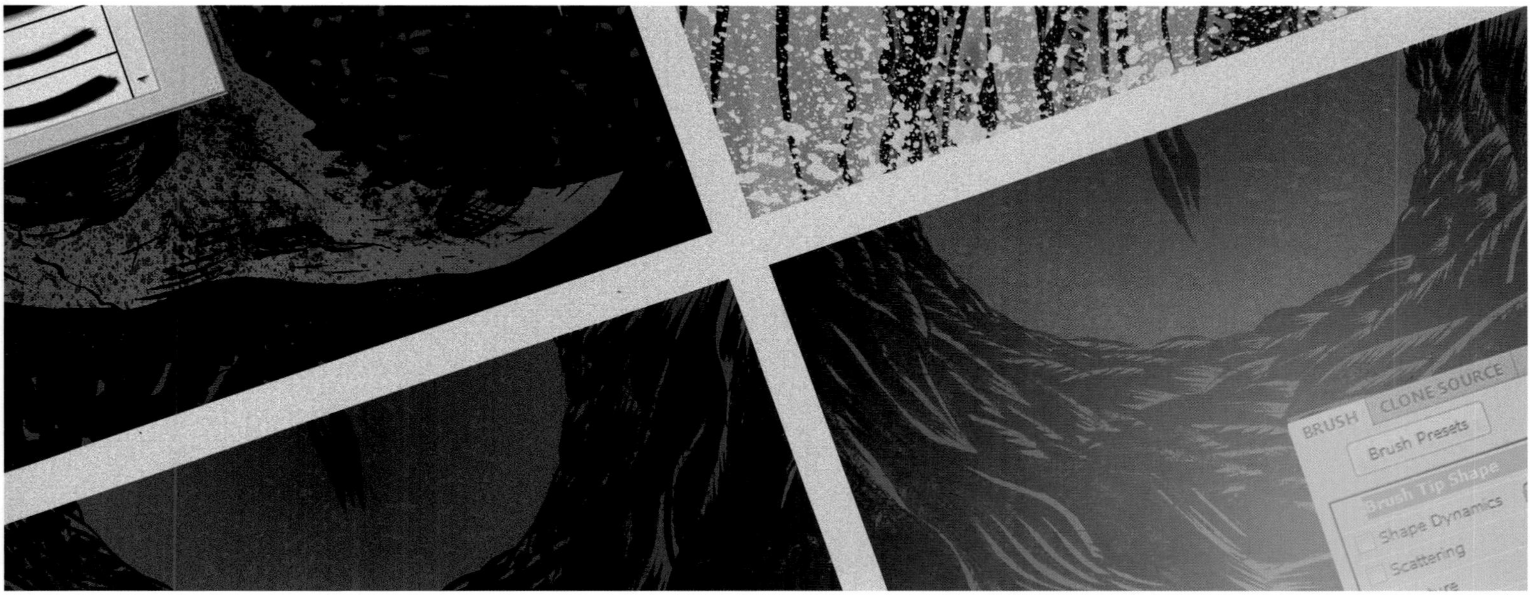
BRUSH
CLONE SOURCE
Brush Presets
Brush Tip Shape
Shape Dynamics
Scattering

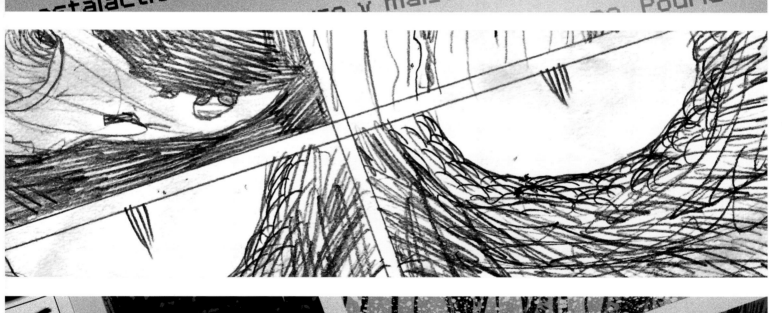

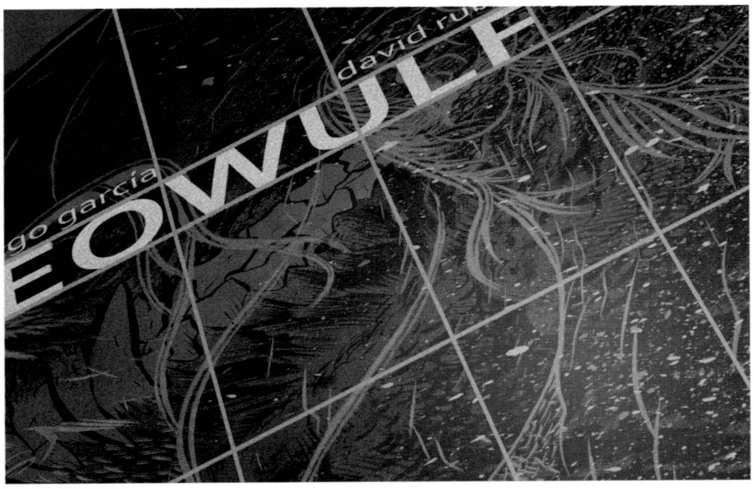
go garcía
david rub
EOWULF

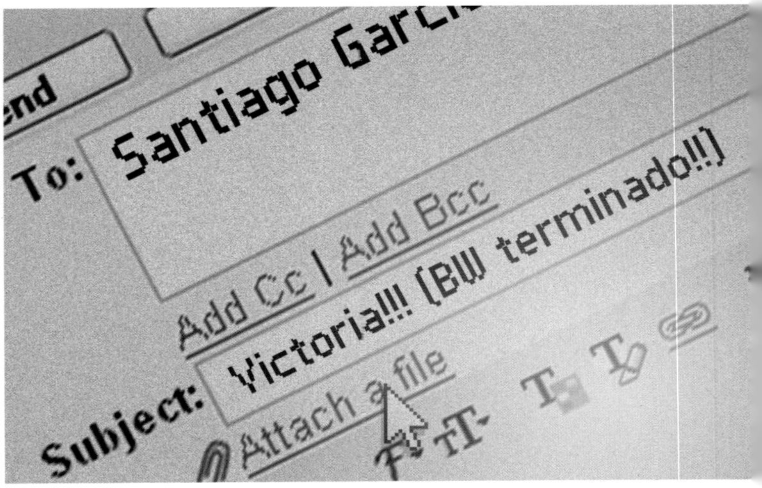
end
To: Santiago Garc
Add Cc | Add Bcc
Subject: Victoria!!! (BW terminado!!)
Attach a file

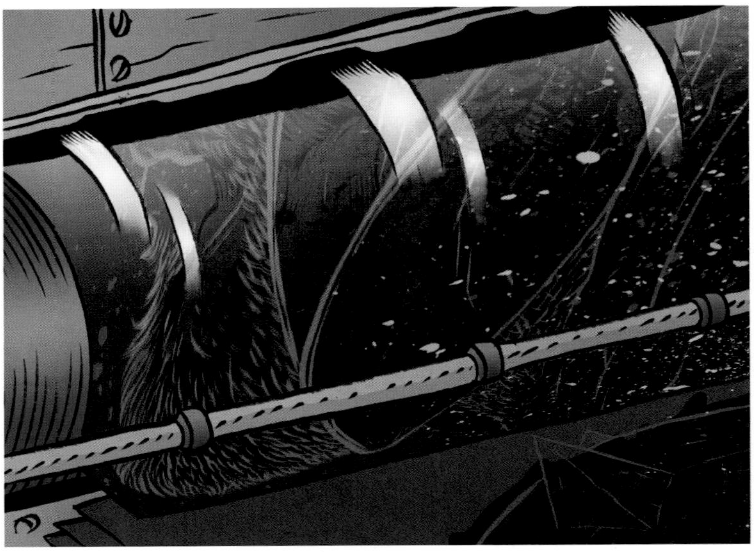

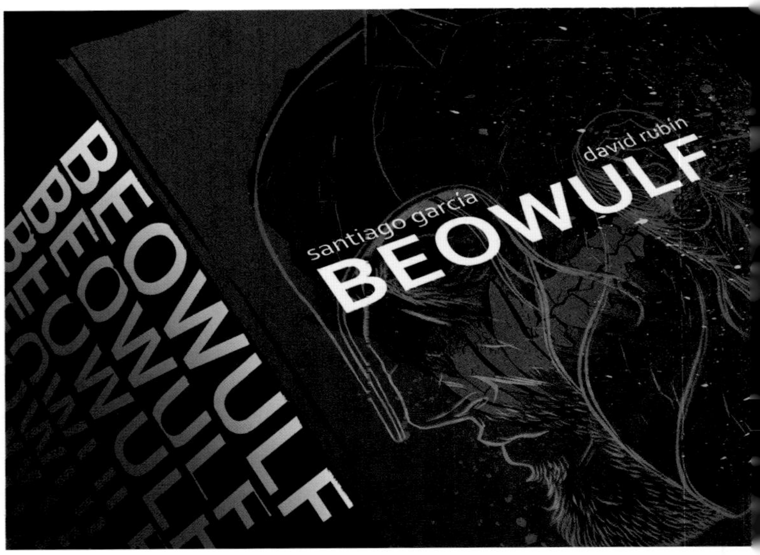
BEOWULF
santiago garcía
david rubin
BEOWULF

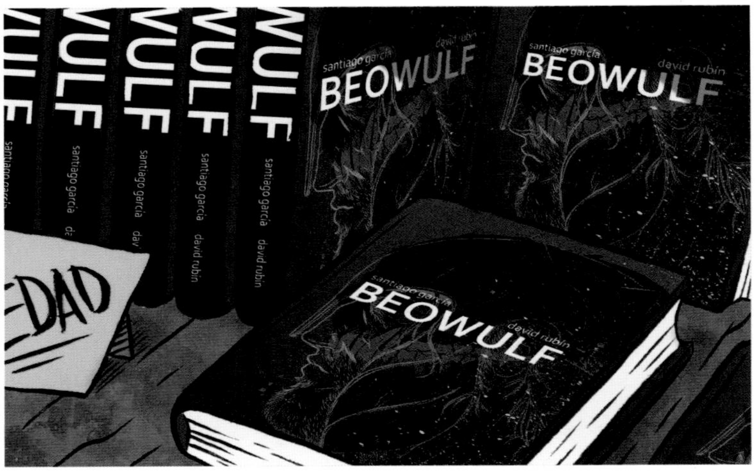
santiago garcía
BEOWULF
david rubin
EDAD

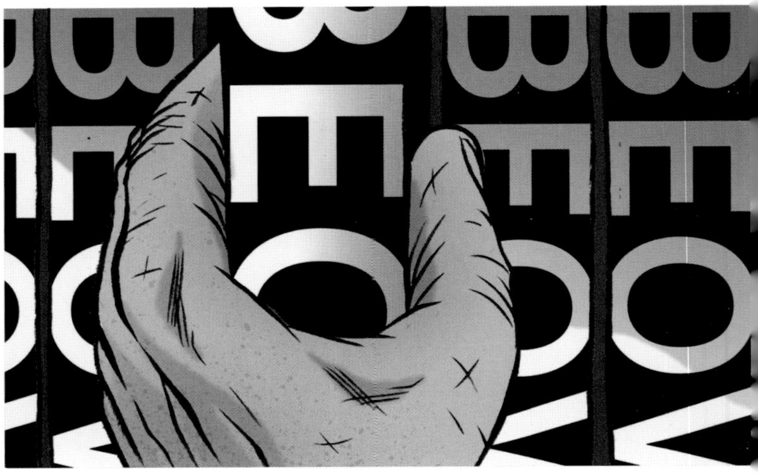

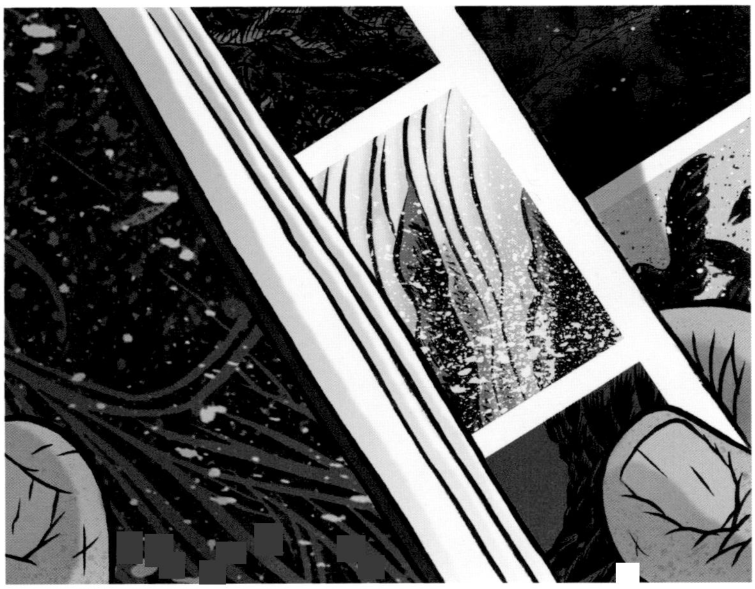

FIN

EPILOGUE THE LONGEST JOURNEY

There's an old Chinese proverb that says... "The longest journey always begins with the first step."

Here I am, an agnostic of epics, faced with the attempt to put on paper the chronicle of a journey that began long ago and contains so many surprising events that my faith in the rational falters and suddenly I find, as I type the end of this sentence with a mixture of embarrassment and impudence, the word destiny.

Destiny that was sealed that day when Santiago and I sat in the living room of his house more than ten years ago and, in that precise moment, he pitched to me a project by the name of BEOWULF.

This script, that Santiago gave me with all the illusion that it was his first attempt to work on it professionally, became a challenge for me, a true hero's journey that I began with the enthusiasm of one unable to discern the difficulty which I faced. And since we are already presenting an epic tale, let's say this young hero prepared so well and was so conscientious of his journey that he exhausted his strength before he even left the fjord. He came to battle and the cunning dragon of time devoured him in two bites.

The moral was so clear that it startled me and when I saw it, it was already too late. The lesson learned came in the form of a scar that runs through my entire drawing arm.

The fact that I'm the one that finally writes this epilogue for Santiago and David's work makes me think that this text could be a good way to close an old wound, professionally and (especially)

personally, that I've been dragging along for more than ten years.

Knowing the usefulness of ancient funeral rites and the importance of staging our losses in a real way, over a year ago, Santiago himself wrote in his blog "Mandorla" a post that told of all the vicissitudes in the attempt to create our version of BEOWULF. It was a complete postmortem whose purpose was to close, publicly and once and for all, that rough and unfinished chapter of our biographies.

But it was clear that this idea had been a childhood obsession of Santiago's that I had derailed it masterfully (or taught it lessons somewhere in the middle) and it would not be stranded for too long and its mythical power would resonate again, resurging from the ground like a Grendel, altered this time by the silence, and caught by the throat by a promising new adversary.

For me, the fact that it was precisely David Rubín who offered to take up idea of adapting the ancient epic poem ended up making sense at the time. Now I know that it wasn't an agony but a wait.

Suddenly, he had not only resurrected the project, he was the young squire who was the logical candidate to remove the sword from the stone.

I've closely followed David's career since its beginnings, from those early days where he drank from some of the same fountains from which I drank and, since then, I've seen him crow and become the solid author he is now. His work has exhibited his own personality for a long time but the fact that he belongs to the same clan by origin and brings a